Ishtaq
The Second Vial

Thomas G. Fournier

Thomas G. Fournier

The characters and events in this book are fictitious.
Any similarities to real persons, living or dead, is coincidental and not intended by the author.

Acknowledgements

My sincerest thanks to my sister Sharon, daughter Leah, and Tammy, my friend. Without their fervent interest and honest criticism, this story would be a lesser work with a terrible ending.

To my sons, Matthew and Andrew, who kept the story, and my dream of writing it, alive until I recognized the time was right for telling it.

To my daughters, Emily and Julia, who sacrificed their computers and the dining room table to the cause for seemingly endless months.

To my beautiful wife, Mona…who spent far too many nights alone on the couch at the far end of the room while her husband fulfilled his dream

May 9, 1993

Agnetha cowered in terror behind the console as the frantic screams of her co-workers reverberated through the cold metal corridors. Clamping her shaking hands over her ears muffled the horrible sound but couldn't completely block it out. She wished she were courageous enough to rush to their aid but her body absolutely refused to respond.

She was still in shock over how quickly their exciting adventure had gone all to hell.

She'd arrived with the advanced team from their base camp – a joint Norwegian – American research facility – only a week ago to secure and conceal the newly unearthed alien spacecraft an aerial survey team had stumbled upon during a recent flight.

A recent quake along the eastern coast had knocked out a couple of beacons at two of their unmanned sites. They'd been on their way to reactivate them and assess further damage when the pilot had noticed a newly formed crater in the distance only a few miles from the closest site. A quick overflight was enough to convince them that the malfunctioning beacons no longer mattered.

The screaming ceased abruptly leaving a silence that was just as terrifying. Agnetha lowered her hands and strained to hear. Something soft and heavy was being dragged across the floor out in the corridor. She struggled to determine if the sound was approaching or receding.

Blood pounded loudly in her ears as a shadow formed against the wall opposite the doorway. Someone or some *thing* was standing at the junction of the main corridor and the short passageway leading into the small room where Agnetha was hiding. The shadow paused, swaying slightly from side to side, its owner apparently considering its options.

Agnetha held her breath and prayed that it would continue along the central corridor toward another part of the spacecraft. The dragging sound resumed and the shadow grew smaller and more distinct.

It was moving towards her…

Agnetha searched frantically for another way out of the room. As she scanned the bare metal walls, she couldn't remember seeing this room before during their initial foray into the vessel. But the small space *was* unremarkable and they'd been so focused on re-concealing the spacecraft that it would have been easy to overlook.

It had been quite a feat, but they'd done it. Less than three days after its discovery, the treasured relic was sufficiently covered to keep it from prying eyes, thanks to a large quantity of winter camouflage netting the company had commandeered from an Army base in Washington state. It would have to do until a more permanent structure could be assembled.

They'd done a quick survey of the vessel, gaining access through a hatch that had remained open since the vessel had landed or crashed who-knew-how-long ago. A thick layer of frost and ice encased everything inside the ship underscoring the fact that it had been buried in the Antarctic ice for a very long time. There was no sign of the spacecraft's other-worldly crew…at least not right away.

Then the weirdness began…

Agnetha shook her head rapidly, trying to focus on her immediate situation. She realized with a sinking feeling that the door through which she had entered the room a short time ago was the sole point of entry…and exit. There would be no escape. The metal walls had turned instantly from a sanctuary to a prison. She silently cursed them as they stared back at her – cold, impassive, and devoid of anything she might use as a weapon.

Hiding was her only option. With any luck, there would be nothing of interest in the small space and the creature would quickly move on.

A low, guttural growl came from the doorway less than ten feet away.

Agnetha began to shake uncontrollably. Fear was beginning to overwhelm her. It would subdue her into inactivity if she let it. She'd seen it happen more than once to soldiers on the battlefield during her time in Iraq. She fought it as she crouched more tightly against the base of the console, desperately trying to blend into it as she searched frantically for a better solution. But there was simply nothing else that she could do right now.

There was a heavy thud very close by followed by the unmistakable sound of a man groaning in pain. It was Cobain…

Agnetha felt a twinge of guilt at having abandoned her friend just moments ago to save herself. Mustering all her courage, she moved slowly toward the edge of the console to peer around it.

Cobain was lying on the floor across the door's threshold, his body half in and half out of the room. Bjorn stood over him, his back to Agnetha. …only it wasn't really Bjorn. There was no doubt about that now.

The Bjorn imposter positioned himself at the top of Cobain's head. Reaching down, he placed both hands against the side of Cobain's head like a vise and lifted it slightly off the floor. Cobain groaned and stirred.

Bjorn opened his mouth and mechanically directed his gaze downward. His jaw wriggled slightly from side to side then yawed open far wider than was humanely possible, like a snake preparing to swallow an oversized kill. His head lunged forward slightly and a thick, deep black fluid poured from his mouth, forming a syrupy puddle in the midst of Cobain's face. The unconscious man convulsed as his body instinctively reacted to the blocking of his airway by the gooey fluid.

The puddle of viscous fluid suddenly vibrated and shattered into a thousand individual droplets. Agnetha watched in horror as each immediately sprouted several tiny legs and flowed rapidly across Cobain's face, entering his mouth, nostrils, and ears. Some of the tiny, tic-like creatures seeped into his eyes beneath his eyelids or plunged directly into his skin leaving small black scars.

Cobain convulsed violently as the skin of his face and neck immediately turned a sickly blue-grey hue. The tiny creatures crawled with ease just beneath his skin and multiplied rapidly as they spread throughout the rest of his body.

Cobain's head jerked suddenly sideways and Agnetha found herself looking into his eyes. She recoiled but couldn't avert her gaze from the grotesque spectacle. Cobain stared back, his eyes screaming silently with agony as they pleaded for help.

Agnetha slinked backward until the cold steel wall prevented her from retreating further, her heart pounding wildly in her chest.

She calculated quickly.

The Bjorn-creature was standing with its back to her, weaving trancelike from side to side. With surprise on her side, she might be able to bound over Cobain's prostrate body and dash down the corridor before the Bjorn-thing could react. But weaving her way through the heart of the vessel's complicated interior to reach the exterior hatch before it caught up with her…*that* would be a much bigger challenge. Even if she did succeed, without their pilot – one of the creature's first victims – she'd be stranded alone out on the arctic tundra, hundreds of miles from anywhere.

The odds weren't very good…but it was her only shot.

vling sensation washed over his tongue as though fire
uring into his mouth, biting him fiercely as they plunged
roat. The feeling spread rapidly as hostile alien cells
mach and lungs with searing flame. His body seized
spasms as the creature consumed him from within.

≈ O ≈

moment for Robert to realize that the scream had been his
ooked frantically around the dimly lit room, trying
to comprehend what had happened. But the sweat-
ets clinging to his body and the incessant pounding in his
kly revealed the harsh truth...it had been just another
. They were growing more frequent and certainly more
longer he remained at Langstadt Station. He felt lately
s teetering on the brink of some great abyss as the edge
mbled beneath his feet.

swore aloud and threw the top sheet to the foot of the bed.
d over to his nightstand and fumbled in the darkness for
The top drawer was ajar, just as he always left it before
into bed. In the dim light, he could just see the dark gleam
tol resting inside. Robert exhaled and felt himself relax a
y how he could find so small a thing to be so soothing.
dn't comfort him quite like it used to.

up and gulped down some water, running his hands through
s he glanced around the room. He'd been through his
nnumerable times and none of them were attractive.

ld simply stay and learn to cope with his fears. Maybe he
t Doc K to prescribe him something that would help him
something that could take the edge off. But Robert cringed
ought of Armand, or anyone else for that matter, knowing
ng about him that was so…personal. The mere thought of it
m flush with embarrassment.

PART ONE

ONE

Present Day

The image blurred as Robert peered into the eyepiece of the microscope. He arched his back and rubbed his eyes, cursing the fatigue. Although he had been up for over thirty hours, he couldn't tear himself away from studying the organism.

It was scary as hell. But it was also thrilling, watching the speed with which it took over its host.

He stood and walked over to the coffee mess, hoping a seventh cup would charge him enough for another hour or two of research. He *should* call it a day *now*. But he wanted so badly to crack the code that enabled its cells to replicate so rapidly. If he could glean that knowledge while weeding out the far less desirable aspects of the organism, he would be a hero.

Across the room two of his colleagues were intent on the very same thing while, ironically, microbiologists across the hall were studying the organism with the opposite purpose – seeking ways to quickly neutralize it… just in case.

"You look like hell."

Robert shrugged his shoulders, "Hey, Martin. Yeah…I should probably go get some rest. You guys making any progress?"

Martin scoffed, "You kidding? This thing is tenacious! The only way we've been able to kill it off with one-hundred percent certainty is with prolonged and intense heat."

Robert set his cup down and stretched. He really was in no mood for small talk. "Guess I'll go to my room for a while," he said stifling a yawn. He waited for his colleague to move out of his way but Martin didn't budge. Instead, he stared into Robert's eyes with an intensity that was highly unnerving.

"Excuse me." Robert tried to step
closer. A strange, warm sensation be
and Robert realized with a start that M

"What the hell are you doing?" Rob
himself. "Let go!"

But Martin stood transfixed, grippin
and staring at him intently. His grip gr
suddenly felt afraid.

As he watched in disbelief, several th
beneath the skin of Martin's wrist like e
moist evening soil. They rapidly snakec
through his fingers, and wound themselv

Robert screamed and shook frantically
the wispy tentacles raced over his hand u
point just below his elbow. They linked
forming a matrix that encapsulated his fo
net.

The tentacles suddenly tapered and plun
his flesh like hot copper wires. Robert scr
more desperately. He could see and feel th
crawling just beneath his skin.

The organism had escaped. It had someh
of the others, one of whom had just reached
he could do now to stop it. It would surge i
body until it had completely taken him over.
utmost certainty. He'd watched the process
the lens of his microscope.

Intense pain erupted from deep within his a
suddenly heavy and limp. He tried again to s
himself unable to breathe. Martin had clampe
Robert's nose and mouth.

That left only two other options. He could put in for a transfer back to the states, where he would surely be relegated to some not-shit desk job. They might even just let him go.

…or he could simply resign.

Either of these options would pretty much eliminate any chance of finding further employment in his field. He was sure that they would see to that.

But microbiology was all he'd ever known…all he ever *cared* to know. There was something serene about observing microbes as they swam about in the confines of a petri dish, blissfully ignorant of the larger world beyond. There was something powerful about manipulating life at the cellular level…it was intoxicating.

He hung his head and sighed. There was no getting around it…he was stuck here at Langstadt.

"Shit," he mumbled. As much as he hated to admit it, his best option was to just tough it out here. He'd made it through fourteen months already. If he could just hang on for another ten, he would simply rotate back to some cushy job back in Seattle or an outlying site to finish up his time. "Ten months," he whispered to himself. It didn't seem like such a long time when he said it.

But there was no question about it. If he stayed, he was going to have to talk to Doc. He'd already given Robert a sleeping aid on a couple of occasions in the past. Yeah, he would just tell Doc that he was having trouble sleeping again.

Robert looked again at the half-open drawer of his nightstand. He reached in and felt the cold, smooth steel of the gun barrel, caressing it delicately with his fingertips and allowing himself to be comforted simply by the presence of the weapon. It had been awhile since he'd last fired it, but he loved how powerful he felt holding it in his hands.

Robert bolted upright and swung his feet over the side of the bed, stunned by the plainness of his epiphany.

He would suggest a competition…a shooting match. Most of the crew carried a pistol and all of them enjoyed shooting. Hell, half the crew was downright fanatic about their second amendment rights. Yet no-one had shot a weapon since they'd arrived at this godforsaken place. Surely, they'd jump at the chance! It would be a welcome break from the routine.

Robert closed his eyes and imagined the weapon recoiling in his hands. He could almost smell the cordite of the spent rounds and see the targets shattering into a thousand pieces.

He opened his eyes, surprised by how the idea of it had filled him with a sense of peace, at least momentarily. Maybe he wouldn't need to talk to Doc after all.

The chirping of his clock suddenly jolted him back to reality. He brought his hand down hard to silence it, cursing it for ruining the moment. He scowled as he remembered what was scheduled for today. Cold dread seeped back into his veins as he made his way to the bathroom. He'd be late now if he took time for a shower, but he didn't really give a rat's ass.

He caressed the pistol for a moment longer before tossing it onto the bed. He focused on his plan as he got himself undressed, sure now that the suggestion would be well-received.

Robert paused on the way to the bathroom, surprised by his reflection in the mirror. He was smiling. He couldn't remember when he'd last done that.

"*Maybe today won't be so bad after all,*" he thought, as he entered the steaming shower.

≈ O ≈

PART ONE

ONE

Present Day

The image blurred as Robert peered into the eyepiece of the microscope. He arched his back and rubbed his eyes, cursing the fatigue. Although he had been up for over thirty hours, he couldn't tear himself away from studying the organism.

It was scary as hell. But it was also thrilling, watching the speed with which it took over its host.

He stood and walked over to the coffee mess, hoping a seventh cup would charge him enough for another hour or two of research. He *should* call it a day *now*. But he wanted so badly to crack the code that enabled its cells to replicate so rapidly. If he could glean that knowledge while weeding out the far less desirable aspects of the organism, he would be a hero.

Across the room two of his colleagues were intent on the very same thing while, ironically, microbiologists across the hall were studying the organism with the opposite purpose – seeking ways to quickly neutralize it… just in case.

"You look like hell."

Robert shrugged his shoulders, "Hey, Martin. Yeah…I should probably go get some rest. You guys making any progress?"

Martin scoffed, "You kidding? This thing is tenacious! The only way we've been able to kill it off with one-hundred percent certainty is with prolonged and intense heat."

Robert set his cup down and stretched. He really was in no mood for small talk. "Guess I'll go to my room for a while," he said stifling a yawn. He waited for his colleague to move out of his way but Martin didn't budge. Instead, he stared into Robert's eyes with an intensity that was highly unnerving.

"Excuse me." Robert tried to step around but Martin stepped in closer. A strange, warm sensation began to spread through his hand and Robert realized with a start that Martin was grasping it firmly.

"What the hell are you doing?" Robert asked, struggling to free himself. "Let go!"

But Martin stood transfixed, gripping Robert's hand even harder and staring at him intently. His grip grew tighter still and Robert suddenly felt afraid.

As he watched in disbelief, several thin strands erupted from beneath the skin of Martin's wrist like earthworms punching through moist evening soil. They rapidly snaked up his hand, weaving through his fingers, and wound themselves around Robert's wrist.

Robert screamed and shook frantically, trying to free himself as the wispy tentacles raced over his hand until they had reached a point just below his elbow. They linked together in several spots, forming a matrix that encapsulated his forearm like a slimy, leathery net.

The tentacles suddenly tapered and plunged into his skin, piercing his flesh like hot copper wires. Robert screamed and shook his arm more desperately. He could see and feel the searing tentacles crawling just beneath his skin.

The organism had escaped. It had somehow infected at least one of the others, one of whom had just reached *him*. There was nothing he could do now to stop it. It would surge inexorably through his body until it had completely taken him over. He knew this with utmost certainty. He'd watched the process dozens of times through the lens of his microscope.

Intense pain erupted from deep within his arm, which grew suddenly heavy and limp. He tried again to scream but found himself unable to breathe. Martin had clamped his hand over Robert's nose and mouth.

A hot crawling sensation washed over his tongue as though fire ants were pouring into his mouth, biting him fiercely as they plunged down his throat. The feeling spread rapidly as hostile alien cells filled his stomach and lungs with searing flame. His body seized with violent spasms as the creature consumed him from within.

≈ O ≈

It took a moment for Robert to realize that the scream had been his own. He looked frantically around the dimly lit room, trying desperately to comprehend what had happened. But the sweat-soaked sheets clinging to his body and the incessant pounding in his chest quickly revealed the harsh truth...it had been just another nightmare. They were growing more frequent and certainly more severe the longer he remained at Langstadt Station. He felt lately like he was teetering on the brink of some great abyss as the edge slowly crumbled beneath his feet.

Robert swore aloud and threw the top sheet to the foot of the bed. He reached over to his nightstand and fumbled in the darkness for the light. The top drawer was ajar, just as he always left it before climbing into bed. In the dim light, he could just see the dark gleam of the pistol resting inside. Robert exhaled and felt himself relax a bit. Funny how he could find so small a thing to be so soothing. Still, it didn't comfort him quite like it used to.

He sat up and gulped down some water, running his hands through his hair as he glanced around the room. He'd been through his options innumerable times and none of them were attractive.

He could simply stay and learn to cope with his fears. Maybe he could get Doc K to prescribe him something that would help him manage, something that could take the edge off. But Robert cringed at the thought of Armand, or anyone else for that matter, knowing something about him that was so…personal. The mere thought of it made him flush with embarrassment.

That left only two other options. He could put in for a transfer back to the states, where he would surely be relegated to some not-shit desk job. They might even just let him go.

...or he could simply resign.

Either of these options would pretty much eliminate any chance of finding further employment in his field. He was sure that they would see to that.

But microbiology was all he'd ever known...all he ever *cared* to know. There was something serene about observing microbes as they swam about in the confines of a petri dish, blissfully ignorant of the larger world beyond. There was something powerful about manipulating life at the cellular level...it was intoxicating.

He hung his head and sighed. There was no getting around it...he was stuck here at Langstadt.

"Shit," he mumbled. As much as he hated to admit it, his best option was to just tough it out here. He'd made it through fourteen months already. If he could just hang on for another ten, he would simply rotate back to some cushy job back in Seattle or an outlying site to finish up his time. "Ten months," he whispered to himself. It didn't seem like such a long time when he said it.

But there was no question about it. If he stayed, he was going to have to talk to Doc. He'd already given Robert a sleeping aid on a couple of occasions in the past. Yeah, he would just tell Doc that he was having trouble sleeping again.

Robert looked again at the half-open drawer of his nightstand. He reached in and felt the cold, smooth steel of the gun barrel, caressing it delicately with his fingertips and allowing himself to be comforted simply by the presence of the weapon. It had been awhile since he'd last fired it, but he loved how powerful he felt holding it in his hands.

Robert bolted upright and swung his feet over the side of the bed, stunned by the plainness of his epiphany.

He would suggest a competition…a shooting match. Most of the crew carried a pistol and all of them enjoyed shooting. Hell, half the crew was downright fanatic about their second amendment rights. Yet no-one had shot a weapon since they'd arrived at this godforsaken place. Surely, they'd jump at the chance! It would be a welcome break from the routine.

Robert closed his eyes and imagined the weapon recoiling in his hands. He could almost smell the cordite of the spent rounds and see the targets shattering into a thousand pieces.

He opened his eyes, surprised by how the idea of it had filled him with a sense of peace, at least momentarily. Maybe he wouldn't need to talk to Doc after all.

The chirping of his clock suddenly jolted him back to reality. He brought his hand down hard to silence it, cursing it for ruining the moment. He scowled as he remembered what was scheduled for today. Cold dread seeped back into his veins as he made his way to the bathroom. He'd be late now if he took time for a shower, but he didn't really give a rat's ass.

He caressed the pistol for a moment longer before tossing it onto the bed. He focused on his plan as he got himself undressed, sure now that the suggestion would be well-received.

Robert paused on the way to the bathroom, surprised by his reflection in the mirror. He was smiling. He couldn't remember when he'd last done that.

"*Maybe today won't be so bad after all*," he thought, as he entered the steaming shower.

≈ O ≈

TWO

Charlie was working at the far end of the lab, hunched over something, and hadn't heard Brian when he entered.

"*Excellent*," he thought as he tiptoed toward her, a huge grin on his face.

"Don't even try it," Charlie warned, sticking her middle finger into the air without even looking up.

"Well you don't have to be so nasty about it," he retorted, chuckling inwardly.

"After last time? I most certainly do!"

He moved up close behind her, placing his hands on her hips as she peered into the centrifuge. "Well maybe you'd like to get to know me a little *better*."

"You don't take your hands off me and you'll be sipping dinner through a straw for a month." Without warning, Charlie slapped her hand down and grasped Brian's wrist, twisting it awkwardly.

Brian gasped in pain and fell to one knee, lifting his remaining hand into the air in resignation. "OK! OK!"

"That's a good boy." Charlie turned on her stool and looked down at him over her glasses as she gave his wrist another twist, evincing a final howl from him.

"Man! You are bru-tal!" He got up slowly, rubbing his hand.

"Mm-hmmm."

Brian glanced around again, "No Hildy yet?"

"Not yet. Should be here any minute though."

"Damn. Was hoping for a little more lovin' before I, you know, put my nose to grindstone," he said, using his best Don Juan voice.

"Yeah, guess you're out of luck."

"Well I can see that I won't be getting any sympathy in here," Brian said in mock resignation, turning to leave.

"Hold on there, hotshot." Charlie hopped off her stool and grabbed a small box from atop the refrigerator. "I believe this is yours," she said, balancing it in her hand.

"Ah! Perfect! My man on the other side came through for me again."

"What exactly is this?"

Brian grinned broadly, 'This, Miss Charlie," he said, taking it from her, "…is the secret to making really good beer."

"Oh. Well, then I suppose there's no chance that *that* thing is going away any time soon, hmmm?" Charlie asked, gesturing toward one corner of the room.

"Not unless you want a mutiny on your hands," Brian replied.

Charlie's stern face finally softened into a wide grin, "Ain't that the truth."

Brian's makeshift brewery was not only his personal pride and joy, it was also a big hit with the crew. He was constantly experimenting with different recipes and had gotten quite good at it. The crew eagerly awaited each fresh batch. Frank had even softened the restrictions on drinking, allowing them to have a full-out bash every month or two as each new batch matured.

Brian was the star of this particular show and he played the part well. He'd prepare for each impending bash weeks in advance and talk it up endlessly to heighten the anticipation.

When the big day came, Brian would organize a contest, usually some silly or humiliating game design for maximum laughs, with the winner getting the honor of drawing the first beer. Nobody else could even sample the new brew until the winner had fully quaffed the last sip. Of course, the lucky crewman would make a huge production of it, slowly sipping the concoction and providing a running commentary, with much exaggeration, on how each sip tasted finer than the last.

The parties were a welcome distraction. Minimal work got done for a day or two after a bash but the revelry released pent-up tensions so management considered it a good trade-off. Anyone foolish enough to take that away, as Charlie had teased, would probably end up as a missing person.

"You know," Brian remarked dryly, "you really ought to show a little more respect for my craft."

"Yes, yes… I know…," Charlie said derisively, "The Egyptians or Greeks or *some other old people* have been brewing beer for thousands of years blah blah blah...."

"Actually, it's the Chinese that have the oldest known recipe," Brian replied, ignoring the barb. "Some of their oldest surviving concoctions date back over 7,000 years."

Charlie laughed and rolled her eyes.

Brian was a human sponge. He was always rattling off some bit of trivia and seemed to know some obscure fact regarding just about everything. While most of the others spent much of their free time watching some movie that they'd already seen a hundred times or quietly viewing porn, Brian would while away the hours watching documentaries. Later, he would spontaneously spout off some weird fact that was apropos to whatever it was that they were doing at the time in a valiant but futile attempt to educate the rest.

The crew mocked and needled him endlessly because of it but it never seemed to faze him. He'd just take it all in stride and continue through his explanation while the others jeered at him or told him to shut up. But Charlie knew that the crew really enjoyed it despite, or perhaps *because of* their light-hearted objections.

"Mind if I just keep this here until we're done today?" Brian asked, returning the box to the top of the fridge.

"Ok by me," Charlie replied, returning to the centrifuge.

"Thanks." Brian made his way to the exam room and peered in. Doc had allowed him to set up his brewery in the unused exam room three years ago as the lab offered a far more suitable environment for the fermentation process. The rig had quadrupled in size over the years but still took up only a small fraction of the room. Not that that mattered. There were two other exam rooms that provided ample space for Doc and the girls to treat any sick or injured crew. Besides, even Doc, who didn't normally drink beer, was impressed at the quality of Brian's product.

It hadn't been so good at first but he'd refined his technique over the years and would routinely churn out a respectable brew, especially since he began receiving his secret ingredient from a friend at McMurdo a year or so ago. But Brian knew the real reason Doc allowed it was because he appreciated the positive psychological impact that this particular hobby had on the rest of the crew.

"Hey, Char. Can I ask you something?"

"Um, sure." Charlie cringed inside and pretended to be focused on her task. She was pretty sure that she knew what was coming next and didn't like the thought of having to lie. She waited several seconds for him to speak and then turned to face him when the silence dragged on just a little too long.

Brian shuffled his feet and looked away. "Is everything…I mean, does Hildy…" Brian's face grew red as he struggled to find the words. Charlie just sat there, staring at him blankly. He immediately regretted having started the conversation. But at the same time, it had been bugging him for some days now and he really needed to know.

"It's just that, Hildy has seemed so…distant lately. I just thought, as her best friend, you might…"

Charlie exhaled heavily. "Brian," she began, "We're dealing with a potential outbreak here and we've all been working long hours. Hildy, Armand, me… We're all just tired and cranky right now."

Brian slumped his shoulders and exhaled. "Yeah, I guess you're right."

"Listen, we should know what we're dealing with in another day or so. It'll probably turn out to be no big deal. Just some nasty virus that'll have to run its course. But until we figure it out…well, we're all going to be a little stressed."

"Yeah," Brian sputtered.

Charlie couldn't tell whether or not he was buying it. "Look, I'm sure she's fine. Give her a couple of days. I'm sure she'll be back to normal once this blows over."

Brian smiled wanly. "Yeah, ok. Thanks." He snatched a small rag from the counter and began furiously wiping down the shiny copper casing of his contraption. "Who the hell has been in here?" he asked indignantly.

"Don't look at me," Charlie yelled, holding up her hands like a cornered fugitive.

Brian grunted in dissatisfaction. As he wiped the metal casing, he suddenly caught sight of his watch. "Shit. I'd better get to work. Big day, you know."

He rubbed down the casing one last time, "I'll be back later, my baby," he said lovingly, as he patted the contraption.

Charlie rolled her eyes and chuckled to herself. "Yes…and I'll be sure to let your other 'baby' know you stopped by."

Charlie could tell that Brian was preoccupied and upset by their awkward conversation and wished she could think of something to say that might lighten the mood before he left. But he was out the door before she could say anything more.

She dropped her head, resting her chin on her chest, and breathed a sigh of relief as the door snapped closed. She'd dodged a bullet and she knew it.

"*Oh, Hildy…you're going to have to tell him.*" She winced at the thought, knowing that it wasn't going to be easy. But it was already unfair that she'd kept it from him this long. It had to come out soon.

She retrieved the small box from the top of the refrigerator and mulled over the situation, absent-mindedly hefting the package in her hands. She sniffed at it but could smell only packing paper and glue.

She scrutinized every inch of the box. It would be so easy to break into the package. She knew she could reseal it so that he'd never know it had been opened. She could have so much fun dangling it over his head, threatening to reveal his secret. Or maybe she could replace the box's prized contents with some innocuous substance like baking soda or salt.

But the thought faded quickly. Ruining a batch of beer would be grounds for a lynching in this environment. Besides, with a crew that constantly worked and lived in such close quarters, it was important to respect the privacy of others. It would be better for the secret to remain with Brian.

Secrets… The thought brought her back to Hildy's looming bombshell and how Brian would likely react once he found out. "Damn secrets," she scowled, tossing the box roughly back onto its perch atop the fridge.

THREE

Kelly entered the cafeteria and looked around. The place was busier than usual as everyone filled their bellies prior to the field test. It was bound to be a long day for the crew, the kind where they wouldn't get a lunch or possibly even a dinner.

The cafeteria was always open for light grazing. But during off-hours it was self-serve, the selection was limited, and, more often than not, the fare wasn't exactly fresh. Breakfast and lunch were the only times during the day that a real meal was served and they'd all learned to take advantage of it whenever possible.

'*Shit, they're not here.*" Kelly frowned, irritated. He was about to turn and leave when he noticed a hand shooting up from a table at the far corner of the room. Viktor was waving him over.

"Ah, good," he said to himself, his previous good mood instantly restored.

"Look at him. He's practically skipping over here," Viktor said, smiling. "He seems pretty optimistic to me."

He watched as Kelly wove through the crowded room on his way to their table. "Wouldn't it be something if he turned out to be right?"

Viktor turned back toward Frank, who sat at the table staring down into the warehouse below through the large Plexiglass window.

"I'm sorry…am I boring you?"

Frank looked up and over at Viktor, "What's that?"

"Good morning, gentlemen," Kelly bellowed before Frank could answer. He placed a clipboard filled with forms atop the table, "I'm thinking it's going to be a fine day!"

"Yes, I was just saying the same to Frank here," Viktor said, a hint of sarcasm in his voice.

"Whatcha got, Kel?" Frank asked, picking up the clipboard and ignoring the jab.

"We're all buttoned up…. except the main hatch, of course. I'll be closing that one behind me. Cables have all been cleared, all other hatches have been secured, and the additional recording equipment is in place and operating. Henrik says we can begin any time you're ready."

Frank smiled weakly, "You really think this is going to do it?" He sipped his coffee, "Seems like a stretch."

Kelly deflated a little, "Maybe so. But we've pretty much tried everything else."

"I'm actually excited to try it," Viktor said with enthusiasm. He, too, had his doubts about Kelly's suggestion. It just seemed too simple. Still, Viktor didn't want to douse the guy's spirits, which had already taken a hit thanks to Frank's nonchalance. "I think he may be on to something. And, we *have* tried just about everything else."

Frank smirked, "Yeah, I know. I'm just jerking your chain."

"Why don't you get these boys rounded up and tell Henrik we'll start in half an hour."

"You got it," Kelly replied, beaming once again. He wasn't exactly fooled by Frank's half-hearted attempt at enthusiasm but he was too excited to let it drag him down.

He turned and strode toward the door, his thick voice booming, "All right now. Let's get a move on! Boss-man says we're kicking off in twenty minutes!"

Most of the crew immediately rose from their seats, just as eager to get started. They were usually limited to experiments of a much smaller scale. It wasn't often that they conducted an all-out operational test.

Frank and Viktor waited as Kelly yelled at a few stragglers to get the lead out.

"What's up with you today?" Viktor asked, as the shouting receded down the hall. "You feeling alright?"

"Me? Yeah, just thinking…." Frank trailed off.

"Anything you'd care to share?"

Frank shrugged and rose from his seat, "Not really. C'mon, let's get a move on," he said with slightly more enthusiasm.

Viktor remained unconvinced but simply nodded, "Right." He looked up at the clock, "I'm going to make a quick stop to shed some coffee then I'll head right down. In the meantime, would you at least *try* to appear to the rest of the crew like you give a shit?"

Frank chuckled, "Alright. See you in a few minutes. Here," he said, extending his hand, "I'll take care of that."

"Thanks." Viktor handed his tray to Frank and made his way to the exit.

Frank walked over to the conveyor and set the trays onto the belt. He turned to leave but was distracted by the bright yellow wrapper on the tray. He stared at it for a moment then reached down to pick it up. He held it for a few seconds, gently running his thumb over the name brightly embossed in the plastic. "Sara Lee," he whispered.

He was surprised at how much it still hurt. "*Has it really been that long?*" he thought. But he knew even as he asked himself that it would be exactly three years tomorrow.

His eyes moved from the name on the wrapper to the ring he still wore on the hand that held it. Kate kept telling him during their periodic on-line video chats that he would never be able to move on as long as he wore it. His answer was always the same, "I'm not ready to move on, sis."

"But it's what Sarah would've wanted," Kate would insist.

"I know," he would admit.

They'd go round-and round for a minute or two but it always ended in the same stalemate. Deep down he knew she was right, but he just couldn't bring himself to let go.

The wall clock chimed the hour, breaking Frank from his reverie. He tossed the wrapper back onto the tray just before it disappeared into the wall on the conveyor.

He was the only one in the cafeteria now and he allowed himself a moment of peace, knowing that he wouldn't have that luxury once they starting things up. Then, he donned his cap and headed to the Observation Deck.

≈ O ≈

Less than half an hour later, the observation deck was humming with barely concealed excitement. The entire crew was pumped by the first significant success that they'd had in a very long time. Still, each crewman kept their thoughts to themselves, fearing any spoken word might jinx things.

Brian quickly scanned the readings displayed on his monitor, hardly believing what he was seeing. Until just moments ago, all he could think about was his earlier conversation in the lab with Charlie. Something hadn't quite seemed right. But the sudden developments aboard the spacecraft immediately drove all other thoughts from his mind.

He was trying to be cool, to project a calm professionalism, but it seemed his every movement was betraying him. He could feel his temples pulsing with every heartbeat. He grimaced in annoyance and pulled his headset forward in a lame attempt to mask them. This irritating little quirk had cost him alot of money over the years. He'd only recently stopped participating in the weekly poker matches when he finally realized that the other players could read him like a billboard when he got excited over a good hand, thanks to his 'flashing' temples.

"It's looking good here." Brian scowled, annoyed that he couldn't stop his excitement from reflecting in his voice.

"Yes. It's looking pretty good in here too," Henrik replied from within the vessel. Brian glanced up at the monitor that displayed the interior of the ship. Henrik looked cool and professional as he directed the experiment from inside the spacecraft. This heightened Brian's annoyance at his own giddiness, which he just couldn't seem to mask. Still, he clearly wasn't the only one. Other members of the crew seemed just as animated as they scrambled about checking and re-checking equipment.

Brian peeked to his left trying to get a glimpse of the vessel through the Observation Deck window but the glare from the interior lighting prevented him from getting a good look from this far back in the room. He could just make out the aft end the spacecraft at the far end of the warehouse.

"Can't see a friggin' thing," he mumbled between clenched teeth. He glanced over at Parker, who was in the best position within the O-deck for viewing the entire ship directly below. Brian was stuck with a view of only the instrument panel before him.

"Ho-lee shit!" Kelly's baritone whisper was just audible through the speaker. The entire O-deck crew suddenly craned toward the monitor.

From this angle, Brian could just make out the image on the screen. Every man aboard the vessel was on their feet, their bodies oriented toward something at the center of the compartment. But it was impossible from this angle to tell what had captured their attention. Brian removed his headset, which allowed him to lean back further for a better look. Even then, the image of the ship's interior on the monitor was dark and it took several seconds for him to see it.

Inside the ship, the normally subtle glow at the upper and lower sections of the wall had grown to an appreciable intensity and the bridge was now bathed in a comfortable, uniform light. Kelly and Henrik stood in the center of the room beside a translucent column of shimmering light that stretched from floor to ceiling.

The column was comprised of thousands of individual shining tiles that blinked in various shades of white, grey, black, and tan. Most glistened from a fixed position within the column but numerous smaller segments were alive with movement. These shifted more vibrantly in repeated patterns within invisible boundaries, each like a small animated picture trapped within an unseen frame. One larger segment near the center of the column flashed even more frequently in quick, seemingly haphazard flashes.

Henrik slowly approached the column as the rest of the crew stood transfixed, mesmerized by the graceful shimmering and shifting of the light. He stopped abruptly and reached toward the column. "I can feel its energy," he said, his voice teeming with amazement. He rotated his hand slowly as it hovered within inches of the column, "It's like a low-voltage tingle."

Kelly moved closer to the column and reached out slowly. "Yeah. That's it exactly. It's like a mild electric shock, but…not unpleasant."

He waved his hand slowly along the column, being careful not to touch it, and paused for a moment near one of the more animated segments, his eyes widening in surprise. "The energy's different here. It's…subtle, but definitely more defined. I get the distinct feeling that there is a sense of 'purpose' here," he said, continuing to wave his hand over the shimmering section.

Henrik shifted his hand, waving it over a similar section. "Yes. It definitely feels different here. It's hard to describe, but Kelly's right. The rest of the column seems to emit a more general energy. It's much more specific…more 'refined' here. It's like it's 'wanting' me to reach out and touch it," he said, his fingers probing closer to the column.

"For God's sake, stop!"

The 0-deck crew jumped in unison as Viktor's thickly accented voice boomed over the speaker and reverberated through the room.

On the screen, Henrik had stopped in mid-reach and slowly withdrew his hand.

"Now's not the time to get careless. We've been waiting for this for a long time. Let's not screw it up now."

Brian looked around the O-deck. The entire crew stood frozen, enthralled by the images on the monitor.

"Yes," Henrik said sheepishly, "There'll be plenty of time to analyse this later." He gazed up at the monitor and flicked his eyebrows skyward, "Sorry."

"Kim, how's the video feed?" Frank asked, forcing the crew to focus on their individual tasks.

"Feed one looks good and clear. Feed two…" Kim turned to Sun Ah and mumbled something to her in Korean. Sun Ah typed furiously at her terminal and the focus on the monitor beside her suddenly sharpened. "Clear," he finally shouted back.

Brian looked over at Erland, who had already been squinting over in his direction. "Wow," Erland mouthed. Brian raised his eyebrows in agreement.

Frank cleared his throat, "Vik's right. We don't need another casualty so let's all stay focused."

During the last four years, two separate tests had ended disastrously. A crewman had been electrocuted when she unintentionally contacted an energized tellurium node. A second member of the crew died trying to rescue her. In another instance, a hung-over electrician misread a gauge and mistakenly overloaded the vessel's power distribution network, damaging almost a third of the circuits on the upper level. The mishap had destroyed several tellurium nodes, components they had neither the knowledge nor the raw materials to repair or replace.

Brian watched as the crew responded to Frank's urging, working zealously to ensure that everything was exactly as it should be.

"Care to join the rest of us?"

Brian looked at Frank, who was eyeing him from just a few feet away. He felt his face flush as he realized he was the only one who hadn't returned to his terminal. He'd actually been holding his breath as Henrik had reached towards the column and was disappointed that Viktor had stopped him. He quickly sat back down at his computer but could barely stay seated.

"*This is friggin' awesome*," he thought as he took his seat, barely able to contain his excitement. His eyes darted back and forth from his equipment console to the vessel's interior monitor. He wanted so desperately to know what was going on below them.

The desire to be more connected with the action overwhelmed him, impairing his judgement and causing him to neglect the oscilloscope beside his console. Ordinarily, he wouldn't have missed the large, bright green electronic spike shining so prominently on its display.

FOUR

Andre snapped several more photographs of the penguins as he balanced precariously on the rocky outcrop, smiling at his own ingenuity. The outcrop provided the perfect vantage point for capturing the bulk of the group against a backdrop of the coastline, a single majestic peak accentuating the shot in the near distance.

The angle of the sun so low on the horizon illuminated the orange bands circling the necks of the males, clearly identifying the penguins as Emperors. It was a cover shot that would command a pretty sum from National Geographic or some other nature-centric magazine.

Andre swore as the ground beneath his foot suddenly gave way. He released his grip on the camera and reached frantically for a handhold, just managing to grab onto a sharp peak to arrest his fall. Below him, Adeline gasped loudly.

"It's ok, dear! I'm alright!"

He could hear her breathe a sigh of relief. Andre smiled, knowing that she'd be looking up at him angrily. She had been against the climb and had begged him repeatedly to stay with her on the shore. She would surely let him have it now once he was safely back down.

A glint of sunlight reflected by the camera lens caught his eye. He held it up to inspect it as soon as he had stabilized himself.

"Damn!"

"What is it, love?"

"It's nothing. I'll be right down."

Andre placed the plastic protector over his freshly cracked lens. He'd surely catch hell now.

A loud din suddenly arose from the waddle below as the penguins seemed suddenly agitated. Andre stopped his descent to watch. Something seemed to have spooked the group, which was now nervously moving away from him. Andre scanned the area but could see nothing obvious.

The waddle suddenly surged with renewed vigor as if the threat had suddenly grown more imminent.

"What's that noise? You hear it, that high squeal?" Adeline shouted from below.

Andre could hear nothing but the racket of the penguins as they scampered away. The leading edge of the group had reached the ledge of the low cliff at the shoreline. Without hesitating, the leading penguins jumped into the water even as several Leopard seals could clearly be seen broaching the surface of the icy waters nearby.

Andre hurriedly removed the cap from his lens, wishing that he'd had a video unit with him instead. The headlong plunge of the penguins into waters infested with one of their fiercest natural predators was highly peculiar. Surely none of his peers would believe such behaviour without convincing evidence.

He angled the camera and rapidly snapped off several shots through the cracked lens. He dropped the camera from his eye and peered over it at the sight before him, searching for a better view. Thousands of penguins continued to surge over the edge of the cliff and into the sea. Andre expected to see the waters swirling furiously with activity as the seals converged on easy and plentiful prey. But surprisingly, the predators were nowhere to be seen.

Andre searched the waters, finally spotting them in the distance swimming rapidly away from the bay. The bizarre behaviour of the penguins had been fascinating enough. But combined with the equally odd behaviour of the seals, Andre found himself suddenly feeling uneasy. He swung the camera around his neck and onto his back as he hastily retreated from his perch.

"Did you see that?!" he asked excitedly, once he was safely on the shore.

Adeline nodded as she scanned the now empty beach. She kept opening her jaw wide and moving it from side to side as though trying to unblock her ears after a long flight.

"What's wrong?"

"Don't you hear it?"

Andre stood quietly and strained to hear. "I don't hear anything."

"You don't hear it? …that high-pitched squeal?"

Andre paused again and listened.

"It's coming from over here," Adeline said as she walked slowly down the beach toward the area just vacated by the penguins.

Andre followed her. After several yards, he began to hear it as well.

"It's getting louder."

Andre nodded, "I hear it now."

After several more steps, Adeline stopped and placed her hands over her ears. "It hurts. Let's get out of here."

It was certainly louder now but not to the point where it was causing him pain. Several yards in front of them a slight dune rose to obscure their view of the beach. "You go back, dear. I want to look around a bit." He walked with her, supporting her by the arm as he pointed her back toward the boat.

"Andre, something ain't right here. I am leaving right now, with or without you."

Andre peered over his shoulder desperately wanting to see what was beyond the dune. Instead, he nodded reluctantly, "Alright." He placed his arm around her gently and led her back. He'd jot down the coordinates back at the boat and return later with a few others to investigate further.

He glanced at his watch and frowned. It would be at least three hours before he could get back here. He hoped that whatever it was, it would still be there.

Less than fifty yards from where they'd stopped, in the area where the waddle of penguins had been concentrated just moments ago, the ground shimmered in the fading sunlight. Innumerable shiny black pebbles strewn across the beach vibrated along zig-zagging paths toward an innocuous spot on the shore, where they jockeyed for position atop each other like iron filings on a magnet. Those in the center of the pile jumped like popcorn, resonating from the frequency of the barely perceptible signal broadcasting from the object awakening just beneath the sand.

FIVE

Robert lingered at the far corner of the O-deck, sulking as he stirred his fifth cup of coffee. How quickly his mood had changed.

Several of the crew had commended him earlier for his idea regarding the shooting match. It seemed everyone was genuinely excited by the prospect of a break in the routine. For a brief moment, the crew seemed to treat him as an equal, patting him on the back and offering to buy his next beer. That had felt awesome.

But it had been a fleeting moment.

The small knot in his stomach that had been there earlier in the day had grown exponentially during the last hour, aggravated by the recent events aboard the vessel.

He eyed the room warily and shook his head in disgust. "*Fools! They have no idea...*"

But he did. He was one of the few at the site that knew the craft's ugly secret.

He'd been working at the home office in Seattle, cultivating a new strain of bacteria that rapidly broke down petroleum into harmless base constituents. They'd tested it recently with excellent results against a small oil spill in a nearby bay. Within days, all that had been left of the mess was a floating, sponge-like muck that could be easily scooped up and disposed of safely. It even worked well on small animals, eliminating the need to scrub them by hand. Just spray them with a fine mist and release. The bacteria would do its work and they'd be completely normal in a day or so. Except for a few dead fish, you'd have never known that a spill had occurred.

He'd gone to work as usual that Thursday morning when, without warning or explanation, they'd suddenly and unceremoniously dispatched him to some small research facility ninety miles away. He hadn't even been aware of the site's existence.

He'd been glad for the change, actually. He hadn't been getting along with many of his co-workers since he'd succeeded in developing the bacteria. While it had put him in exceedingly good standing with his superiors, and placed him among the top microbiologists in the country, it had the opposite effect among his peers. Many of them had grown distant and aloof, apparently resentful of his success.

So, Robert found himself suddenly working at the Dunford Research Center, a small facility tucked away in an isolated area of Lewis-McChord Air Force Base in eastern Washington State. Despite its small size and obscure location, Dunford contained some of the most advanced laboratory equipment that Robert had ever seen. When he first arrived, he'd felt like a kid in a candy store except that he could actually touch all the goodies that surrounded him. He almost didn't know what to touch first.

He had been just as intoxicated as everyone else when the first tissue sample had arrived.

Robert felt his skin erupt in goosebumps as he recalled the first time that he'd actually handled the alien flesh.

They'd been informed only the day before that it was coming. And they had been repeatedly warned about how dangerous it was, although it was never quite specified in what way.

He hadn't found that strange at the time. Every scientist at the site worked with dangerous biological microorganisms daily. They were all quite used to working under exceedingly rigorous biohazard precautions.

But the higher ups had droned on incessantly about protective measures…like the highly-trained scientists had never heard it before. It was only later, once Robert had seen what the alien flesh was capable of, that the company's omission of the details regarding the dangers of the specimens began to gnaw at him. But at the time, he'd wished that they'd just shut up and let them examine it.

His attitude changed completely the first time he saw it in action.

He'd been among the first to witness its capabilities. It was he who had been operating the glove box, slipping his hands into the heavy butyl rubber gloves on the outside of the contraption and manipulating the cells contained within it on the other side. He heard the gasps of the other scientists, who were watching on the monitor behind him, as he combined the samples.

It had taken less than a minute. Before their eyes, the alien flesh absorbed the test cells he'd introduced into their presence. All subsequent tests had the same result. Insect, rat, goat, pig, human…it didn't matter. It assimilated them all with equal ease, violently and with frightening speed.

Within minutes the alien cells had completely assimilated the host cells and formed an exact replica. Once the process was completed, the resulting copy was nearly indistinguishable for the original, even at the cellular level. He'd never seen anything so amazing…and so utterly scary.

Robert sipped his coffee and studied the crew on the O-deck. It annoyed him when they'd talk about how exciting it would be to come across a frozen alien. They'd speculate for hours about what the damned things might look like based on the layout of the ship and what they could learn from it, if they could revive it. They all knew, of course, about what had happened when the team had first found the vessel in 1993. But the company had seen to it that they knew only the vaguest of details.

'*Things would be different if we were to come across one now,*" they'd argue. "*Clearly, any being intelligent enough to build a vessel that could traverse the galaxy could be made to understand that we meant them no harm.*"

The consensus was that the creature had attacked back then because of its circumstances. Awakening from a long, deep sleep on an unfamiliar world and confronted by strange beings with questionable intentions, who wouldn't be defensive?

When he'd first arrived on-site, Robert would quietly scoff at their ignorance. He'd gloat inwardly about the things he knew about the vessel's inhabitants, things about which the rest of the crew had no idea. But eventually his derision turned to envy and he wished that he, too were as ignorant as they were about the organisms terrifying capabilities.

"Excuse me."

Robert jumped, sloshing coffee all over his hand as Shifty squeezed by him on his way to the coffee mess.

"Sorry," Shifty mumbled feebly.

"No problem," Robert replied, trying to sound nonchalant but feeling foolish as he wiped the spilled coffee from his pants. He'd been so lost in thought he hadn't even heard the man approach.

Shifty stumbled as he grasped the top of a water cooler and poured himself a cup.

"Are you alright?" Robert silently cursed himself for asking.

Shifty gulped down the water in one swig and poured another cup. "Yeah. Just dying of thirst…and I have a wicked headache."

"Oh." Robert breathed a sigh of relief and turned away. He was in no mood to even attempt being sociable – which he knew he sucked at – and was glad that the situation called for no further action or conversation. He pretended to be captivated by something on the other side of the room near the oversized window as he waited for Shifty to go away.

"*Why the hell am I even here?*" His role in the current experiment was pretty insignificant, a fact for which he was both glad and annoyed. He didn't really *want* a part in this and would've preferred to be just about anywhere else. But for some reason, Frank wanted him here. He sensed that the rest of the team on the O-deck were well aware of his lack of a purpose in the current endeavour and that embarrassed him.

Erland looked up at him and gave him a terse nod. Robert gave him a weak wave and Erland returned his attention to his terminal. Robert sighed. His discomfort with people seemed to get worse every time he changed jobs. "*I should just…*"

The equipment rack directly in front of him was suddenly rushing toward him as a loud crash reverberated from behind. Before he could react, he'd smacked his head hard on the edge of the rack's metal frame and fallen across someone's lap. A woman screamed shrilly and jumped up from her seat hitting Robert with her knees and causing him to hit his head again on the underside of the keyboard tray.

Robert was on the verge of passing out and was only vaguely aware of a commotion happening somewhere in the vicinity of where he had just been standing. His mind flashed back to a moment ago, when he'd been recalling his days at Dunford, filling him with a sudden dread.

He fought to push himself up, more concerned now with what was happening behind him than he was with the pain. He felt dizzy and balanced precariously on his hands and knees, attempting to steady himself before rising further. He sensed rather than saw the dark shadow looming toward him and turned his head away just as it smacked into his side, throwing him again into the rack of equipment.

Robert's head snapped back sharply as it connected for a third time with the cold metal frame and darkness enveloped him.

Charlie entered the lab juggling a cup of coffee, a corn muffin, two books, and three vials of blood. Armand watched her as she glided over to the counter and gracefully put everything in its place, even managing to sip her coffee in the process. As usual, she was lightly humming to herself, seemingly oblivious to everything else.

"I don't know how you do that," he finally said.

Charlie jumped, placing her hand delicately on her chest. "Dammit, Armand!"

"Sorry. Didn't mean to startle you."

She exhaled deeply, "No, it's fine. You know me.... off in my own little world."

Armand glanced behind her toward the door, 'No Hildegard this morning?"

"She's right behind me. Just had to make a little 'pit-stop' first," Charlie replied making a squeamish face.

Armand winced. "Still hitting her pretty hard, huh?"
Charlie nodded, "Just tried having breakfast with her but she says that the smell of food still makes her sick. She can't even go near the kitchen."

"Well, it should pass in a couple more weeks."

Charlie smiled. It was almost funny hearing that coming from a man. Although it had been a while, she could still remember the gut wrenching intensity of her own morning sickness. There had been weeks when she could barely even get out of bed. But she could just as vividly remember the joy she felt, once the sickness passed, of having a life growing inside her. It had been almost overwhelming at times and made the nausea and vomiting pale in comparison. Even now, years later, she longed to feel it again. She felt her eyes beginning to mist.

"Are you alright?"

Charlie turned her head away suddenly, "Yes. I'm fine," she said feigning a sneeze and reaching for a tissue on the counter. She blew her nose noisily and then walked toward a waste receptacle on the far end of the room, dabbing her eyes along the way.

"You sure?"

"Yes. Yes, I'm fine."

Armand nodded, "Before I forget, would you be a gem and refill Robert's Ambien? He's looking pretty ragged lately and I suspect he's having trouble sleeping again."

Charlie exhaled in relief, *"Good. He fell for it."*

She laughed lightly, "OK, but I don't think it's going to do him any good. That guy is wound so tight…"

Armand paused. "He is, isn't he?" he asked quietly, as if just realizing it. He made a mental note to dig into this a little more later on. Between the isolation, the harshness of the Antarctic environment, and the psychological stresses of the unique work in which they were engaged, the crew already had enough to deal with. The last thing they needed out here was for someone to 'lose it'.

"Are those from Matteus?" he asked, pointing to the vials she'd brought in.

"Mm hmm. He's says he's feeling fine but I told him that he needs to lay low until we know for sure. He's still in indoc so it should be easy for him to limit contact with the rest of the crew. I feel bad for the guy though. Been here less than a week and he's already making quite an impression. And you know they're not going to let him off lightly."

Armand laughed, "No, these guys will needle him every chance they get. It took me two years to live down the 'Novocain incident'."

Charlie laughed aloud. She hadn't been at the warehouse during the episode but she'd heard more than once since her arrival the story of how he, the site's doctor, had passed out from an injection during a routine dental procedure. The attending physician had tried to keep it quiet but Armand had been one of four people that had arrived at McMurdo that day from the site for an exam. Somehow, the others had learned of it and the story had spread like wildfire once they returned to the warehouse. The crew had razzed him mercilessly for months.

They learned later that the Novocain injection had caused a dangerous drop in Armand's blood pressure, which was already low due to an undiagnosed bout of Mononucleosis. But he'd taken over as the site physician just two months prior to the incident and the crew had no intention of taking it easy on the new guy, even if there was a valid medical reason behind it.

"Well," he said, moving over to the counter. "We don't really know for sure if he's the culprit, although all signs do seem to point to him."

Just then, the door swung open and Hildy entered, clutching her stomach. Her eyes glistened from freshly-shed tears and she leaned to support herself against the wall.

Charlie rushed over to her and the two women hugged as Hildy wept silently on Charlie's shoulder. After a brief moment, she regained her composure and gently pushed away.

"Hildegard, come sit," Armand said pulling his chair from behind his desk.

Hildy looked up at him from her chair, her eyes wrinkled with a mixture of anxiety and tenderness. Armand was the only one of the crew who called her that. To everyone else, she was 'Hildy'.

She smiled weakly as she eased into the chair, grateful for his thoughtfulness. Armand's leather chair was the only one in the lab that offered any comfort. The others were cold and uncomfortable, the tripod-type metal stools typical in any medical lab. The three of them bitched constantly about how the company had spared no expense in equipping the rest of the facility but had gone so cheap in the 'stool' department just to save a few bucks.

Charlie knelt beside Hildy and placed her hand gently on her arm.

"I almost told him this morning," Hildy said, so weakly that they'd barely heard her. "I don't know what it is. I've tried to tell him a number of times but when he's sitting there across from me I can't seem to get the words out."

"Hildegard," Armand exhaled, "I know you're doing your best but you're going to have to tell him. And you're going to have to do it soon. I've held off on saying anything but I'm not going to be able to do so much longer. I can give you to the end of the week but, by Saturday, you know I'm going to have to inform Frank. I'm sure you'd rather Brian hear it from you than from someone else."

He touched her hand. "And, you've got to decide what you're going to do," he said gently.

Charlie looked up at him suddenly. "What do you mean?" she asked, sharply. She rose to her feet and looked down at Hildy, "Are you thinking of aborting?" she asked incredulously.

Hildy looked up from her chair, surprised at Charlie's hostility.

"You can't be serious!"

"No, you don't understand," Armand said firmly, placing his hand on Charlie's shoulder.

She brushed him off, shooting him an angry look. She opened her mouth as if to say something then abruptly turned and left.

Hildy sobbed quietly. "Look, Honey," Armand said, turning back to face her, "It doesn't matter what anyone else thinks. You've got to do what's right for *you*. Just make sure that, whatever you decide, you do it for the right reasons."

Hildy nodded, "I know, "she said quietly. She stood and gave him a hug, "Thanks."

Armand winked and gave her a smile, "And don't worry about her," he said gesturing toward the door.

Hildy nodded and smiled. She knew what was going on in Charlie's head right now. They'd spoken of it only once, just after Hildy had confided in her friend that she suspected she was pregnant. Charlie had smiled weakly and tried to be supportive and encouraging but had suddenly burst into tears. After several minutes of sobbing, Charlie told Hildy of her own experience several years ago.

She had treasured every minute of it, despite the terrible sickness in her first trimester, and had looked forward eagerly to having a child. She'd cherished the feeling every day of the little life growing inside her. Every little movement inside her flooded her with joy and amazement. She knew that she'd miss those feelings terribly once the child was born and wished she could prolong her pregnancy.

Yet the actual birth of her daughter had been just as overwhelming. Clutching the small warm body of her little girl close to her chest…hearing the little 'coos' and feeling her soft breath against her skin. Charlie had felt like she was in heaven. Losing her so unexpectedly just days later had been a terrible blow and she still bore the emotional scars. For her to be thinking that Hildy was considering an abortion – which couldn't have been further from the truth - must've been just too much for Charlie to bear.

The phone on Armand's belt buzzed suddenly. He glared down at it for a moment before answering it, annoyed by the interruption. "Damn thing," he said through gritted teeth.

Hildy smirked. She found it funny that he was so technically savvy when it came to the advanced equipment and machines that supported his medical work yet so repulsed by something as simple as a cell phone. But he hated having to wear the infernal device and griped about it often, calling it an invasion of his privacy.

The fact was that every other member of the crew found the system to be incredibly convenient. They were glad that the company had installed its own self-contained mobile phone system to ease communications within the facility, allowing anyone at the site to readily contact any other member regardless of where they were. The Americans had all taken to calling their phones 'cellulars' in mock deference to the Norwegians.

Due to the relatively small size of the site, the system's power requirements were pretty minimal, which meant that it didn't create a large communications footprint. Of course, the company had also ensured that the system was encrypted, just in case.

Hildy watched as he strode toward his desk. He'd been there for her ever since she showed up at the site over a year ago. They'd hit it off right away and he'd since become a wonderful mentor to both her and Charlie. But he'd also become a very special friend, a bond that had certainly grown stronger during these last few weeks as he listened patiently while she babbled on endlessly about relationship issues. He never judged.... never pried or pushed. Just listened. Then, when she'd thoroughly exhausted herself, he would begin.

It was amazing really.... He'd enquire about things that he surely knew the answers to already. He would deftly ask her a stream of seemingly unrelated questions, subtly causing her to reflect on her own thoughts and feelings until the answer to her present issue seemed just as obvious to her as it had clearly been to him from the beginning. He would tenderly guide her through her self-inflicted maze of confusion bringing her around to the one inescapable conclusion.

Hildy had spilled her guts to him so often that she felt he knew her better than anyone, including Brian. All *he* ever wanted to talk about was this friggin' place.

But Armand...he was different.

He'd chat with her often while they worked and seemed to know something about everything. They shared many of the same views on life and had developed the ability to anticipate each other. Things she didn't say aloud he seemed somehow able to guess. It was tremendously stimulating. In fact, she'd realized recently that she was greatly attracted to him. She'd even fantasized, more than once, about making love with him...about what it would feel like to run her hands over his taut, bare chest as he pushed himself inside her. She felt her face flush at the thought.

Hildy jumped as Armand slammed his cell phone onto his desk. "Sorry," he said, reaching for his coat and a medical kit, "but we are urgently needed elsewhere." He rushed by her and then paused at the door, "You know what...why don't you stay here and finish processing those vials. Charlie's going to meet me there so there's really no need...."

“No,” she said, grabbing her coat. “I’m alright. Let’s do this.”

Armand nodded and held the door for her as she slipped by him, purposely brushing against him in the cramped doorway and hoping she hadn’t been too obvious about it.

SIX

Robert felt two distinctly separate sensations as he regained consciousness; the cold tile pressing against his face and a warm, wetness that covered much of his backside. A third sensation, a splitting headache, revealed itself only when he tried to move. He lay there quietly for a moment and listened.

The din on the O-deck had died down some but he could hear the others tending to another co-worker who also must've been injured by…whatever-the-hell had happened. Muted voices were urgently shouting instructions. Slowly, the voices grew clear.

Robert opened his eyes and found himself staring at a ventilation grid just inches from his face. The bump on his head was screaming for attention but, oddly, he felt nothing else. He rolled slowly onto his back and was surprised to see Sun Ah kneeling beside him.

She placed her hand gently on his leg, "Don't move." She turned her head and spoke in Korean to her husband, who immediately came over.

"How are you doing, Robert?" he asked, slowly and deliberately. "Try not to move. Help is on the way."

Robert nodded weakly and closed his eyes. It annoyed him how Kim spoke, enunciating every syllable as if each were a separate, stand-alone statement.

A flurry of activity was happening on the floor behind Sun Ah. As much as he wanted to know what was going on, he didn't dare move. Doing so only sent pain coursing through his head and neck. He opened his eyes just as Sun Ah placed a cool, damp compress on this forehead.

"What happened?" he asked weakly.

She turned to look behind her, "Shifty," she mumbled.

"*What the hell is that supposed to mean?*" Robert scowled. He should've known better than to ask her. Her English sucked. She wasn't all that great a technician either and was at the site only because it was the only way that her husband would agree to *his* assignment.

Despite the pain, Robert propped himself up on his elbows, eager to find out what had happened and alleviate his fears.

Shifty was lying on the floor and moaning. Charlie was gently supporting Shift's head between her knees as Armand quickly sized him up. Although disoriented, Shifty didn't seem to be badly injured.

Robert scowled then winced as his outward display of displeasure sent fresh pain slicing through his head. He was both offended and angry. His own injuries seemed much more serious yet Shifty was the one getting all the attention. His head was covered with welts from his collisions with the rack and was throbbing furiously. He was also pretty sure that he'd thrown his back out.

Robert stiffened, suddenly aware of the warm, wet sensation he'd felt when he first regained consciousness. He inched out from beneath the instrument console, wincing from a sharp pain that sliced through his hand. Blood oozed from a small cut on his palm. He noticed shards of glass littering the floor around them, remnants of the snack plates and beverage cups that had occupied the counter near the door until just moments ago. One shard had made a small cut on Shifty's face as he'd writhed around, smearing the floor near his head with blood. Robert froze at the sight of it as the warm stickiness soaking the back of his shirt suddenly took on a new significance.

"I'm bleeding," he choked.

Kim and Sun Ah looked down at him curiously.

"Are you deaf *and* blind?! I said, I'm bleeding! Get the doctor over here!"

Sun Ah brought the cold compress over to one side and began dabbing his face.

"It's ok," Kim said, as Sun Ah continued tending to Robert's face, "It's just a small cut."

"Not there, you idiot! My back! My back! Get the damn doctor over here!"

Kim looked at him dubiously then gently shoved his wife aside. He cautiously rolled Robert onto his side and ran his hand carefully along his co-worker's back. Near the small of his back, Robert's shirt was indeed wet and sticky but even in the poor lighting Kim knew it wasn't blood. He brought his hand to his nose and whiffed, the familiar odor confirming his suspicion.

"Is it bad?" Robert asked, now on the verge of panic.

"It's coffee," Kim said dismissively, as he turned his attention back to Shifty.

Robert felt his heart sink in his chest as his face flushed. Sure enough, the shattered coffee pot lay on the floor just a few feet away. No doubt they'd all get a good laugh over that one later.

He lay there brooding, relieved now that no-one else was paying him any attention.

≈ O ≈

Brian was anxious to get back to work now that Shifty's condition appeared to have stabilized. He'd done what he could to help care for the guy, which wasn't much. But now that they'd loaded him onto the stretcher and Doc was working his magic the whole thing seemed more like an annoying distraction rather than a true crisis.

He moved to the rear of the small knot of men and women still tending to Shifty, looking for a way to get back to the real excitement without seeming like he didn't care. It had only been a few minutes but it seemed far longer.

He craned his neck to scan his terminal. It was difficult to tell for sure at this distance but everything seemed to be normal.

Doc and Frank were talking in muted tones at the foot of the stretcher, where Shifty lay idly. Hildy had finished inserting an IV line and was monitoring Shifty's vitals for what must have been the fiftieth time as Charlie drew some blood.

Two guards entered the O-deck. "He's all set to go," Armand instructed. "Take him to his quarters, though, not to medical. I'll be right behind you."

"Finally," Brian murmured to himself as he started back toward his station.

"Thanks for getting here so quickly, Doc." Frank said, turning toward his station.

He'd taken about half a step but stopped as Armand grabbed his arm.

"I need to talk to you."

Frank opened his mouth to protest but the seriousness of Armand's expression caused him to reconsider.

Frank turned to Erland, "Check in with Henrik. I'll be right back."

"Right," Erland acknowledged, striding over to Frank's terminal.

"*What the hell is this all about?*" Brian thought.

He hung his headset over his terminal and walked over to Erland. Halfway there, he noticed Kim and his wife still tending to Robert on the floor.

"Hey, man. You ok?"

Kim turned to him and nodded, "Doc says possibly a concussion but nothing life threatening."

"Ooooh," Brian groaned, noticing the large welt on Robert's head, "Yeah, that's gonna hurt in the morning."

"It hurts *now*," Robert stuttered, causing the others to chuckle. "Hey, listen," Brian said, turning to Kim, "I can monitor both positions from here. Why don't you get him up to medical so Doc can have a look at him?"

"I can't. I've got an anomaly," Kim said, gesturing toward his terminal. "Frank asked me to run a diagnostic."

Brian cursed under his breath. "OK. I'll take him then. Keep an eye on my position til I get back."

Kim nodded as he and Sun Ah helped Robert to his feet.

In the hallway, Armand watched as the two guards wheeled Shifty toward the elevator.

"What's going on Doc?" Frank asked with obvious impatience.

"I'm not positive yet but I think we may be facing an outbreak of meningitis. I think we need to isolate him right away."

Frank's eyes widened momentarily in surprise as Armand continued, "This is the third case in as many days. James and Henna are stable right now. I can give them stuff for the pain but, if this is meningitis, they're going to need more than that. And, I'm afraid we're pretty low on what we really need to fight it. We've taken some blood and should know for sure within the next twelve hours."

Armand took a deep breath before continuing. "Frank, this could be real bad. If it is meningitis, it looks to be bacterial rather than viral. Much more dangerous and much more communicable."

"Shit," Frank muttered, "What do you need me to do?"

"We'll, for starters, we need to quarantine anyone who has any symptoms…severe headache, nausea, fever or any combination. We should also quarantine the new guy."

"Matteus?" Frank asked doubtfully. "He seems fine."

"Perhaps. But he's probably the carrier. Meningitis doesn't just spring out of nowhere. He must've brought it here with him."

Frank scratched the back of his head as he thought. "OK. You do what you can. Soon as we're through here, I'll be sure to pass the word."

Frank turned, anxious now to get back to the experiment, but stopped as Armand grabbed his arm again.

"Frank...we don't have enough pharmaceuticals here to treat a large outbreak. I suggest you contact McMurdo ASAP to get more. They should also be warned. Lord only knows how many people he may have infected during his stay there."

"Alright, Doc," Frank said, somberly. "I'll get Anders right on it."

Armand nodded as he turned to leave. "One other thing. I need to speak with you later on about a private matter, when you've got a moment. Nothing pressing."

"Sure thing," Frank replied, "Anything else."

"I think that's enough for now," Armand said. "I'll be either in the lab or on Deck 2 checking on our patients."

"OK, I'll track you down."

SEVEN

Brian entered the O-deck and took a quick look around. He hadn't been gone long but the team had apparently settled back into a smooth rhythm during his absence. Some of the crew actually seemed bored. He frowned and started making his way back to his seat but was distracted by the aroma of fresh coffee and moved to get a cup.

'Why the hell couldn't I have been assigned to Henrik's team?' he thought as he stirred in some creamer. He glanced around the O-deck. Everyone seemed focused, each diligently monitoring their respective terminal. On the monitor showing the vessel's interior, Kelly stood beside the shimmering column, slowly shaking his head. Brian smiled. At least Kelly had been aboard the vessel this time rather than up here in the O-deck. It was he who had had the idea two days ago that led to their latest, tremendously exciting breakthrough. It was only right that he be there to experience it in person.

Brian sipped his coffee and closed his eyes for a moment as he savoured the flavor. "Mm-mmm," he moaned, exaggeration his pleasure as he sipped the brew. "Now *that's* good coffee," he belted out in his best television-announcer voice. He stretched and glanced over at Frank, expecting a comical reaction. But the chief was engrossed in something on the screen in front of him and hadn't even heard him.

Brian shrugged and snuck over to the window. "*Guess it won't hurt if I'm away a minute or two longer*," he thought looking down at the scene below.

He never tired of looking at it and was amazed that they'd been able to keep it a secret for so long, especially given the size of the facility. Between the false buildings topside and the underground warehouse area, the site covered over 25 acres.

Brian looked up at the expansive ceiling that covered the underground complex. He found it comical that it was constructed in the very same way as the ceiling of the Wal-Mart Super Center back home. In fact, were it not for the thick icicles hanging like stalactites from the white steel girders, he could easily imagine himself being there now, shopping for dog food or something.

But this particular ceiling covered a much greater prize than flat screen televisions and other insignificant consumer goods.

Once the camouflage netting had been emplaced to hide the spacecraft when they'd first found it, they'd quickly erected the more permanent structure directly over the expansive canyon. The steep icy canyon walls formed a natural enclosure leaving no need to construct artificial ones. It had been like placing a lid on a pre-existing, natural cauldron.

Immediately beneath the ceiling's massive expanse at one end of the canyon were the crew's living and working spaces; pre-fabricated structures jutting out from the icy walls and suspended high over the warehouse floor. Deck 2, immediately above them, held the sleeping quarters, a large cafeteria, a well-equipped gym, and two recreation rooms where the crew would usually gather at the end of the day. These spaces were unexceptional and would seem ordinary in any apartment building back home were it not for the oversized windows overlooking the vessel below.

The company had constructed the interior spaces to offer a breathtaking overhead view of the vessel from multiple vantage points on either level. Every inch of space along the innermost boundary of Decks 2 and 3 – where each room or hallway sat exposed and suspended over the spacecraft – was capped by a heavy Plexiglas wall, providing a nearly full view of the warehouse interior below and the amazing artifact that had come to rest there ages ago.

The Observation Deck, where the team was busy at work behind him, was on the Deck 3. This deck housed the various laboratories, medical facilities, and other work spaces they'd initially thought they would need to unlock the spacecraft's secrets. They actually turned out to be of little use, with the exception of the medical spaces and the O-deck. Most of the real work was done on Deck 4, directly inside the vessel.

Brian looked down into the dock, taking in the spacecraft below. The ice had been excavated from around it decades ago and the ship was now supported by metal framing. The icy canyon walls formed by the vessel's crash untold millennia ago rose sharply along the periphery of the silvery craft encasing it like a giant crystalline fishbowl.

A cargo elevator rose from the warehouse floor, running upwards through both decks before terminating at ground level within the helicopter hangar. It served as the primary mode of transportation not only for equipment and material, but also for the staff, who found the metal stairway running adjacent to the elevator to be far too strenuous and time consuming. It was, after all, more than six stories from the warehouse floor to the Deck 3 landing.

A small landing had been built halfway between the O-deck and the warehouse floor, level with the top of the spacecraft, affording direct access to the vessel's main hatchway via a narrow catwalk. It was by far the elevator's most used destination as the crew constantly shuffled equipment and materials into and out of the ship's interior via an overhead crane.

As Brian watched, the crane moved away from him along its rails, transporting a load of the metal tubing from the landing toward the open hatchway, where another crewman was busy directing the crane's operator.

"Still quite a sight, huh?"

Frank startled him and Brian almost spilled his coffee.

"I never get tired of looking at it," he replied, trying to sound casual.

"I was only twenty-three the first time I saw it," Frank said, his eyes glazing over. "My God, how the time does fly."

He stared out at the cavernous enclosure, his eyes fixated on something on the canyon wall at the far end of the dock. "It's amazing what we've done through the years to keep it under wraps." He fell silent as he surveyed the pit below them.

Brian said nothing. It was moments like this, when Frank grew melancholy, that he had the best chance of learning more about the early history of the site. Despite his best efforts to learn the details, discussion of the vessel's discovery and the initial construction of the site seemed taboo. But at times like this, when Frank got lost in the recesses of his own mind, Brian could sometimes glean a new tidbit or two.

"I can't believe we did it," Brian whispered, sensing that he was losing the moment. He could sometimes prod Frank into revealing more by unobtrusively inserting himself into the experience as if he, too, had been there.

Frank chuckled, "Turned out to be pretty simple, really. Commandeered some winter camouflage netting from some army base in Washington and simply covered the whole thing with a giant canvas blanket until we could erect the permanent roof." Frank glanced upward, the distant look still clouding his vision.

He chuckled again, "Hardest part was bringing in the huge amount of construction materials without attracting attention." He sipped his coffee and shook his head slowly then stiffened suddenly and looked around the room.

"*Shit,*" thought Brian, "*He's back.*"

Frank's gaze finally settled on Brian and the younger man cringed inwardly, sensing that perhaps he'd pushed a little too far.

Frank eyed him for a second then visibly relaxed. "Think about it. Antarctica is home to a very small, tight-knit scientific community. A man can't fart out here without hundreds of researchers from dozens of countries knowing about it. Building a site like this in total secrecy? Damn near impossible."

Frank wiped the back of his hand across his brow. "But we pulled it off. I don't know how…but we did."

He went to take a sip of his coffee, then realized that he'd drank it all. "I don't know what's more amazing actually," he said, staring into his empty cup. "The fact that we could build this facility right under their noses or the luck we had in finding her first. I mean, there were teams from all over out searching for that missing chopper in '93. Any one of them could've found her. Fortunately, we got to her first."

Frank looked through the Plexiglas at the spacecraft below and fell silent.

Brian felt his pulse quicken. This was unfamiliar ground. It was the first time that Frank seemed to be *consciously* volunteering information. He stared in silence at the vessel, vacillating between his desire to probe further and the fear that doing so might cause his boss to suddenly clam up.

"A remarkable woman, really. Took some coaxing, but in the end, she led us right to it."

Brian stood speechless, realizing suddenly that Frank was not talking about the alien spacecraft lying dormant on the floor below them.

"My God…. Coming face-to-face with an alien life form…such a hideous one, too. I'm not so sure I could've handled things as well as she did. It took me almost two years to sleep normally again, after the stories she told."

Frank studied Brian. The young man stood wide-eyed, coffee dribbling over the side of his cup.

"That's right," Frank said softly as he chuckled lightly, "You don't know…"

"I don't know what?" Brian asked the question a little too loudly, causing some of the O-deck crew to glance curiously in their direction. A stern look from Frank was enough to quickly turn them back to their tasks.

Frank's firmly clenched jaw and the pulsing of the veins in his neck told Brian that he'd unintentionally crossed the line. He couldn't help it. He'd simply been too stunned by the implication of Frank's latest revelation.

"There was a survivor?!" Brian blurted out.

Frank's glare pierced right through him and Brian felt himself grow suddenly cold and uneasy.

Frank's cell phone suddenly vibrated, breaking the awkward silence.

"Yeah?" Frank answered. The tone of his voice had softened but his gaze remained firmly fixed on Brian.

"What is it?" Frank snapped after several seconds.

Frank blinked several times rapidly, his eyes widening in surprise, "I'm on my way."

Frank stood for a moment, sizing Brian up. "You and I need to have a little chat later," he said suddenly, turning to leave.

Brian felt his heart sink. He'd definitely overstepped his bounds this time.

Frank paused at the door, "Erland, you've got this. I'll be right back."

Erland nodded and moved over to the central monitor, pulling the headphones over his ears.

Brian cursed under his breath as he watched the door close behind his boss, berating himself for his lack of restraint. He knew that he'd just messed up big time, possibly sealing the vault to any future information he otherwise might have learned about the site. After several minutes his anger turned to awe as Frank's latest revelation began to sink in.

"*Of course! ...the Langstadt woman*," he thought. "*What was her name...Allaina? ...Aretha?*"

"Agnetha."

The thought leapt out at him from the far reaches of his memory.

"Holy shit," he mumbled to himself. It had been right there in front of him the whole time. There had been seven members in the team that had originally discovered and explored the spacecraft in '93. For years, they'd been led to believe that the entire team had perished when the organism had been inadvertently released.

"*...but Agnetha must've survived. That explains why they named the damn place after her*," he realized, feeling foolish now that he hadn't before made the connection. He always felt it odd that they'd chosen to name the site after her rather than the expedition's leader.

He couldn't yet be certain, of course. But, it all seemed to add up. He was determined now to find out for sure.

Brian smirked. Even if he wasn't *completely* correct, the conclusion was inescapable.

Despite the company's continued insistence to the contrary, there had been at least one survivor of the 1993 encounter with the alien life form.

EIGHT

“Priority one,” Viktor said. “Haven’t seen one of those since we fried Section 7.”

Frank grunted and leaned over to switch on his computer. "Yeah. Comes at a great time, too," he said, not bothering to hide his annoyance. "Seems like any time we make progress, they come along to screw it up."

The site’s video teleconferencing capabilities were very rarely used and Frank was surprised that Anders had it up and running before he’d even gotten there from the O-deck. He made a mental note to commend his Security Chief for it later.

The blue background of the screen was suddenly replaced by the image of a well-dressed and meticulously-groomed African-American man.

Frank broke into a wide grin, “X-ray! It’s good to see you, my friend!” he said with unrestrained delight. “What’s it been now, two years?”

“Good to see you too, Frank. Looks like life out there is treating you well.” He shifted his gaze to Frank’s left, "Viktor,” he said with a nod, acknowledging the Norwegian’s presence.

"Charles," Viktor said, nodding in return. Unlike Frank, he didn’t know the man on the screen all that well and the guy rubbed him the wrong way.

Charles Xavier Raymond had been the Site Chief for 6 years before being promoted to Vice President of Operations three years ago. Frank assumed command of the site shortly thereafter. The two had been friends for almost 10 years, working together at the site for much of that time. Frank spoke of Xavier often and always with fondness. He was the only one who could get away with calling him 'X-ray', a nickname that Charles disliked but tolerated from his friend.

The sound of a man clearing his throat off-screen informed them that Charles wasn't the only outsider one on the line. The screen split into quarters, each displaying a person or small group at various locations.

"Yes," Charles continued, "With us on the line are George Perlise from Seattle, Terry Huffman from Chicago, and Steve Westcott from the National Security Agency." The group briefly exchanged pleasantries.

"Listen, gentlemen, I need to get right to the point," Charles said, suddenly growing serious. "We need you to immediately shut down power to the vessel."

Viktor and Frank jumped up from their seats.

"You can't be serious" Viktor blurted out, incredulously. "Do you have any idea..." Viktor stopped as Frank grabbed his forearm. Viktor shot him a venomous look but got the message and fell silent.

"Gentlemen, this is Steve from NSA. A couple of hours ago, we picked up a new and quite unique transmission emanating from your location."

Viktor and Frank looked at each other, wondering why they hadn't noticed it on-site.

"Now, the signal is damn strong. We'd like to have you shut it down before it's detected by… um, others." Steve uttered the last word with barely concealed disdain, as if he were talking about some unpleasant hairy critter on his bathroom floor. "We're dispatching a tech team out there right away so that we can isolate it but, until then, I'm afraid you've got to shut it down."

Viktor started to protest again but another squeeze from Frank, still clutching his forearm, held him off again.

Frank coughed, "You realize that we run the risk of not getting this back if we completely shut it down right now. This is the most success we've had in getting the system powered up. We haven't had much experience in how to properly shut it down without damaging the tellurium nodes. If we lose any more…"

"Tellurium nodes?" The woman's voice on the telecom line surprised them both and they turned their attention to the section of the screen showing the feed from the Chicago office.

"I'm sorry, miss…?"

"Huffman. Terry Huffman," the woman replied, positioning herself now so that the lights could better capture her image. A hint of a smile crossed her lips as she moved into view, as if she were enjoying the fact that her gender had caught them by surprise.

"Tellurium nodes," Viktor interjected, struggling to contain his annoyance. "They act as transducers or power regulators for all of the ship's functions. Super-conductive, but also very sensitive. We've inadvertently destroyed a number of them over the years trying to get things working."

"Can't you just manufacture replacements?" The woman's tone was condescending, pushing her firmly into Viktor's 'dislike' column.

"Unfortunately, no," Frank jumped in, sensing his friend's growing annoyance. This woman was clearly enjoying pushing their buttons. Frank couldn't be sure what was driving her agenda, but he knew without a doubt that they were dealing with a first-class bitch. And she was working at the main office in Chicago…that made her a *dangerous* first-class bitch.

"Tellurium is exceedingly rare. Few other metals come even close to matching its conductive properties. The original...uh, *'manufacturers'* of these components have either found an abundant supply of it somewhere or they're somehow able to manufacture it."

Frank chose his words carefully to avoid using terms that might provide any unintended listener with the idea that they were talking about an extra-terrestrial technology. The complicated encryption algorithms the company employed in its communications were touted as unbreakable but he was always skeptical of such claims.

"This is all very interesting, and I am truly looking forward to learning more about it," Steve interrupted. "However, our immediate concern is to prevent others from investigating the signal. We simply have to shut it down until we can contain or disable it."

Viktor snatched the phone from its cradle on the wall beside him before Steve had finished speaking, "Anders, patch me through to Henrik right away."

They waited in silence as Viktor instructed Henrik to shut down the experiment. Henrik's irate voice was audible through Viktor's receiver even to those on the far end of the conference line. Charles cleared his throat to underscore the fact and Viktor moved a few steps away to take him out of range of the system's microphones.

"We should be off-line in about ten minutes," he reported as he hung the receiver back into its cradle. "If you'll excuse me," he said with barely concealed disgust, "I'll go see to it."

"Hold on, Vik," Charles said. "There's something else."

The two men listened intently as Steve dropped an even bigger bombshell on them. Three minutes later, Charlie brought the meeting to a close, scheduling another one for later on in the day.

The two sat in stunned silence, considering the implications of what they had just heard as the conference screen grew dark.

Learning of the signal's re-appearance from persons half a world away had surely been a surprise, but it was an exciting one. It meant progress and bolstered the hope that greater discoveries, things that had long eluded them, were now within their reach. But this last tidbit was disconcerting to say the least.

Each sensed the unease of the other as they sat in silence while the light faded from the room.

"Son of a bitch," Frank mumbled as he reached over to flick on the small desk lamp.

Viktor grunted and reached into his shirt pocket, extracting a thin plastic container. He flicked open the top with his thumb and drew a toothpick from the small hole, inserting it into his mouth while Frank watched him absentmindedly. "*He's always sucking on those things,*" Frank thought silently. He did a quick calculation and figured that Vik had gone through about ten-thousand of the little wooden slivers in the years they'd been together.

"You know…it's funny," Viktor said, breaking the heavy silence. "I've long wished for this. But now that it's here…"

"Yeah," Frank agreed. He could think of nothing else to say at the moment.

"Well, we'd better pass the word and start developing a strategy," Viktor said, rising from his seat. "You know damn well that they're going to want us to go out after them." He paused at the door and turned to face Frank, "Too late to ask for a transfer?" he asked in jest.

Frank chuckled. "If it isn't, I'll work one up for me too."

Viktor smiled, "How about I meet you in the cafeteria at 3:30?"

"Yeah…see you then."

Frank sat there and listened as the sound of Viktor's footsteps faded. He swivelled from side to side in his chair as he considered his staff, weighing who was best suited for each of the tasks that surely lay ahead.

"My God," he whispered. "Two more..."

He got up and pushed his chair back under the table, replaying Steve's words over in his mind. Due to the unique characteristics of the signal, its strength, and its duration, NSA had been able to pin-point each transmitter with great accuracy.

The strongest was emanating from the warehouse. No surprise there. But similar signals were also transmitting from two distinctly separate sites at least twenty-five miles away.

"How the hell are we going to handle two more alien vessels?" he thought. But it wasn't the newly revealed vessels that bothered him most. That distinction was reserved for a more sinister thought, one that kept fighting its way to the forefront of his mind despite his best efforts to reign it in. He didn't want to think about this right now and fought consciously to beat it down.

They'd been lucky so far and he knew it. In all these years, despite intense systematic searches within and around the outskirts of the warehouse, they'd discovered no more of the frozen terrors that had been responsible for the horrific deaths of the original advanced team over twenty years ago.

Frank had caught Viktor's gaze as he was leaving and knew instinctively that his friend was thinking the very same thing.

"What if we aren't so lucky this time?"

≈ O ≈

Hildy blew her nose for what must have been the hundredth time and dabbed the corners of her eyes. It had been a long and stressful evening, followed by a fitful night's sleep. Brian had been in a foul mood all night, supremely angry that the experiment had been brought to a screeching halt.

They'd had a tense dinner together, with him complaining the whole time. By 7 o'clock she feigned a headache and retreated to her own suite seeking a peace that never came. Between her whacked out, prenatal hormones, the potential for an outbreak of meningitis, the creepiness of the alien vessel – which had grown all the more so since she'd realized she was pregnant – and her growing desire to leave this place, she was exhausted. The fact that Brian remained unaware of her pregnancy only magnified the enormity of it all.

She'd plopped into bed by eight hoping the sleep would bring her a short reprieve from thinking. But the new day carried with it all of yesterday's baggage.

"*What the hell am I supposed to do?*" she fretted.

She slammed her hands onto the countertop and arched her back, "*You haven't got time for this,*" she reasoned, "*You've got work to do.*"

But the attempt to refocus her thoughts failed again as various scenarios kept running through her mind, none of them good.

Keeping the baby would mean certain redeployment or, worse, termination of her employment with the company. There was no way that Syneco would even consider allowing her to stay on site with a child, not that she'd want to anyway. Already she felt herself growing more fearful and protective of the helpless child growing within her, especially given the weirdness of her surroundings. She actually *wanted* to leave now, which was fortunate. The company would surely send her back home to Trondheim the second they found out, regardless of any desire she might have to stay.

Actually, being thousands of miles away from this place wouldn't be such a bad prospect if she were sure that Brian could handle it. Given the circumstances, he could request a transfer too. That would allow them to remain together if Axis, Syneco's U.S. counterpart, would agree to send him to Norway. There *were* a few Americans working there.

But would he? Was it even fair of her to ask that of him? He loved working at the site more than anything. It was a passion, really. He loved the secrecy and excitement of working on an alien spacecraft. Hell, when he wasn't working, he often spent hours chatting about it, usually with Erland and Parker. They'd ponder the discoveries that still awaited them within the vessel or speculate about the size and shape of its builders. Brian would grow especially animated as they fantasized about the extent of the aliens' knowledge and lament the fact that they'd never discovered one of the creatures frozen somewhere. He rarely talked about anything else, except perhaps one of the endless documentaries he was always watching. Would he really leave this place?

Her heart ached at the thought of their son growing up without his father. She pressed her palms gently across her tummy. Yes.... she felt more certain every day now that it was a boy. *"What if he simply chooses not to come with me?"* Could he really give up all this to go sit behind a desk somewhere? And if he did, would he grow to regret it and perhaps resent her for making him leave?

Her vision grew cloudy again as she dropped her head to the counter.

It was several seconds before she became aware of Armand's gentle touch on her shoulder. All morning long he'd had been a true gentleman, alternately comforting her then giving her space as he worked silently at the other end of the lab. He'd check on her occasionally and even surprised her half an hour ago with a cup of green tea and some wheat toast with honey. Of course, the gesture started the waterworks flowing again, but she was grateful for his calming presence anyway. He would simply smile sympathetically before retreating to his corner.

At first, she was glad that he hadn't stayed to talk, she was in no mood for that. But, as he walked away, she found herself fighting the urge to chase him down, wrap her arms around him, and just cry on his shoulder. He was such a sweet old man.

Hildy almost giggled at the thought. "*Old man.*" While he *was* actually old enough to be her father, he looked much younger than his 55 years, despite his snow-white hair. She paused for a moment and watched him as he worked. He had the sexiest physique. She and Charlie were in complete agreement on this and discussed it often when they found themselves alone in the lab. Charlie would call him 'luscious' and lick her lips as they both laughed like school girls.

But it was true. Every inch of his body seemed perfectly proportioned and was marvellously toned. Hildy especially loved how the trapezius muscles connecting his neck and shoulders curved so gently, almost elegantly, while unambiguously displaying strength and power. He worked out regularly, watched what he ate, didn't smoke, and drank only an occasional Grand Marnier. A couple of the guys had even taken to openly calling him Dr. Viceless due to his seeming lack of character flaws. Armand didn't mind it. He'd once told her that as long as the crew was cracking jokes he didn't need to worry about their psychological state.

Hildy took a sip from her water bottle, her eyes never straying from Doc's silhouette on the other side of the room. "*Yes*," she thought, "*He's got it all…almost too good to be true.*"

But deep down, she knew better.

Hildy knew about the pain and self-doubt he still felt over patients he'd lost on the operating table. She knew about how he'd turned to drugs for a while to escape from it. She knew how he still blamed himself for his wife's death years ago from a violent car accident as she'd sped away from him following a nasty argument over his drug use. She knew that it had almost driven him to kill himself.

The very thought of it made her heart instantly ache. He seemed such a huge part of her life now. She couldn't imagine him not being there.

Armand turned from his work suddenly and looked over at her, giving her a wink and a smile. Hildy smiled weakly and returned quickly to her task. Her face was hot and she hoped that he hadn't noticed the flush in her cheeks.

She clattered the test tubes noisily as she pretended to be engrossed in her work while covertly peeking at Armand's murky reflection in the glass door of a nearby metal cabinet. But Armand had resumed his work and was paying no attention to her at all, filling her with both relief and disappointment. Stupid hormones, she thought, laughing quietly at herself.

"Damn!"

Hildy looked over at Armand, who was peering intently into a microscope.

"Come take a look at this," he said, squinting his eyes.

The image in the microscope seemed to leap up at her and she quickly lifted her head in surprise, wondering if she had actually seen it. But already the image had burned itself into her mind, sending a chill down her spine. "Oh, no," she quietly whispered.

"Exactly," Armand said seriously.

Hildy shuddered involuntarily. She'd seen this only once before, when she was working as an intern at John Hopkins University in Baltimore. As a naïve lab technician, fresh out of school, she'd been so excited at first to recognize it. It was her first brush with something truly significant out here in the real world.

Bacterial meningitis. It had sounded so exotic at the time. She felt proud and important as she rushed to let them know what it was that they were dealing with. She even gloated over her discovery later as she sat with her peers around the lunch table. They'd all been impressed and perhaps even envious.

But the ravaging effect of the infection on that helpless nine-year-old girl erased all that. The awful outcome still made her cringe in fear and shame on those occasions when she was unfortunate enough to remember, which, thankfully, had grown less frequent over the years.

"Better get Charlie down here and begin preparing. I've got to go see Frank. Be back soon as I can."

"I don't think we have much Claforan left in stock. We used a lot of it for Cholsu's kidney infection and when Kelly sliced his arm open a couple months ago. We haven't made a run to McMurdo in a while so we still haven't restocked."

"Shit. Well, prep what we've got. Let's hope we won't need any more than that."

Without another word, Armand abruptly turned and exited the lab, leaving Hildy in stunned silence. She reached for the phone and dialed Charlie's number, willing her girlfriend to answer.

NINE

Robert glanced at his watch. The Trac was supposed to head out in less than two hours and it looked to him like they weren't even half done getting it loaded.

He scowled in disgust at the bright yellow tracked vehicle. He hated them. Trac Crawlers were slow and uncomfortable and he was damn glad that he didn't have to ride in them often. On this particular trip, the Trac would transport its unfortunate crew for several hours just to get to the closest reported site, where another alien craft was supposedly transmitting. The beast drank gas at an incredible rate, especially when loaded as heavily as this one would be. But this would be a one-way trip, so fuel wasn't going to be a factor. The out-going crew would set up a fake field research camp to deflect the interest of other parties that might be drawn to investigate the signal. They would wait for reinforcements from the warehouse to retrieve the craft later, once the weather had cleared.

Robert stood by the door pretending to concentrate on his clipboard while two crewmen worked at the far end of the garage loading equipment into the Trac. They chatted in hushed tones as they labored, laughing frequently. He frowned at their slow progress and felt certain that they were intentionally dragging things out just to keep him out in the cold. He didn't really know these two that well but that was just the sort of thing that the guys were always doing to him.

"You guys almost done?" he yelled from across the room. "I don't know about you guys but I've had enough of this cold."

One of the men stuck his head out from within the vehicle, "Well, we'd sure finish quicker if you'd give us a hand," he yelled back.

"I've got my own work to do." Robert looked at the man and tried to recall his name. Was it Hugh? He thought so but wasn't quite sure.

The man eyed the clipboard in Robert's hand and shot back, "Yeah. Must be tough," he replied before retreating back into the vehicle.

Robert cursed under his breath. He'd meant to be funny but knew that he'd come off as condescending.

The two men laughed and continued their muted conversation, much to Robert's annoyance, as they resumed their task at the same leisurely pace.

"Why should THIS place be any different?" he thought to himself. He'd moved repeatedly over the years in a fresh attempt to forge a relationship of mutual respect with his peers. It would start off just fine but it always ended miserably, leaving him feeling isolated.

The two crewmen – he was sure now that the first one was called Hugh – seemed to get along great. Sure, they constantly bitched and moaned about their work and the cold but their incessant joking and easy laughter readily belied their good nature. Robert's heart sank. He'd seen it everywhere he'd been but was never able to a part of it.

He strained to hear what they were talking about but could catch only an occasional word such as 'putz' or 'loser'. He was tired of having words like that directed at him. People were always enjoying themselves at his expense. He could feel the anger rising inside. He fought hard to control it as it bubbled to the surface.

"Not this time," he yelled, slamming the clipboard onto a fuel barrel. The clang echoed through the garage and Robert jumped, surprised by his own uncharacteristic outburst.

"You say something?" asked the second guy, whose name Robert couldn't recall.

"Uh, just talking to myself," Robert replied trying not to sound sheepish but failing miserably.

"Huh! Looks like he's finally found someone who'll listen to him."

Hugh hadn't meant for Robert to hear him, but he *had* heard. Robert felt himself growing hot as the unknown guy fought to suppress a laugh as he leaned into the vehicle.

"Well, you got about ten minutes to get this finished up," he stated, trying to sound authoritative. "We don't have all day."

The nameless guy paused deliberately, shooting Robert a dirty look. He said nothing but Robert got the message. He'd work at his own pace, no matter how much Robert might bitch and moan. After a tense moment, the man returned his attention to his work and Robert knew that he'd lost again.

Robert silently cursed Frank for having put him in this position. *"Why the hell does he insist on putting me in charge of anything?"* Sure, it was *easy* for Frank. Every single member of the crew respected *him.*

Robert could never decide which made for a better leader, fear or respect, and waffled hopelessly back and forth hoping to attain one or the other and ultimately getting neither. He seemed to harvest nothing but contempt and just couldn't understand why. He sighed loudly and glanced at the checklist.

He felt hot anger wash over him as a fresh burst of laughter erupted from inside the Crawler. He flung his clipboard, knocking over some empty cans of motor oil and stormed out of the room, slamming the door forcefully behind him.

Hugh peered out from inside the Crawler. "What's up with him?" Peter asked from behind him.

"Beats me. Maybe he doesn't like the show.'

"How can anybody not like 'Seinfeld'? It's the best show *ever*!"

"Beats me. Anyway, at least he's out of *our* hair for a while."

"Amen! Man, that guy needs some serious help."

"Aw, he's not so bad. It's not *his* fault. Some people are just born without people skills," Hugh said as the two men resumed packing the Trac.

"You know," Peter chuckled, "No matter how many times I've seen that episode, it's still hilarious every time."

Hugh laughed, "Yeah. I'm telling you, that show will go down as one of the all-time best sitcoms in television history."

They laughed more loudly now with Robert gone, as they reminisced about the crazy antics of Jerry and the rest of the '*Seinfeld*' cast.

TEN

"Mind if I join you?"

"Hhhmm?" Armand glanced up at Hildy, who stood holding a sparsely populated food tray.

"Oh. Um, please," he said, tentatively gesturing toward a chair.

Hildy studied him for a moment. "Are you sure? You seem preoccupied. I don't want to intrude."

"Don't be ridiculous," Armand replied, rising from his own seat. "C'mon and sit."

Hildy placed the tray onto the table as he studied its contents.

"Well, it's not much but it's something."

Hildy laughed. "Unfortunately, it's all I can handle right now."

Armand sat in silence as Hildy splayed out her silverware and napkin. "You're especially quiet this morning," she said hesitantly once she was settled.

"Mmmm," he acknowledged, "I'm just tired is all." He looked up at the wall clock, "Charlie and I are going to make our rounds in about ten minutes. I'll get some rest after."

On the far side of the room, Frank sat sipping a cup of coffee by himself, his back to them.

"He seems off today too. Barely said two words to me as we were getting lunch."

Armand set down his cup and stared at Frank. "Well, in the last few hours he's learned that there's a nasty and very dangerous outbreak in the makings here and that we're scary low on the supplies we need to fight it."

He sipped his coffee and resumed, “Kevin also just came in and told him that the weather’s going to prevent McMurdo from sending us any meds for at least the next 48 hours. And, I’m not sure what went on during yesterday’s tests, but it seems they suffered a significant setback.”

“Yikes. Sucks to be him right now.”

“That’s not all,” Armand said, leaning in close. “Do you remember me telling you about Sarah some months back?”

“Vaguely.”

“Well…it’s three years ago today.”

“Three years?” Hildy asked, as she buttered a toast. “Since what?”

She scraped the knife noisily across the bread several times then stopped when she realized he hadn’t answered. She looked up to see Armand peering at her over the rim of his glasses.

“Oh! Right!” Hildy cringed, suddenly remembering. “Oh my god, how could I have forgotten?”

“I sure wish he’d take some time off and just get away for a bit. You know, I think he’s left this place once in the last four or five years. That’s not healthy. Not with all we have to deal with out here.”

Hildy crunched loudly into her toast. “It must be hard for him,” she said, her words barely discernable as she chomped her food.

“Must you?” Armand said with mild annoyance, as he held out a napkin for her.

She cowered slightly as she wiped her mouth. “Sorry,” she said sheepishly, still chewing. “It’s been a little while since I’ve been able to keep anything down. I’m starving.” She tore into the toast again with zeal.

“Did I tell you that they were supposed to be married? Had this elaborate ceremony planned in Barbados. That’s where they’d met. I didn’t know Sarah well but, from what I hear, it would’ve been one hell of a party.”

He swirled his coffee around inside the cup before taking a sip. "I can't imagine losing someone like that."

Hildy nibbled absent-mindedly on some bread. Armand had told her before about how Frank's fiancé had died in an accident but that was all she really knew.

"Poor girl. She wasn't even supposed to be there. Made the trip back home for just a couple of weeks to help them with some dire situation. I have no idea what. She'd only been there a week when the pilot lost control of the plane." Armand cocked his head and glanced up at the ceiling for a moment, "Or was it a mechanical malfunction?"

"Well, either way," he continued, "…came down right on top of the facility. Completely destroyed the place."

Hildy dropped her toast onto her plate. "Oh, my god! That's terrible!"

"Yes," Armand leaned to one side as if trying to get a better look at Frank in the distance.

Hildy sat there with her mouth hanging open as she looked over at Frank. "When you told me before that she'd died in an accident, I thought you meant a car crash. Not that *that* isn't just as bad but…" She exhaled loudly and shook her head. She paused suddenly, "How many died?"

Armand shook his head, "A fully fueled B-1 bomber makes one hell of a fireball when it lands upside down. There were thirty-six working in the building at the time. Killed everybody."

"Oh my god!" Hildy could think of nothing else to say.

Frank arose from his seat, glanced at his watch, and picked up his tray to leave. Armand and Hildy sat in awkward silence as he headed for their table. They both greeted him as he walked by but Hildy couldn't look directly at him. She was afraid she'd burst into tears.

He'd returned their greeting but otherwise said nothing as he made his way to the exit.

He dropped his tray onto the conveyor and stopped for a moment to chat with Pamela and Stephan who were also on their way out. They left together, the couple dropping behind Frank as they approached the door. Hildy watched as Pamela glanced about quickly then gave Stephan's butt a playful squeeze. He pushed her hand away quickly and mouthed for her to stop, peeking into the cafeteria to see if anyone had noticed.

"Uh, oh," Hildy said quietly.

"What?"

"Nothing," she said, stuffing more toast in her mouth. She watched them until they disappeared down the hallway. Everything about their interaction with each other seemed a little too intimate. Cliff, Pamela's husband, surely wouldn't like that.

"It's ironic, actually."

"Wha…?" Hildy asked. It took her a second to realize that Armand was resuming their previous conversation.

"They picked Dunford for a number of good reasons. It was isolated in some obscure corner of an Air Force base so security wouldn't be a problem. It was small so it was more manageable than any of our facilities around Seattle and they could restrict knowledge of it to a handful of researchers. They wouldn't have been able to do that in Seattle either. It was just some unremarkable building."

"So, where's the irony?"

He looked at her thoughtfully for a moment, "All those precautions to protect it and the site inadvertently gets taken out by a damn plane crash."

He looked away and sipped his coffee, "Funny."

"Well here you are!"

Hildy jumped in her seat. She'd been so focused on Armand's story that she hadn't noticed Charlie approaching.

"Oh, shit," Armand rose, looking at his watch. "I'm sorry. I totally lost track of the time."

"No, it's ok," Charlie laughed, "Actually, I'm a little early." She brushed a lock of hair away from her face, "I was hoping we could finish early. I'm bushed."

"Good idea," Armand replied. "In fact, it would do us all a world of good to get a good night's sleep tonight, if we can. We're going to get pretty busy until we get this outbreak contained."

"Sounds good to me," Hildy agreed, suppressing a yawn. "Why don't you let me give you guys a hand so we can finish up quickly?"

"That's not really a good idea," Charlie said, glancing at Hildy's abdomen.

Hildy started to protest but Armand cut her off, "She's right. Let's not take any chances."

"But I could stay outside their rooms and do the prep work for you. It would expedite the process. I could also do the paperwork while you two tend to them."

"It would be quicker, actually," Charlie agreed.

"Ok, you can come," Armand said reluctantly. "But you stay outside with the mobile unit. We'll talk, you type and catalogue."

They chatted idly as they made their way to the door.

≈ O ≈

"This is such bullshit!" Brian was pacing aimlessly around his suite and griping. Every now and then he'd pick something up off the counter or shelf only to slam it back down.

Hildy sat at the edge of the bed wishing now that she hadn't come to his room. She should've just gone right to bed as Charlie and Armand had as soon as they'd finished their rounds.

But she'd thought about it all afternoon as they'd cared for the sick crewmen and had finally psyched herself up to tell him about her pregnancy and her decision to leave the site. She had steeled herself the best she could for whatever reaction Brian might have. And though she honestly had no idea what to expect from him at this point, she knew that she couldn't wait any longer. The stress was just getting to be too much.

But with Brian in such a foul mood, now was clearly not the time.

"You should've seen it, Hil," he said in exasperation. "It was amazing! Things were happening! There were new things popping up everywhere inside the vessel! And I was beginning to wonder if we'd *ever* make any headway on cracking this thing."

"That's great, Hon," Hildy said, trying her best to sound interested.

"...then they go ahead and shut us the hell down." Brian flung a knickknack down, shattering it against the leg of the bed and sending shards of glass everywhere.

Hildy jumped then scowled at him. "Did that really help anything?"

"Yes," he shouted through clenched teeth. "Those corporate idiots! We're sitting out here in the shit-ass cold waiting.... working our asses off and *dying* for some new breakthrough. We struggle to get things done under all their bullshit constraints because these assholes sitting ten thousand miles away are afraid we're going to scratch their precious ship. The thing's flown a billion miles through interstellar space for God's sake! And, just when we finally, *FINALLY* make some real progress, they pull the plug. Unbelievable!"

Hildy slid down off the bed to the floor and began picking up the remains of the ill-fated knickknack. "I'm sure there's a good reason, Brian," she said calmly. "Maybe they're just trying..."

"WHAT?!" he shouted at the top of his lungs. "What possible freakin' explanation can there be?!"

Hildy stood and dropped the shards she'd recovered back onto the floor. "I'm not going to stand here and get barked at," she said firmly. "You need to calm down and…"

"I don't *want* to calm down! What I want to do is smack some corporate headcheese right in the mouth!" He swept a few more unlucky knickknacks from a small shelf with the back of his hand. Hildy winced and grabbed her knee as a small picture frame that had been sent flying by his outburst struck her.

Brian dropped his shoulders and walked over to her, "I'm sorry, babe…This just makes me so damn mad."

Hildy smacked his hand away and stood there rubbing her knee.

"Hey," he said defensively, "I *said* I was sorry."

"Oh! That just makes it all better now, right?!" She hobbled over to the bed and grabbed her bag. "You know, this is just like you. All you ever care about is yourself. Poor little Brian can't play with his spaceship," she said derisively.

"What the hell is up with you?" he asked angrily.

"You think you are the only one dealing with shit? Are you so full of yourself that you can't see that something's been bothering *me* for the last week? I've told you at least twice since last weekend that I needed to talk to you about something. Have you made *any* effort or set aside *any* time for us? All you give a shit about is that damn ship out there!"

"I have so made time for us," Brian retorted half-heartedly. He thought frantically, trying in vain to remember an occasion that he could use as an example and realizing that he couldn't. He bit his lip, realizing that he was on shaky ground.

"Bullshit!' She turned suddenly and marched toward the door, limping slightly. "I'm sick of coming in second to that hunk of frozen metal. Call me when you get your priorities straight…*if* that ever happens!"

She slammed the door behind her and strutted triumphantly down the hall toward her own suite. But her pace slowed and then stopped altogether just a few yards down the hallway as the weight of her words began to sink in.

"*What the hell just happened*?" Hot tears welled in her eyes and she fought hard to hold them back. "*Did we just break up?!*"

She fell into the wall, leaning on it with her shoulder for support. "*Oh my god*! "*I'm in this alone now,*" she thought, tears spattering at her feet. She stiffened at the sound of an approaching voice. A rush of adrenaline surged through her at the thought of Brian chasing after her. But a second voice responding to the first quickly shattered that illusion.

She cringed as the voices grew nearer and searched desperately for a place to hide. The only thing close enough was a men's room just a few feet away. She hurried over, praying silently that it was unoccupied.

ELEVEN

"You should've felt it," Kelly said with unrestrained enthusiasm. "It's like nothing I've ever felt before!"

"Kel, I'm really glad you got to be there. I mean, I wish I had been there too, but you really deserve it."

Parker slapped Kelly on the back, "Who would've thought it would turn out to be something so simple?"

Kelly was beaming, a huge grin spread from ear to ear. Brian was truly happy for his friend, but he was also jealous. He felt robbed, having had to experience their latest breakthrough from the remoteness of the O-deck. While it was only a hundred feet or so from the action, it had felt like miles. And just when things begin to get interesting, the corporate pricks back home shut them down. Finally, he ended up getting chewed out by Frank for having missed the signal on the o-scope.

God, he was pissed and wanted to lash out at somebody or something.

But he *had* lashed out at someone. He cringed inwardly, his anger partially trumped by guilt. Hildy had been right earlier. He realized that now. He vowed silently to make it up to her at the earliest opportunity.

"I can't believe they shut us down," he said irritably. "Probably over some corporate happy horse shit, too."

"Yeah, but now we know," Kelly replied. "Man, I can't wait to see what we find out next time around!"

They clinked glasses and chugged their beer.

"This is like the coolest thing that's happened since I've been here," Parker said. He tipped his head back and let out a loud whoop.

Brian backhanded him in the chest and shot him an angry look.

"Keep it down," Kelly hushed, trying hard not to laugh. "There'll be hell to pay if we get caught."

The three sat in the far corner of the lab illicitly chugging down some of Brian's latest brew from a couple of medical beakers that had recently been sterilized. Brian opened the refrigerator door, moved aside some flasks filled with God knew what, and grabbed another unmarked brown bottle.

Kelly grinned even more broadly, "I almost feel bad, cheating like this."

"Who gives a shit?!" Brian twisted off the bottle top, filled each beaker with a healthy sampling, and handed them back to his friends.

"I set these bottles aside this morning for just this moment," he said. "Somehow, I just knew you were going to be right."

He stood and offered his 'glass' in salute and the three men downed the cold brew in one long gulp.

"Ah," Kelly exhaled, "My friend, I think you've outdone yourself this time."

Brian shrugged, "It's definitely good, but I think the flavor has been enhanced somewhat by your vindication."

They laughed and, for the first time since he left the O-deck, Brian actually began to loosen up.

Parker put his arm around Kelly's shoulder, "How the hell did you come up with it anyway?"

Kelly cocked his head and eyed the empty beaker. Brian took the hint and poured the rest of the bottle into it.

"Well, I had just finished shaving on Tuesday and as I stood there admiring myself in the mirror I got to thinking about my boy."

He hopped down from the counter and swilled the last of the beer. "A few years back, we were trying to get his go-cart running. I'd gotten it for him for Christmas. We were having a hell of a time getting it started so I finally grabbed the operator's manual and read through it."

Kelly smirked, "Turns out the damn thing had a safety feature that we didn't know about. See, it had this little, pathetic looking door that was supposed to help keep the driver in his seat. We thought it looked ridiculous so we decided not to attach it. Turns out that the guy who designed the thing had foreseen this and had constructed the door to be part of the electrical circuit. Bottom line…the door had to be in-place and latched for the damn thing to run!"

Kelly walked over to the sink and rinsed out the beaker he had been using. "As I stood there chuckling to myself in the mirror, it suddenly seemed so obvious. I thought maybe the damn thing wouldn't 'start' because we've got every damn hatch hanging wide open. We've got electrical cables and ventilation ductwork laying across every hatchway leading into the ship, for crying out loud! I mean, if you think about it, we wouldn't send out own guys out into space unless they were safe inside a hermetically sealed compartment, right?"

"I just can't believe it was something as ridiculous as that," Parker marveled. "I mean, a whole bunch of really smart scientists have been trying to figure it out for almost 30 years."

"Right?" Kelly asked, a hint of derision in his voice.

Brian moved over to the refrigerator and grabbed the last bottle. He cracked the seal and refilled each beaker, "Well, here's to you, my friend."

They polished off the bottle in silence, each replaying the events of the day.

"I gotta tell you, man," Kelly finally said, "You've really gotten good at this." He held the empty flask up to the light studying the color of the beer before chugging it down.

"Yeah, not bad at all," Brian replied smugly. He snatched the package from its perch atop the refrigerator. "It's all thanks to this stuff."

Brian's face suddenly lit up. "Oh hey! That reminds me! There's something I've been wanting to try."

They watched him curiously, sipping their beer as Brian skittered around the lab grabbing things.

"Check this out," he said finally, handing each of the others a pair of safety glasses.

They crowded around a deep sink as Brian poured a clear fluid into a flask followed almost immediately by another. He swirled them gently to mix them. Next, he ripped open the package and retrieved a small brown bottle. Unscrewing the cap, he used the attached dropper to squeeze a small amount of a ruddy brown liquid into the solution already in the beaker then quickly popped a cork into the opening to seal it.

He dropped the beaker into the deep sink and waited.

A small wisp of smoke or steam shot toward the top of the beaker. Seconds later, the men dropped to the floor as the top of the bottle exploded, sending shards of glass everywhere. Fortunately, the deep sink funneled most of the glass upward to be embedded into the ceiling panel.

"What the hell, man?!" Parker yelled. "You trying to kill us all?"

Brian grinned triumphantly. "Maybe I overdid it, but it was pretty cool, right?"

"What the hell was that?"

Brian laughed as he began sweeping shards of glass off the countertop. "I saw this program a couple weeks back about the various defense mechanisms used in the insect world. One of the bugs they covered was the bombardier beetle. This little guy manufactures hydrogen peroxide, hydroquinone, and catalase inside its body and stores them in special chambers. When threatened, it secretes them into another chamber where they mix."

He paused for a moment to focus on removing a splinter of glass from a hard-to-reach corner.

"By themselves, the peroxide and hydroquinone don't react all that violently. But, you add catalase to the mix and…BAM! In a fraction of a second, it turns the mixture into a scalding hot fluid. The beetle shoots the steaming liquid through a nozzle in its abdomen and into the face of any unfortunate predator giving it a nasty burn."

Brian dumped a dustpan full of shattered glass into the trash. "Ever since I saw the program, I wanted to give it a try. Kent uses hydroquinone to develop his film so it was easy enough to 'acquire' a little. And there's plenty of peroxide here in the lab."

"So where did you get the other stuff? …the catalyst?" Parker asked.

"Not catalyst…'catalase'. It's a naturally occurring enzyme. I use it as a 'secret ingredient' when I brew my beer. Gives a little kick to the fermentation process. Just another tip I learned from one of those documentaries that you guys are always mocking."

"Of course," Kelly laughed.

"I get a shipment every six months or so from a buddy at McMurdo." Brian knelt on the countertop and began pulling glass shards from the ceiling tile. "But please don't tell nobody."

He squinted at the ceiling, admiring his handiwork. "Guess I used a little too much, eh?"

"Yeah, no shit!" Kelly said sarcastically.

They quickly cleaned up the mess.

As they finished, Brian looked at his watch. "I should probably go find Hildy. She's not real happy with me right now."

Brian flipped the bottle of catalase to Kelly, "Do me a fav and put this in my suite for me."

"Sure thing." Kelly slipped the small bottle into his jacket pocket. "Hey, man," he said, rubbing his stomach. "Thanks. That really hit the spot."

Brian smiled and shook his head, "Are you kidding me?! Thank *you*! We'd probably be no closer to getting this thing going than we were yesterday if it hadn't been for your epiphany."

Parker slapped Kelly again on the back, "So true. I can't wait to see what happens next. Wonder when they'll let us have another go at it."

"Sure the hell hope they don't keep us waiting…. corporate pricks," Brian scowled.

"Well, one thing's for sure," Kelly said, "Things are going to be a lot more interesting around here in the near future."

"Amen!" Brian agreed, as they made their way to the door.

TWELVE

"So, what's the plan now?"

"Well, now," Frank said, glancing alternately at Viktor and Anders, "We continue with what we're doing. We've got no choice but to focus on retrieving the closest of the pods. That's going to be challenging enough as it is. If someone else has gotten to one of the others, there's not much we can do about it."

"Frank's right," Viktor said, "The others are definitely too far away for us to retrieve."

Anders exhaled deeply, "Man, this is all happening way too fast."

"Yes," Viktor sighed, plucking the toothpick from his mouth and flicking it into the trash.

They sat in uneasy silence for a moment.

The teleconference with Xavier had been short but packed with foreboding. Steve Westcott, their NSA friend, informed them that high resolution satellite photos showed 'foreign activity' at the pod furthest from the warehouse. There appeared to be two tractors at the site with about a dozen people milling about.

"Someone else has found it then," Frank had said, stating the obvious.

"Well, given the cloud cover the images aren't exactly crystal clear but it sure looks that way. We're thinking they're from Mizuho Station."

"The Japanese," Viktor grunted, "Better them than the Russians. They're more likely to cooperate."

"Yes, well we don't know yet for sure who they are but neither scenario is advantageous."

"So, what exactly would you like us to do?" Frank had asked. "Given the weather right now and the distance we're really not in the position to do much of anything about it."

Xavier shifted uncomfortably in his chair, "We'll take care of the Japanese on this end. We just wanted you to be aware. Right now, the most important thing you can do is retrieve the pod closest to you. We may still be able to keep a lid on this thing with the Japanese involved. But if the Russians get involved too, it's going to be damn near impossible. We can't give them the chance."

"Excuse me, but I think keeping the Japanese and Russians quiet is the least of our problems right now. Given what we already know, it's pretty damn likely that these are *escape* pods, which means that it's also very likely that *something* was *escaping* in them."

"Which is why you'll keep them frozen once you get them back and wait for the tech team to arrive," Xavier snapped.

The silence in the room was palpable.

"I'm sorry guys," Xavier said, softening his tone, "We've been putting in the hours here too, trying to figure out how best to support you."

He sighed, "Look, the last thing *any* of us want is an unexpected encounter with these creatures. We all know what happened before. But this time, we have the advantage of knowing what to expect *and* we have more control over the situation. What I mean is we can keep these things frozen until we are better prepared to unfreeze them."

Anders slammed his fist onto the desktop, "Yeah, well I don't want to be on this continent when that happens."

Xavier regarded him for a moment, "All right, Anders," he nodded, "Once the tech team arrives, you can take one of their choppers back to McMurdo and we'll get you stateside on the next available vessel. Until then, I trust we can count on your support?"

"Of course, you can count on my support," Anders shot back, the edge in his voice somewhat lessened.

Frank couldn't tell if Anders' tone was the result of his taking offense to Xavier's question or was borne out of embarrassed at his own outburst.

"OK, gents," Frank chimed in, "we all know what we've got to do. Let's get on it."

A moment later the teleconference ended.

"I'm sorry guys," Anders said as soon as Xavier's image went dark. "I shouldn't have… I mean, I was…"

"Don't worry about it," Viktor assured him, smacking him on his shoulder. "He'll get over it."

"Vik, why don't you go check on things in the hangar. We've got a small window to do this, with back-to-back shitty weather heading our way. We'd better be ready to move as soon as these winds die down."

Viktor nodded, "I'll go check but I think we're ready to go."

"Thanks. I'll meet you in the cafeteria in half an hour."

"Is there something else bothering you, Anders?" Frank asked as soon as the door closed behind Viktor.

"No. Nothing else," Anders replied. I just…well… Before I took this assignment, this place had been operating for two decades with no further contact with these creatures. I knew there was always the potential that we'd find another one day. I guess I just thought that after all this time the odds were remote. And I certainly didn't think it would be during my time here."

"I know. Listen, you can be damn sure that we're going to do everything we can to keep these things contained. What I'd like *you* to do is develop a contingency plan."

"You mean, like, for if something goes wrong once we get them here?"

"That's exactly what I mean," Frank said quietly.

"Yeah." Anders seemed to have perked up again now that Frank was speaking his language. "Yeah, ok."

"Keep your work crew small. The fewer who know of it, the better."

Anders put his cap on and turned toward the door, then paused," What do you think they'll do about the Japanese?" he asked.

Frank blinked and cocked his head to one side, "I'm not sure what they *can* do."

He jumped down from his perch on top of the desk, "But we have to focus on what *we* can do, right?"

Anders nodded and exited the room.

A moment later, Viktor returned.

Frank looked at him quizzically.

"Everything good?"

Viktor nodded and sat on the edge of the desk. "I was just thinking…Anders made a valid point."

Frank sighed, "I know. I'm uncomfortable with it too."

"It just all seems to be happening so quickly. I just start to accept one bit of news when another gets thrown at us. I can't help wondering if we're missing something."

"Me too." Frank picked up his mug and brought it to his lips, then realized that he'd already finished his coffee. The minor oversight seemed to accentuate Viktor's point.

"You know, the potential for an encounter with one of these this is disturbing enough. But there's something else."

Viktor nodded almost imperceptibly and swore in Norwegian, "Do tell."

"Well, Steve said that, based on their size and shape, the pods were likely attached at one time to the larger vessel."

"Uh huh. No surprise there I suppose. We've long suspected that something was once attached to the underside of the spacecraft. Each of the four large indentations were clearly designed for some detachable device. It stands to reason that…"

Viktor's eyes suddenly widened, "Oh shit."

Frank nodded. He knew it wouldn't take Viktor long to work it out.

It was pretty clear now that the voids in the hull beneath the spacecraft had been occupied at one time by the newly discovered pods. The problem was that there were accommodations for four pods but they could account for only three. One pod was missing.

"Do you think they realize?"

Frank pursed his lips. "I'm sure they do."

Viktor mumbled something in Norwegian as he hopped off the desk. He looked at Frank and shook his head in resignation.

Frank shrugged but didn't speak.

Both men made their way to the door without another word. There was nothing more to be said. They knew what they had to do to handle the immediate situation. This new knowledge did nothing to change that.

Frank opened the door and stepped aside to allow Viktor through. He followed close behind, feeling less confident about the situation than he cared to admit.

≈ O ≈

"I think we're about as ready as we're ever going to be," Anders reported, "Here," he said, spreading out a diagram of the facility. "Let me show you what we've got."

Frank leaned over to study the chart. A clear acetate sheet marked with various symbols had been juxtaposed over a diagram of the topside buildings. Several orange rectangles formed a ring around the garage, with a number of green circles interspersed among them. Two much larger red triangles occupied fully one half of the building's interior. While the orange and green symbols required some explanation, everyone in the room knew exactly what the red triangles represented.

Only with considerable difficulty had they succeeded in getting the two pods back to the site. They'd been surprised to discover that the nearest site actually concealed more than one. They lay buried in the ice within just a few yards of each other.

Extricating them had been easy enough but transporting them to the base hadn't gone so smoothly. The turbulent weather and equipment malfunctions presented them with challenges several times. A couple of crewmen had also fallen ill with Meningitis during retrieval of the first pod, leaving them short-handed.

It had taken them a couple of days but they'd eventually managed to move and secure both pods within the confines of the garage. Headquarters was working on a strategy for recovering the third. Unfortunately, it was now clear that the Japanese *had* found it.

"OK, so we've rigged the garage with explosives here, here, and here," he said, pointing to various points on the diagram. "We've positioned the charges near high combustibles to maximize the incendiary effect if we have to blow them, which we can do from the CDC or from a couple remote riggings. Every man in my team is familiar with the locations of the remotes."

Frank studied the diagram for a moment. "Aren't some of these a little close to the hangar?" he asked, pointing to some of the charges.

"Not at all. These are shaped charges, designed to direct the blast and flame toward the center of the garage. It'll be thousands of degrees for several seconds after the initial blast before it settles into a nice steady heat. Should be enough to roast anything alive."

Anders flipped the chart over for a different view, "We can let the flames burn for as long as we want before extinguishing them. In the meantime, we'll have guards with flame units stationed at multiple points between the garage, the CDC, and the hangar. They'll also have thermite grenades. We've taken special care to preclude the use of any weaponry that would result in spattering or dismemberment. We can't afford to let any small fragments of the creature survive. Using this plan – if we are forced to – is about as close as we are going to get to ensuring the creature is one-hundred percent, completely annihilated."

Frank grunted his approval. Anders knew his stuff. The charges and incendiaries were well placed. His backup plan, too, seemed calculated to ensure the complete destruction of the organism in the unlikely event that anything survived the initial blast.

Frank looked over at Viktor, who had been silently scrutinizing the diagram. “See anything they missed?”

“No. I think it looks good. Nice work,” he said to Anders.

Anders nodded but the furrows on his brow belied the apprehension that still plagued him.

Frank dropped his mechanical pencil onto the diagram and stood up. He arched his back and let out a groan. Well, gentlemen,” he said, I think we’ve done about all we can to safeguard things until the tech team arrives. We’ve just got to remain extra vigilant now.”

“I think we ought to assemble the entire crew in the rec room this evening and give them an update on where things stand,” Viktor said. “They’ve gotten pretty restless since we brought those things back here. Could probably use a little reassurance.”

“Good idea. Arrange it so that anyone on duty in the CSC can listen in on the monitor.”

“Any word on Lance and Suzanne?” Anders asked.

“Doc says they’re stable for now. He’s got them isolated in their staterooms like the others.”

“How many does that make now?”

“Five,” Viktor replied. “Probably be a good idea to ask everyone to keep to themselves for the next few days, until this blows over or at least until we get the medicines we need from McMurdo.”

“Yeah, I guess it’s come to that,” Frank sighed. “We’re going to need every member of the crew to help us keep an eye on these things until the tech team arrives. Can’t afford to have any more falling ill.”

Anders began rolling up the diagram, “I’ll keep this in my office in the CSC, in case either of you needs it.”

“OK, Frank replied. “Let’s go eat before we brief the crew.”

THIRTEEN

Hugh eyed the craft warily and sipped coffee from his thermos to warm himself. The garage door was partially opened and the frigid winds blew into the interior through the gap, turning the garage into an over-sized freezer. The arctic air seemed oblivious to his heavy parka and the steaming hot coffee and he cursed it as he stood there shivering.

But it wasn't only the cold and wind that caused the goose bumps all over his body right now. The menacing looking pods made him uneasy and he wished desperately for some company. Although the spacecraft below within the warehouse still gave him the creeps sometimes, he'd gotten used to it to the point where those moments weren't all that frequent anymore. He'd been here long enough for the sight of the alien vessel to become familiar, despite its strangeness. But these new craft…they were a complete unknown and everything about them seemed threatening.

The two pods were identical and were slightly larger than the Trac Crawlers, three of which had been moved outdoors to make room for the new arrivals. They'd been unable to move the fourth Trac, which lay in pieces on one side of the bay. Between the disassembled Trac and the newly arrived vessels, the normally spacious garage had grown quite cramped.

The fuselage of each pod was shaped like an elongated tear-drop, with the forward end coming to a point six feet or so above the garage floor. Three large fins protruded from the blunted rear of the vessel, projecting backward at a steep angle then abruptly changing direction and tapering to form spires that angled toward the nose of the craft. Each spire ended in a sharp point several feet beyond the vessel's nose. Two of them ran beneath the craft to form the skids that supported the vessel.

"*Looks like a damn over-sized fishing lure*," he thought, as he tightened his parka around his neck. He chuckled as he realized that one of the three-pronged lures in his tackle box back home actually did look pretty similar.

Hugh set the thermos onto a workbench and studied the nearest pod. The main body was a metallic silver. A dull, dark gray pattern enveloped the entire rear of the craft and stretched forward for half the vehicle's length, forming slightly raised ridge-like sections that were offset from the spires at equal angles. The spires themselves were a glossy black and had the same velvety texture as the dark gray pattern. Deep, narrow creases covered every inch of the fuselage, forming sharp edges at the crests between them that ran longitudinally along the vessel's length.

Hugh lit a cigar and jumped down from the workbench, where he'd taken a seat to shelter himself from the wind behind a large toolbox. He checked his watch and frowned. He still had the better part of an hour before his replacement would be coming in. He took a couple of puffs and exhaled the smoke directly into the lens of a security camera, smirking as he did. He knew he'd probably catch hell later for smoking in here but, between the cold and his anxiety over the craft, he was beyond caring. He resented the fact that he had to pull a shift out here watching these frozen lumps of metal while the others lounged around in the warmth and security of the CSC.

Emboldened by this act of rebellion, he walked through the debris of the torn-apart Trac, careful not to upset the deliberate placement of its parts, until both vessels were directly in front of him.

The two craft had been placed nose to nose with a space of about eight feet separating the tips of their spires. He walked over and stood in the gap between the vessels and peered right then left.

Despite the cold, he removed his glove and reached out cautiously to touch the end of one. The metal against his bare hand was not as cold as he'd expected. As he ran his hand along its surface, he was surprised by how astonishingly smooth it felt.

His hand glided effortlessly along the spire, which seemed to offer no resistance to his touch. He quickly removed his hand and took a step back, unnerved by the unnatural lack of friction. Then, just as quickly, he stepped boldly back in and placed both hands onto the spire as the gentle clicking and whirring of a security camera scanning the room reminded him that the guys in the CSC were watching.

The metal felt more 'slippery' the more firmly he tried to grip it until finally it seemed to repel his hand altogether. He did it again with the same result. The tighter he squeezed, the stronger the metal seemed to push back with a smooth, almost liquid motion. It was like trying to bring together the similarly charged ends of two powerful magnets.

A fresh gust of wind howled through the garage and a loud clanking behind him caused Hugh to jump involuntarily. A pry bar that had been leaning against the remaining Trac had been jarred by the wind and now lay beside the vehicle in a pool of oil or lubricant.

"This is bullshit," he said, peering up at the cameras and feeling suddenly embarrassed. He turned and made his way back to the workbench, tripping and falling over a segment of the Crawler's track that lay on the floor. He swore loudly as he got to his knees, rubbing his elbow and searching the floor for his stogie. Picking it up, he stuck it back into his mouth only to taste the foulness of the lubricant that now saturated the end. "Wouldn't you friggin' know it," he spat, holding it out to inspect it.

He scowled, bemoaning the loss of his tasty and expensive cigar. "*No doubt the security guys are laughing it up right now.*"

The two vessels looked more mocking now than sinister. "Screw you," he yelled at the top of his lungs, flicking the remnant of his smouldering stogie at the nearest pod.

The cigar bounced harmlessly off the hull, showering the vessel with sparks, and skittered across the floor before coming to rest beneath the Trac. He thought for a second about retrieving it but balked at the thought of crawling awkwardly on the cold floor underneath the vehicle as his buddies in the CSC laughed on. He dismissed it with a wave of his hand and resumed his trek back to the workbench, muttering obscenities the whole way.

He heard the muffled 'whump' just as he reached the bench and knew instinctively what it was even before he saw the bright orange flash of the flames reflected in the shiny stainless steel cabinetry. Hugh hit the ground and curled into a ball, waiting for the flames to rush over him. He waited for several seconds before realizing that he wasn't about to be engulfed then peered out cautiously from behind his hands.

Tall flames were leaping up from beneath the Trac, turning the vehicle black with soot. Hugh scrambled to his feet and frantically scanned the room for an extinguisher, finally seeing one on the other side of the burning vehicle. As he broke into a sprint toward the device, another muffled 'whump' and flash filled the room as the flames ignited another container, filling the space between the Trac and the workbench and cutting off his path. His eyes widened in dread as he spotted the tall metal bottles of acetylene and oxygen leaning against a welding machine in the midst of the flames.

"Oh shit," he yelled, looking for another extinguisher. He estimated that he had only seconds before the flames ignited the canister's rubber hoses and could only guess at how powerful the detonation would be it the bottles themselves went off. At a minimum, the garage itself would be obliterated, and he along with it.

Hugh spotted another extinguisher on the other side of the two pods and dashed toward it now in all-out panic. He cursed the bulkiness of his clothing and the fresh gusts of wind rushing under the garage door that fanned the flames and seemed to slow his progress. "*I'm not going to make it*," he thought.

In desperation, he reached out with his left arm hoping to use the spire of the nearest pod as a fulcrum to propel himself more quickly between the two craft. He lunged for the spire, readying himself for what would surely be a dicey landing on the other side.

As he flew through the air, Hugh realized that his angle was all wrong.

As his body twisted through the air, he recognized that he had failed to account for the strange properties of the metal. It propelled him forward, causing him to pick up too much speed. His body twisted slowly and he flailed about desperately grasping for anything that might protect him from the inevitable collision with the second vessel. His mind raced, calculating the angle of his flight through the air and adjusting his body to lessen the damage of his impending impact. He closed his eyes and braced himself, hoping that he wouldn't injure himself too badly.

He felt the dull thud of the impact against the small of his back, the shock of it reverberating through his body. Oddly, though, he felt no pain.

He wouldn't live long enough to understand why.

Before his back even made contact with the fuselage, the sharp point of the upper spire had penetrated his neck, instantly severing his spinal column and mercifully sparing him the worst. The spire sliced through his brain stem and punctured his nasal passages before erupting through the flesh of his face between his eyes.

As his body hung there limply and the synapses of his brain rapidly fired off thousands of random impulses in the final climax before his death, a canister of gas in the midst of the flames exceeded its maximum pressure and exploded in a tremendous fireball.

≈ O ≈

Anders happened to glance at the garage monitor just as the initial conflagration erupted. He immediately hit the fire alarm and could only watch as the flames spread rapidly around the Crawler.

"Get your asses in here," he yelled as the first members of the response team burst into the CSC moments later.

The words had barely escaped his lips when the blast rocked the building, shattering glass, disrupting computers, and knocking most of the crew to the floor. The lights flicked out immediately pitching the room into an inky darkness.

≈ O ≈

"I don't care what you say, those things give me the creeps."

"Are you kidding me? This is an incredible opportunity!"

Parker wiped his oily hands on a rag and threw it down at Brian from atop the helicopter. "Yeah, well, you can shove this 'opportunity' up your ass. I didn't sign up for this shit. I just want to do my time and get the hell out."

Brian swatted the rag aside, "What the hell is wrong with you? How can you not want to see what they look like? How many times have we talked about this very thing?"

Parker stopped and peered intently at his friend, "It was all cool when it was still a remote possibility." He leaned back under the open canopy and began tweaking something along the side of the helicopter's turbine. "Now," Parker straightened up and began closing the canopy. "It just feels like things are spinning out of control and we're just being dragged along for the ride. I don't like it one bit."

"I'm with him. This whole situation just smells wrong."

The two looked over at Robert, who had appeared out of nowhere on the other side of the helicopter.

"You of all people," Brian exclaimed in exasperation. "You're a biologist, for cryin' out loud! I'd think you'd be chomping at the bit to examine these things!"

"I don't want any part of 'em. I've seen all I care to see of these things."

"What are you saying?" Parker jumped down alongside Brian and eyed Robert through the open fuselage. "You telling me that you've *seen* these things before?"

Robert glanced around nervously. "I… I don't know anything."

"I think you do." Brian said, skeptically. He jumped into the cabin and moved through the aircraft toward Robert. "What are you not telling us?"

Parker had moved around the nose of the chopper cutting off Robert's only exit. "You've seen these things before, haven't you?! I think the company recovered one of them and you got the chance to play with it."

Robert backed against an oversized mechanics chest as Brian jumped to the floor from the helicopter's passenger door, effectively cornering him. "Listen, guys," he said, nervously, "I really don't know anything. I was just going by what happened in '93. I mean, between that and the creepy spaceship downstairs…I just don't *want* to know any more."

Parker squinted at Brian. "I don't know about you, man, but I think Robert here is full of shit."

Brian nodded, shuffling over to the door and dropping to the ground. The two men inched closer until they were far too close for Robert's comfort.

"Honest, guys! I don't know anything!"

Parker slammed his open palm loudly against the chest, "Bullshit! You'd better start talk…"

The force of the explosion outside knocked them to the ground. Ice rained down from the ceiling and shattered on the floor all around them. They cowered for a moment until they were sure the danger had passed then got to their feet, looking each other over in the dimness of the emergency lighting.

"You guys ok?" Brian asked.

"I'm good."

"Me too," Robert said, his voice shaking. "What the hell was that?"

"I have no idea. We'd better go find out."

Parker reached into the chopper and pulled out a flashlight. "Wonder if it's just here or if the power's out all over the camp."

≈ O ≈

The low rumble shook the warehouse and the lights flickered momentarily.

Kelly looked up then quickly grabbed Matteus and flung him into the empty elevator shaft as thick icicles shattered and clattered all around them. A moment earlier, the two men had been unloading equipment from the cargo elevator and onto large pallets. The overhead crane had been making its way back to them after delivering a loaded pallet to the platform atop the vessel near the upper hatch. It stopped along its track and swayed gently as Matteus and Kelly balanced precariously on a narrow ledge.

They glanced up nervously as they waited for the man-made hail storm to pass.

The elevator itself had come to a halt just below Deck 3 trapping Jakub, its sole occupant. Its heavy cables swayed from the concussion, smacking noisily against the interior of the shaft. Matteus wasn't sure which was the better of his options – standing on the slick metal beam inside the shaft with a powerless elevator dangling overhead or the risk of injury from the ice daggers falling out on the catwalk. But since Kelly's heavy frame had him pinned to the wall he really had no choice.

He closed his eyes and waited helplessly to see what fate would dictate.

≈ O ≈

"Where the hell are the emergency lights?" someone asked.

The response team entered the room from opposite the hangar entryway, shedding some light into the room.

"Jam that door open," Anders yelled, "We need some light in here."

He hurriedly organized the team and led them outside.

Most of the flames had already died out by the time they arrived at the remains of the garage. A few barrels of fuel continued to burn, the only things that could overcome the strong arctic winds.

As the team spread out to extinguish the remaining fires, Anders stood off and assessed the damage.

The only recognizable features left in what had once been the garage were the burned-out hulk of a Trac and the two alien pods. The latter sat slightly askew from their original positioning but otherwise seemed unscathed except for some minor charring.

"Nice job, Hugh," he said sarcastically under his breath. He regretted the comment immediately as he caught site of Hugh's charred body still hanging limply from the spire.

He stood for several seconds surveying the scene, incredulous at the destruction but realizing that it could have been far worse. The positioning of the two alien craft had actually deflected much of the blast, preventing any real damage to the hangar. All the exterior lighting had been obliterated by the explosion leaving the area lit only intermittently by the flames.

Anders grabbed a crewman who was running by, snatching the extinguisher from his hands. "Get to the hangar and grab some tarps," he yelled over the wind. "We've got to get these things covered up as soon as the fire..." He squinted in the pale light. Something about the nearest craft didn't look right.

It was tough to see it in the semi-darkness – the flickering of the flames providing the only light – but something was clearly different. He peered at the spot on the furthest vessel but the smoke, haze, and dim lighting made it difficult to get a clear view. He walked slowly over to the side of the two pods, his eyes fixed on the vessels, leaving the puzzled crewman standing there alone.

As he got closer, he realized that the seemingly charred areas formed clearly defined, straight edges. He shone his flashlight up at the craft but a low, still-smoldering section of the garage wall blocked too much of his view. Anders made for one of the still-intact Tracs that had been fortunate enough to be outside of the garage. He opened the door and climbed quickly into the cab then swung himself up onto the vehicle's roof, scarcely taking his eyes off the craft as he maneuvered for a better vantage point. As he stood atop the vehicle, a shift in the winds momentarily cleared the smoke allowing him to confirm his earlier suspicion. The dark blotches weren't caused by charring. They were voids where the vessel's hatches or doors had recently been. The pod had somehow opened.

Anders tried to shine his light into the openings but he was too distant to make out anything inside. He slowly lifted the radio to his mouth as he realized the implications of what he was seeing.

"Frank. Viktor. Come in."

"Go ahead," Viktor replied, barely audible over the wind. "What's going on out there?"

"Vik," he said, scanning the area slowly with his flashlight, "We've got a real big problem."

≈ O ≈

FOURTEEN

Parker panned the dim light across the workbench. "Look for another flashlight. This one is dying already."

"Over there, Robert," Brian said, pointing to the far end of the bench.

Robert made his way over to the flashlight hanging in its charging stand, tripping over some debris along the way and almost falling down.

"Shit! It's dark as hell in here. Why are the emergency lights so dim?" He snatched the light from its perch and flicked it on.

"That's a good question," Brian wondered as he looked around the dark interior of the hangar. There were few windows in the hangar. They weren't much use in the extreme Antarctic environment. Still, with the numerous exterior floodlights that ringed the compound, he would have expected at least some light to filter in through the few windows they did have. But the only thing they could see or hear from outside was the low droning of a fire alarm somewhere in the distance.

"Guess we don't need this thing anymore," Parker said, switching off his flashlight and setting it down. "Useless piece of shit."

Robert aimed the light so that Parker and Brian could make it safely over to where he was near the front of the chopper. The jar from the explosion had knocked tools and hardware as well as grease and other fluids onto the floor from the nearby workbench. Ice that had fallen from the ceiling also littered the floor. In the low lighting, it would be easy to slip or trip and suffer a nasty fall.

"Holy shit, "Brian muttered, "There's crap all over the place."

"Yeah. But look at that." Parker pointed to one small window across the hangar bay. A faint orange glow flickered along the top edge of the pane. "We'd better go find out what the hell is going on," Parker said urgently. "Lead us to the door, Robert. I can't see a friggin' thing."

When Robert turned away from them, Parker quickly reached out in the darkness and grabbed Brian by the shoulder. "You realize what's out there, right?" he whispered.

Brian's nod was barely perceptible in the faint glow of Robert's flashlight, which was now pointed away from them. "You bet your ass I do," he murmured. "Not good."

After a few steps, Robert turned and shone the light onto the floor to allow them to catch up. "Careful now," he said mustering some false bravado. "There's ice all over the place."

Once the two men had caught up to him, Robert turned back toward the door to resume the trek.

"I can't believe how damn dark it is in here," Parker said, somewhat nervously. He was trying to concentrate on just getting to the door but kept looking up at the window to his right. The bright orange glow seemed to be diminishing but clearly something out there was on fire.

"Yeah. What the hell is up with the emergency…"

Robert's sharp yell echoed through the hangar, which went suddenly dark again as the flashlight crashed to the floor. Brian and Parker crouched instinctively in the darkness as Robert continued to yell repeatedly.

"Shut the hell up," Brian finally yelled after several seconds. He could hear Parker on the floor frantically searching for the flashlight, which had gone out upon hitting the floor. He cursed repeatedly under his breath as he tripped on the debris and ice littering the area.

"Did you see it?! Did you see it?!" Robert was in full panic mode, as he retreated in the darkness toward the sound of Brian's voice.

"Did I see what?" Brian yelled back. "Calm down, damn it!" He could hear Robert scrambling blindly in his direction and gauged him to be just a few feet away now, based on the sound of the stuff he was kicking around.

"Got it," Parker said suddenly, the relief evident in his voice. The immediate area was instantly illuminated once again as he turned the flashlight back on. The light was dimmer now. Some of the LCDs were no longer working due to the light's impact with the floor. Still, it was tremendously comforting to not be completely in the dark.

Robert immediately changed direction and scrambled over to Parker and the perceived safety of the light.

He grasped Parker sleeve, "Did you see it?! It was right there! Right fucking there!"

Robert was pointing in the direction of the door to which they had just been heading.

"See what?" Parker asked loudly, quickly flashing the light around the hangar. "You need to calm the hell down!"

"It was huge! And I'm telling you right now that it wasn't one of us! It was huge! HUGE!"

Patrick shined the light across the room then aimed it at Robert. "I don't see anything."

Brian put his hand on Robert's shoulder and looked him deliberately in the eye. "Robert, calm down! Look. It's pitch dark in here." Brian gestured for the light. Parker eyed him curiously but complied, handing him the flashlight.

"Look," Brian said, shining the light toward the doorway. "See? The shadows made by the flashlight make everything *seem* bigger." He purposefully held the light up close to the handle of a floor jack beside them casting a large shadow along the wall at the far end of the room that swayed in the flashlight's beam.

"See? It was only your imagin…"

Every inch of his skin suddenly erupted in gooseflesh. At the far end of the room, a very large and distinct shadow was slowly making its way along the far wall. Brian blinked rapidly several times to assure himself that he wasn't just seeing things. But there was no mistaking it.

The flashlight's beam began to quiver against the far wall as Brian's hand began to tremble. He slowly panned the light until it shone directly on the shadow. The creature seemed to take no notice of them as it continued to creep inexorably toward the door.

"Holy mother…" Parker whispered as the creature reached the door.

Robert panted rapidly but said nothing.

The creature's silhouette was about two feet taller than the top of the door frame. Brian couldn't make out its lower section but from its midsection the thing grew wider toward where its head should be. Only, there was no obvious head… just a mild rise or bump at the top that was, as best as they could tell, devoid of any recognizable facial feature.

The creature made no sound at all as it glided along the wall. Two thick, multi-jointed appendages rose from behind the creature like the legs of a spider and began rapidly rummaging through the items on the work bench, indiscriminately flinging things aside.

Robert emitted a hoarse croak and clung more tightly to Parker's arm. Parker reached out to steady himself but otherwise barely noticed. His full attention was on the great bear of a creature less than 40 feet away. "Turn the light out," He whispered urgently.

Brian moved his thumb over the switch, but then reconsidered. The creature hadn't reacted to the light at all and seemed intent on searching for something. Either it hadn't noticed them or didn't care that they were there. He kept his thumb resting lightly on the switch, just in case.

Brian peered intently into the darkness trying hard to make out the creature's face but it just didn't seem to have one. He could hear his heart pounding in his ears and everything seemed to be moving in slow motion.

The creature picked up a sledge hammer, seemed to study it for a moment, then slammed it down sharply on the corner of the bench, buckling the forward leg. The three men jumped as the noise reverberated through the hangar. Brian could hear one of his co-workers, probably Robert, crawling along the floor toward the helicopter. He doubted that hiding beneath the aircraft would stop this thing for long if it were intent on getting at them.

The creature resumed its search along the bench with its one free hand as it continued to grip the sledge in the other. It whirled around suddenly as a light came on in the hallway leading to the CSC.

"Someone in here?"

Brian opened his mouth to shout a warning but it was too late. The creature dashed into the hallway with shocking speed.

There was no scream, just a sickening dull thud of something heavy slamming into the wall followed by a muted shuffling noise. Seconds later, the creature returned to the hangar. It scanned the hangar quickly then sprinted through the blast door and into the tunnel leading down into the warehouse.

The two men quickly made their way to the door leading to the CSC. As they got closer, they could faintly hear someone outside yelling, although they couldn't make out what was being said over the howling of the wind. "*Sure hope it's not another one of those things*," Brian thought. The sudden reality of an encounter with the alien creature – especially one so large and terrifying – had instantly shattered the idealistic fantasies that had built up in his mind over the years.

They peered cautiously into the hall. A crewman was doubled over and motionless on the floor. With a sickening feeling, Brian realized that the poor guy was bent in half the wrong way, his spine clearly broken. An indent in the wall above him and a large spatter of blood marked the area where the creature had thrown or slammed him.

As they drew closer to the man, it was clear that he'd taken a heavy blow to the head too. There was just no way the guy could've survived. They did a quick check of just to be sure.

The emergency lighting came on suddenly in the hangar. "Whew! Thank God for that, anyway," Brian said, switching off the flashlight. "C'mon. We'd better let them know."

"That *thing* went down into the warehouse," Parker said. "Shouldn't we take care of *that* first?"

"With what?! This?!" Brian asked, holding the flashlight out to emphasize his point.

An alarm began to shriek within the hangar and they could just make out a flashing yellow light reflecting off the side of the nearest helicopter. A mechanical clanking noise began to reverberate noisily through the hangar. It sounded like an old rusty piece of heavy equipment being suddenly operated after years of neglect. Although they'd never heard it before, they understood immediately what it must be.

They rushed back into the hangar and collided with Robert, who had been running full speed in their direction. The three men tumbled to the floor.

Robert quickly got up and sprinted again into the hallway leading to the CSC, yelling incoherently at the top of his lungs.

Parker and Brian sat on the hangar floor for a moment, dazed by the collision, then got to their feet. They watched dumbfounded as the last several inches of the heavy steel door descended to the floor. There was some additional clanking and knocking as the locking mechanism engaged, then silence.

The huge steel door had been installed during the early days of the site's existence but it had never before been used. They called it the 'blast door', as if its function was to protect the warehouse from a crash or fire that might occur within the hangar. Its real purpose was far more unsettling.

The failsafe door, its official name, was designed to seal off the warehouse in the event that the crew uncovered another of the horrible creatures that had decimated the advance team in 1993. It was meant to trap the creature below, containing it within the icy canyon walls, where it could be captured and exterminated.

In the two-plus decades that they'd been working at the site, there had never been a reason to activate the door other than to perform routine maintenance, which had grown less frequent over the years once it was obvious that the buried spacecraft contained no further specimens.

By activating it now, Robert had just entombed the alien creature below – along with an unknown number of the crew.

Brian and Parker stood for several seconds listening in disbelief to the faint whirring of the yellow emergency beacon rotating above the doorway.

"You're right," Parker finally agreed, "We'd better let them know."

PART TWO

FIFTEEN

Kelly put his cell phone back into its sheath on his belt and turned to face the group. He took a deep breath as fifteen anxious faces stared back at him. During the last half hour or so, he'd been on the line frequently with topside getting updates on the situation and working to get the trapped crew out of the warehouse. He was doing his best to sound positive for the sake of the crew but each conversation with those above seemed to bring fresh bad news.

They'd found the elevator's cab, doors, and framing in a twisted wreck shortly after the explosion. There had been no sign of Jakub, who had ridden the elevator up to the 3rd deck to grab some coffee. At the same time, they'd discovered that the blast door had sealed off their only means of escape. Kelly had gathered the men in one of the rooms adjacent to the elevator shaft since then to keep everyone together while they worked out a plan.

"So, here's where we stand," he said, trying to sound confident. "They still can't get the door open so we can't return topside through the tunnel."

"You gotta be friggin' kidding me!' Codi griped loudly, "How the hell can that be? It's just a metal door, for God's sake! How hard can it be to lift it open?"

Several of the others joined in, loudly grumbling their dissatisfaction.

"Shut the hell up!"

The voice emanating from the back of the room was unfamiliar and the group turned in unison to see who had spoken.

Matteus jumped down from countertop where he'd been sitting. "Bitching about things isn't going to get us any closer to getting out of here. Why don't you listen to what he's got to say before going Cro-Magnon on him?"

"Who the hell are you? You've been here all of what…a week? What makes you think…"

Codi fell silent as Kelly's heavy hand came to rest on his shoulder.

"The door was built as a safety feature. It's eight inches thick and secured by six steel pins, three on each side, that are six inches in diameter. It's like a damn bank vault. Once it's been activated, it can only be re-opened by entering a specific code that must be provided by headquarters, and only after *they* deemed the situation to be under control. As far as *they* are concerned, the situation is *not* under control."

"You're damn right it's not under control," one of the men shouted. One of those 'things' is running around out there!"

"Yeah!" a second man joined in, his voice thick with resentment. "And those corporate dicks are back there, ten thousand miles away, while we're stuck down here with it!"

The room erupted in chaos as each crewman fought to be heard, many using outrage to mask their fear.

Kelly held up his hand and waited for the men to grow silent. But as he waited for the din to die down, he realized that he, too, was angry.

He had understood the logic behind it when it hadn't really mattered…when the odds of a brush with the creature after all these years had seemed so remote. It made sense that any decision to re-open the door, once it had been activated, would be made by men who were far removed from the immediate situation.

Preventing the escape of this creature, even at the expense of some of the crew, must always be the top priority. The consequences of failure were far too dire. Any on-site manager would be much more likely to make the decision based on an emotional response, as the lives of friends and co-workers were threatened, rather than a logical one.

Yeah, he got it.

But suddenly, it was all too real and it *did* matter.

"So, there's a plan, right?" Matteus asked, tentatively.

"Yeah. There's a plan," Kelly replied, suppressing his anger. Best to redirect their energies into something productive. He paused and exhaled, "It isn't going to be easy."

"OK," Matteus said. He made his way to the front of the crowd, ignoring the sneers of the veterans. "So, what do we have to do?"

Kelly outlined the plan, pausing several times to overcome an objection or clarify a point. The room was silent when he finished speaking. The plan was dangerous but workable.

Kelly allowed the men a moment to digest it. Then he began assigning tasks to get them focused on preparing for their trek. He also wanted to keep them from focusing too heavily on the risks.

"Do you really think this will work?" Matteus asked him quietly once the team dispersed.

"It's got to," he answered. "There's no other way."

Kelly watched as the men readied themselves. There was a look of grim resolution on the faces of some, but fear pervaded the rest. It would be a real challenge to maintain order once they were on their way, especially if the alien creature made an appearance when they were out in the open.

Their escape route would leave them exposed and vulnerable and retreat would not be an option. "*Same as Jake*," a small voice nagged from inside his head. Kelly squirmed and grit his teeth again at the thought of his friend's fate.

From what they'd seen of the wreckage of the freight elevator, the creature must have cornered Jakub inside just as it reached Deck 3. The metal caging at the front of the lift had been completely twisted out of shape and half torn from its track. The heavy wire mesh had been stretched outward as though some mighty animal had beaten itself against it repeatedly from within while attempting to break out. Except the forensics of the scene - the way that debris was scattered about, the angle of the twisted doors, the pattern of some unknown white fluid spattered along the back wall - all clearly indicated that something had broken *in*.

The thick, milky white substance that covered the floor in and around the lift was especially odd. It appeared to be a mucous of some sort, with small dark spots sprinkled liberally throughout like grains of scorched brown rice. The fluid was smeared in a way that indicated that something or *someone* had been dragged through it.

Except for a single red leather work glove, there had been no sign of Jake.

Kelly shook his head and stared at the wall. It had been a lousy scenario for Jake, for sure. The guy had never stood a chance. At least the team he'd assembled would have a few more options. Still, based on what they'd already seen, it was likely that the outcome of any encounter they might have with the damned beast would end the same.

Kelly looked at his watch. "We're heading out in three," he said, trying to sound confident. Several of the men grew noticeably more anxious but Kelly had already done everything he could to calm their nerves. It'd be up to each man now to conquer his own fear.

As he rose to his feet, even he couldn't ignore the large knot forming in his own stomach as the moment of truth drew near.

≈ O ≈

"Ooooo, Right there." Hildy exclaimed mildly. She winced as Armand pressed lightly on her abdomen.

"Have you noticed anything else? Headache? Dizziness? Nausea?"

Hildy cocked her eyebrows, "Nausea? Seriously?! There hasn't been a day in the last two weeks that I haven't felt that!"

"What I mean is…" Armand dropped his hand to his side and sighed. "Never mind."

He stepped back and looked her up and down. "Well,' he finally said, "I don't think it's anything urgent. I'll have to look you over real good once we get topside. In the meantime, you let me know right away if it gets any worse."

Hildy nodded but suspected that Armand wasn't being up front with her. "*Maybe I'm just being paranoid,*" she thought. She looked around the room. They were stranded, sitting in a dark, unfamiliar room with no electricity and no idea what the hell had happened to knock out the power and the cell phones. It only made sense that Armand would be preoccupied.

She dropped her head to her chest then arched it all the way back in a long, slow stretch in an effort to relax. "So, what do we do now? Just wait?"

"I'm working on it,' he replied.

"I don't understand," Charlie intervened. "How can it be that we don't have comms with anyone? I thought the cellular system was designed to work even during a power outage."

"It should. But the earthquake, or whatever it was, obviously knocked it out along with the power."

They sat in silence for a moment in the semi-darkness, lit only by a flashlight and by the faint light filtering in through the open door from the hallway, where the emergency lighting had kicked in. Armand had tried repeatedly to reach someone, *anyone* via his cell phone but had gotten nothing but static. They'd ultimately taken refuge in Carlson's suite, the room closest to Shifty's, as they waited for the power to come back on. They didn't feel right about leaving their patients until then.

But it had been twenty minutes or so since the jolt and, with both the main power and the cellular system still out, Armand was getting anxious.

"Can we please get the hell out of here?" Hildy asked, eying Carlson's terrarium in the corner of the room.

"Hildegard, will you please relax?! That thing isn't going anywhere."

Hildy shuddered. "Who in their right mind keeps such a gross thing as a damn pet?"

"You'd be surprised. Tarantulas make interesting pets. Their coloring can be quite beautiful and they're an interesting conversation piece."

"I've got to agree with Hildy on this one," Charlie interjected.

They glanced at the ceiling as a muted thump echoed from somewhere overhead.

"Sure hope everyone's alright up there."

Charlie scanned the ceiling, "It sure is quiet. I guess that's a good sign."

Armand grabbed the flashlight from the table top. "I think we ought to make our way back. Someone could be hurt up there."

Charlie shrugged, "It's better than sitting here, waiting for them to come to us."

"That's for sure," Hildy chimed in, standing up from the couch.

"I'm dying for some…."

"Sshhhh!" Armand put his ear to the door and pressed a finger to his lips.

"What?" Charlie asked, mildly annoyed. "I'm hungry."

"Quiet!" Armand whispered urgently, cocking his head to one side. "Either of you hear that?"

Before either of the women could respond, a low, mournful hooting noise came from the hallway, warbling rapidly before fading.

"What the hell is that?" Charlie asked under her breath.

Armand held up his hand and the sound pierced the silence again, more loudly this time. It was clearly not mechanical and appeared closer than before.

"I've never heard anything even remotely like that," Hildy said, anxiously.

"Wait here," Armand whispered.

He walked cautiously out the door, shining the light both ways as he searched for the source of the sound.

"Armand, I don't think that's a good idea. Let's just wait."

Armand pressed his finger to his lips then held it out toward them. "One minute," he mouthed silently. A second later, he was creeping cautiously down the hallway toward the sound, crouching close to the wall.

Charlie and Hildy huddled together in the darkness scarcely making a sound.

"What do we do?" Hildy asked, her voice quivering.

Charlie hugged her close and glanced at her watch. Barely half a minute had gone by since Armand left but it already seemed much longer. "I don't know," she replied.

The words had barely left her lips when Armand leapt through the door, slamming it shut behind him and bolting it. He was breathing heavily as he looked at them, wide eyed and mouth agape.

"What is it?" Charlie asked, urgently.

He studied them for a moment, torn between the urgency of the moment and a desire to keep them from panicking.

"I have no idea," he finally replied.

SIXTEEN

Kelly peered down the hallway, looking for anything out of the ordinary. But except for the absolute silence, everything seemed normal. Their undertaking had gone well so far but it was far from over. He'd chosen to divert the group from the original plan, stopping in at the armory for some weaponry. They'd originally set out with none so it hadn't taken much to convince the men to make the detour. He was glad they'd diverted. Already it was clear that the men felt more secure, having the means now to defend themselves.

Kelly stood at the top of the stairwell as the rest of the group streamed behind him down the hallway. Some were getting restless. Just below, they could see the twisted metal framing of the elevator shaft where Jakub had encountered the creature.

"What's the hold-up?" Codi asked, snaking his way to the front of the line.

"We're waiting for Drew's group."

"What the hell for?"

Kelly glared at Codi and the smaller man fell silent.

"Get back there and wait," he ordered gruffly. "You know what the hell for. We'll head out together as soon as they get here."

"We should just go and let them catch up."

Kelly grabbed Codi by the nape of his neck and forced him to look down. "They're carrying wounded men and heavy equipment up all nine flights," he hissed, pointing down at the steep metal staircase spiraling its way to the warehouse floor. "They're going to need our help once they get up here and *we're* going to be here to give it to them. Now, get your ass back there before I kick it back there."

Kelly gave the man a shove to make sure he got the point.

Codi grumbled but moved reluctantly back along the wall midpoint down the hallway.

Kelly had actually thought about sending Matteus ahead with some of the others while he waited with the rest to help Drew's group once they got to the top of the stairwell. But he ultimately realized that it wouldn't have done them any good. If they'd had the blow torches they needed to cut through the steel doors on the other end of the catwalk, things would've been different. They could have gone ahead to get started.

But the blow torches had to be brought up from the machine shop on the warehouse floor by Drew's crew so it made no sense to send a team ahead. They'd have just ended up waiting at the far end for the rest of the crew without really accomplishing anything. And splitting the group up just didn't seem like a good idea at this point. If *that thing* showed itself, there might actually be safety in numbers.

He reviewed the plan to himself again as they waited for Drew's team to start making their way up.

He'd completed a brief recon of their escape route just moments ago and it seemed straight forward enough. From their current position, they'd enter the cab of the overhead crane through the access door adjacent to the elevator shaft on the Deck 3. Once inside, each man would climb the short ladder that led out the top of the crane and onto the catwalk that ran along the length of the track from which the crane was suspended.

The track and catwalk spanned the entire length of the warehouse, ten stories above the spacecraft, before terminating at a small building on the far side that housed the crane's support machinery. At the remote end, they could theoretically exit a service door and climb a staircase that led up and out of the complex and into the Antarctic wilderness, where Trac Crawlers would be waiting to pick them up.

It seemed simple enough. Still, Kelly had his doubts. The catwalk was narrow and ran along the track on only one side. Once they started across, they'd be extremely vulnerable. Even if they made it to the far side without incident, they still had to get through a solid steel door that had been welded shut years ago when it had outgrown its usefulness. The group would remain vulnerable for an hour or two while an opening, one large enough for them to squeeze through, was cut through it with an acetylene torch.

Kelly gazed below at Drew's team as they assembled at the base of the stairwell. Between carrying the heavy acetylene and oxygen tanks, the cumbersome hoses and nozzles, and the wounded men, they were sure to be exhausted by the time they reached the 3rd deck. It was a lousy time for the damn elevator to be out of commission.

Kelly's cell phone buzzed silently. "We're here," he said quietly into it. "Yes, we can see you. We'll be ready for you."

Some of the men inched closer to get a better view of what was happening below. They watched as the small knot of men began ascending the staircase almost a hundred feet below them. The lighting was brighter on the warehouse floor so they were easy to see.

Kelly quickly scanned the rest of the warehouse floor for any sign of the creature. He was thankful that Deck 4 still had power and that the large expanse below remained lit by the primary lighting. He shuddered involuntarily at the thought of them having to attempt their escape under the emergency lighting, which only covered the main areas of the facility. He was sure that would've been enough to completely unnerve some of them.

They watched for several minutes as Drew's small group snaked their way up the staircase. The first four crewmen carried a wounded man on a makeshift canvas stretcher, each awkwardly grasping one corner of the impromptu device. From the chatter he'd heard on the radio, Kelly gathered that the man had broken both of his legs when falling ice jarred loose from the explosion had knocked him from a scaffold. He'd fallen twenty feet, landing on top of a welding unit and suffering a compound fracture in both legs.

Three other men followed behind the stretcher crew, one man supporting himself by draping each arm around the neck of a crewman on each flank. He was limping badly but was at least somewhat mobile. At the rear of the group, two men were carrying the tanks and other components to assemble the torch that they'd need to cut through the steel doors.

After several minutes, the group had gotten only about a quarter of the way up. From their perch at the top of the stairwell, Kelly and his team could make out an occasional grunt as the crewmen labored to maneuver the wounded men and heavy equipment around the sharp, narrow corners between each flight of stairs. The man on the stretcher yelped occasionally when the ride got a little too rough.

"Shit, I think that's Warren on the stretcher. Shouldn't we go down and help them?"

"No, Phil" Kelly replied reluctantly, "It's already too crowded on the stairway. We'd only make things worse. They'll probably rest for a minute at midpoint landing before making it the rest of the way. Once they get up here, we can take over."

Phillip nodded. He, too, had been frequently scanning the expanse of the warehouse as they waited for the small group below to reach them and was getting nervous about how long it was all taking. Their agonizingly slow progress was getting slower by the minute as they grew tired from the effort.

Kelly could tell that Phillip was torn between his desire to help his friend and the need for self-preservation. "They'll be ok," he said, trying his best to sound reassuring. "Soon as they reach the top, we'll be here."

Phil nodded and forced a weak smile.

"What the hell is that?"

Kelly froze, peering intently into the area where the crewman was pointing but seeing nothing.

"I see it! It's right there!" another man yelled. "Below them, in the elevator shaft! It's moving up toward them!"

Kelly still couldn't see what the others had spotted but he quickly grabbed his cell phone from his belt. The men surrounding him began murmuring in agitation, backing slowly away from the stairwell and retreating into the hallway behind them.

Kelly could see the green light blinking on Drew's belt as the small group rounded the corner at Midpoint landing. But the maneuver required the use of both of his hands and he was unable to answer.

"C'mon! *C'mon*!" he urged.

The group paused at Midpoint, setting the wounded man down on the walkway that lead out to the hatch at the top-center of the spacecraft. The four men that had been carrying the stretcher, including Drew, collapsed against the railing clearly exhausted from the effort.

Kelly watched as Drew, panting and sweating profusely from the climb, slowly reached for the phone attached to his belt.

It was then that Kelly saw it, the broad shadow emerging from the darkness. It was easily twice as large as even the largest man on the landing.

He dropped his hand to his side, the cell phone still ringing, as he realized that his warning would be too late.

The creature sprang from the elevator shaft without warning, hurling itself into the air like a large gorilla and landing with a loud thump on the walkway behind the men. The beast grabbed Drew by the front of his jacket and flicked him effortlessly into the air. It had happened so fast that Drew had had no time to react. He fell silently, letting out a stiff grunt only when impacting the edge of the spacecraft thirty feet below. He rolled along the sloping edge of the vessel before plummeting another five stories to the warehouse floor.

Kelly shouted and waved his arms over his head in an attempt to distract the creature. He grabbed his rifle and aimed it downward but there was just too much metal framing between him and the landing at midpoint for a clean shot. He looked around frantically for a better vantage point.

The crew on midpoint landing tried to scatter but there were few places to hide. One man leapt into the elevator shaft as the creature approached. He landed precariously on the metal framing and groped frantically for a handhold as he struggled to maintain his balance. He ultimately lost his footing on the slippery metal and plunged screaming down the shaft. Several sickening smacks marked his progress as he careened off the gantry on his way down, followed by one loud, final whack as he hit the thin metal flooring at the bottom.

Two men sprinted down the catwalk leading to the spacecraft. The wounded man yelped in pain as they dropped him and he struggled frantically to get to his feet. His wounded leg collapsed beneath him just as he gained his footing and he tumbled down the stairwell to the landing below.

The creature turned toward another man who stood with his back pressed to the railing, frozen in fear. One enormous limb arched up and over the creature from behind and grabbed the unfortunate man by his face, lifting him several feet into the air. The crewman clawed at the giant paw encapsulating his face and struggled wildly, his muffled protests barely audible.

Kelly fired several shots down into the warehouse in an attempt to scare the creature off. It glanced upward briefly but seemed to recognize that Kelly was no immediate threat and continued its pursuit of the next nearest crewmen.

"Come on!" Kelly yelled behind him. He jumped down onto the metal landing and bounded down the steps two at a time. A few of the others followed while the remainder huddled against the wall, too terrified to act.

The creature bounded toward its next victim, who was frantically scrambling up the staircase. Another powerful limb grabbed the man by his leg, yanking him harshly back down. The man clanked roughly along several of the steps as he struggled hysterically to free himself. The beast lifted him over its head, dangling him by one ankle as he screamed and flailed about.

The creature sized up its prey then turned suddenly, surprised by gunfire coming from immediately behind it.

Kelly paused, trying to determine where the shots were coming from. On the landing below, Warren was firing a pistol at the creature as he lay sprawled along the walkway, still partially wrapped in the make-shift stretcher. He hit it several times but the impacts had no apparent effect. The creature effortlessly hurled the second crewman away and out into the void.

Even from his position on the stairwell several stories up, Kelly felt the impact of the man's body as it hit the floor.

Warren continued to fire, hitting the thing with every shot as it bounded toward him. When it was clear that the pistol was no match for the creature, he turned the firearm on himself just as the beast grabbed him.

The noise of the shot in such close proximity seemed to startle the creature. It immediately underhanded Warren's limp body away and toward the elevator shaft. The lifeless figure arced rapidly through the air, crashing through the fencing that protected a high voltage electrical panel. The force of the impact collapsed the panel's metal door, shorting it out in an explosion of sparks and bright blue arcing.

Kelly had gotten only halfway to the landing when the warehouse went completely dark.

SEVENTEEN

The small group congregated around the console and contemplated the new developments.

Brian stood behind the main console in the CSC glowering at Robert, who cowered at the far end of the room. Things had seemed far more hopeful just minutes ago. But the loss of both main power and part of the communications network within the warehouse would greatly complicate the escape attempt. The grim reality of the survivors' desperate situation hung over the CSC like a dark cloud.

"So, we've got at least thirty-two trapped below, right?" Viktor asked suddenly, his mind clearly calculating.

"Yes," Anders replied, handing him a printout. "Here's what we've been able to confirm, based on the reports from Kelly and Drew. We haven't heard anything from Doc or anyone else on Deck 2."

Brian darted across the room and grabbed Robert with both hands by the front of his shirt.

"You fucking idiot," he yelled, his face just inches from Robert's. "If anything happens to her, I'm going to kill you!"

He slammed Robert several times against the wall before Viktor and one of the security guards were able to pull him away.

"I mean it," Brian said through gritted teeth, "I *will* kill you..."

"Knock it off," Frank shouted. He walked over to Brian, who was still being restrained. "We have enough shit to deal with right now without being distracted by your personal vendetta. If you're not going to be a part of the solution, I'll have you locked up!"

Brian nodded and slumped his shoulders as Viktor and the other crewman released their hold on him.

"For the record," Viktor said, "Robert did exactly what he should have done. By closing the hatch, he trapped the creature below where we can contain it."

Robert nodded rapidly, “That’s right!” His eyes darted about the room, seeking affirmation and acceptance from anyone to quell his guilt. Perhaps he *had* acted out of duty and it hadn’t been panic that had prompted him to seal the hatch. “*Yeah,*” he thought, taking some solace in Viktor’s words. “*I did the right thing!*”

Brian glared at him and the guilt, which had been trumped momentarily by a wave of self-righteousness, reclaimed its throne in the pit of Robert’s stomach. As much as he’d like them to think that he’d acted out of duty, Brian and Parker knew better. They’d been with him in the hangar when he’d sealed the door and witnessed his panic first hand. It wouldn’t be long before the rest of the crew would know too.

Brian looked at Frank, "Hildy is down there..."

"So are dozens of others," Frank shouted. "And we're working on getting *every single one* of them out," he said softening his tone.

Anders cleared his throat, "Believe it or not, it could've been alot worse.”

“How you figure that?” Brian asked scornfully.

“Under normal circumstances, just about everyone would’ve been down there. But with the extra security needed to keep an eye on them things,” he said, gesturing toward the two pods outside, “a good number of the crew were diverted up here from their regular duties. We *could* have almost twice that many down there right now."

Viktor looked at his watch, "Drew must've started out by now. With any luck, that's at least twenty who should be making their way to the service entrance. And,” he continued, looking directly at Brian, “it’s entirely possible that some of the others have joined them since we last spoke with anyone down there.”

“Well, we’re not going to just sit here and wait.” Frank interjected. “Anders, get as many men as you can assemble to the hangar.”

"Are you considering going in?" Viktor asked incredulously. "I'm not so sure that's a good idea at this point."

"Maybe not. But I'm not going to stand by and just *hope* for the best. They need help down there and we're going to give them as much as we can."

"What if it's already too late?! All we'd be doing is putting more of the crew in harm's way. We may also be giving that thing a way to escape, if we open up those doors."

"Do *you* want to just leave them down there, Vik? Cause *I* sure as hell don't! ...and I *won't*!"

Viktor paused. "No," he finally relented, "I sure don't either."

"Ok, then. Once we get them up here, we keep them segregated until we can test them. None of them re-join the crew until we've verified that he *is* who he *says* he is." Frank deliberately avoided using any female pronouns to avoid agitating Brian further.

Frank turned to Anders, "You set it up."

"Right. We'll keep them in the conference room. It's the only place besides the hangar big enough to hold that many."

"You work with Anders," Frank said turning to Brian.

Brian stared at Frank, "If it's all the same to you, I'd rather be part of the rescue team," he said with considerable restraint. He was doing everything in his power to control himself, knowing that he couldn't afford to anger Frank further.

Frank eyed him for a moment. "Alright. Go. But you do exactly as you're told."

Brian nodded and quickly turned away before the others could see his face flush. He was annoyed and embarrassed at being chastised like a child but glad nonetheless that he'd gotten his way. The thought of being stuck up here waiting was unbearable.

He shot Robert one last look when he was sure that nobody else was paying attention, drawing his finger across his throat.

Robert turned away.

Frank looked at his watch, "Ok, let's be ready to roll in five."

"We are going to catch hell once they realize back home that we've circumvented the safeguards," Anders said, "That is, *if* we succeed in getting them out".

"They'll make it," Frank replied. "And as for headquarters, I really don't give a shit."

≈ O ≈

The tension in the small room was palpable. Armand was doing his best to downplay what he'd seen. But it was clear to the two women that he'd been shaken by his brief encounter with the creature.

He'd attempted to describe it to them but they looked at him as though he were crazy. He couldn't really blame them. Hell, he was still struggling himself to accept what he'd seen.

Part of him fought for an alternative explanation. Perhaps it had been just one of the larger Norwegian crewman decked out in a heavy parka and man-pack. Maybe the guy was preparing to go outside to check on things...to see if the earthquake had caused any exterior damage.

It could also have been one of the chopper pilots, fully suited up for a jaunt out to McMurdo to collect the additional medicines they needed to fight the meningitis. Their flight suits and helmet always did appear bulky and cumbersome to him. Could it have been either of these, made all the more foreign-looking by the poor lighting?

But the more logical part of him slowly asserted itself, forcing him to finally admit to what he'd seen.

The thing had bolted down the hallway with amazing speed and agility. Nothing on this earth that big could move so swiftly and silently. He'd also never heard anything that sounded even remotely like it. If it hadn't intentionally 'spoken' – if that's what that strange, warbled hooting noise had been – Armand wouldn't even have seen it until it was too late.

It had been lurking in the shadows, its black and gray coloring melding perfectly with them. In the split-second it took for him to recognize what he was seeing, Armand hadn't been able to make out what it had been doing. Running from it had seemed far more urgent.

A chill ran up his spine as he realized just how close he'd come to it.

He knew of the organism's horrific abilities. As the site's physician, they'd allowed him to read up on the Dunford team's earlier efforts as they'd experimented with the alien flesh. He had insisted on this before accepting the job. They were reluctant at first to allow him, but he argued that he needed to be prepared in case they came across another specimen of the organism. He needed to know how to counteract it.

Like everyone else, he'd been enthralled at first. But this quickly turned to anxiety and fear as he realized the implications.

Armand had actually known one of the doctors involved in the early research. They'd even spoken a couple of times during the man's tenure at Dunford. At first, he had been reluctant to discuss their work and faithfully abided by the non-disclosure pact that he'd signed with the company. But one day he just suddenly opened up. "*This thing makes Ebola look like the sniffles*," Daniel had told him, clearly shaken by what they'd already learned. A month later, he had become so terrified that he refused to work at the site any longer.

They'd transferred him back to Seattle, where he'd taken to drinking heavily. Within weeks, upper management decided that he was too much a liability and they quietly let him go, with a severance package sizable enough to buy his continued silence of course. He ended up taking some menial job at a local hospital and Armand had since lost touch with him.

At about the same time that Daniel had vanished into obscurity, Robert had shown up at Langstadt Station. Once he realized that Robert had worked at Dunford, Armand questioned him constantly about the organism, hoping to glean some new tidbits about the organism that hadn't been included within the seemingly innumerable status reports from Dunford. As scary as it was, as a doctor and a scientist he found it incredibly fascinating. He wished to learn all he could about the organism from a purely scientific perspective.

Robert had discussed it with him eagerly at first. But quite suddenly and inexplicably something changed and he grew increasingly more reluctant to talk about it. Finally, he told Armand in no uncertain terms that he no longer wished to talk about it and had since deliberately avoided the subject altogether.

Over time, Armand had come to piece together a thorough understanding of the organism. He shuddered again as he thought about how close he'd come to what surely would have been a terrifying end. Yet despite the creature's unparalleled adaptability, it had seemed just as frightened of him as it sped away. Armand found *that* to be most perplexing.

He'd began again to describe the creature but suddenly stopped when he noticed how pale Hildy had become. Even the normally unflappable Charlie had grown noticeably agitated.

After he had bolted the door, they moved one of the dressers in front of it for added security. Armand knew instinctively that this would do nothing to prevent the creature from coming through the door, if that was its intent, but had suggested the move anyway in an attempt to alleviate the girls' fears.

He chastised himself for his earlier behavior and vowed to present a brave face until they got out of their current mess. But inwardly the experience had unnerved him, filling him with a deep though poorly defined sense of foreboding.

The muted but unmistakable sound of gunfire erupted from somewhere below them just as he'd gotten the girls to relax a little. The three stood in the center of the room straining to hear and eyeing each other anxiously.

Behind his back, Armand fingered the sturdy steak knife, a soiled relic left over from one of Carlson's lone dinner in his suite, which the three of them had commandeered. Despite a thorough search of the room, it was the only weapon that they could come up with.

As quickly as is erupted, the gunfire ceased. The silence seemed all the more oppressive in its wake.

Charlie and Hildy stared intently at Armand. He knew that they were waiting for him to comfort them but he honestly had no idea what to say.

His mind raced in a dozen different directions...his close call with the creature just minutes ago...the results of the research at Dunford...their current predicament, which left them trapped and isolated. He was also desperately contemplating what to do about the five sick and incapacitated members of the crew. How were they possibly going to get them all to safety?

"Armand!" He grew aware of Charlie's insistent calling only after she'd already called his name a few times. Hildy and Charlie were staring intently at him, their faces masked with anxiety and doubt. Hildy had both hands over her mouth as if trying to stop herself from vomiting.

Armand felt a sudden resolve wash over him like a warm blanket. He cursed himself for what he was about to do despite knowing that he really had no choice.

"Ladies," he said firmly, as he discretely slipped the knife into his pants pocket, "Let's get the hell out of here."

EIGHTEEN

Kelly leaned against the wall breathing hard from the climb. It had been an exhausting few minutes and he was actually surprised that they'd made it.

"Nice job, guys," he said between pants.

Trond, Phillip, and Matteus nodded as they, too, struggled to catch their breath.

The emergency lighting had come on right away when the main power had gone out. It had initially been very dim but by now had grown noticeably brighter. They'd remained frozen in place on the stairwell for a minute or so until it brightened sufficiently for them to move around safely.

From their position on the stairwell a couple of flights above the Midpoint landing, they could see that the creature had gone. Unfortunately, so were all the men that had comprised Drew's team. The canvas stretcher that had carried Warren was the only thing that indicated they'd even been there a minute ago.

Kelly thought for a moment about continuing down to Midpoint to check for survivors but then reconsidered. It was clear from his perch on the stairwell that all of Drew's men were gone.

They'd just started the climb back to Deck 3 when Phillip suddenly stopped and cursed, remembering that they needed the torch if they were to have any hope of getting out. They reluctantly climbed back down, quickly collected the components that they needed, and then practically ran up the stairwell to Deck 3.

A couple men ran over as they collapsed onto the floor. One of them held out a water bottle and they took turns gulping down the cool liquid as they slowly caught their breath.

“I don't want to do that ever again,” Matteus said between gasps. He'd had the misfortune of grabbing the heaviest of the tanks and had barely made it to the top of the stairwell.

Phillip got up from the floor and began examining the equipment. "Looks like we've got everything we need." He stopped suddenly and picked up the nozzle and hose. "Shit! The damn nozzle is dented. Must've happened during the…" He cocked his head in the direction of Midpoint, unable to say it.

"Can we use it?"

"I don't know, Kel," Phillip replied, "Won't know til I try it."

Kelly shrugged, "We're screwed if it doesn't…" He regretted the words the moment he said them and cursed himself silently. The last thing he wanted was to give the others a reason to despair.

He sat up suddenly, "Where's everybody else?"

One of the men scowled and pointed with his thumb toward the overhead crane. "They bolted for the catwalk as soon as that *thing* appeared."

Kelly scowled but said nothing. He'd deal with those cowards later.

"Idiots!" Phillip said loudly, "They're not getting anywhere without this," he said, tapping the nozzle as he hefted it.

"Stanley, Trond? You guys mind carrying these for a while?" Kelly asked, pointing to the tanks.

Trond slung one of the heavy tanks over his shoulder without a word. Stanley did the same with the other tank while a third man grabbed the hoses.

"Listen!" Phillip was standing motionless near the stairway that led up to Deck 2.

The rest of the group stood motionless, straining to hear.

"I don't hear it now," Phillip whispered after several seconds, "but I definitely heard something up there."

"What did it sound like?" Kelly asked.

"Who gives a shit?!" Stanley whispered, making no effort to mask the alarm in his voice.

“I agree! I’d kinda like to get going now,” Matteus said nervously.

Kelly nodded. Under normal circumstances, he’d prefer to investigate. But these circumstances were far from normal.

“You take lead,” he said to Matteus, “I’ll hang in the rear.”

In less than a minute, all six of them were walking along the narrow catwalk that stretched into the darkness toward the far end of the warehouse.

≈ O ≈

Armand stopped at the hallway junction and cautiously peered around the corner. When he didn't see anything obvious, he shined the flashlight down the hall in both directions.

"Ok, let's go." He motioned to the two women to follow, taking the hallway to his right.

He forced himself to ignore the voice in his head that was berating him for leaving the sick crewmen behind. Hildy and Charlie had been mortified at the thought, too, but had ultimately agreed that they had no choice. The three of them wouldn’t have been able to move all five of the patients. Two of them had already been so debilitated by the meningitis that they were barely coherent.

Armand crept along the wall as silently as he could, using only the faint emergency lighting to light their way. He used the flashlight only when necessary, telling the women that this was to conserve the battery. In truth, he didn't want the flashlight's beam to alert the creature to their presence.

Armand stiffened at the sound of a low groan. He raised the steak knife and poised himself, ready to strike. He heard it again, more faintly this time. It took him a second to realize that this wasn't the same sound that he'd heard before when he’d encountered the thing. He turned quickly to look behind, surprised to see that the women weren’t there.

Armand ran the few steps to the corner and flicked on the flashlight. Hildy was doubled over along the wall, using it for support, as Charlie crouched beside her.

Charlie looked worried, "It seems to be worse than before."

"I'm ok," Hildy gasped. "It's subsiding."

Armand felt her abdomen, gently pushing in several places.

Hildy winced as he gently probed.

"She also complained of being dizzy just before she doubled over."

Armand nodded at Charlie and forced a smile. He grabbed Hildy's wrist to assess her pulse as he glanced nervously around the corridor. "Can you walk?" he finally asked.

"Yeah. I think so."

"We'll help you," Armand said as he gestured to Charlie.

Hildy wrapped her arms around their shoulders as they got her to her feet.

"Ready?" he asked.

"Ready," Hildy gasped.

It took them several steps to coordinate their efforts but they were moving fluidly enough by the time they'd reached the next junction.

"We're almost there," Armand said, satisfied that he hadn't seen or heard anything. He started out but was immediately jerked back by the weight of the two women, neither of whom had moved with him.

"What's wrong?" he whispered.

He heard it before they could answer…the unmistakable sound of a creaking door hinge. It had come from somewhere very close.

"Get down," Armand urged. They hurriedly crouched along the base of the wall, Charlie huddling over Hildy like a protective mother. Armand hovered over both of them, knife at the ready.

Hildy suddenly groaned loudly and dropped to the floor, dragging Charlie with her. Charlie balanced unsteadily with one hand along the wall, trying to prevent herself from falling on top of Hildy. She slid slowly along the wall for a moment then suddenly fell forward as she lost her battle with gravity.

Charlie flung her foot out in a last desperate attempt to regain her balance but succeeded only in knocking the flashlight out of Armand's hand. It rolled toward the doorway across the hall, shining its beam directly on the three of them as it came to a stop.

A door across the hallway suddenly flung open and a large shape charged out at them, arms flailing wildly about. Hildy screamed just as the figure smacked into Armand, who collapsed onto both women.

At the bottom of the pile, Hildy struggled to breath. The blow had knocked the wind out of her and the weight atop her made it impossible to breathe. Her contorted position sent waves of pain throughout her abdomen. Every fiber of her being urged her to protect her unborn child but she could already feel her strength ebbing. She pushed with all her might against the floor to keep from being crushed as Charlie screamed above her. Finally, the last of the energy seeped away and the cold floor rushed up to meet her.

Hildy sank into the blackness silently pleading for forgiveness from her unborn child for the life it would never see.

NINETEEN

The end of the catwalk immediately over the crane's cab was lit by an emergency light. Matteus could see emergency lighting at the far end as well but the majority of the catwalk's length was not very well lit. The walkway presented a dark silhouette that stretched out in front and away from him, lit mainly from below by the emergency lighting at the ground floor. "*Well, if this isn't piss poor planning,*" he thought, as he shuffled forward a few steps.

"Guess the ShurShine Emergency Lighting Company didn't give a shit that some guy might be stranded in the crane," the guy behind him mumbled quietly, as if reading his mind.

Matteus grunted, "Remind me to file a complaint with them when we get out of here. Their product sucks." A second later, he felt a tap on his shoulder and turned to see the shiny silver casing of a flashlight being offered from behind.

"Thanks," he mumbled quietly. He wished he could remember the guy's name but he'd only met him once since he'd gotten here. He took the light and flicked it on, shining it down the length of the catwalk. The beam illuminated only a fraction of the catwalk's length but it was better than making the trip in complete darkness. He looked again at the far end of the walkway but could see nothing moving. "*Where the hell are the others*?" he thought.

"Guess we'll never get there if we don't get going," Matteus mumbled to himself. He took a deep breath and started out. He walked silently, alert for any unusual noises. Behind him, he could hear only the shuffling of feet and an occasional grunt from the guys that were carrying the heavy tanks.

When they'd gotten about a third of the way across, Matteus stopped and turned the flashlight behind him where the others were strung out, Kelly at the very rear of the line. He could almost feel the apprehension that was reflected in their faces.

The man behind him set the heavy cylinder down and rubbed his shoulder. Phillip crept silently up to him. "Stanley," he whispered, tapping him first on the shoulder and then tapping the top of the cylinder. Stanley nodded and tilted the tank forward, allowing Phillip to grab it by the bottom while he grasped it from the top. The fourth and fifth man took the cue and did the same with the other.

Matteus flashed the light on Kelly at the rear of the group, who was shining his own light along the catwalk behind them. Kelly turned around and waved him on.

Matteus turned around and resumed his slow shuffle along the catwalk, relieved for some inexplicable reason that he now knew the name of the guy behind him. It was somehow comforting. He was careful to avoid the icy patches that were scattered along the metal grating, formed by the moisture that dripped in some spots from the ceiling. The walkway was clearly seldom used but he found himself growing annoyed that it hadn't been kept free of ice. That was just plain careless.

Through the metal grating beneath him, he could clearly make out the silhouette of the spacecraft ten stories below, its periphery lit by more effective lighting below. "*Looks like they put the cheap lights up here*," he thought to himself.

Matteus jumped as a loud clanking resounded behind him. He whirled around and leapt out of the way just in time as something small and shiny clattered along the catwalk past him. It slid to the edge of the catwalk then dropped off, falling into the darkness below.

Matteus tried to follow it with his light but the object was too small for him to get a bead on it. It impacted with a loud smack against the top of the spacecraft, then shattered into several pieces that skittered and scraped along the vessel's metal skin. A second or two later, the pieces rained noisily onto the warehouse floor, echoing loudly.

Matteus' heart was in his throat and he could feel the blood surging through his veins. He shined the light on the men behind him, who stared back at him wide-eyed.

"What the hell was that?!" Kelly hissed from the rear.

“My cell,” Stanley answered. “Came…came out of my pocket,” he stuttered, clearly shaken.

No-one spoke. They waited just long enough for the adrenaline rush to subside.

“Anyone got a spare set of drawers?” someone asked quietly from further down the line.

A few of the men chuckled quietly and the tension ebbed.

“Keep moving,” Kelly urged from the rear.

Matteus turned and started again toward the far end of the catwalk, a slight smile still on his face from the crewman’s wisecrack. They were approaching the halfway point now. The smile faded quickly as he realized that their destination still seemed so far away. The catwalk seemed to have grown more narrow and confining, too, since the falling cell phone had so loudly announced their presence. There was no way that the creature could have missed hearing it.

As he shuffled along slowly down the walkway the unease grew like a mushroom within his gut as he realized the precariousness of their position, his own in particular. He was acutely aware of the fact that he was one of only three on the walkway that was holding a flashlight. It could act like a beacon, guiding the creature directly to him. He fought the urge to turn it off.

Matteus also fought the urge to quicken the pace. He didn’t want to risk having any of the guys hitting a patch of ice. The catwalk had no toe-board so it would be easy for someone to slip beneath the railing and fall to his death. The only thing to stop a fall would be the top of the spacecraft or the warehouse floor.

They trudged along as silently as they could, Matteus occasionally turning the light behind him to check on the others, concerned for their safety. Although he wouldn’t admit it, he also found it tremendously comforting to see them back there.

A couple of minutes later they had gotten close enough to the end of the walkway for Matteus to clearly see the open area immediately in front of the machinery building. He paused for a moment and studied the landing. There should be at least four men waiting there, the four cowards that fled when the creature had attacked Drew's team. But there was definitely no-one on the far landing.

From the other end of the catwalk, and even during most of the journey to this end, the fact that he couldn't see anyone waiting for them at this end hadn't seemed quite so odd. There were plenty of places where they could've been waiting just out of sight. But now that the others clearly weren't here, it was highly disturbing.

His flashlight began to dim just as he reached the end of the catwalk. He turned it off and stuck it into a cargo pocket, thankful that an emergency light had been installed above the doorway to the machine room. The catwalk terminated at a small platform that spanned the length of the machinery building. At least they would have more room now as they worked to cut through the doors.

"Where the hell are they?" Phillip asked quietly as he set down his end of the tank.

Kelly was pushing his way through as the group began to crowd the small platform.

"Where the hell are they?" he echoed, looking around.

"I'm gonna get to work on those doors," Phillip murmured. "I want out of here ASAP."

Kelly smacked Stanley on the shoulder and pointed to the small building, "Cover me."

Stanley looked at him quizzically but did as he was told. As they walked out to the extreme far end of the platform, he suddenly understood. The machinery room door was ajar.

Stanley took up a position immediately in front of the doors. Kelly positioned himself slightly to the side, looked over at Stanley, and nodded. Stanley shouldered his weapon and peered down the sights as he moved slowly forward.

The rest of the men backed away anxiously as Kelly reached for the door handle. He flung the door open, shining his light inside.

Stanley kept his weapon trained on the area illuminated by Kelly's light, ready to fire. But there was nobody there.

Kelly shined the light more slowly around the small room but there was just no sign of the others. He stepped inside, intent on illuminating the far side of the large generator that occupied the center of the room. Kelly moved in one direction while Stanley moved to the opposite side. The space inside the room was cramped, every square inch seemingly crammed with machinery. He'd have a better shot without Kelly in his way, if someone or something was hiding there.

Stanley stopped before he'd gotten very far into the room. "Why is the floor sticky?"

Kelly shined the light at Stanley's feet. A thick, milky white substance covered the floor. Several thick strands stretched from the sole of Stanley's boot to the floor like a wad of gum that had been lying on warm asphalt.

Kelly felt a chill go down his spine. "Get away from it," he whispered urgently.

Stanley backed toward the door. "What is it?"

"I don't know."

Stanley scraped his boot along the ground, trying to remove the goo. After a quick check behind the machinery, they backed out of the small building and returned to the group, firmly closing the door behind them.

Phillip had finished assembling the torch and was giving the damaged nozzle one last look. He opened the flow to the acetylene and oxygen tanks. "Here goes," he said, flicking his head to lower the glare shield.

He sparked the flame and the torch glared a brilliant blue flame.

The men gave a collective sigh then caught their breath as the torch sputtered, threatening to go out. But with a few rapid adjustments, Phillip got it operating smoothly and immediately began to cut.

Two men instinctively took up a position at the far end of the platform to keep watch as the rest assembled along the catwalk again. They turned their backs as Phillip began to cut to avoid the glare.

"Where could they have gone?" one of the men asked aloud.

"I don't know. But, I'll tell you what…I ain't never coming back down here," another replied quietly.

Kelly walked over to where Matteus was looking down over the railing.

"See anything?" Kelly asked, as he scanned the floor below.

"No," Matteus replied. "What the hell happened to them? It's like they just vanished."

"You know that white shit we saw sprayed all over the busted elevator? It's all over the place in there," he said, jerking his head toward the shed.

"Oh, man," Matteus uttered, shaking his head. "Why don't…"

A commotion on the catwalk suddenly demanded their attention.

Several of the men were gesturing animatedly as they retreated onto the platform.

"What is it?" Kelly asked one of them.

"There's something coming this way," the crewman replied nervously.

Kelly saw immediately that the guy was right. Although the walkway itself was not illuminated, he could clearly see a large, dark shadow silhouetted by the lighting in the distance behind it. It was easily two or three times as wide as a man and was moving with a slow, awkward gait.

"Shit! Spread out!"

The men fanned out along the edge of the platform, each aiming his weapon down the length of the catwalk.

Kelly whispered, "Soon as it gets close enough, I'm gonna hit it with my light. Hold your fire until I give the word."

One of the men that had positioned himself at the far end of the platform came running over. "What's going on?"

"Get back there and stay alert. Something's heading our way."

The man's eyes widened in alarm and he quickly made his way back to the far edge.

Phillip had stopped cutting and was looking at them curiously.

"Just keep cutting!"

Phillip flicked the face shield back down and resumed his work.

Kelly stationed himself at the mouth of the catwalk, in the center of the group.

He checked the safety of his rifle, ensuring it was ready to fire.

"Screw this!" One of the men lost his nerve and dashed toward the far end of the platform.

The move seemed to unnerve some of the others. They looked to Kelly, suddenly unsure of themselves.

"He'll be no safer there," Kelly said. "We don't stand a chance unless we hit this thing together."

One man cocked the handle of his shotgun and got down on one knee. Others followed suit, preparing their own weapons.

Matteus crept up beside Kelly, "These things didn't seem to do any good before," he whispered, displaying his own rifle.

Kelly had already thought of that, recalling the failure of Warren's pistol to stop the creature. He tapped his shotgun, "This thing's got alot more punch to it than a nine-mil," he said confidently.

"And if that's still not enough?"

"Then we'll just have to overwhelm it with numbers," Kelly replied.

≈ o ≈

A crewman approached Anders and yelled something. Although he was only a couple of feet away, Anders could not hear him over the howling of the wind.

The man moved closer still until the openings of their parka hoods were physically touching. "I can't get the torch lit!" he shouted again, slowly and deliberately.

Anders shouted several obscenities then walked over to the steel doors. He scowled at the gray metal protrusions sticking out of the ice. The bottom third of the door was covered with packed ice and snow, the product of years of relentless pounding by the incessant arctic winds. He ran his hand along them, feeling the strength of the steel through his glove. They were meant to be opened only from inside and had no exterior features. He gestured to the others to get back to the Trac.

With the door closed behind him, he took off his hood and gloves to feel the heat inside the cab of the vehicle. It still surprised him sometimes how quickly cold this intense could work its way through the human body regardless of how much clothing one wore.

"What's going on," Brian asked.

"Igor can't get the torch going. I'm not sure if it's the wind or because the damned thing is just not working."

"Well we gotta do *something*! If we don't get those doors open then they're screwed!"

"No shit, Brian!" Anders yelled back. "But unless you've got a spare torch on you, and one that will light, we're not cutting our way through."

"Hey, what about these chains back here?" asked a man from the back of the vehicle.

"You think we could *rip* them off?"

The man hefted the end of the heavy-duty chain for the rest of the group to see.

Anders scrutinized it. The chain *was* pretty thick. Still, the doors were sturdily built and had been spot welded together from inside when they'd sealed the entrance years ago. He couldn't see it, of course, but he knew that a steel bar had been placed horizontally across the doors, wedged tightly against the inside jamb for added strength and security. This made it highly unlikely that they be able to rip the doors away.

Anders considered sending one of the Tracs back to the hangar for another torch but decided it would simply take too long. The Crawlers were too slow. As it was, they'd been forced to take a circuitous route due to the rough terrain and were already about as far away from the forward end of the compound as they could get.

Anders eyed the chains again. He had his doubts that they would be strong enough but they didn't have much choice.

Anders picked up the field radio, "Geoff, you there?"

"Yeah," the voice crackled through the speaker.

"You got any chain in the back?"

"Yeah. Why?" Geoff replied after a short pause.

"Change of plans. I'm coming over"

"I'll be here," Geoff replied sarcastically.

Anders set the radio into its stand between the seats. "Grab all the chain we've got back there. We're going to try to yank these things open."

"What are we going to attach the chain to? There isn't even a door handle for us to get a grip on."

"I'm working on it," Anders replied, exiting the vehicle.

TWENTY

An unfamiliar warbled hooting echoed through the warehouse. Kelly shifted his position, trying to determine where it had come from. But the sound echoed throughout the cavernous spaces making it impossible to tell. Still…it seemed to have come from somewhere other than the catwalk.

"Easy," Kelly hissed. "Let it get just a little closer."

The shadow continued its awkward hobble toward them. Its size blotted out the light in the distance behind it and its outline blended in with the darkness, making it more difficult to see the closer it got. …and it was very close now.

A loud clanging echoed behind them. Kelly didn't have to look to know that Phillip had succeeded in cutting through the door. The heavy steel cut-out had fallen inward, slamming onto the metal flooring on the other side.

The creature paused momentarily along the catwalk then resumed its march forward, its pace seemingly quicker than before.

Kelly drew a breath and raised his light, flicking it on with his thumb. Immediately, a single shot rang out from behind him. Fortunately, the rest of the team exercised a surprising restraint as the creature's true identity was revealed.

Hildy was stooped on the walkway flanked by Stephan and Charlie, who were doing their best to support her as they walked. The narrowness of the catwalk forced Stephan and Charlie to twist their bodies sideways to enable the three of them to fit side-by-side. It was clearly awkward and uncomfortable and had greatly slowed their progress.

Stephan's face was contorted in pain from the lone bullet, which had struck him in the chest. He crumpled to the cold metal surface revealing Armand and Pamela behind them.

Thrown off balance by the loss of Stephan's support, Charlie and Hildy fell against the railing in the opposite direction. Charlie managed to grab hold of the railing and was fighting frantically to secure her footing as she and Hildy fell forward.

Armand grabbed Charlie by the back of her heavy sweatshirt just as one of her legs slipped over the edge. She teetered on the brink of falling as Armand struggled to pull her back onto the walkway. At the same time, Pamela seized Hildy by both feet and the two of them tumbled forward onto the center of the walkway.

Kelly dropped his weapon and ran to help but collided with Matteus and fell to the floor. As they scrambled back to their feet, Stephan's shoulders slipped slowly over the edge of the walkway opposite Charlie.

Kelly lunged and grabbed Stephan's leg just as the rest of his body spilled over the edge. He stretched out awkwardly on his side, his arms arched over his head as Stephan dangled beneath him. He fought to pull him back up but his own body was twisted clumsily and he could get no leverage.

"I can't hold him," Kelly cried out.

Matteus grabbed Kelly by both legs to steady him but could do nothing else to help. The narrowness of the walkway and the number of bodies already occupying it left him no room to maneuver.

Kelly strained to support Stephan's weight. His body twisted from the effort, jamming his back into the vertical railing support. He gasped in pain but fought with all his strength to hold on. His body suddenly surged several inches, scraping his back along the handrail support bar.

Matteus gripped Kelly's legs tightly but there was nothing more that he could do to help. His mind raced, frantically searching for something else that he could do to keep Kelly from being dragged over the edge. He pulled himself forward, climbing Kelly's legs until he had reached his midriff. He quickly wrapped one arm around Kelly's waist and seized the railing support with his other hand.

Kelly grunted then suddenly relaxed, twisting his body forward to relieve the strain on his back. Matteus knew instinctively that Kelly had released his grip. Pamela's scream, followed seconds later by the loud smack of Stephan's body hitting the spacecraft below, quickly confirmed it.

"I…I couldn't…," Kelly gasped through clenched teeth as he arched his head back in pain.

"Kel, there was nothing more you could do."

Kelly looked up at Armand, who was kneeling next to him.

"Can you stand?"

Kelly grunted continually as he slowly got to his feet with the aid of Matteus and Armand.

"Didn't realize you were still down here, Doc," Kelly groaned between gasps.

"We had just finished checking on our patients when the power went out because of the earthquake…or whatever it was."

"An earthquake," Kelly moaned, arching forward to stretch his bruised back. "That would've been far more pleasant," he said as they made their way back to the platform.

≈ O ≈

"So, what's wrong with her, Doc?" Matteus asked, gesturing discretely toward Hildy with his chin.

Hildy was sitting on a small wooden bench that they'd retrieved from inside the machine room. She huddled forward, cradling her stomach in her hands.

"Probably gestational hypertension," Armand replied, absentmindedly. "But I won't know for sure until we get her topside, which we'd better do pretty damn soon."

"What the heck is…"

"You mean she's pregnant?!" Kelly interrupted.

Armand paused for the briefest of moments then resumed his examination of Kelly's back. A moment later he was done.

"I don't see any serious damage," he said, ignoring Kelly's question, "But you are going to be quite sore for a week or so anyway."

"Doc?" Kelly turned to face Armand now that the doctor had completed examining him.

Armand sighed, "Look, keep it quiet, OK? It's still a fairly new development and she didn't want anyone to know just yet. I don't think she's had time to come to terms with it herself."

"Sure, Doc," Kelly answered. "She going to be ok?" he asked.

"It's pretty common, "Armand replied, "but if I don't start treatment pretty soon, *if* that's what it is, it can turn serious very quickly."

"Like life-threatening?" Matteus asked quietly.

"Possibly." Armand shifted uncomfortably. He had already said too much and wished they'd just drop it.

Kelly grunted and lurched backward, slamming his head lightly against a support beam.

"Shit, that's all I need right now," he said sarcastically, "Back spasms."

Armand put his hand on Kelly's shoulder, "I can give you some powerful muscle relaxers once we get topside but I'm afraid I don't have anything to offer you at the moment."

"They back yet?" Kelly asked, gesturing toward the gaping hole in the door.

"Not yet," Matteus replied, turning to face the door. "I'd better go check on what's taking them so long."

He'd gone only a couple of steps when Stanley poked his head through the hole in the door. He quickly pulled himself through the rough opening, snagging and tearing the back of his jacket on the jagged edge.

He cursed loudly as his feet hit the platform. "Dammit! This is a brand-new jacket," he bemoaned.

Phillip emerged right behind him, more mindful of the sharp rim.

"The stairway's clear all the way to the top," he reported, as soon as he'd cleared the opening. "It's dark as hell but it's clear. But," he hesitated for a moment.

"Yeah?"

Phillip shrugged, "They still haven't cut the opening in the topside door."

Several of the crew cursed silently and mumbled to themselves.

"I know they're up there, though. I could hear them banging on the other side. I tried to yell to them but the door is just too thick. I couldn't make out anything they were saying and I seriously doubt they could even hear me at all with the wind howling. Still, they did respond to my banging so they at least know we made it this far."

"How much fuel have you got left in these tanks?" Kelly asked him.

Phillip eyed the tanks, "Not much. Why? You want me to start cutting from inside?"

A harsh shriek from somewhere down below suddenly filled the warehouse. The crew jostled about, eyeing each other nervously.

"I'm gonna start cutting from inside," Phillip affirmed, hastily disconnecting the hoses from the tanks.

"Good idea," Kelly affirmed. "You two give him a hand," he said, pointing to two nearby crewmen. Both nodded rapidly and raced over to help.

The creature shrieked again, a shrill, high-pitched tone that pierced their ears. It proved to be too much for one of the crew, who sprang toward the opening and the door and dove through it. Others followed him, jockeying for the next spot nearest the door.

"Stop!" Kelly hobbled toward the door. They paid no attention to him as they jostled one another to be next.

"There's no exit up there," Kelly yelled. "If that thing makes its way up here, there will be nowhere else for you to go."

The man nearest the door faltered, obviously torn between his desire to get out and the logic of Kelly's argument.

"We send these guys up," he said, pointing to the team dismantling the torch, "then, once they've made us an exit, the rest of us follow. Until then, we're better off here."

Phillip bounded past followed by the others carrying the torch equipment. "Don't worry, boys! I'll have us through that damn door in no time," he said confidently.

"Lickety-split, man," Kelly whispered to him as he passed. "I think we're running out of time here."

Phillip gave Kelly a wink then eased though the hole.

≈ O ≈

Brian cursed loudly and stared at the dent he'd made in the door. It wasn't nearly deep enough.

Anders moved him aside to scrutinize his progress while another man reloaded the bolt gun. "Hit it again," he instructed as the other crewman handed the gun back.

"I still don't see why we aren't using *these* to blast a hole through the door," Parker yelled, tapping on the stock of his rifle.

"Ricochets," he yelled back. "Rifle ammo isn't strong enough to penetrate the steel. We fire that at the door and we'd end up dodging our own bullets."

Parker scrutinizing the door then shrugged and walked away.

Brian placed the barrel into the divot created by his first attempt and pulled the trigger. The bolt gun recoiled violently in his hands, stinging them despite his gloves. The spike fell again at his feet, its shaft bent and its nose blunted by the impact with the steel door. He removed his glove and ran his fingers into the divot. It was definitely deeper than before and there appeared to be some slight cracking in the metal at the center of the small crater left by the previous impact.

He hurriedly held the gun over his shoulder for a reload. “It just might work,” he yelled over his shoulder.

Anders smacked him on the back enthusiastically. Still, the outcome was far from certain. The bolt gun itself was certainly powerful enough. Phillip had devised it a couple of years ago as a way to easily drive a steel spike into the ice. It had come in handy on numerous occasions when they’d needed to install cabling or secure equipment to the walls within the warehouse, where the ice was used as a natural partition to contain the facility.

The problem was the spikes. They simply weren’t made to penetrate steel. The first two had buckled and bent while making only a marginal dent in the door. They needed to ram a hole through the first layer of steel if they were going to have any chance of yanking the doors open. Anders still has his doubts about that part of the plan as well. Even if they succeeded in doing that, he wasn’t so sure the chains would be strong enough for the next step – ripping the door from its frame.

Anders glanced back at the cargo box, squinting to see through the wind-blown snow. They only had four charges left. If they couldn’t get one of the next four spikes through the door, then the ability of the chains to stand up to the strain would be a moot point.

≈ O ≈

TWENTY-ONE

The shrill shrieking reverberated through the warehouse every few minutes but they still couldn't tell where it was coming from. Kelly had spread the group out along the periphery of the platform as sentries while he roved among them offering encouragement. Others had joined them since they'd first arrived at the far end of the warehouse and it was beginning to get crowded on the small platform.

"How you guys hanging?" he asked, approaching two men at the far end of the platform.

"Wish they'd hurry the hell up," Stanley replied, motioning with his eyes toward the door.

"What? You don't like it here no more?" Trond chided lightly.

Kelly raised his brow, surprised and impressed that the guy could maintain his sense of humor under these circumstances. In fact, everything about the guy had impressed Kelly during the last hour or so. He'd volunteered without hesitation to go down to Midpoint landing after Drew's group had been attacked and had carried the heavy equipment up to Deck 3 without complaint. He had kept his cool throughout their ordeal and frequently encouraged the less valiant men. Even now, as he joked, his eyes continued to scour the area.

Kelly looked at his watch and frowned. Phillip's team had been gone for less than 10 minutes but it already seemed like hours. With the time it would have taken for them to climb six flights of stairs and reassemble the torch, they were probably just now beginning to cut.

"They want out of here just as bad as we do," Kelly said. "I'm sure they're going as fast as they can."

"Hey, you guys game?" Trond whispered conspiratorially. The mischief in his voice was unmistakable, even through his thick Norwegian accent.

Trond backed slowly into the shadows where the light didn't quite illuminate the landing, gesturing with his head for them to follow. When they were out of sight of the others, he opened his jacket to reveal a shiny metal flask.

Kelly threw his head back and smirked.

"Got to stay warm somehow," Trond said, his eyes gleaming with mischief.

Kelly extended a hand and grabbed the flask from Trond's pocket. Trond beamed with approval as Kelly took a swig. He did the same then offered it to Stanley, who declined.

Another odd sound pierced the air. It pulsated rhythmically for several seconds then slowly faded. It was nothing like the creature's shrill shrieking yet was just as alien.

"You guys stay sharp now," Kelly admonished. "If you see it, don't shoot at it unless you have to. The last thing we want is to provoke it."

They nodded as Trond slid the flask back into his pocket.

Kelly turned and walked away, headed for the other end of the platform.

"Where is the damn thing?" Stanley asked quietly.

Trond muttered under his breath in Norwegian. Stanley knew just enough of the language to recognize most of it as profanity.

Although the lighting was better on the warehouse floor, there was enough equipment down there to cast long, dark shadows everywhere. Directly below them, a couple of aerial man-lifts were parked side by side, their booms extended upward and away from them. The area of the floor immediately surrounding the two machines seemed especially dark and menacing.

They scoured the area below them, looking for any movement.

They should've been looking up.

≈ O ≈

“How you doing, honey?” Charlie asked as she knelt beside Hildy, who was sitting on the bench with her back against the steel door. She looked pale and was shaking from the cold.

“I could use some water,” Hildy replied, her voice dry and cracking.

“I’ll be right back.”

Charlie returned a minute later with a water bottle that she’d confiscated from one of the men. The guy had been kind enough to offer her his jacket as well. “Here you go, kiddo.”

Hildy took a long, slow drink. “Thanks,” she said, wiping her mouth with her sleeve. “Want some?”

“No. I’m good.” Charlie wrapped the jacket around Hildy’s shoulders.

Hildy looked across the platform, “Thank you,” she mouthed to the crewman.

He winked at her then focused again on the warehouse floor.

“How’s Pamela?”

Charlie sighed, “She’s a wreck. Seems to think that what happened to Stephan is her fault. I’ve been trying to calm her down but…” Charlie shrugged and shook her head.

Hildy looked across the platform. Armand was treating Pamela for a gash in her shoulder as she leaned against the front of the building below the light.

“She’s lucky to still be alive. Armand could’ve easily killed her.” Charlie said seriously. She suddenly chuckled, “She sure scared the hell out of me!”

“Right?!” Hildy agreed. They laughed together quietly.

“Why did she *do* that?” Hildy asked.

"I guess she was just so relieved to see us," Charlie replied, suppressing another laugh.

They grew serious again as one of the crew approached them.

"Hey Spence," Charlie greeted him.

"Hey," he replied, holding out another jacket, "Courtesy of Mr. Jenks over there."

Charlie draped the jacket over Hildy's legs.

"May I?" he asked, pointing to the water bottle.

Charlie handed it to him and he took a drink.

"What happened to her?" he asked, motioning with the water bottle to where Armand was treating Pamela.

"Oh, uh…she hurt herself when she was climbing up through the crane." Charlie answered.

"What the hell would do that to her *in there*?"

Charlie shrugged and took a drink from the water bottle.

"I see," he said skeptically. "Well, you let me know if you need anything, ok?" He patted Hildy on the leg and walked away.

"I don't think he believed you," Hildy said when he'd gotten far enough away.

"Well, what was I supposed to say?" Charlie asked defensively.

"It's not Armand's fault…"

"I know," Charlie interrupted. "It's not that. It's…"

Hildy nodded. She knew exactly what it was.

Pamela and Stephan had been in his quarters when the power went out. They'd seen the creature when they had peeked out into the hallway to investigate after the power had failed and promptly locked themselves in his suite. Later, when they'd heard Armand's voice in the hallway, Stephan had opened the door a crack.

In her excitement and relief to see them, Pamela had rushed out the door. Armand hadn't recognized her at first in the dim lighting and had prepared himself to defend the girls from what he'd thought was the creature. By the time he understood the true nature of the threat, Pamela was already on top of him.

Fortunately, Pamela had thrown him off balance so his aim was off. She didn't receive the full force of the blow as he brought the knife down. They'd all ended up in a tangled pile on the floor. Luckily, other than the gash in Pam's shoulder, no-one had been seriously hurt.

But it wasn't the fact that Armand had stabbed Pamela that made them uncomfortable. That was merely the result of an unfortunate set of circumstances. The tricky part was the affair. Stephan, Pamela, and Cliff, her husband, were all well liked. Any nastiness between them could end up being more divisive than a typical marital row.

Charlie watched as Spencer made his way over to where Armand was treating Pamela.

"Uh, oh."

Charlie placed her hand gently on Hildy's leg and sighed as she watched Spencer chatting with Armand. "It's OK, Hil. They were going to find out about the two of them eventually anyway."

Charlie felt Hildy stiffen suddenly.

"Oh, my God! Oh, my God!"

Charlie turned quickly. Hildy's face was pale and her eyes were wide and fixed on something at the far end of the platform.

Charlie turned to look.

She saw nothing unusual at first. Two men were standing against the railing, looking down into the warehouse. A third man was behind them and appeared to be dangling from a rafter, his feet swaying gently just above the platform. The man was mostly in the shadows just beyond the illumination of the emergency lamp at the front of the shed.

As she watched, his boots slowly descended to meet the platform. Only then did the strangeness of it all hit her.

Although he now stood on the platform, the man's arms continued to stretch up into the darkness of the rafters. Charlie looked up and gasped. The closest rafter was easily more than ten feet above them. She could clearly see his hands against the bright white background of the metal framing, still grasping the rafter high above him. His arms stretched from the rafter to his torso like soft, sinewy taffy.

The man released his grip on the rafter with one hand. The free arm shortened in a smooth, fluid motion as it retracted, rolling and curling like a cobra intent on mesmerizing its prey just before striking.

Charlie jumped to her feet and shouted to the men at the far edge of the platform. They looked in her direction but didn't see the man lurking in the darkness. She shouted again and pointed.

In a flash, the snake-like arm surged forward, wrapped itself around Trond's neck, and lifted him off the ground. It stretched and pulsated like the bulging, sweaty arm of a weight-lifter as it spun Trond around to coil itself around his torso. Trond pulled and beat at the appendage trying to release its grip.

Stanley dropped his weapon and dove under the outstretched arm to keep from being crushed against the railing as several men came running from the other side of the platform. They stared in shock and disbelief as the man emerged from the shadows, both arms still grotesquely out of proportion to the rest of his body. He turned his head slowly revealing Codi's face, which stared at them impassively.

Several large blisters formed suddenly along the length of the Codi's arm as Trond struggled to free himself. Almost immediately, the blisters burst, releasing a thick black fluid…except it didn't *behave* like a fluid. Instead of running down the arm and dripping to the floor like blood oozing from a laceration, the substance concentrated in globules that pulsed and writhed with intricate movement, like thousands of tiny spider hatchlings swarming over the remnants of the egg sack from which they had just emerged.

All at once, the globules shattered into thousands of tiny tic-like creatures that scattered rapidly in every direction. Most made their way upward along the length of the arm toward Trond while others fell to the cold steel floor. Those that reached him spread out over his face and surged into his nostrils and ears. His terrified screams were quickly cut off as the tiny creatures poured into his mouth and forced their way down his throat.

The crew finally overcame their shock, shooting a torrent of bullets at the Codi-creature, which shrieked wildly as the hot lead tore through its body. Blood and flesh spattered the side of the shed and covered the floor of the platform. The creature threw its head back and wailed. After several intense seconds, the crew ceased firing.

The Codi-creature stumbled, then dropped to its knees. It knelt on the platform emitting a low growl as both arms swayed in the air above it. The numerous cavities left behind by the blackened blisters were already filling in with new flesh.

Trond continued to dangle from the one appendage, which sprouted fresh blisters. The tiny creatures that spewed from them clung together as they poured to the floor in four distinct pillars. As soon as the lower part of each teeming column touched the steel decking, the creatures comprising it melded together and solidified into a misshapen, leg-like protrusion.

New eyes – black as coal – formed on the lower part of the arm that held Trond aloft. They blinked slowly as they coldly studied the numerous antagonists arranged in a line, rifles at the ready. Codi's eyes also remained locked on his former teammates. Unlike the cold and impassive eyes of the alien creature, these still looked human and seemed to be pleading, as if Codi still existed somewhere within the creature and was begging to be saved.

The tiny creatures continued to force their way into Trond's body. They pierced him everywhere, brutally penetrating the exposed flesh of his face, neck, and hands once his facial orifices became clogged.

The creature let out a shrill screech, a mixture of high and low harmonic tones that penetrated the flesh of the human crew. Their bones resonated to the perfectly tuned frequency resulting in intense pain everywhere. The crew writhed on the cold steel flooring, helpless against the pain as their innards vibrated energetically. Finally, one of the men struggled to his feet and began firing again in a desperate attempt to silence the thing.

The creature shrieked again as a fresh round of bullets tore into it but, mercifully, the bone shattering wail ceased. Freed from the torture, the rest of the crew quickly resumed firing, filling the creature with more hot lead.

Fresh blisters sprouted beneath the creature's arm as Trond's body began to spasm and thrash about. In seconds, four fresh limbs stretched to the floor and the arm detached itself from the main body of the creature at the shoulder with a sickening crack, like a tree branch that had grown too heavy to support its own weight. Several eyes budded randomly along its length as it wobbled unsteadily on its new legs.

A thick tentacle abruptly sprang from the back of Codi's neck. It spiralled around Codi's head like ivy climbing the trunk of a tree and shot upward toward the ceiling. As the crew continued to fire, the Codi-creature pulled itself quickly up into the rafters, seemingly oblivious to the shells still tearing through its body, and disappeared into the darkness above them.

There was a pause in the shooting as the crew scrambled to reload, not taking their eyes off the partial beast that remained on the platform. The hideous appendage resembled a leopard on overgrown, spindly legs and with its skin turned grotesquely inside out. It took several short steps toward the darkness on the far side of the shed, sauntering across the platform with an ungainly, unsteady gait as it sought to escape with its prey.

Trond's skin had turned black where the tiny creatures had penetrated him and had begun to assimilate his cells. He stared blankly up at the ceiling, his eyes tearing and filled with pain. In several places, his flesh melded indistinguishably with that of the thing, flowing together like warm wax from two adjacent candles.

The creature wrapped a freshly grown tentacle around the handrail then sprang over it. It hung there for just a second, its black eyes regarding the crew on the far side of the platform, then lowered itself and its captive out of sight.

≈ O ≈

Phillip flipped up his mask and glanced down nervously at the landing below. He could easily hear the sound of gunfire over the noise of the torch.

"Should we go check it out?"

"No," Phillip replied. "If they can't stop it with what they've got, I doubt we'll make any difference. We need to focus on getting through this damn door."

He eyed the gauge on the blowtorch warily. He didn't say anything but he was beginning to doubt that he'd have enough gas to cut a big enough hole for them to escape.

"How much longer you think you'll need?"

They jumped as a loud bang rang out from the metal door and reverberated through the stairwell. Jackson flashed his light onto the door. "What the hell are they doing out there?"

Phillip inched closer to the door and ran his hand along the smooth steel in one spot. He'd noticed a small bump in the metal there earlier but it seemed much more pronounced now. He hurriedly lit the blowtorch as he realized what it meant.

"I think they're trying to punch a hole through the door!"

"What?! Why aren't they cutting? They're supposed to be cutting!"

"How the hell am I supposed to know, Jackson?! But I'm going to see what I can do to help them from this end! You two get that bar out of the way," he said, pointing to the metal crossbeam as he concentrated the heat of the torch in the center of the dent.

≈ O ≈

Brian pried the spike from the door and peered into the small hole. The tip of the spike had definitely driven into the second layer of steel this time but it was difficult to tell just how far.

"How's it look?" Anders asked.

Brian shrugged, "We're hitting the second layer but…" He peered into the box, "I've only got two shots left. Even if I manage to punch through, the hole's not going to be nearly big enough for us to force a hook and chain through."

Anders looked into the box at the two spike charges. He'd been wracking his brain on this very problem since Brian had started and was nowhere closer to a solution.

Brian suddenly cocked his head sideways and sniffed the air. "You smell that?" he asked.

Before Anders could answer Brian leaned into the door and sniffed again. A small wisp of smoke wafted through the small hole and dissipated quickly in the wind.

He peered into the hole and saw that the spot surrounding the indentation caused by the last spike was glowing a bright hot red.

Brian looked up at Anders excitedly, "I think they're trying to burn through from the other side!"

Brian quickly grabbed a spike from the box.

"Wait," Anders shouted, putting his hand on Brian's arm. "Let them burn through! They can make a bigger hole than that thing can."

≈ O ≈

TWENTY-TWO

The air was thick with smoke that hung like a cloud over the cold platform. The ensuing silence was every bit as deafening as the gunfire had been just a moment ago. The crew stared at one another, each man searching for someone among them who could make sense of what they had just seen.

"Reload!" Kelly yelled as he began to slip ammunition into a blank clip. The crew stared blankly back at him. "I said reload," he yelled. "That thing may be back."

Most of the men removed the firing clips from their weapons and began frantically fumbling for extra ammo. One of them dropped several rounds on the platform, which rolled to the edge and dropped onto the warehouse floor.

"They're not going to do us any good down there," Kelly said firmly. The man nodded and resumed reloading, his pace a little more deliberate and careful.

One of the crewmen swore loudly. "What the hell are we reloading for? These things didn't do shit," he said, throwing his rifle to the floor.

"Because these things are all we have," Hector replied, as he chambered a fresh round. "Maybe they didn't kill it but they sure as hell made it think twice about wanting to be up here."

"Hey! Need some help over here!" A crewman was kneeling beside a man on the floor halfway across the platform.

Armand looked up from the bench near the door, where he was still tending to Hildy, who lay across the bench and appeared to be unconscious. Kelly looked at Matteus, "Go check it out. I've got to get these guys ready, in case that thing decides to make another go at us."

"Right." Matteus took off at a jog. Armand met him halfway.

"She alright?"

"For now," Armand replied. "But if we don't get her up there soon..."

"It's Stan," the crewman said as they reached the injured man. "I think he's been shot."

Stanley lay on his side shivering uncontrollably, his back toward them. A large pool of blood had collected beneath him from an unseen bullet wound.

"Damn! Help me turn him over," Armand instructed.

They slowly rotated Stanley onto his back. Blood poured from his thigh near his groin and his face was already deathly pale. Once on his back he began to tremble violently.

Matteus flung his body across Stanley's torso in an attempt to pin him down and stop the trembling. "It's his femoral artery. Jonas, rip his pants open and apply pressure to the wound," Armand shouted to the other crewman. "Press as hard as you can! We don't have much time." Jonas nodded and reached for the knife on his belt.

Stanley suddenly lurched violently upward, flinging Matteus across the floor. He arched his back, his stomach rising slowly until his body formed a perfect arc suspended by his head at one end and his feet on the other. His outstretched arms hung limply beneath, swaying from side to side. He turned his head sluggishly and looked at Armand, who was quickly backing away.

Stanley opened his mouth slowly and emitted a deep, breathy hiss. His jacket roiled with movement across his chest from some unseen activity beneath.

Armand and Jonas tripped over each other as they scrambled to get away and fell headlong onto the cold floor of the platform. They quickly sprang to their feet and bolted.

Matteus got to his feet and searched desperately for his rifle. He spotted it on the floor on the other side of the Stanley-creature.

Three small finger-like appendages sprouted instantly from the back of Stan's skull. A round, lidless eye quickly formed at the tip of each appendage, each budding like some ugly petal-less flower. They regarded Matteus impassively as Stanley's body continued to jerk and twist from unseen activity beneath his clothing.

Two larger appendages tore through his jacket at the top of his shoulders. In seconds, they grew into thick legs that lifted his head off the floor until the three bulging eyes were level with Matteus'. The creature simultaneously rotated its body on its four new legs, aiming itself toward him to block his retreat.

Matteus found himself trapped against the handrail at the opposite end of the platform. Stanley lurched upward again as all four legs doubled in height and girth. They came together beneath the creature until Stanley was folded completely in half. Fresh protrusions were budding and sprouting all over the creature, molting into eyes, tendrils, and arms, each terminating in three clumsy looking fingers.

Matteus sought desperately for an escape but there was none. The creature began walking toward him in a smooth, almost graceful way, despite being so ugly and gangly. It stopped after only a few steps and shrieked as its flesh suddenly erupted all over as the sound of gunfire filled the air.

He was directly in the line of fire, with only the Stanley-creature to shield him. The sharp ping of metal striking metal and the concurrent flash of sparks off a nearby steel beam underscored the precariousness of his position. Several ricochets had already hit too close for comfort.

The creature suddenly lurched toward Matteus as dozens of rounds continued to slice through its flesh, spilling blood and slivers of flesh along its path. It shrieked wildly and turned its head to glare behind at its antagonists as it charged toward Matteus.

Matteus searched frantically but could find no way to avoid the inevitable. With the creature less than two yards away, he turned, grabbed the top railing and hurled himself over. He twisted his body like a gymnast on a high bar to face the platform as he fell, managing to grab the middle bar of the railing as the creature sailed just inches over him.

The ghastly beast streaked through the air and collided with a steel support column almost 20 feet away. It paused and glared at its would-be prey clinging tenaciously to the handrail before it wrapped itself around the column like a giant boa and slithered down its length into the darkness below.

Matteus clung doggedly to the bar but his strength was already beginning to ebb. While his acrobatic maneuver had saved him from the clutches of the beast, it had not been without cost. Once he'd grabbed hold of the railing, the arc of his swing inevitably caused his chest to slam heavily into the platform's support beam cracking several of his ribs and knocking the wind out of him.

He grunted repeatedly as he fought to gain a better hold of the railing and struggled to breathe, his shattered ribs protesting painfully. The impact had loosened his grip on the bar and he felt it slowly slipping through his thick gloves.

Adrenaline surged through him as he realized that he was fighting a losing battle. He looked up just as his fingers separated from the bar and his stomach heaved as he began to fall. He closed his eyes and waited for death to claim him on the warehouse floor.

Kelly cringed as he watched Matteus' hands slip from the bar. He hadn't known the guy very long but had really grown to like him.

"What the hell is happening, man?!" one of the crew shouted after several seconds of stunned silence.

"What the hell happened to Stan?! ....and Codi?"

"It wasn't Codi...or Stanley. At least...not anymore." Armand leaned against the wall, still trying to catch his breath.

Hector threw his rifle onto the platform. "What the hell are you talking about, man?! We all saw him...I mean, them! I mean..." He trailed off, not knowing what else to say.

"It wasn't them," Armand said firmly.

"What the hell are you talking about," Spence demanded. "I was just talking to Stanley! We bullshitted for almost half an hour! I didn't notice *anything…*"

Armand eyed the rest of the crew warily. He had thought before that he'd understood the organism's capabilities…but the horrible things he'd just seen starkly highlighted the danger far more clearly than any amount of reading about it ever could.

He studied every man closely, searching for any clue that one of them wasn't who he appeared to be. But each man appeared to be perfectly normal. "*Stan had appeared perfectly normal too until just two minutes ago*." The thought seemed to leap out of nowhere and he felt his flesh erupt with goosebumps.

"Doc?"

Armand swallowed hard. All eyes were fixed on him, each gaze reflecting desperation and fear. They were on the verge of panic and needed some answers. But he knew they wouldn't like *his* answers. Hell, *he* didn't like them. But it was important that they all understand the nature of the threat.

"I need everybody to listen very carefully."

≈ O ≈

"Okay, everybody but Spence and Jonas into the stairwell."

"Wait a minute! You said before that that thing could trap us in there," Hector protested. "Why go in now?"

"Because *now* we're low on ammo. Standing out here, that thing can get at us from anywhere. We get everybody into the stairwell, then it can only attack us through this hole," Kelly said, tapping the rim of the cut-out.

"Everybody who has ammo left, hand it over to these guys," Kelly ordered, gesturing to the two he'd chosen.

"What?! I'm not giving up my ammo! If Doc's right, any one of us could be one of those things! You saw what it did to Stan…and Codi! What if we go into the stairwell with it?! What are we supposed to do then, huh?!" The man held his rifle close to his chest and glared menacingly at the rest of the crew.

"I ain't giving up my ammo either," another shouted, waving his rifle threateningly. "And I don't want none of you coming anywhere near me!"

In three strides, Kelly reached the man, parried the barrel of the rifle aside, and grabbed him by the throat. "This isn't open for discussion," he yelled. "You'll hand over your ammo or I'll break your damn neck!"

Kelly released his grip and took a step back, snatching the rifle out of the crewman's hands.

"The only way we *might* be able to fight this thing off again is if we consolidate what little firepower we have left. We get everyone behind this door so it can't pick us off one at a time."

Kelly quickly examined the rifle he'd just acquired then surveyed the crew. The group had collectively dispersed along the platform, remaining close enough to the door to allow a quick retreat if necessary but distant enough from each other to give a margin of safety from any other undetected replicants.

Kelly removed the clip from the weapon and checked the ammo. He slammed the clip back in, chambered a round, and tossed the rifle to a nearby crewman.

"Konrad here will take one rifle behind the door with the rest of you. At least one of the men up there with Phil is armed too, so that gives you two. The three of us will stay out here in case that thing returns."

"Why the hell does Konrad get the rifle?! What if he is one of those things?! I don't remember seeing him earlier. All of a sudden he shows up all by himself just when things go to shit?!"

"Yeah, Konrad! Where the hell were you?!" Hector demanded.

"Go screw yourself," Konrad yelled back. "I was in the damn john, man! So, it's *my fault* that this thing got loose when I'm taking a crap?!"

Other members of the crew began shouting, objecting to him having the weapon. Kelly grabbed the nearest objector by the front of his jacket and slammed him roughly into the wall, silencing the rowdy group.

"We don't have time for this shit," he screamed. "Next guy that opens his mouth is gonna find it full of my fist!"

"What about Doc?" Spence suggested calmly. "Seems to me that if he was one of those things he'd have kept quiet about it."

Kelly paused. The man had a point. He reached out and Konrad reluctantly surrendered the rifle.

"You're going to have to be ok with this, Doc," Kelly said to Armand quietly but firmly. "Spence is right. Right now, you're about the only one here that these guys can reasonably trust. Keep them all together and get them to the top of the stairwell. Give us a shout when Phil gets the door open."

"I…I'm not so sure..." he began.

Kelly inched closer, "Doc, *these people right here* are relying on you," he said firmly. "If you don't do this, it's going to be every man for himself…and that's the last thing we need right now."

Armand nodded, trying his best to display confidence. He knew Kelly was right. "So much for my Hippocratic Oath," he mumbled.

Kelly looked at him quizzically.

"First do no harm'. It's the first tenet of…never mind."

"No, I get it," Kelly replied. "But right now, maybe it would help if you thought of it as 'first *allow* no harm."

Armand nodded. Oddly, that did make him feel better about his unwanted task.

≈ O ≈

The platform was eerily quiet now that the majority of the group was on the other side of the steel door. Kelly leaned against the wall and surveyed the far end of the landing where three of his comrades had fallen victim to the beast. Spence and Konrad were to his right, forming a shallow defensive arc in front of the door. They'd be ready to hit the thing with everything they had if it was foolish enough to show itself again. Hopefully, it would be enough.

"Creepy as shit out here," Konrad muttered as he bit off of chunk of chewing tobacco.

"Sure is," Kelly whispered. He studied Konrad, crinkling his face in disgust as the man launched a wad of ruddy brown spit onto the floor. Kelly never really had liked the guy and this disgusting habit was one of the reasons why. He found him to be generally crude and obnoxious.

Kelly had really wanted Jonas out here with him. The man was reliable and fearless. But the widespread mistrust displayed earlier against Konrad had forced him to reconsider. The group was already on edge. Removing Konrad from among them might alleviate some stress. Besides, Kelly shared their misgivings about Konrad and preferred to keep him where he could keep an eye on him.

"Are you guys hearing that?" Spence asked.

Kelly felt his heart rate increase at the mere suggestion that something odd was happening. He strained but heard nothing but an occasional sharp but subtle cracking, as if someone nearby was noisily chewing gum.

Konrad sniffled and wiped his nose on his sleeve. "I think it's just the steel flooring re-freezing. It got pretty heated up here for a bit, you know…with all the firing and stuff."

He kicked a spent shell casing near hit foot to underscore his point, sending it clattering toward the equipment shed.

"That's not what I'm talking about," Spence replied. "Listen."

They stood silently, listening intently to the silence.

"I don't hear anything," Kelly whispered. As if in reply, a muted groan came from somewhere nearby.

"Right there!"

It had sounded human, like a man suffering from a hangover. Kelly couldn't be sure but it sounded like it had come from the far end of the platform.

The three men huddled close together directly in front of the doorway. "You want me to go check it out?" Spence asked.

Kelly *did* want that…but his instincts spoke against it. "No. We stay here, together."

"What's that?!" Konrad yelled.

"Sshhh! I see it," Kelly hissed back.

A dark, narrow form was slowly rising above the lip of the flooring at the far edge of the platform – a short, stubby rod with a small knob-like bulb at the top.

Spence quickly raised his rifle, using his scope to get a clearer picture. After several seconds, he abruptly lowered his weapon. "It's human," he said firmly.

As if in reply, the knob opened up into the unmistakable shape of five fingers. It firmly grasped the lower railing and a short, sharp groan once again filled the air. As they watched, a second hand rose from the darkness and latched onto the same railing. A man was pulling himself up onto the platform.

"Shit! It's Matt," Kelly said in surprise. He started toward the man then stopped abruptly.

"You two stay here. I'm going to help him."

"What if it's not really him?" Spence urged nervously, grasping Kelly by the arm.

Kelly hesitated. It was entirely possible that the alien beast had replicated Matteus. It seemed unlikely, given the short amount of time that had gone by since the guy had gone over the railing. But hell, a lot of things that seemed impossible just an hour ago were suddenly grim realities.

They really knew nothing about creature… and it *had* morphed astonishingly fast from one form into another during its attacks on Trond and Stanley. Still, he reasoned, it was one thing for the beast to assume its original ghastly form and quite another to mimic the form of something different such as a man…at least that's what logic seemed to dictate.

"It's him," he said with more conviction than he actually felt. "But…. cover me."

Kelly ran over and grabbed Matteus' arms. "I got you," he said reassuringly.

Matteus pulled himself up with Kelly's help until he was standing on the platform. He panted heavily from the effort and his face was contorted with pain.

Kelly slipped his arm beneath Matteus' armpit and wrapped it around him. Seconds later both men were standing together on the platform.

"You alright?" Kelly asked.

Matteus nodded, "Thought I was dead for sure. Turns out that there's another catwalk right below us." He gasped for breath, "Must have been left over from the original construction of the place."

Kelly looked Matteus over but saw no obvious injuries.

"I think I broke some ribs," Matteus replied, noticing Kelly's scrutiny. "Having a hard time breathing and it hurts like a bastard."

"Let's get you back," Kelly responded, gingerly lifting Matteus' arm and wrapping it around his own neck.

After a couple halting steps, Matteus suddenly stopped.

"What's wrong?" Kelly asked.

Matteus signaled with his eyes, gesturing for Kelly to look down.

Kelly heard it before he actually saw it. The strange crackling noise that he'd heard earlier was more pronounced now and was occurring more frequently. The floor in front of them seemed to be alive with movement. Kelly squinted and focused on one spot.

The platform gleamed with the flesh and blood shed by the creature earlier as dozens of bullets had torn into it. Each sharp crackle was accompanied by a rapid flash of movement as small bits of flesh sprung into the air like popcorn. Kelly tried to make sense of what he was seeing but the light from the front of the equipment shed was shining directly in his face, allowing him to see only vague silhouettes.

"Get back!"

Kelly looked up. Armand was leaning halfway out through the hole in the door and gesturing wildly for them to back away.

Kelly and Matteus moved to their left giving the bloody patch of flooring a wide berth as they returned to the doorway.

"What the hell is going on?" Kelly demanded, never taking his eyes off of the soiled flooring.

"It's reconstituting," Armand replied in amazement.

"What the hell does that mean?" Konrad demanded.

Armand stared at the blood-soaked floor. "Every part of this organism is capable of being an entity all its own. Every piece of it is able to form a self-contained, self-aware and fully functioning creature. But it has to achieve a certain critical mass before it can morph into something large enough to give it mobility."

"What?! What the hell does that mean?!" Konrad demanded.

"The parts of the creature that were blasted off are coming together to form a bigger, more cohesive being...one that can move…one that can do more than just slither along the ground."

They watched as several small bits of flesh sprang upward several feet, jumping through the air like popcorn toward a central spot on the floor. As they landed near each other, the individual pieces slithered together and merged into a single, larger piece of flesh. Even the pool of blood covering the floor was changing shape as it, too, flowed toward the central location where is was rapidly absorbed by the ever-growing lump of flesh.

"It *means* that we need to get the hell out of here," Kelly said. "What's the story with the outer door?" he asked.

"They're almost there," Armand replied. "Phil's in contact with the crew on the outside. Think they'll have it opened soon."

"Great," Kelly replied. "What do we do about *this* in the meantime?" he asked, gesturing toward the flesh reassembling before them. "These rifles aren't going to do us any good against that."

"Flame," Armand answered. "It's the only thing that will complete kill it."

Without a word, Spence sprang forward and disappeared into the equipment shed. Seconds later he emerged carrying a plastic 5-gallon container. He lopped off the spigot with his Bowie knife and cut a gash onto the opposite side of the container. As the others watched, Spence splashed kerosene all over the floor, wetting as much of the contaminated area as he could.

Numerous chunks of alien flesh jumped and assembled with renewed urgency in response to being doused with the cold, oily liquid, as if sensing their impending demise. When the container was more than half empty, Spence slid it across the floor into the center of the infected area. He grabbed a cigarette lighter from his pocket, struck the wick, and threw it onto the puddle of fuel.

The kerosene caught quickly, spreading flames over the far half of the platform. A high-pitched, shrill shriek filled the air as the alien organism, still in various stages of assembly, writhed and sputtered amidst the flames. Almost immediately, a loud screeching emanated from somewhere along the warehouse floor, as if in response to the tortured wailing of its dying associate. Each screech from below seemed closer than the one before.

The men backed toward the door and stopped, acutely aware that there could be no further retreat. As long as the outer door remained in place, there was simply nowhere else for them to go.

They watched in silence as the fire raged. In less than a minute, the shrieking protests of the organism ceased. They waited anxiously for any further sign of the creature from below, half expecting it to rush them at any minute.

"Better get back inside, Doc," Kelly said quietly.

Armand ducked back into the stairwell without a word.

"You, too," Kelly said to Matteus. "You're not going to be any help out here."

Matteus gingerly made his way through the opening. Seconds later, a loud crash erupted from inside the stairwell followed by several unintelligible shouts.

"I told you Matteus couldn't be trusted," Konrad yelled. "The damn thing must've gotten to him! We should've wasted him when we had the chance!"

Kelly rushed for the opening, cursing himself for his decision earlier. If Matteus *was* infected, he may have just doomed everyone back there.

As he placed his hand on the jagged edge of the cut-out, the creature on the warehouse floor shrieked again, seemingly from directly below.

Armand suddenly stuck his head through the opening, almost colliding with Kelly. "Gentlemen," he said, his voice dripping with relief, "They got the door open! Ripped it right off its frame! Let's get the hell out of here!"

Konrad practically dove through the opening in his haste to leave the warehouse. Spence followed him even before Konrad's boots were completely through.

Kelly suddenly felt especially vulnerable, the sole occupant now on the platform. He fought the urge to rush. As he handed his weapon through the door, he paused and stared at the flames on the platform, their intensity diminishing quickly as the kerosene was consumed. Something about the sight bothered him…something he couldn't quite put his finger on. As he stuck his head through the opening, he wondered why he found himself suppressing an overwhelming sense of dread rather than enjoying a profound sense of relief at their escape from the warehouse.

TWENTY-THREE

l crouched in the cab of the forklift and peered up at the a hundred feet above him. Following a period of intense there was now no sign of movement…no sound at all from the far end of platform above. “*Where'd they all go*?” ht anxiously.

e hundredth time, he cursed the co-workers who had left him d stranded as they fled to save themselves.

l been working within the vessel's interior, adjusting some of the test equipment for the next series of experiments, when the foreman had sent him to one of the lower decks to retrieve a spectrometer. When he'd returned, he'd found that the others had disappeared. A thorough check of the surrounding areas of the ship revealed no sign of them.

It was only when he'd passed the opened lower hatch that he'd heard the blaring of the klaxon.

He'd spotted a small group of men making their way up the stairwell as he exited the vessel through the lower hatch. The sight of them filled had him instantly with relief. Finding himself alone inside the alien vessel had spooked him.

But his relief was short-lived. Almost immediately, the creature had attacked and the warehouse had gone dark.

Erland crouched beneath the spacecraft and watched in horror as the beast ripped the group to shreds. Several of the crew fell to their deaths nearby on the warehouse floor. One had landed with a loud smack just a few feet away. A green and black work glove from the unfortunate man had landed practically at his feet. The image of the bloodstained glove, the last thing he saw before the lights had gone out, was still seared into his brain.

When the emergency lighting kicked in, Erland had quickly climbed into the cab of a nearby forklift to hide.

Erland glanced at his watch, covering the timepiece with his hand to prevent its light from revealing his position. It had been over two hours since he'd heard anything more and he was growing more distressed at the realization that he was now truly alone.

He cursed his inaction earlier when he'd heard some of the crew on the platform above. He had just worked up the courage to make a run for it to join them when he heard the gunfire. He shrunk further back into the dark cab too afraid to move. He wished now that he'd risked it. Any fate he might have met would surely have been better than his current one.

Erland caught his breath at the sound of a shuffling noise nearby. He rose just enough to peer over the lower lip of the window.

He saw nothing at first. But it distressed him even more to see that the emergency lights had grown noticeably dimmer now that they had been on for a couple of hours.

A man suddenly appeared from behind a generator dragging something behind him.

Erland surged with relief. He flung open the forklift's door and jumped onto the floor, startling the other man and causing him to drop his load.

"God, Jakub! Am I ever glad to see *you*!" Erland spoke in hushed tones, fearful of alerting the creature to their presence if it remained nearby. His voice trembled, a mixture of fear and relief.

"What the hell is going on?" he asked, pulling away. "Is anyone else still down here?"

Jakub studied Erland for a moment. "I haven't seen anyone else," he finally replied. "Is anyone else with you?"

"No. Just me," Erland answered. "We gotta get the hell out of here, man! Did you see it?! Do you know what's going on?"

"It okay," Jakub said quietly, putting his hand on Erland's shoulder. "We'll be alright if we stick together."

Erland jumped at the sound of a low muffled groaning. It seemed to have come from behind Jakub. He was shocked to see that Jakub's load had actually been an injured crewman. His heart sank as he noticed that one of the man's hands was covered by a green and black glove. The other was gloveless.

Erland started toward the man but stopped as Jakub grabbed his hand.

"He isn't going to make it," Jakub said casually. "He's busted up pretty bad."

Erland paused and stared at the wounded man, uneasy with the way Jakub was so callously dismissing their dying comrade. Whoever the injured man was, he was still a member of the crew…a man with whom they had, until very recently, lived, worked, and horsed-around.

Jakub was staring directly at Erland, his face blank and dispassionate. Erland found it highly unnerving. A warm, wet sensation began to spread through his hand and he realized with a start that Jakub had seized it and was holding it far too firmly. He looked down at his hand. A dark black fluid was oozing from beneath Jakub's sleeve and spilling over his skin.

"What the hell…" Erland struggled to free his hand. "Let go!"

Jakub lunged forward, backing Erland forcefully against the side of the forklift with surprising strength. He pinned both of Erland's hands against the side of the machine near his head, using the rest of his body to press Erland into the cold steel frame.

Erland stared in disbelief as the black fluid fragmented into hundreds of tiny droplets. They burned his skin like small embers as they began crawling all over him. He tried to scream and shook frantically as the tiny creatures began burrowing into his forearm, piercing his flesh like superheated syringes.

Erland screamed. The insect-like things climbed higher up his arm, crawling just beneath his skin. His arm was on fire from within and seemed to grow suddenly heavier, as if the marrow in his bones had been displaced by molten lead.

The skin of Jakub's forearm bulged along its entire length with blisters that released countless more of the tiny creatures. They streamed upward and onto Erland's jacket, spreading out in every direction.

Erland instinctively turned his head away to protect his face and found himself looking into the side mirror of the forklift. In the reflection, he saw that several droplets of murky black blood from Jakub's mangled forearm had spattered onto his cheek.

He watched helplessly as the droplets unfurled tiny legs and crawled rapidly up his cheek toward his left eye. He wanted desperately to turn away from the image in the mirror but the compulsion to watch was somehow stronger.

The insects swayed rapidly from side to side as they probed their way up his face. Upon reaching the corner of his eye, the first one pried its way into his tear duct. His lower eyelid expanded briefly like a bloated tic then subsided. The organism released millions of alien cells from its burrow within Erland's flesh, turning the white of his eye instantly black and opaque and causing searing pain.

Erland screamed loudly again and again and thrashed about wildly. He could actually feel the organism spreading inside him as it made its way along his optic nerve into the depths of his brain.

Jakub released his grip on Erland's other hand and clamped his free hand over Erland's mouth. He stared at him impassively, unaffected by the violence of the ordeal. Jakub's hand grew suddenly very hot, melting into the flesh of Erland's face to form a tight rubbery seal. Erland felt his face flush with heat as Jakub pumped more alien cells into his mouth and the flesh of his cheeks.

Every second brought fresh agony as the creatures rummaged relentlessly through him. His whole body was wracked by violent spasms as the molten sensation hit his spine and the alien cells surged unimpeded through his central nervous system.

Erland suddenly remembered his gun. He could see the bulge of the ankle holster through his pants leg, easily within reach. He would end the misery.

But his free arm and leg refused to respond. In an instant, he understood that he'd already lost physical control of his body. It had taken only a moment for him to become a mere spectator to the nightmare, able to see and understand what was happening but powerless to do anything to affect the outcome.

Erland's head lurched back involuntarily, slamming into the forklift's steel frame, as the searing sensation spread through his brain. Darkness began to close in on him. The prospect of death, once scary and uncertain, was welcome now. He closed his eyes, praying it would take him quickly and end his agony.

But the darkness began to recede as quickly as it had approached. Strangely, the pain, too, was receding rapidly.

He opened his eyes and was amazed by the acute sharpness of his vision. Everything stood out with amazing clarity, as if his brain's ability to process visual input had improved ten-fold.

Jakub stood several feet away. His ruptured forearm was already healing itself, rapidly re-forming into a normal looking human appendage.

Erland stared at his own reflection in the mirror. He was amazed to see himself just as he had been only minutes ago. There was no sign of the violent intrusion that had wracked his body just moments ago.

He was also surprised when his body began to move. He tried to stop himself but his body refused to obey. A few steps later he was looking down again at the injured man. His foot kicked the man's gloveless hand, which twitched then fell listlessly back down.

"This one is useless. He will not live long."

Erland heard the voice coming from his own mouth but he hadn't intended to speak them. "*What the hell is going on?*" the thought echoed inside his head. The thought was immediately and forcefully suppressed. The harder he tried to push it through, the stronger it was held back by some force operating just outside his consciousness. Erland despaired as he began to understand his transformation.

This thing had invaded his body and assumed control. It had replaced his physical cells with its own, shaping them to look and act as *he* normally would. As the organism spread throughout his body, it developed a collective mind like a colony of ants working toward the survival and propagation of the hive. He had sensed it during his transformation but the terror and agony of the moment had prevented him from understanding it. Now, free now from the pain of his assimilation, he began to comprehend the scope of it all.

The alien cells that first penetrated his brain began immediately to absorb his intellect. They instantly shared it, using Erland's central nervous system as a conduit, with the trillions of other replicant cells already scattered throughout his body, arming each with the knowledge and skills it would need to survive within this host. The organism's desire to survive bordered on paranoia.

As the replicants began to outnumber his original cells, he'd felt it beginning to grow…a foreign, alien consciousness developing rapidly beside his own. In several areas of his body, the replicant cells reached a critical density and underwent a form of mitosis, splitting into two or three smaller, independent groups, each with its own 'consciousness'. Major muscle groups, extremities, and internal organs became essentially self-aware, gaining the ability to form an independent entity, if necessary, while retaining their ability to operate normally as part of their host.

For a brief moment, Erland had actually sensed and understood the purpose of each new 'intelligence' now scattered throughout his body. Any physical part that became separated from the main body – an arm, a leg…a damned *kidney* – could survive, armed with both the physical and intellectual means to form a wholly separate being. But until such time, the multiple organisms would function within him as part of a collective mind.

But the wonder of it all quickly passed.

In short order, a superior consciousness began to box him in, wresting almost total control of his mind. It compressed and suppressed his consciousness, banishing it to an almost inconsequential sector of his brain. Even as it was happening, Erland had understood the purpose behind it. From the alien organism's perspective, it made perfect sense.

While the organism could replicate him physically and control the chemical and mechanical processes that allowed his body to function, it couldn't eradicate the one thing independent of these processes…his mind. Confining him was the only way for the organism to assume complete control and operate with full autonomy.

'Consciousness' was all that remained of his former self, a small sphere of intelligence imprisoned somewhere deep within. The realization of it was maddening. As long as this *thing* lived, his mind would be a helpless, unwilling witness to whatever the organism did to survive and propagate.

TWENTY-FOUR

The security guard looked up from behind his desk, “Good morning, Mister Westcott. What brings you in on a Sunday?”

“Good morning, Jimmy. Oh, you know...the usual. Making the world safe for democracy. How’d the O’s do last night?”

Jimmy laughed, “Won, seven to four. Game was tied through the eighth but then the birds came alive.”

“Glad to hear. Two more wins and they’ll have clinched a playoff spot, right?”

“That’ll be sweet! I’ll be going to at least one of those games for sure!”

Steve laughed, “Good for you! Must be nice to be rich!”

Jimmy chuckled, “Oh yeah…I’m just rolling in it,” he said sarcastically. “Hope you’re not here too long. Supposed to be a beautiful day.”

“I figure an hour or so. Should be plenty of day left to enjoy. I’ll catch you on my way out.”

“Sounds good. See you later.”

Steve pressed his badge to the reader and the turnstile opened, allowing him to enter.

He actually didn’t mind coming in on a Sunday morning. The halls of the National Security Agency were quiet but still seemed to hold an air of anticipation. Steve knew that, come Monday morning, all hell would break loose as thousands of analysts returned and reacted to the many regional and worldwide crises that had occurred since they’d gone home on Friday.

A hint of a smile crossed his lips at the many memories he had of having once been one of those analysts. Work had gotten less fun, the higher he'd risen in the agency's hierarchy. But his involvement in this Antarctica business had revived the excitement he used to feel when coming to work. There were too few specialists cleared for the operation so he'd been assigned primarily as an analyst. That suited him just fine.

Steve didn't bother removing his jacket as he made his way down the hall. He didn't expect that he'd be here all that long. Although the crisis in Antarctica continued, there just wasn't much that NSA could do to support them now that things had gotten out of hand at the warehouse. At this point, the agency's main focus was to look for signs that the situation had spread beyond the site's confines. Not much chance of that, given the harshness of the surrounding environment and the remoteness of the site's location. He entered the code into the cypher pad and the heavy lock unlatched with a noisy click, allowing him to enter.

A special office had been set up within the National SIGINT Operations Center for their exclusive use until the crisis in Antarctica abated. The NSOC was the nerve center of the agency, where specialists from various disciplines kept their fingers on the pulse of the world twenty-four hours a day, ready to raise the alarm to the highest military and government officials should current events indicate an impending crisis.

An attractive woman approached Steve as he entered the room.

"Hi Cheryl. Things quiet?"

"Relatively," Cheryl responded curtly. She handed him a small bright red envelope. "Here's today's package."

Steve thanked her and headed for their office. He knew Cheryl, the Watch Officer for this shift, would watch him until he closed the office door behind him. Like her predecessors, she had undergone a rigorous qualification process to be in her position, which granted her access to the most sensitive of the Agency's secrets.

The Watch Officers made decisions daily, sometimes hourly, that could significantly impact the military and political interests of the country. In order to do this successfully, they had to know about everything that was going on in the intelligence world. They were understandably unhappy about being kept in the dark, clueless about the project and its potential implications as the unfamiliar crew operated in their sphere.

Steve ripped open the envelope along its perforated edge and dumped the small plastic card into his hand. The card contained the several passwords that he would need to access the heavily compartmented data associated with Archway, the codename given to the current situation in Antarctica.

Given the extra-terrestrial nature of the project, less than a dozen managers and analysts were knowledgeable of it. The passwords for the various databases they needed were changed automatically every eight hours and provided to each Archway analyst as he or she came on duty. They were determined by a complicated algorithm and printed and sealed by a special machine to keep them free from human eyes. On their way out, each analyst was required to verify that the Watch Officer slipped the re-sealed envelope into a special high-speed shredder that would pulverize it into dust.

Steve poured a cup of coffee and sat at his desk to quickly scan the files he'd received overnight from the various country desks.

Radio chatter from two days ago revealed that the Japanese had conducted several helicopter flights from their Showa research facility to Mizuho, another research site that they'd abandoned years ago. Not a good sign. The Japanese had abandoned Mizuho almost twenty years ago and hadn't been back there since. For them to do so now, with one of the alien pods still transmitting quite near the abandoned facility, was more than just suspicious.

He turned to the report that they'd gotten from the National Geospatial Intelligence Center, the arm of the intelligence community that performs high resolution satellite photography of key ground-based targets.

The Center's imagery was so good that, under the right circumstances, an analyst could determine which side of a quarter was facing up in a man's palm based on a photograph taken from a satellite ten miles above the earth. The NGIC had placed all of the sites in Antarctica, including the areas where the un-recovered pods now lay, on its priority tasking list and was providing fresh pictures of each location every twelve hours.

Steve quickly scanned the NGIC photos. Two of them showed signs that the Japanese had re-opened Mizuho. Snow and ice had been removed from some outbuildings and at least a dozen men could be seen scattered about the facility. One shot even captured a helicopter in-flight, apparently departing the facility.

He flicked rapidly through the photos, looking for one in particular. As soon as he saw it, he swore under his breath and picked up the STU, the enciphered telephone.

After making his notifications, he sat back in his chair and went through the pictures more slowly. There wasn't much of anything to see in most of them, just barren snow-covered landscapes punctuated by an occasional mountain peak. But the two from Mizuho and another from site AA34672 – the resting place of the third unrecovered pod – were alarming.

Photos from the site from twelve hours ago showed nothing…just a barren white landscape and a fuzzy dark, teardrop shaped object just below the surface of the ice. Unfortunately, the most recent picture was a little more interesting.

Two large tents had been erected and boxes of equipment were strewn about in an arc around the spot where the object lay buried...except the dark tear-shaped shadow was no longer present. At least six men were assembled beside a nearby helicopter.

The signs that the pod had been recovered by the Japanese couldn't have been more obvious.

PART THREE

TWENTY-FIVE

Frank switched off the monitor and stared with disbelief at the darkening screen. Even after all they'd been through recently, what they had just heard was too unbelievable…too terrible to contemplate. He looked up at Viktor, who stood there silently – the usual toothpick sticking out of one corner of his mouth – and couldn't help wondering if his own face was so deeply etched with the same worried furrows.

"Man, if I look anywhere near as bad as you, just shoot me now."

Viktor raised his gaze from the monitor and stared at him. Without a word, he reached down and snapped open his holster, wrapped his fingers around the grip, and slowly lifted the pistol several inches.

Frank had to chuckle despite the seriousness of their situation. "Thanks."

Although he'd witnessed it a number of times in the years that they'd worked together, Viktor's ability to deflate a tense situation still surprised him sometimes. It had certainly kept them focused during the last few days, as things had grown more and more desperate.

"It's what I'm here for," Viktor replied dryly, grabbing for a metal chair and dropping the gun back into the leather. He flicked the chair around and straddled it while flicking the toothpick rapidly from cheek to cheek.

"Listen. We can't worry about that," he said, motioning with his head toward the monitor. "We've got more than enough to handle right here."

"But if they're right…. if that boat is already on its way to Moscow or Tokyo…"

"That's *their* fight! *Ours* is here!"

Frank stared back at Viktor, surprised by the forcefulness of his tone.

Viktor let out a long deep sigh. "Sorry."

"Forget it," Frank said, forcing a smile, "…and you're right, of course. It's just…" He groped for the words then dismissed the thought with a wave of his hand. By now, everyone was on edge. His own mind was growing more cluttered with each passing hour as the recent, strange events competed for his attention like giant, grotesque floats in some morbid parade. Almost a dozen of his crew remained trapped below, including one of his closest friends. They knew of at least four dead and suspected many more.

Viktor ran his hand through his hair, muddled and oily now for lack of a recent shower. "Anders says that they finally got the blast door opened. I'm going to send Tom below. A few others have volunteered to go with him. We need more medicine and we've got to get some more food up here."

"Yeah…this place wasn't really built for long-term habitation." A sudden chill ran through him, despite the warmth of his parka.

Viktor sighed in exasperation, "We also need… well… we're pretty much out of everything."

Frank shrugged and looked around the room, which contained little more than a small desk, a couple of wooden folding chairs, and a computer. Like almost everything else topside, it wasn't much to look at. But the facilities up here had been crucial to maintaining the ruse and he couldn't help but be impressed that their secret remained intact after all these years, despite several close calls.

The topside facilities were, in fact, largely a façade; a group of empty shells arranged to look like any other Antarctic research site. The lights were computer controlled, turned on and off at random intervals to make the buildings look occupied. Security teams occasionally cleared the pathways that meandered between the buildings to give the impression of normal research activity. They'd even dispatched scientists to other nearby sites on occasion, ostensibly to conduct joint research but, in truth, mainly to bolster the illusion.

But up here, few of the buildings served any real purpose. The real work had, for decades, been happening below in the warehouse, the cavernous structure built over the spacecraft soon after its discovery to hide it from prying eyes and prevent intrusion by 'undesirables'. For almost 30 years they'd been operating under its umbrella, which protected them from the harsh arctic environment and provided them with the privacy they needed to examine every aspect of the alien craft at their leisure.

Frank looked around and tried to remember the last time he had been up here…that is, before the recent circumstances had driven them all to the surface.

The Spartan appearance of the topside facilities stood in stark contrast to the warehouse facilities below, all of which were top-notch. In addition to the superbly outfitted research facilities, everything else the crew needed was supplied within the warehouse's interior spaces, deep below the icy surface. Comfortable and spacious living quarters, a well-stocked kitchen, all kinds of recreational distractions…. *'Not to mention HEAT,'* he thought as a shiver ran through him.

They'd only been topside for a few days but already these comforts seemed like distant memories. And, unfortunately for the members of the crew now living topside, the last of the food, toiletries, and precious few comforts had quickly run out, depleted by a contingency for which no-one had planned. Getting supplies from below, especially food and medicines, had definitely become a priority.

"OK. How're they fixed?"

"Four flame units, two per team. Rifle and pistol each."

"Give them each a radio too. I want every one of them to check in *individually* every five minutes. Tell them anyone out of comms for longer than that or anyone getting separated from the group won't be allowed back in."

Frank sighed deeply and dropped his head to his chest. "Shit…we should've been prepared for this."

"Based on what?! We've been in business here over 30 years and this place has been absolutely clean! There's been no shred of a threat whatsoever…and you know damn well that we've been careful!"

Frank jumped from his seat, flinging it aside, "We knew the risks when we brought the damn things back here," he shouted. "We knew the danger! It almost completely annihilated the advanced team in '97. Wasn't that warning enough?! But no! We had to go and bring them back here and now they're running loose!" Frank threw his empty coffee cup against the wall raining shards of glass over the far end of the room. "What the hell will this thing be able to do if it reaches Russia or Japan or friggin' Timbuktu?! They'll be no stopping it!"

Frank slumped into his chair and threw his arms into the air, letting loose a string of mumbled obscenities. "We should've left the damn things alone… Better yet, we should've blown them to pieces right where they were."

Viktor leaned forward and said calmly, "You know that those weren't viable options." He paused, waiting for Frank's tantrum to pass.

It didn't take long. "I know. You're right," he sighed in exasperation.

"Frank, the decision to retrieve them was made echelons above our pay grade and over the objections of us both. We did all we could to ensure that any potential occupants remained safely frozen. We set thermite charges. We posted guards and set up video surveillance to keep an eye on the damn things 24 hours a day.

Frank dipped his head, "I know... But, God, I can't believe how fast this all went to hell." He stood there shaking his head. As always, it had been the smallest of details…the stupidest, one-in-a-million, freakish damn things that had rendered moot all their precautions.

"Yes," Viktor replied quietly as if reading his mind, "And now, here we are."

Viktor rose from his seat and headed for the door. "Well," he sighed, "we may still be here for a while so I'd better see to those supplies." A gust of wind howled outside, causing the corrugated metal sheeting that comprised the walls to creak and groan. The harsh noise seemed to validate Viktor's assessment and underscore the direness of their situation.

Frank grabbed him by the arm as he passed by, "Vik…" He sighed and shook his head rapidly from side to side as if he could shake away his grogginess.

The big Norwegian stopped and placed his hand on Frank's shoulder. "I know. What a mess, huh?"

"Yeah, and we're both getting a bit edgy. I'm going to try to get some sleep in the CSC. You should probably do the same once the supply detail gets back here."

"I'll try." Viktor turned to leave but then paused in the doorway, "What's the latest on the storm?"

"Kev says we're looking at another 24 to 36 hours before it lets up. But there's another storm front right behind it. The tech team is going to have less than a day to get their asses out here."

Viktor rolled his eyes and frowned, then flipped up the hood of his parka with a sharp whip of his head. "Better get back," he said, waiting at the doorway.

They'd head back to the command center together following the same rule they'd insisted on for everyone else. No-one was to go anywhere unless accompanied by at least one co-worker…preferably two. They'd be far less likely to become prey that way.

At the outer entrance, Viktor stopped suddenly and turned, "You know if that ship *does* make it to another shore…"

"God help us," Frank said, closing the inner door behind them.

"Yes…. God help us." Viktor spit the toothpick onto the floor as he pulled on his gloves. "Well, given this recent revelation, they've certainly got bigger things to worry about now than our little 'deviation' from the security protocols. Maybe we'll end up dodging that bullet after all." He pulled his goggles over his eyes, "Sweet dreams, eh?" he said, lunging into the wind and snow.

'Oh, yeah," Frank scoffed. "I'm sure I'll sleep like a baby." He hurried to catch up to Viktor, whose large silhouette had already disappeared into the darkness.

≈ O ≈

"What the hell are they thinking?!" Frank shouted as he cleared the last of the steps into the tower.

"I have no friggin idea," Jonas replied as he quickly handed Frank his binoculars.

Frank grabbed them brusquely and peered out at the snow-covered landscape. He'd only been asleep for an hour when he was abruptly shaken awake and informed that a chopper was on final approach. He was still feeling pretty groggy and was hugely annoyed.

He could just barely make out the shape of the helicopter, its silhouette camouflaged almost perfectly by the ridge it had just flown over on its way in. Despite the distance, the bucking of the small craft in the high winds was obvious.

"How the hell do they expect to land in this?!"

Frank turned, acknowledging Kevin's arrival in the tower with barely a grunt before resuming his scan of the horizon.

Kevin glanced at Jonas over his shoulder. "Winds are gusting at over 40! This is insane!"

Frank scowled and grit his teeth. "I'd like to know whose bright idea *this* was," he yelled, slamming the expensive binoculars down on the countertop.

Jonas and Kevin look at each other uncomfortably. Neither of them had ever seen Frank pissed off. His reaction to the unexpected arrival of the helicopter seemed a bit extreme. It was unusual for sure for the site to receive an unscheduled flight, but it certainly wasn't the first time that it had happened.

Frank stared out the window, oblivious to the awkward silence. It wasn't the flight itself that had gotten him this angry, not even under these extremely foolhardy conditions. It was the fact that HQ hadn't even alerted him to the inbound flight, and they certainly could have done so during their last teleconference just a few hours ago. They would have had to have known about it at that time. He'd barely had time to digest the latest news about the Japanese recovering one of the pods and now he had to deal with this. He wasn't exactly sure which event was more unsettling at the moment.

He listened as Jonas guided the chopper in and provided the pilot with the latest meteorological data. The aircraft actually got more difficult to see the closer it got to the site due to the ground haze formed by the wind-blown snow. Frank would occasionally catch a glimpse of the black fuselage as the aircraft bucked and swayed above the ground. Only the pilot's anxious voice would occasionally break the silence in the tower while they waited tensely for the aircraft to touch down.

"Man, this guy is earning his pay this time out," Kevin marveled. A chopper pilot himself, he was keenly aware of the war the pilot was waging with the controls in these conditions. He drew a breath suddenly, "Geez, I think his tail just came within inches of that pole!"

"Tower, uh, I'm gonna swing around and put her down west of the hangar. These winds are just…"

The chopper veered suddenly to the right and the tail rotor erupted in a shower of sparks as it slammed into the wooden utility pole.

"Shit!" The pilot yelled frantically as the chopper began to spin uncontrollably, still 20 feet or so over the landing site.

The crew in the tower could only watch in disbelief and listen in shock as the pilot frantically urged his passengers to hang on.

The nose of the aircraft dipped suddenly as it dove into the ground, sheering off the main rotors and sending shrapnel flying in every direction.

Frank suddenly found himself on the floor as the groaning and thumping of the chopper's heavy frame slamming into the ground filled the air. He lay still for several seconds until the noise subsided, then nudged Kevin to get off of him.

He rose cautiously to his knees.

"You guys ok?"

The others nodded.

Two of the tower's windows had been shattered by flying debris from the stricken chopper. A good-sized piece of the main rotor was lodged in the ceiling above them. Frank shivered involuntarily, unsure if it was from the cold now pouring into the room or from the realization that Kevin had likely saved him from being seriously injured or killed.

"I owe you one," Frank muttered at Kevin, who merely nodded back.

Below them, the chopper had come to rest on its side. The crew and passengers were already scrambling out of the wreck with the help on the ground from some of the site's crew.

"You two start patching things up in here," Frank instructed, "I've got to go see what else these *idiots* destroyed."

"Easy, dude! You're gonna break something."

Brian scowled but forced himself to slow down. He'd been grabbing bottles indiscriminately from the shelves and carelessly heaving them into Parker's shoulder bag.

"Are you sure we're grabbing the right stuff?" Parker asked, eyeing each shelf.

"Yeah. I already grabbed the rest of the meningitis stuff. That was that shit in the pink bottles that I loaded into the side pocket first thing."

"Should we grab some of those?"

Brian glanced at the rolls of gauze and medical tape, "Nah, Christian's taking care of that."

They could hear Christian in the adjacent lab noisily shuffling through drawers and shoving supplies in his bag.

"Wonder how the other guys are making out," Parker asked nervously.

Brian looked up at the clock above them, "Let's finish loading our own shit and then we'll give Tom a call." He dropped to one knee and started grabbing stuff from the lower shelves.

"Man…it's so quiet down here," Parker said, looking over his shoulder. "Least they got some of the lights back on though."

"I know," Brian murmured quietly in agreement. He'd jumped at the chance to come down here with the others to get supplies. Hildy needed medicine. Perhaps he was being selfish, but he wanted to be sure that Armand got what he needed to treat her…and his kid. He exhaled at the thought, whistling lightly. A kid…he was still struggling to get used to the idea.

As soon as they got to the lab, he'd searched for the medicine Armand said she needed. Once he'd gotten it, the rest of the stuff suddenly seemed less urgent. Now, he was just grabbing anything else he thought Armand might need. But the bag was getting full.

Brian grabbed his cell and lobbed it up to Parker. "Why don't you check on Tom and the others while I check out those cabinets," he said, pointing behind them.

Brian rummaged through the drawers and cabinets looking for anything else that might be useful topside while Parker spoke quietly on the phone. When he finished, Parker walked over to the cabinets and handed the phone back to him.

"Tom says they just got to there. I told him we were already almost done here and he said to go on up without waiting for them."

Brian paused. The original plan called for his group to wait in the lab until Tom's team returned from the pantry so they could go back as a group. But they were pretty much done in the lab and Tom's group was just getting started. It seemed pointless for the three of them to wait.

"What you think?" Brian asked.

"I say we get the hell out of here," Parker replied without hesitation.

Brian was relieved. He would've waited if that was what the others had wanted but, now that they had what they'd come here for, he wasn't in the mood to hang around. Not with that *thing* lurking about.

A loud thump from above startled them both. They stood quietly, looking up at the ceiling and straining to hear.

"What's above us?" Parker whispered.

"Crew's quarters," Brian whispered back.

Parker's eyes widened and he clenched his jaw.

Five ill members of the crew had been abandoned in the spaces above them. It had been a few days now and there had been no contact from any of them. Armand had initially insisted on mounting a rescue but Frank had overruled him. At the time, the blast door was still firmly sealed. The only way to reach them would've been along the same catwalk by which they'd escaped from the warehouse and he thought that it was too dangerous.

Once they'd gotten the blast door open to give them a direct route below, they'd already given up hope of rescuing the sick. It had already been too long. They'd probably long since succumbed to either the meningitis or….

Brian fought unsuccessfully to keep his mind from going there. He walked silently over to where he'd dropped the flame thrower and slung it over one shoulder. The small blue flame of the pilot light still hissed at the edge of the nozzle. He wanted so badly to give the trigger a quick squeeze to reassure himself that the unit was still working but the lab was not a good place to release a burst of flame.

"C'mon," Parker whispered, grabbing Brian's arm. "Let's get Christian and get the hell…"

Parker froze. Brian was holding his finger to his mouth and looking at him urgently as he craned his neck toward the door connecting the two labs.

Parker listened but heard nothing. It took him several seconds to realize that it was the silence itself that was disturbing Brian. Now that he was aware of it too, he found it equally unsettling. Until moments ago, they'd been able to hear Christian rummaging noisily through the cabinets and drawers in the adjacent lab.

Brian crouched low and slowly made his way toward the doorway. Fortunately, they'd left the glass door panel separating the two rooms wide open. He slowly stuck his head around the corner then fell back onto his butt as an object hit the door frame just above his head.

He scrambled to his feet. Behind him, Parker was on his hands and knees wavering unsteadily from the force of the object, which had ricocheted off the steel door frame and struck him in the face. Blood poured over his nose, staining the glistening white tile.

Brian quickly threw his free arm into the remaining strap of the flame unit and charged into the second lab, slamming his back against the wall.

At first, he could make no sense at all of what he was seeing.

He recognized the clothing and the brown hair woven into a long erratic ponytail. He knew the face that stared back at him impassively. But his brain struggled to comprehend the inhuman things that Shifty was doing to Christian.

Shifty's tattered and bloody frame hovered over Christian, who was sprawled out in a heap on the floor. It looked as though Shifty had recently been on the wrong end of a shotgun. His intestines seemed to have poured from a gaping wound in his chest and spilled all over Christian…except the appearance of Shifty's flesh was all wrong. Intestines weren't supposed to be black.

The fleshy strands stretching between the two men surged and pulsed slowly and rhythmically, as though a viscous fluid was being pumped through them. They'd attached themselves to various parts of Christian's face and torso, turning his skin a dark grayish blue.

Shifty glared at Brian, opened his mouth wide, and let out a loud, guttural growl. A milky white substance streamed forcefully from Shifty's mouth toward Brian, who raised the nozzle of the flame unit and fired without hesitation. The flame connected with the slimy mucous midway between the two driving it to the floor where it solidified and writhed like a fiery serpent.

Brian raised the nozzle further and sent a long blast in Shifty's direction. Shifty screeched and flailed as the flames engulfed him. With a sickening snap, each tendril released its grip on Christian, who slumped lifelessly to the floor.

Brian continued to fire flame at both men, shouting at the top of his lungs in terror. Shifty staggered a few steps away and fell to the ground in a burning heap as Christian writhed on the floor nearby, the flames cooking his flesh. In less than a minute, both men fell silent and still.

Brian watched for a moment as the flames burned wildly, searching for any signs of movement. Only when a few bottles of peroxide exploded on the counter from the heat did he relax enough to look for an extinguisher.

He gave both carcasses a wide berth, maneuvering around them to extinguish the burning lab.

Finally, the room was silent again.

Brian stared, still struggling to comprehend what he just saw. He'd heard the warehouse survivors describe it a couple of times in the days since their rescue, but the actual experience of it was far more horrific than he'd imagined. None of the survivors had said anything about the inhuman sounds and the sickening stench.

Brian spun around quickly, startled by a rustling noise in the adjacent lab. He raised the nozzle of the flame unit then abruptly let it fall as he rushed to the door.

"Park?" he called out tentatively.

Brian froze as he sighted his friend.

Parker sat on the floor, his back propped up against a wall. Blood smeared the floor, a small pool marking the spot where he'd initially been struck by whatever it was that the creature had thrown. It continued to stream from the deep gash in his forehead.

Parker had removed the shiny silver implement from his head and held it loosely in his hand. Blood covered it to the midpoint of its shaft like dark, dirty oil on a dipstick. Parker's skull had been impaled deeply by the device causing a wound that would have killed a normal man. But a low, raspy growl coming from Parker was proof enough that he was no longer a normal man.

Brian stared at him in shock as he tentatively raised the nozzle and pointed it at his friend. A hundred questions clamored for answers in his mind. "*When the hell did it happen?*" He'd been with Parker almost constantly since the others had been rescued from below a few days ago. "*How could it have gotten to him?*" Parker's dark eyes watched him impassively as Brian reviewed the last couple of days, struggling to remember when they *hadn't* been together. Those times were few and hadn't been for longer than a few minutes. "*How was this possible?*"

Brian shuddered as it dawned on him how close he had come to becoming another victim.

There was movement beneath Parker's clothing, his jacket writhing with movement all over.

"*There's just no way!*" Part of him continued to deny the obvious even as the rest of him fought to accept it.

The unnerving growl grew louder and more menacing and Brian steeled himself for what he knew he had to do. He waited as long as he could, squeezing the trigger only when the blisters erupted from Parker's flesh.

TWENTY-SIX

"What the hell are they up to?" Frank asked angrily.

"I don't know," Viktor replied, "But I sure don't like it."

Frank continued to mumble obscenities as they walked briskly down the hallway, slamming his fist into a trash bin along the way. "This is still *my* site, dammit!"

Viktor said nothing. This was one of those times when Frank just needed to vent. He insinuated himself between Frank and the hangar door and paused. "Let's just hear what he has to say," Viktor suggested. "Maybe there actually *is* a reasonable explanation."

Frank issued a sarcastic grunt but nodded reluctantly in agreement. He turned the handle and pushed on the door but it didn't budge.

"What the…?"

He jiggled the handle rapidly and pushed again with the same result.

Suddenly, the door swung open. Two men stood just inside the door, blocking the entrance into the hangar. A small, wiry guy stepped between them.

"Gentlemen, I'm Richard Werthers. I'm here to provide corporate with a fresh assessment of the situation."

"I think we're more than capable of providing…"

"Perhaps under better circumstances," Richard said, interrupting Frank.

They stood in awkward silence for several seconds.

"Look, gentlemen," Richard resumed, softening his tone. "You guys have been dealing with this now for over a week. No doubt you've gotten very little sleep since this crisis began. You get tired, you make mistakes. It's that simple really. And, given the consequences of failure here, I think you'd agree that a fresh perspective isn't a bad idea."

"Fresh perspective, my ass," Frank hissed. "What's with these?" he asked, tapping on the freshly installed deadbolts. "If you think you're going to march in and take over *my* site…"

"*Your* site?" Richard asked, the edge returning to his voice. "This site is the property of Axis Corporation. They've given you the *privilege* of running it but make no mistake…this is *their* site. And they will do everything they deem necessary to protect and preserve it. You've already made one egregious error since this whole thing began. You can't blame the board for…"

"Egregious error?! What the hell are you talking about?!" Frank lunged forward then stopped as the man next to Richard instantly planted himself firmly in front of his boss. His hand rested on the sidearm attached to his belt and he glared defiantly at Frank.

"It's ok, Scott." Richard said. "He may be pissed…hell, I would be too. But he's not stupid."

Scott took a step back but remained glued to Richard's side.

Richard regarded Frank and Viktor coolly, "I am referring to your unwise decision to circumvent the blast door's built-in security. Those protocols were in place for a reason. Your decision to override them has heightened the risk to the facility and jeopardized the lives of everyone working here."

"Lives were already in jeopardy," Frank shouted.

"We needed food and medicine," Viktor interjected before Frank could respond further. "That creature isn't the only threat we're facing. We've had three more crewmen come down with meningitis in just the last two days. We weren't about to just sit back and watch them die."

"Yes. Well, it doesn't matter now, does it?" Richard stated flatly. "Look, Frank... You're still in charge. But I've got my orders too and they require me to provide headquarters with *my* assessment of things here. My men will stay out of your way."

Frank glowered at Richard for several seconds. "I'll have Anders show you where you can settle in."

"That won't be necessary," Richard replied. "We'll set up shop right here in the hangar, if that's alright with you, of course." Frank turned to leave without another word. Richard's demeanor made it quite clear that they were going to set up in the hangar regardless of whether or not it was alright with him.

"What about the medicine?" Viktor asked.

"What?"

"Medicine. ...for the meningitis?" Viktor strained to keep his cool but couldn't completely hide the disdain in his voice.

Richard blinked several times rapidly and, for the first time since their encounter began, appeared flustered. "Oh...yes. Of course. It's still in the chopper. I'll send one of my men out to get it.

"You didn't bring it in with you?" Frank asked incredulously.

"In case you missed it, we had a bit of a rough landing," Richard snarled back.

Frank scoffed, "Don't bother. We'll go get it ourselves."

"You'll stay away from my chopper!"

Frank erupted, "I don't know what the hell you're up to but I will go where I please on *my* site! It IS *my* site until they take it away from me!"

Scott and the other man flanking Richard inched closer to their boss, weapons drawn. The two groups stood in silence, glowering at each other. Finally, Frank spit on the floor and turned to leave.

"One more thing," Richard blurted out.

"Until we know for sure the extent of the….issue, please see to it that you keep your crew away from my team. If you haven't already done so, it would be wise to keep them together and sequestered somewhere to keep an eye on them."

Frank paused for just a second then charged back down the hallway toward the CSC.

Viktor sighed heavily. "I suggest you change your tone, Mr. Werthers. We're all a bit frayed right now. The last thing this crew needs right now is attitude from some arrogant corporate prick."

He turned and stepped through the door. "Let me know if you guys would like some extra pillows and blankets," he said sarcastically over his shoulder.

Scott closed the hangar door and slid the newly-installed latch bolt, locking it.

"Have you secured the rest of the doors yet?" Richard asked.

"Deadbolts will be in place shortly."

"Good," Richard replied, "I don't want any of them unexpectedly wandering in."

"What about our cargo?" Scott asked.

Richard thought for a moment and glanced at his watch. "It's ten now. Wait an hour, then go back out to the chopper and retrieve it. I want to get them installed as soon as possible. No need to tell you that this must be done discretely."

"No need," Scott affirmed.

"How's their chopper?"

"Looks good. Plenty of fuel. Dodson says it's a fairly new machine."

Richard glanced at his watch again. "Good. We absolutely have to get this done *tonight* if we're to have any shot at hitting Mizuho before the next storm hits."

Scott nodded grimly as he turned away to go check on the team's progress.

≈ O ≈

Viktor caught up with Frank just as they reached the door to the CSC.

"Something about this whole thing really smells," Frank muttered.

"I agree," Viktor replied. "What are we going to do about Tom's crew?"

Frank swore and stopped in his tracks. He was so pissed off that he'd forgotten about the men they'd sent below. They'd gone back down into the warehouse via the hangar just minutes before the unexpected arrival of the helicopter and would be returning the same way.

He glanced at his watch. They'd been gone for less than half an hour but with all that had happened since they'd gone below it seemed much longer.

"Soon as we're back in the CSC, get in touch with Tom. Find out how much longer they expect to be down there. And you'd better warn them about *the Dick* in the hangar," he said, his voice seething with venom.

Frank reached for the door but paused, hearing no reply from Viktor. He turned around to see his deputy just standing there, his brow wrinkled with worry.

Frank shot him a quizzical look but said nothing. Viktor was clearly contemplating something heavy and he didn't want to break his train of thought.

"I don't know what they've got up their sleeve," Viktor finally said, "but I can tell you one thing for sure…they didn't bring any medicine with them."

TWENTY-SEVEN

Brian stared at the flaming carcass on the floor in front of him, his mind still reeling from the events of the last few minutes. The flames were beginning to climb up the walls and threatened to engulf the lab if he didn't do something about it soon. Yet, he found himself unable to act, stricken by shock.

What had just moments ago been one of his closest friends now lay in a twisted, burning heap filling the room with a sickening stench. The organism has somehow gotten to him during the last few days. He had had no clue, no inkling whatsoever, that Parker had been anything other than his friend. "*How could it be?*" The answer seemed leapt at him immediately. "*Someone topside is infected.*"

With that sudden realization, Brian jumped to his feet. He scanned the room frantically, looking for the radio or his cell phone, both of which he'd lost during his encounter with the creature.

He felt a growing sense of panic at the thought that Hildy was again in grave danger. He dropped to his hands and knees and began feeling around beneath the cabinets and tables. His hand brushed against something under one of the cabinets, knocking it further out of his reach. He swore and dropped onto his back to extend his reach. His hand closed around something he recognized immediately as his phone.

He stood and examined it. There didn't appear to be any obvious damage. He pressed the screen, exhaling loudly in relief as it lit up normally.

Something shiny flashed briefly off to his right. Brian instinctively side-stepped and threw his hands up to protect himself. But as he felt the creature gripping him, he knew it was already too late.

The immense shadow rapidly filled his vision, enveloping him in darkness. He found it suddenly difficult to breathe. Images of Christian's horrible demise were still fresh in his mind as he struggled frantically to keep from suffering the same awful fate. But he was powerless against the incredible strength of the creature.

A searing pain suddenly filled his left eye. Brian tried to scream but whatever had forced its way into his mouth prevented any sound from escaping. As the creature held him tightly in its grip, he found himself strangely overtaken by a sense of calm in the face of his own death. The pain in his eye subsided as quickly as it had come. In fact, he really felt no pain whatsoever.

He felt himself slipping into unconsciousness. He was glad for it. He'd fought it at first, knowing that Hildy needed him. But his strength left him so suddenly that he quickly surrendered. With the last of his energy, he reached out telepathically to his unborn child, urging it to survive to ease her pain.

≈ O ≈

"So, we're still short on medicines then, Viktor stated to no-one in particular.

Tom sighed and hung his head. "I'm sorry. Once we realized what had happened, we thought it best just to get the hell out of there. I guess we should've looked around but…"

Frank rose from his seat, "It's OK, Tom. You did the right thing. Losing the three of them was bad enough. If you'd lingered, we might've lost you guys too."

Frank closed his eyes and shook his head. Parker, Christian, and Brian…gone, just like that. Already the first whispers of blame were echoing through his head. He shoved them aside, forcing himself to focus on keeping the rest of the crew alive. "Thanks guys. I know it was tough. At least now we've got enough food for a few more days. Kevin says that the winds should diminish overnight. I expect McMurdo will send another chopper as soon as they can fly. How's Henrik doing?"

"Doc's got him quarantined with the rest. Not sure why he went down there with us. He must've been feeling it already, by the time we headed down."

"He's a good man."

Henrik was the most recent of those topside who had gotten sick. He'd collapsed in the CSC almost as soon as Tom's team got back from their foray into the warehouse.

"There's one more thing," Tom said hesitantly.

Frank nodded for him to continue.

"We got a pretty cold reception from the headquarters guys in the hangar when we came back through. Not surprising, I guess. But I got the feeling…actually *we all* got the feeling that they were hiding something. And Peter here saw something."

"That's right," Peter said. "These guys were on us from the moment we came back through the blast door. They kept their distance but did their damn best to corral us through the hangar as quickly as they could. Pretty clear that they were doing something that they didn't want us to see. Well, I'm not one hundred percent sure but," Peter shifted uncomfortably on his feet as he paused.

Viktor approached him, "Peter, what did you see? We need to know what we're up against."

"Well, as we were making our way through the hangar I caught a reflection in the helicopter canopy. I could be wrong but it looked to me like they'd removed some of the Halon bottles from the main equipment room. I'm pretty sure I saw at least five cylinders standing against the wall *outside* of the equipment locker."

"Halon? The firefighting stuff? I thought that stuff was banned years ago."

"It was," Frank replied. "Our fire suppression system was installed decades ago and they never updated it. Too costly and inconvenient, given our location."

"Why the hell would they deliberately disable the fire suppression system?" Tom asked. "You think they're planning on torching the warehouse to kill this thing off?"

"No," Frank replied. "That would destroy their prize. An alien spacecraft isn't something that you find every day."

Viktor cursed in Norwegian, "They replacing the Halon with something else…some other gas."

Frank nodded. "It's the only thing that makes sense. They've got a gas or chemical agent of some kind that will kill the creature while leaving the spacecraft intact."

"Why wouldn't they just tell us then, if that's their plan?" Tom asked.

"Probably cuz we've still got men down there," Peter suggested. "They probably figure we'd fight 'em to save our guys."

"I don't think that's it," Viktor said quietly.

"No. At least, it's not the *only* reason," Frank agreed.

"What?!" Tom asked, perplexed and annoyed that he hadn't reached the same conclusion that the others clearly already had.

Frank stroked his chin, "It all adds up. They disconnected the security cameras in the hangar so we can't see what they're doing. They installed deadbolts on the doors so that they can only be opened from inside the hangar. Dick seems intent on keeping us away from what's left of their helicopter…probably wants to keep us from seeing what they brought in here with them. Hell, we weren't even informed of their inbound flight."

"They're also doing everything they can to keep their crew from mingling with ours," Viktor chimed in. "Minimizes the risk of them getting infected and allows them to remain cold and aloof…prevents them from seeing us as human beings."

"Right."

"What the hell are you guys talking about?!" Tom shouted.

Frank inhaled deeply, exhaling slowly and deliberately. "They're going to gas the place. They don't intend to let any of us make it out of here alive."

TWENTY-EIGHT

"How you feeling, Hil?"

Hildy sat up in her cot and smiled weakly. "I'm doing ok," she replied as Charlie sat down beside her.

"You sure had me worried." Charlie brushed Hildy's bangs from her face with the back of her hand. She grabbed a brush from the makeshift nightstand and started fussing with Hildy's hair.

"Yeah, well…Armand's fixing me up," Hildy replied. "The drugs seem to be doing their job. At least I'm not cramping anymore. He gave me something to help me sleep too but," she paused and sighed, "I haven't done much of that."

"Me either."

"You want to talk about it?" Charlie asked, hesitantly.

"Not at all," Hildy immediately replied.

Charlie exhaled with obvious relief, "Good. Me either…"

They sat in silence. It was the same throughout the camp. Those who had witnessed the events in the warehouse during their escape were still trying to deal with the reality of what they'd seen. They kept mostly to themselves, in no mood to talk. Unfortunately, those who *hadn't* been there were intensely curious and pressed them incessantly for details. They resented the fact that the warehouse survivors were reluctant to share information that could be crucial to their own survival. The tension in the air between the two groups was palpable.

"So, Brian knows about the baby now, huh? How'd that go?"

Hildy smiled. "Better than I'd hoped."

"I'm glad." Charlie caressed Hildy's arm. "I know you were really worried."

"I told him I was leaving. I'm sure of that more than ever now." Hildy buried her face in her hands. "My God! That thing! It's so….horrible!"

Charlie swallowed hard as she struggled for something to say. She tried to drive the images from her mind but they wouldn't leave.

"I can't believe he went back down there!" Hildy shouted angrily. "What the hell is he thinking?! He's always got to get involved! Why didn't he just let the others go?"

"Calm down, Hil! Brian didn't go down there out of morbid curiosity. He went down there because he had to. He's really worried about you! And, there weren't exactly a ton of volunteers, you know."

"I know," Hildy said quietly, tears running down her cheeks. "I'm just…so afraid."

"We all are. But we'll get through this. We'll get out of here soon," Charlie said, trying her best to sound reassuring. "There's supposed to be a break in the weather by this time tomorrow. I'm sure they'll get a helicopter out here right away. And you'll be the first one on it." Charlie nudged Hildy with her elbow, "I plan on being right there beside you."

Hildy smiled wanly and then broke into tears. Charlie hugged her for a moment, fighting back her own.

After several minutes, Charlie backed away and grabbed a box of tissue. She dabbed her eyes and extended the box to Hildy.

"Ok," she said firmly, "Pity party is over." She stood and walked over to the other side of the bed where a dinner tray lay atop the counter, its contents untouched.

"What have we got here?
"Soup, I think," Hildy replied. "Anders brought it in about an hour ago."

"Let's get this heated up for you," Charlie said, grabbing the tray.

Hildy started to protest but thought better of it as Charlie shot her a stern look.

Charlie placed the bowl in the microwave, closed the door, and began pressing buttons.

"You'll feel better with some hot soup in you. In fact," she said, punching the last button with flair, "I'll share it with you, if that's alright."

Charlie rolled a small table next to the bed as the microwave hummed behind her.

"Crackers?" she asked.

The two jumped at the sound of a loud bang nearby. Charlie turned just in time to see the microwave oven leap up several inches from the countertop and slam back down with another loud bang. A blackish red lump inside the oven slammed into the glass and slid to the bottom of the door leaving a slimy, bloody residue on the pane. The messy lump leapt against the glass pane again screeching in a shrill, high-pitched tone.

Hildy screamed and leapt from her cot. Charlie grabbed her by the arm and hurried her toward the door. The microwave continued to bump and jerk as whatever was inside it thrashed about wildly. It flailed violently and with increasing desperation as the electromagnetic energy cooked its cells. Finally, the oven slipped over the edge of the countertop. It hung there by its cord as the spasms of the dying creature began to ebb, its flesh sputtering and snapping like bacon on a hot griddle.

Unable to avert her eyes from the spectacle, Charlie tripped over a metal chair and fell to the floor, dragging Hildy with her. Both women screamed as they scrambled to their feet and hurried to the exit. They tripped over each other again at the threshold and spilled out into the hallway, nearly colliding with a couple of crewmen that were hurrying over.

"What the hell is going on?!" one of them asked.

"Good God! What is that awful smell?" the other man asked, burying his face in his jacket sleeve.

Armand forced his way into the room between the two men just as the electrical cord slipped free from the outlet. The microwave crashed to the floor and landed squarely on its front rupturing its faceplate. Black sooty smoke seeped from the seams around the door.

One of the men rushed into the room toward the shattered appliance and bent down to pick it up.

"Don't touch it!"

The man stopped and stared at Armand, unsure of himself.

"Quickly! Back away from it!"

The man did as he was told.

"What's going on, Doc?" Brent panted, winded by his sprint.

Armand pointed to the battered microwave, "Burn it."

Brent hesitated for just a moment then fired a blast.

They watched in silence as the microwave burned. A minute later, Brent approached the charred shell, flipped it onto its back with his boot, and shot another short burst directly inside.

Finally, Armand directed them to extinguish the flames. They carefully poked and prodded at it, searching for evidence that any part of the organism had survived.

Several men were milling about now, drawn by a mix of curiosity and anxiety. No one spoke.

Viktor forced his way through the small crowd and entered the room. He quickly surveyed the scene. "What the hell is going on?"

Armand swallowed hard, "We need to get everyone together and accounted for," he said nervously, not taking his eyes off of the charred hulk on the floor. "Somehow, the organism has made it topside."

≈ O ≈

The fear in the room was palpable as each member of the crew struggled to understand what Frank had just told them all.

One crewman finally cleared his throat and rose from his seat. "So, you're saying that this thing can shrink itself? That it can become small enough to fit into a microwave or a shoebox?"

Another crewman swore loudly. "No, you idiot! He's saying that someone deliberately mixed some of its cells in the food."

The first man's eyes widened as he realized the implications. "But, that means that someone up here is infected," he stammered nervously as he slowly backed himself away from those nearest him.

"That's right," Frank replied tersely.

"How the hell did it get *up here*?!" a third man cried out apprehensively.

A quiet murmur surged through the room as many of the crew mumbled expletives or pleaded quietly to the Almighty.

Frank held up his hands to quiet them. "Listen! We all need to be calm. Doc has a test that can detect the organism. If it's hiding among us, we'll soon know it…and we'll deal with it.

Viktor approached Frank and handed him an electronic clipboard. Frank grabbed it and scanned it quickly. "We're instituting a few rules for everybody's safety, until we get a better handle on the situation."

The crew listened as Frank outlined the rules. Once everyone was verified 'clean', they'd be assigned to six-man teams. They were to stay within certain areas of the topside compound at all times, avoiding other areas completely. Any work or movement about the facility was to be done in groups of three and only when required. Nobody was to go anywhere alone. They were to eat only canned food and must prepare their meals themselves.

The mood in the room grew more somber as each rule was announced.

When he finished speaking, Frank approached Armand.

"Ready when you are, Doc," he said confidently.

Armand nodded and pricked Frank's finger with a lancet, drawing blood.

He dropped the lancet into a clear pouch along with a small ampule, stripped the paper backing from the adhesive, and pinched the bag shut.

"The ampule in this pouch," he said, holding it up for everyone to see, "contains a gas that will immediately react with the organism, changing any infected blood from bright red to a light purple. The gas will also immediately kill the organism, if it's present, so there's no danger. Normal human blood won't be affected by the gas in any visible way."

"I am going to be escorted outside by these two gentlemen," Frank said, nodding toward two guards as he moved toward the far end of the room. The crowd parted like the Red Sea as he passed by. He pretended not to notice the anxiety on their faces and feigned indifference to their obvious reluctance to touch him. But he was surprised by the depth of their distrust. It was unsettling to think that people he'd lived and worked with for years would suddenly be holding him at arm's length. Still, it was important to set an example so he buried his unease.

He paused at the door leading to the outside and flipped his hood up. "Only if Viktor here indicates that my blood is not infected," he said calmly, "will they allow me back in." Frank exited quickly before any of the crew could ask him the obvious, "*What if his blood is infected?*" He didn't know how to tell them about the two men already stationed outside with flamethrowers.

Armand waited until Frank and the two guards were outside, then he crushed the ampule with a pair of pliers. He shook the pouch mildly and held it up for everyone to see.

"No change," he said. A collective sigh filled the room as every man visibly relaxed, at least for the moment.

Viktor gestured for the men waiting outside to return. "Guess I should be next," he said as Frank removed his parka just inside the doorway.

"No," Frank said tersely. "Anders will be next."

"What? Why me?"

"Because you were the one who brought the food in to Hildy."

"But I wasn't the only one in the kitchen," Anders protested.

"What's your problem, Anders? You got something to hide?" a crewman chided.

"Screw you, Irwin! I didn't do shit!" Anders continued to protest but was drowned out by the shouts of the others. He balled his fists and took several steps toward Irwin. Those in his path scrambled to get out of his way and the room fell silent, even Irwin – as big as he was. He swallowed hard and blinked rapidly, clearly anxious about having any contact with Anders.

Anders stared at the crew for a moment then relaxed his fists and took a step back. "I suppose if I were in your shoes," he said quietly, "I wouldn't trust me either."

Anders turned and slowly approached Armand. "You'll soon see that I have nothing to hide." The guards stood just a few feet away, tense and ready. Only the crinkling of plastic sheeting as Armand unwrapped the next ampule broke the strained silence.

Armand pricked Ander's finger quickly and backed away.

"Outside," one of the guards ordered tersely.

Anders turned slowly and exited the building, followed closely by both guards.

Armand regarded the small package for a moment before delicately snapping the ampule within it. He tried to act nonchalant about it, as he had with Frank's sample, but his apprehension got the better of him. He held the small bag aloft, using the pliers this time rather than his hand, and exhaled loudly in relief when there was no reaction. Everyone else in the room did the same.

Frank signaled the all-clear and the two guards allowed Anders back in.

"Wait a minute. How do we know this works for sure?" someone asked from across the room.

The entire group shifted uncomfortably, many clearly doubtful. Half the crew were murmuring quietly to themselves.

"It's been tested," Armand replied.

"On what?" Irwin asked suspiciously. "The creature was completely destroyed in '93, at least…that's what they *told* us."

"Yeah. And how the hell can Anders be 'clean' when he's obviously the one who handled the food?!" another shouted.

"Now wait a minute, you piece of shit! Doc's test says I'm clear! So, you can just…"

"Knock it off," Frank shouted.

"Really? What makes you so sure this test works, Frank?" Irwin demanded, shouting to overcome the protests of the others.

"I told you…it's been tested," Armand yelled back.

"This is bullsh…"

"It's true. I know because I helped to develop it."

Everyone turned to look at Robert, who, until then, had been sulking quietly near the door.

"It works. I swear it." Robert quickly approached Armand and held out his hand. He turned toward the door, holding a piece of gauze over his fingertip, and marched outside.

Armand snapped the ampule and observed the result, clearing them to return.

Robert crossed the room to where Anders was standing.

"I'm not a brave man. I know it. Hell, you all know it," Robert said, sheepishly. "This thing scares the shit out of me." He gestured toward Armand and the small table set up beside him, "But I know *this* works," he said confidently, removing the glove from his hand, "…or I wouldn't do *this*." He seized Anders' bare hand and began pumping it emphatically.

Anders returned the handshake, hesitantly at first but then with growing confidence.

The room was silent for a moment. Then, one crewman wordlessly rose from his seat and cautiously approached Armand, his hand outstretched. He strode outside to await his fate.

Another crewman stepped up as soon as the previous man had gone outside. Others followed suit. It wasn't long before the rest of the men had formed a line.

"Well done," Frank said privately to Robert after the last of the men had been processed. "I'm not gonna lie, I was getting pretty nervous. Thought I was going to have to start threatening, if they didn't come around."

Robert smiled faintly, "Glad I could help."

Frank looked around the room. The crew seemed much more relaxed now that they'd all tested 'clean'. They milled about, some even chatting quietly, as they awaited their team assignments from Viktor. "Well, I'm sure your confidence in the test is justified," he said.

"I have no doubt at all about it," Robert replied.

"Good. Thanks again." Frank smacked Robert on the shoulder and headed for the exit.

Frank smiled as he moved toward the door. It was barely discernable and lasted for the briefest of moments, but it was there. There hadn't been many occasions since they'd been forced topside for him to give a crewman a kudo of any sort. Experience had taught him long ago that it was essential to maintaining an effective team. But it wasn't long before that other thought – the one that had been plaguing him since they'd finished testing the crew – moved again to the forefront.

None of the crew had tested 'positive' for infection. While everyone was profoundly relieved, the fact remained that *somebody* topside had infected Hildy's food. Once the rest of the crew realized this, the apprehension and mistrust would return, probably worse than before.

He'd been in situations like that before. It never turned out well.

TWENTY-NINE

Random images flashed rapidly through his mind. Memories, many long since forgotten or suppressed, surged forward, flashing by at lightning speed. Some lingered at the forefront of his mind while others whizzed by in the background. Each passed with exceptional clarity as though he'd just experienced them.

His mind was simultaneously flooded with sensations as the scents, sounds, tastes, and textures he'd experienced with every recollection replayed at hyper speed. Yet, despite the overwhelming volume of data, it took no effort at all to reconnect each sensory input with the appropriate experience.

Brian found himself analyzing each occurrence as they whirred by, seeing each as individual happenings while also placing them into the proper context. He delved further into each event than he'd ever done before, asking himself questions that hadn't occurred to him when he'd originally lived it. It was like he had two brains, one to recall his life's experiences and another to analyze, probe, and ponder their hidden, deeper meanings.

The projector in his mind seemed to slow down as events became more recent, the newer images lingering longer. Hildy was suddenly center stage, turning slowly to face him. As she lifted her face from the eyepiece of a microscope, her red, shoulder-length hair swayed slowly and bounced as she turned her head.

Older visions continued to run in the background but Hildy's translucent figure dominated as she walked slowly toward him. Suddenly, she was in the cafeteria seated across from him. She threw her head back as she laughed. Her hair was longer now and bounced more slowly as if gravity had temporarily lightened its hold on her. Then she was lying beside him in bed while the soft light of a candle behind her cast a warm, golden glow over her naked body.

He had his hands on her stomach now, feeling for movement from the fetus that was still too small and fragile to provide it. Hildy cried softly as the strain of keeping her secret finally evaporated.

The image of Hildy disappeared, replaced by a view of the research site from the air – the first time Brian had ever seen it as he flew in from McMurdo. All other visions disappeared as the site took center stage. He scrutinized every inch of the facility, recalling its capabilities, its crew, and its quirks. The image seemed to linger longer at the hangar and the level of scrutiny seemed far more detailed. He spent a lot of time reviewing the aircraft and recalling flights that he'd taken – how the aircraft responded to various conditions.

For the first time since the show began, something felt odd. He'd always loved flying but it was weird that this, of all things, should so prominently occupy the last moments of his life. The same was true of the garage and the Trac Crawlers.

Then, as suddenly as it began, the imagery ceased.

"*So, I'm dead*," Brian thought with a strange sense of detachment. Yet, a dull ache in his left eye and a soreness in his throat refuted the idea. He hadn't exactly been a religious fellow, but even he knew that pain and suffering weren't supposed to exist in death.

He fought to get his bearings. A tiny bright light suddenly pierced the darkness, growing rapidly in size until it filled his vision.

Fresh imagery flashed by just as his own memories had a moment ago. But these images were new and unfamiliar. They were also more focused and defined and lacked the sensory input that had accompanied the previous visions.

He saw a large foreign world from a vantage point high above. The planet was massive and quite beautiful, its oceans glowing a brilliant emerald green from phosphorescing algae where the waters met the shore. The green faded as the oceans grew deeper further from shore until the center of each large body of water was a shimmering gray, as if someone had punched large holes into the planet's surface.

Six similar-sized moons orbited the planet in three distinct orbital planes. The surface of two of the satellites flickered with concentrations of unnatural lighting, marking the numerous colonies that had been established there.

They were the Shem and these were *their* worlds.

The appearance of the planet changed abruptly, the new image showing a darker, less vibrant world. A prolonged war with a neighboring species had damaged their planet, rendering much of its soil incapable of supporting the microorganisms required for sustained healthy agriculture. Their world could no longer support them.

Once they'd repelled the invaders and the plight of their people was realized, thousands of vessels were dispatched to search the cosmos for the elements they needed to cure their world. To abandoning it in search of another was unthinkable.

There were twelve in their crew. This one was called 'Arkt'. Their vessel was designated Femar 9, the ninth of twelve such vessels sent to this part of the galaxy.

They slept. For countless eons they slept, waking only when the machinery of their craft identified a planet that contained the precious mineral and organic resources they sought.

They'd discovered it on a world orbiting a star not far from our own sun, gleaming blue algae that grew prolifically along the walls of the deep, shaded canyons. Where the organism existed, the local vegetation thrived. Trees along the rim of the canyons burrowed roots over thirty bikti to reach it. Brian somehow understood the measurement to equate to almost 60 yards. Trees that succeeded in tapping into the algae grew thicker and far taller than those that failed, leaving the latter looking stunted and bare in comparison.

It was clear almost immediately that its properties could revive the ecology of their home. Within days, they'd confirmed it. Introducing the algae into samples of sterilized soil from their home world quickly rejuvenated it, allowing it to sustain vegetation. Seeds that they'd brought with them germinated four times faster than normal. For the first time in a very long time, they harvested and dined on fresh fruits and vegetables.

They'd been on their way to rendezvous with another of their vessels when it happened. One of their crew, an Ancient One named Darqu Hab, expired suddenly. They'd known his death was coming…they all knew the signs.

There was usually plenty of time, two to three cycles, to prepare for the inevitable once the symptoms began to manifest themselves. For it to strike him down in less than a full cycle – two and a half earth months – was exceedingly rare. To the Shem, it was also devastating.

Darqu Hab had not completed the preparations for the Barquii Fal – the 'Passing of the Mind' – the process through which he would impart selected knowledge to a brother.

The departing one, known as the Gnom or 'Benefactor', spent much of his time during his final cycles in a coma-like trance, sifting through the repository of his mind. He'd select and prioritize the knowledge that he wished to pass on and cordon off the trivial. His mind must be perfectly ordered to ensure that only the most important wisdom, that which would most benefit their species, would be transferred. He would use every last ounce of his strength to keep the data properly channeled – to keep his mind from straying in the least from the task at hand.

He'd relay as much as he could before he passed. There was never time for a full transfer and the process could be interrupted at any time once his strength was sapped.

As his last days drew near, highly sensitive nerves at the tips of his fingers would swell and secrete a substance causing the surrounding skin and flesh to molt. Once physically prepared, the ceremony would commence immediately.

The Gnom would gently probe the eyes of the Ben Him Hist – the Inheritor – with the exposed nerves of his fingertips and secrete another substance to dissolve the eye tissue and expose the optic nerve. The exposed nerves of the two brothers would merge, allowing the Gnom to rapidly transmit his knowledge.

The Barquii Fal was a physically demanding process that resulted in the death of the Gnom within minutes. But it allowed their species to advance rapidly by ensuring that key current and ancient knowledge was retained – knowledge that the Ben Him Hist could further advance through his own lifetime.

The inheritor would spend almost twenty cycles – four earth years – in seclusion, digesting this newfound knowledge and assimilating it with his own as he waited for his new eyes to grow. Once he emerged, his fresh eyes, now glossy and completely black, marked him as a Lum Ha Niq – an 'Ancient One', a position of high honor.

Lum Ha Niq Darqu Hab had perished too quickly, taking his knowledge to the grave with him. The wisdom of a thousand years – intelligence he had formed during his own lifetime as well as that which he'd inherited half his life ago as a Ben Him Hist – was gone forever. The Shem considered this to be the worst of tragedies.

But Darqu Hab's untimely death brought with it a second, equally terrible disaster.

For, as his body fell suddenly lifeless to the deck of the vessel and his knowledge began to evaporate, the sample of the miracle algae that he had been placing into the Life Vault fell from his hands. It was one of thousands of samples that they'd collected along their journey – the DNA and chloroplasts of animal and plant life scattered throughout the galaxy – to be replicated back home for further study. These were frozen and stored within a specialized chamber, like a cosmic ark.

As Darqu Hab collapsed, the algae spilled and mixed with other specimens. The heat generated by its intense cellular activity was enough to thaw several of the tiny samples.

The first mutations grew at an astonishing rate, rapidly overflowing their receptacles and mingling with others on the next lowest shelf. The unique chemical composition of the algae's microorganisms broke down the natural barriers that separated each of the specimens into discrete plant and animal species. Plant and animal matter mixed unnaturally, forming a single living mass.

The extreme rate of mitosis and the abnormal mixture of cellular proteins altered the DNA of the various samples fusing then into a single helix. The result of the newly created DNA was a completely new living organism.

The organism's creation would probably have been nothing more than a scientific curiosity were it not for one unfortunate coincidence. One of the samples taken aboard years ago contained a virus. It wasn't a particularly virulent germ on its home planet and had barely affected the indigenous species. Consequently, it had escaped detection by the Shem as they'd processed the sample for storage.

But as it became a part of the uniquely assembled DNA, several of the virus' previously suppressed traits were activated. It became extremely aggressive and highly tenacious.

The first member of the crew to inadvertently stumble upon the new organism as she rushed to Darqu Hab's aid was quickly infected. The virus spread through her body, mindlessly replicating, feeding, and assimilating.

It happened when it reached her brain.

As it absorbed the flesh of her cerebrum, the replicant cells seamlessly took over, assuming their form and function. Some replicants began serving as synapses, the conduit through which her brain's electrical impulses fired.

As in all living creatures, some of these impulses supplied the energy that caused muscles to contract or relax facilitating movement and manual dexterity. Others directed the operation of her various internal systems, those responsible for the beating of her heart, respiration, and digestion. Still others stored and transferred the knowledge that she'd accumulated through her years. They comprised her memories… her emotions… her instincts. The virus assimilated these too.

And as it did, it learned and understood. It became self-aware.

They called it Ishtaq – '*Doom*'.

Other members of their crew became infected. When their instruments detected the small blue planet along their path, a world clearly teeming with life, the replicant Shem recognized an opportunity. Here they could reproduce and thrive among millions of organisms. They attempted to land.

But those unaffected by the virus fought them. They understood the stakes. Too late, they tried to disable their vessel. But too many had been infected and the healthy were overcome. The remaining few uninfected Shem ejected.

They'd planned to regroup on the planet's surface to destroy the organism. But their hasty departure from the main vessel just moments before impact had left them no time for calculated flight. The barren, frozen wasteland upon which they'd landed had sealed their fate. In the harsh cold environment, there was nothing more they could do.

The thoughts and images faded and Brian found himself wrapped in a pleasant warmth.

The sensation to breathe returned suddenly. He gagged and coughed as the Shem retracted the probe from his throat – a thin, flexible rod that had been regulating his breathing and heart rate while the two of them were 'connected'. His vision remained blurred in one eye while the other had no vision at all. Somehow, he understood that it would remain that way for the rest of his life...and he was ok with that.

Despite the fuzziness, Brian became suddenly aware of Arkt's presence. The Shem held him aloft, firmly but gently, one huge arm wrapped around his torso as one of its smaller forearms supported his back.

His head suddenly exploded in pain. He arched his head back in agony as the creature disconnected itself from his optic nerve. Arkt probed his face softly, gently massaging and secreting a thin film of an oily substance. The secretion acted as a local anesthetic, relieving the pain and pressure in his damaged eye.

The Shem withdrew its hand in a quick fluid motion, opening its palm wide and splaying it out just inches from Brian's face as the larger arm gently set him down. The much smaller bluish hand quickly withdrew behind the thick veil of the biosuit leaving no trace of an opening.

With his one good eye, Brian could just make out the muddled green-blue-gray of Arkt's biosuit just inches from his own. Its skin seemed to flow, shifting fluidly into various random patterns like spilled oil displaying its colors on the surface of a tranquil pond. It was actually quite soothing. It was also very impressive once he remembered that he was looking at an artificial implement. The biosuit was, in reality, an oversized extension of the creature inside…a spacesuit – a protective, highly dexterous shell that provided the spacefarer inside with an atmosphere and personalized habitat.

They stood for a few seconds regarding each other. Neither was afraid. Each now knew the other was not infected and posed no threat.

Parker's flesh snapped and popped grotesquely as the flames continued to burn. The floor and ceiling tiles were blackened but the fire hadn't really spread. Brian glanced at the clock and was shocked to learn that his interaction with the Shem had taken less than a minute. He absentmindedly raised the extinguisher and smothered the flames, only vaguely concerned with preventing the whole place from burning up.

Brian's mind still buzzed with the flurry of activity. He was exhilarated by the knowledge he'd suddenly gained and struggled to process the incredible amount of data.

Arkt had initiated the Barquii Fal without any preparation, leaving him no time to pre-select the knowledge he would impart. As a consequence, Brian had received data covering a wide variety of topics – some highly technical and scientific and some personal and private. He froze and concentrated intently on trying to remember it all, afraid that any movement would shatter his concentration and he'd lose everything.

He was surprised to see that they were now in the main corridor standing between the wrecked cargo elevator and the access door to the overhead crane. He'd been so intent on retaining the information he'd inherited that he'd made the short trek mechanically, blindly following Arkt's lead.

As they'd walked, he'd been analysing various bits of data, focusing primarily on the Shem's scientific achievements. Some of them he understood right away while others would clearly require more effort to comprehend. Some of it he was sure he would never understand.

But the data was there and he could impart it to those who could make sense of it. He looked forward to that.

A loud clanking and the whir of an electric engine jarred him back to the present. Arkt had set the overhead crane in motion, moving it toward them along its track from its previous location directly over the vessel's hatch.

Brian knew instinctively that the Shem was intent on entering the spacecraft. He didn't know exactly what Arkt planned to do but something compelled him to help the Shem even as he somehow understood that neither of them was likely to survive.

THIRTY

Richard rammed the magazine into his assault rifle. He pulled back the charging handle and released it, allowing it to spring forward to chamber a round.

"Go time, gentlemen. Let's get this done so we can get the hell out of here."

"Works for me. The sooner we're gone from this place, the better." Chavez surveyed the hangar suspiciously, "If this thing is even half as nasty as they said it is, I'd like to put some serious distance between me and it."

"We're all set in here," Scott said. "Stilson and I will prep the gas so we can start releasing it as soon as you get back."

Richard craned his neck toward the helicopter, "Don't forget to get the pre-heaters going. I want to get that thing up in the air as soon as the gas is in full flow."

"He's working on it already." Scott gestured toward the rear of the helicopter where one of the team was connecting a piece of ground support equipment to the helicopter.

Richard nodded in satisfaction. "We shouldn't be long. Frank will have most of the crew assembled in the conference room. I told him I wanted to fill everyone in on what we were doing. The six of us will take care of the main body. Chavez and Pruit will take care of any stragglers. Once we're sure that we've gotten everyone, we'll do a sweep of the facility and completely douse it with chlorine." He tapped one of the chemical grenades hanging from his belt. Each man in the team had several hung from their own equipment.

"I'll rig a timer on the closest bottle. Five minutes after we fly out, it'll start filling the hangar and warehouse. That should do it."

Richard scanned the group quickly. His men were ready.

"Let's go"

≈ O ≈

They moved like professional soldiers down the narrow hallway, fast and quiet. Richard scanned the ceiling for cameras. He didn't really expect to see any as they'd only been installed in the main operations areas. Still, the distrust between his team and the site's normal crew ran deep so wouldn't be surprised to see that they'd installed some.

They bunched up behind the door to the CSC, ready to pour into the room as soon as it was opened. The men up front carried silenced pistols so they wouldn't alert the rest of the crew when they took out those on duty in the command center. One of the forward men slid a fiber optic cable beneath the door and scanned the CSC, watching the video on a small wrist-mounted display. He used hand signals to inform his team that there were two men seated at the console directly in front of them. He saw no-one else.

Richard gave the signal and the man closest to the door turned the knob slowly. The door opened silently. The first of the men quietly surged into the room and fired two shots each. The men seated at the console lurched forward and fell to the floor as the rest of the team fanned out inside the room, looking for others. In just seconds, they'd secured the room.

Chavez signaled to Richard, pointing toward one of the monitors on the console. On the screen, Frank was addressing the crew in the conference room.

Richard signaled for Chavez and Pruit to remain in the CSC as he moved the rest of the team toward the far end of the room. The conference room would be just down the hallway.

≈ O ≈

As they approached the conference room, they could hear Frank addressing the group on the other side of the door. Just passed it, on the opposite side of the hallway, was another door.

Richard knew that this was where the sick crew members were being quarantined. They'd be easy pickings once his team had dispensed with the bulk of the healthy crew. The only uncertainty was the pregnant girl. They didn't have good intel on where she was being kept so they'd have to track her down.

Richard cringed inwardly. What a shame to kill such a pretty girl. But as quickly as the thought crept in, Richard pushed it out. The only way to complete this nasty task was to not think of the victims as people.

Richard was pleasantly surprised to see that the entrance to the conference room was through a double door. Somehow, the site's blueprints hadn't reflected that. "*That's just fine*," he smirked. They'd be able to infiltrate the room twice as fast, with that big, wide opening.

Frank's voice continued to drone on. Richard paused and listened. Frank was updating the crew on their food situation and commending those that had risked their lives by returning to the warehouse to get it. "Things finally seem to be looking up," he remarked.

"*How ironic that he would say that just now,*" Richard thought wryly as he tapped the magazine inserted into his rifle.

He took a deep breath and gave a terse nod. The assault team lunged through the door as he hung back. As he fell into place behind the last man, he was troubled by the fact that he heard no gunfire. Most of the site's crew were armed so he'd directed his men to start the massacre as soon as they were inside to prevent any of them from returning fire. As soon as they were inside he understood why they hadn't.

The stunned men gawked in confusion at the empty room as Frank's voice boomed from an overhead speaker, still urging the imaginary audience to cooperate fully with the team from headquarters. A second later, something metallic clattered across the floor behind them in the hall. They recognized the sound immediately and dove for cover just as the concussion grenade exploded with a deafening roar.

The men rose quickly and assessed their surroundings.

"Drop your weapons and *do not* exit the room."

Frank was addressing Richard's crew now from the overhead speaker. One of Richard's team braced himself against the door frame and glanced into the hall, peering down the barrel of his rifle. His body suddenly jerked and twitched as several rounds, fired from somewhere down the hallway, found their mark. The man's weapon clattered to the floor as he spilled back into the room, blood oozing from a wound just below his eye. He twisted and fell dead at the feet of one of his comrades.

"Don't be stupid, gentlemen. There is only one way out of the room and we've got it covered from every angle.

Richard's teammates eyed each other frantically, each weighing their options.

"You will not get a second chance," Frank warned.

Richard seethed, realizing that they'd been duped. His mind raced as he quickly organized a plan to rally his team for a fight. But his crew had already made up their minds and he could only watch as they placed their weapons on the floor.

≈ o ≈

"That was too close." Viktor hoisted one of the captured assault rifles and looked it over.

"Yeah, no shit. It's a damn good thing that we realized their intentions when we did."

Frank was studying one of the grenades that Richard's men had been carrying, "These aren't fragmentation. Chemical?"

Viktor just shrugged.

"Let's go find out."

Anders approached them as they entered the CSC. "We had to take out one of them but we got this one." One of Richard's men was kneeling of the floor, his hands tied behind him.

"What do you want to do about these two?" Anders asked, pointing with the muzzle of his rifle toward the two dead crewmen on the floor at the foot of the console.

"Sure wish we hadn't had to use them like this," Frank said, shaking his head sadly.

"Our deception might not have worked if we hadn't," Viktor replied. "They fooled Dick's team, just as we'd hoped. I think that they would be glad to know that their deaths helped the rest of us to survive."

"I know. It just seems sacrilegious, using their bodies for something like this." He gazed sadly down at their former teammates. They had actually died hours ago, having succumbed to the meningitis. Still, he felt guilty about having used them as bait. It somehow made him feel like they'd just died again.

"Wrap them up and put them outside."

"Where are you going?" Viktor asked, as Frank turned to leave.

"To get some answers."

THIRTY-ONE

The chair hit the wall and shattered, forcing Anders to duck to avoid being hit by debris. The crash resounded through the room and echoed down the hallway as though warning everyone else to stay away.

"Is that supposed to scare me?"

Frank glared down at Richard, who sat on the floor, his back to the wall. Despite having his hands fastened behind his back, he sneered defiantly at Frank, who hovered over him with clenched fists. Pruit sat beside him in a similar pose but looking much more anxious.

"Oh, I'm not looking to *scare* you, Dick…" Frank replied with unconcealed contempt.

Frank reached behind with one hand and grasped the end of a chair leg that had become imbedded in the drywall. He jerked it free and flipped it in the air, grasping the lower part of the leg as it came around. He sized up the piece of wood, tapping the thicker part in his other hand repeatedly like a ball player making his way to the batter's box.

Richard scoffed and spat, the mixture of blood and spittle spattering on the floor inches from Frank's boot. "Come on, Frank. You know this *had* to happen! *You* know it better than *anyone*!"

Richard suddenly arched his back and fell to one side as the blunt end of the Frank's club slammed into the side of his knee. He screamed hoarsely as he rolled around on the floor, his face contorted in pain.

"Screw you!" Frank stood there glowering, pointing the makeshift club at his victim like a gladiator wielding a mace. In a flash, he lifted it across his chest and brought it down again sharply against Richard's shin inciting fresh screams of torment.

Pruit gasped, his eyes wide with fear as Frank moved toward him. "You'd better start talking."

The frightened man nodded quickly, suddenly eager to cooperate.

Anders removed the gag from Pruit's mouth.

Pruit coughed nervously, "Can I get some water?"

Anders put a water bottle to Pruit's lips and let him drink.

Pruit was trembling and breathing heavily. "Please," he pleaded, "we were just following orders."

"What orders?" Frank seethed.

Pruit blinked rapidly, "It was supposed to be quick. We were supposed to be in and out of here in just a couple of hours. But then we crashed…and the damn bottles…" Pruit rambled incoherently as he pleaded with his eyes for help from the others in the room.

Frank swore, "You piece of shit." He poked Pruit hard on the forehead with the end of his club, knocking his head back into the wall.

Pruit cried out nervously and glanced over at Richard, who was still writhing on the floor in pain and clasping his bruised leg.

"What did you expect, Frank?"

Frank slowly turned to look at Richard, who had managed to pull himself up into a semi-sitting position. He squinted as a bead of sweat dripped from his forehead into his eye.

"You know damn well that we've got to do whatever it takes to prevent this thing from making it out of here," Richard half-groaned.

"Yeah?! Well, what about us, huh?! What about those of us who *aren't* contaminated?!"

Richard eyed Anders for a moment and grunted as he leaned against the wall for support. "How do you know you're not?" He paused, letting the question hang in the air. "The point is, there really is no way to be sure."

Anders scoffed. "Doc's tested us all. Everyone was clean."

Richard shook his head and chuckled derisively, "You think you're all 'clean' because you conducted a blood test?! We had tests at Dunford too. Daily at first. Started doing them at the end of every shift following the first accident. They all said that we were clean too. And then one day, somebody wasn't."

Richard coughed, wincing at the pain that it caused in his wounded knee. He glared at Frank, "We still have no idea how or when it happened."

Richard shifted again, trying to find a comfortable position for his battered leg. "We've had three close calls already. This is a fire that we cannot afford to play with."

The room was silent after Richard finished. Finally, Viktor cleared his throat, "What close calls?"

Richard eyed him contemptuously then shifted his gaze to the floor. "The first was obviously in '93…when the advanced team was attacked. We were lucky then that the scientific team that followed them recognized the nature of the threat and managed to destroy it. Of course, they all had to die to do it. But if any of them had made it out then we probably wouldn't be having this conversation right now."

"The second?"

Richard scowled, "Go screw yourself! I'm done wasting my time."

"When we first brought a sample to Dunford," Pruit blurted out. "Even with forewarning, they underestimated the organism. Cost three of our scientists their lives. We got lucky then too. One of them couldn't sleep that night…decided to go in early. She came in just in time to see the last stages of the…transformation. That was bad enough…but it happened in the clean room, *after* they'd already been tested. If she'd shown up just 15 minutes later, we would've let three replicants leave the facility."

Pruit studied the faces of the men surrounding him, anticipating their question. He averted his eyes and sighed, "We burned them."

"Of course, you did!" Anders swore and slammed the butt of his rifle onto the floor.

"The last accident was just three years ago…again at Dunford," Pruit continued, unfazed by Anders' outburst. He spoke more quietly, as though he'd resigned himself to fate. "This one really scared them. They decided that every trace of this organism needed to be destroyed."

Pruit looked directly at Frank then quickly averted his eyes, "The wiped out the entire facility"

Frank stepped back involuntarily, a look of shock on his face. Viktor quickly inserted himself between Frank and the captives, trying not to be too obvious about it. But Frank didn't seem to notice. He stood silently, digesting this new tidbit.

Viktor could only imagine what was going through Frank's mind at this moment. Three years after Sarah's death he was still struggling to come to terms with having lost her in such a terrible accident. To learn now that it wasn't an accident…that she'd been *deliberately* eliminated…

Frank stood motionless and rigid, his arms stiffly at his side. Viktor watched him closely, his body tense and ready to spring into action at the first hint that Frank was going for his pistol. He couldn't blame the guy. He'd probably do the same thing if he were in his shoes.

Finally, Frank relaxed and stepped around Viktor. "Were you there for that too, *Dick*?"

"I was not," Richard answered dryly. "But if I had been, I would've made the very same decision."

Frank looked at Richard contemptuously, "I'll never get assholes like you…so little regard for the value of human life."

"That's *all* I think about! You still don't seem to grasp what the hell it is you're dealing with," he shouted. "I've seen it! I've watched it rip apart a living creature and take its place!"

Richard suddenly lowered his voice and peered at his antagonists, "You see it just one time," Richard scoffed, "…and you never again look at any living thing the same way."

Anders sneered, "So that justifies killing innocent people just to…"

"Yes," Richard shouted angrily. "Yes, it does!!"

Richard coughed and spat on the floor, a mixture of blood and sputum. "Every cell of this organism is a complete entity, fully capable of invading and replicating on its own. If just a few cells make it out of here…" He looked up slowly, locking his gaze on Anders. "Apocalypse. The end of the world."

"Well that's a bit of a stretch," Anders said derisively.

"Not at all! Think about it, you moron! This thing infects just one of you here and remains undetected...? All it has to do it then is contaminate the water supply to infect the rest. An infected man could infect a hundred more just on the plane ride home. A few million cells, a single drop of blood, is enough to initiate the process. Hell, he doesn't even have to touch anyone. He simply walks into the bathroom on the plane and smears some blood on the door handle or the toilet flushing button. The process would take a little longer with such a small number of cells but, so what? Eventually, it *would* happen.

And once the infected are back among the general population, there'd be no stopping it. In less than a year, the entire planet would be contaminated…every living thing."

Frank glared back at him, too numb to speak. The rest of the crew remained silent, contemplating the implications of what they'd just heard. Several of them looked around suspiciously, suddenly unsure of their comrades.

"Yes," Richard uttered quietly, sensing their unease. "I think now you're beginning to see why they weren't going to take any chances."

THIRTY-TWO

Viktor paused just outside the door to the make-shift cafeteria, resting his head against the wall. He was so damn tired. It was really beginning to cloud his judgement and that concerned him. And he knew he wasn't the only one with impaired judgement.

He lifted his head and listened. There was no muted din of conversation from the other side of the door. The crew had grown detached, each distancing themselves from the others as a pervasive distrust poisoned the atmosphere.

He opened the door and entered the room, striding across the floor with far more confidence than he actually felt. The half-dozen or so crewmen scattered about the room watched him warily until they were sure that he wasn't approaching them.

"How you doing, Doc?"

Armand looked up and pursed his lips but said nothing.

"Any change in Hildy?" Viktor asked, switching tactics. He had come in to gauge Armand's frame of mind but that wasn't going to happen if the guy wouldn't talk. He knew that the only way to get him to talk would be to get him to focus on someone else.

"No. Still won't eat or drink anything. She needs a magnesium sulfate drip but she sure as hell won't let me shoot her up. Won't even let Charlie do it, and they've been together the whole time. Her symptoms are getting worse. There's a real danger of preeclampsia if we don't do something about it soon."

They watched quietly as a crewman entered the room and grabbed a can of stew from a stack on a nearby table. He surveyed the room then moved to one side where another man was sitting alone and sat down at the opposite side of the table.

The second man rose and gruffly grabbed his things. "What the hell, Ed…you couldn't just go sit over there?" he asked angrily pointing to another area of the room.

"I have as much right to sit here as you do," Edgar replied just as testily.

They briefly traded verbal jabs and cusses, eyeing each other angrily from across the table. "Just stay the hell away from me," the first man finally yelled as he moved to an isolated corner. None of the others in the room interfered. They just watched silently from their places and went back to their own business once the altercation had played itself out.

"It's like that all over," Viktor sighed.

"It's quite sad," Armand said softly, watching the others. "They need each other more than ever right now." He raised a canteen partway to his mouth and stopped, peering into its mouth. "Can't say that I blame them," he said, placing the canteen on the table without taking a drink.

"I know. I'd kill for a whiskey right now."

Edgar suddenly cursed loudly and slammed the can onto the table, sending his metal spoon flying across the floor. Blood seeped from a small cut on his finger, courtesy of the can's sharp metal lid. He stuck his finger in his mouth, murmuring a continuous string of obscenities.

Armand regarded Viktor, who silently stared back. "You know, it's not that I'm afraid to die. Hell, I figure I deserve to, leaving those men alone down there. If I'd have known what we were in for, I would've stayed…would've casually given them an injection…help them to go peacefully. I only hope they succumbed before *it* realized that they were there."

You can't blame yourself, Doc. You did what you had to. You saved Hildy and Charlie."

"Saved them?! For what?! I think I've only postponed the inevitable."

Armand had raised his voice and some of the crew had overheard. Two of them got up and left the room.

"I'm sorry," Armand said, softening his tone. "But I have never been so afraid of something in all my life. Not for me…but for them…for everyone."

Viktor could think of nothing to say. He watched absentmindedly as Edgar retrieved his spoon and began to eat straight from the can, a scowl on his face. Although there was a microwave on a nearby table, most of the crew ate their meals this way. Since Hildy's close call, nobody trusted the device anymore. They couldn't seem to accept that the microwave had actually been responsible for *revealing* the organism hidden in her food. In less stressful times, the irony of it would be comical.

Viktor inched closer to Armand, "Doc, you know more about this damn thing than anyone else out here. What are we missing? What else can we be doing?"

Armand looked at him somberly, "If it were up to me, I'd drop a nuke on this place…a very big one."

"Is it really *that* dangerous?"

"Yes."

They sat in silence for a moment, observing the men in the room.

"Vik," Armand resumed, speaking slowly and deliberately. "I think it's quite possible that, despite our best efforts to prevent it, one or more of the crew may be infected."

Viktor's jaw dropped and his eyes widened in surprise.

Armand nodded in affirmation. "If what Richard said is true, then it somehow found a way to reproduce and spread itself at Dunford despite all their precautions. We don't have nearly the same level of precautions out here."

Viktor nodded gravely. "What do you know about this thing?" after a moment of contemplation.

"You sure you want to know?"

Viktor nodded.

Armand sighed, “Well…it’s like Richard said…every single cell of this organism is a distinct creature all its own. On their own, each responds to only the most basic of stimuli…the need to survive. And this thing has one hell of a survival instinct. Like a virus, the alien cells ultimately need a host and they’ll quite actively seek one out. That’s when the really scary shit begins.”

Armand paused, waiting for a response from Viktor.

“Go on,” Viktor whispered.

Armand nodded, “The reproductive capabilities of these cells are far beyond anything here on earth. You see, once they’ve latched onto a host cell they undergo an extreme form of mitosis, spawning as many as six *additional* alien cells. Just before the original cell penetrates the host cell’s outer membrane the spawned cells disperse to seek other hosts. The process is incredibly fast. You start with ten million cells – that’s about the amount contained in a single drop of human blood – and in less than a minute there are over sixty million. A minute more…360 million. The rate increases exponentially until all host cells have been replicated. In just a few hours, this small sample can replicate all 100 trillion cells in a typical man. A fully replicated human, carrying trillions of replicated cells, can transfer them to a host at a much greater rate, assimilating another man in as little as 15 or 20 minutes.”

“It’s…uh, difficult to comprehend.”

“Yeah, well, get this...once this thing takes over a host, it not only gains its physical capabilities but its cerebral and mechanical abilities as well.”

“It starts to think?”

Armand raised his eyebrows, “Much more than that. It inherits the cumulative knowledge and skills of its hosts.”

“Um…you’ve lost me.”

"OK. Say some of these cells are lapped up by a house fly. Each alien cell will do what it does, individually invading and conquering a cell from the fly until the whole thing has been physically replicated. But this organism doesn't just take over the fly's appearance. It also inherits the fly's knowledge, experiences, and instincts. In this particular instance, the organism would have ended up inside a host offering very limited capabilities, except for the greatly improved mobility. The replicant fly would be no smarter or more capable than any other fly.

Now, if this replicant lands on and infects some unlucky sanitation truck driver, then the whole process starts all over again. Only this time, the alien cells will ultimately inherit the unfortunate man's knowledge, skills, and experience while retaining what it learned from the fly. When the truck driver assimilates *his* next victim, say a biologist or a nuclear physicist, *this* replicant will possess the knowledge, skills, and experiences of all three. The cells of the alien organism will learn and pass it on."

"Holy shit," Viktor murmured.

"More like 'unholy shit'. It's awe inspiring and terrifying at the same time."

They sat in silence for a moment. Finally, Viktor cleared his throat, "If what you've said is true, and one of us *is* infected, the replicant will want a pilot."

"Unless it's already one of our pilots that's been infected," Armand whispered.

A loud clatter startled everyone in the room as Edgar dropped his food and utensils. He knocked over his chair as he rose hastily, grasping at his throat and coughing. "My throat…on fire." he said haltingly.

Armand approached him quickly but stopped a few feet away as the man recoiled, afraid of him. "It's alright, Edgar" Armand said, raising his hands. "I just want to take a look at you."

Edgar hesitated, torn between the need for aid and the desire to keep away from everyone else. Finally, he relented.

Armand moved in and removed a penlight from his pocket. "Open your mouth."

Edgar swallowed hard, wincing at the pain, then opened wide.

Gooseflesh erupted all over Armand's body at the unfamiliar sight. Several black shiny patches covered the man's mouth and the back of his throat. They glistened and writhed energetically like miniature ant colonies, each swarming beneath a thin black membrane. As he watched, the patches spread, slowly yet discernibly.

Armand stepped back involuntarily as Edgar gagged and coughed. "Help me," he pleaded desperately, falling to his knees.

Armand turned to Viktor, "Get security in here right now!"

Viktor was already barking instructions to someone over his cell phone.

Without warning, the beleaguered crewman lunged forward. Armand jumped back to avoid him, knocking over a table and chair. Edgar latched onto Viktor, wrapping his arms around his waist. Viktor dropped his phone and yelled, twisting and turning violently in an effort to shake free from the man's grasp. He fell backward onto the floor when the crewman unexpectedly released his grip.

Armand grabbed Viktor by his arm and helped him to his feet. Together, they sprang for the door.

They stopped at the threshold when it was clear that Edgar wasn't pursuing them. The terrified man knelt on the floor, pleading for help with his eyes as black splotches began to appear on his face and lips. As if sensing his impending doom, Edgar put a pistol to his head and pulled the trigger.

The sudden silence of the room following the gunshot was almost as deafening as the blast of the weapon. Viktor opened his mouth wide and stretched his jaw in an attempt to clear his ears. The pistol now lay on the floor just a few feet away. Viktor recognized it immediately as his own. Edgar must have stripped it from him during their brief scuffle.

"How the hell did it infect him?! He was eating from a freshly opened can! We both saw him open it!"

"I don't know." Armand contemplated the can on the floor, its contents scattered all over. If Edgar had become infected in the short period of time since he'd entered the room, then this organism was capable of spreading far more rapidly and with less critical mass than he'd previously thought. If he was infected already before he entered the room, then an undetected replicant was freely roaming the facility. He didn't know which was worse.

"I don't know," he repeated, "But they'd better not wait too long to drop that nuke."

THIRTY-THREE

"So, you're sure that he wasn't a complete replicant?"

"I've looked into a lot of mouths in thirty years. I'm positive, Frank," Armand asserted. "I actually saw the infection spreading through his flesh in that one brief moment, right before my eyes."

"I didn't see into his mouth, but there was no mistaking the moment it hit him." Viktor said equally as assertive.

Frank closed his eyes and grimaced. Every minute during the last two days seemed to bring a fresh harbinger of doom and he was running out of ideas for handling each new crisis.

There was a light knock on the door, which opened before anyone could respond. Kelly entered the room and uttered a monosyllabic greeting as he headed in Frank's direction. He handed him a clipboard, "I briefed Pamela and Geoffrey. They aren't too happy about it but they'll be ready to go when you're ready to send us. I'm still not sure it's a good idea though."

Frank held up his hand, "Hold on a sec, Kel."

Kelly grimaced, realizing that he'd interrupted something. "Sorry," he muttered. "You want me to wait outside?"

Frank hesitated for a moment then shook his head, "No, its ok. Just give us a minute to finish up here."

Viktor and Armand glanced at each other uncertainly as Kelly moved toward the back of the room. Viktor finally shrugged as he reluctantly accepted Kelly's presence in the room. He'd have preferred to keep this conversation limited to just Frank, Armand, and himself. But the rest of the crew would soon learn about it anyway.

"Frank, the crew's begun to unravel. I mean, seriously unravel. Everyone is absolutely paranoid. I've given up on trying to get any of them to work together. They're all keeping to themselves. Hell, they're even afraid to eat or drink anything now. For the first time in my life, I'm not sure what to do." Viktor shrugged and shook his head sheepishly.

Frank turned to Armand.

"Don't look at me. I'm about out of ideas too," Armand said. "This is about as extreme a situation as you can get. No psych textbook I've ever read even *begins* to touch upon this level of paranoia."

"You know, everyone is carrying at least one firearm now. With so much stress and distrust, I think it's only a matter of time before someone gets shot."

"I know, Vik. But we can't very well take them away. Having a means to protect themselves is about the only source of comfort these guys have anymore."

"I have to agree, much as I hate to," Armand chimed in. "You take them away now and you remove the only hope they have. Besides, the only way you'd get them to surrender them now is by directly threatening them at gunpoint. That would ignite a serious firestorm."

"Okay. Right now, we've got the crew bunked in several different areas. That's not working. We can't expect them to trust each other when they've got no idea where the others have been or what they've been up to."

"So, we consolidate?" Viktor asked.

"Yes. We move everybody into the hangar…give them the means to keep tabs on each other and hopefully start rebuilding some level of trust. Doc, you have any more testing kits?"

"Not nearly enough."

"What if we tested people in batches…say three or four blood samples at one time?"

"Could work. Only…if there were a reaction, we wouldn't know which of the subjects was the infected one. We'd also have to test at least six samples at a time. There just aren't enough testing kits to handle less than that."

"Wait a second," Viktor exclaimed. "Doc, you mentioned something before about the organism's incredible reproduction rate. Wouldn't that manifest itself somehow?"

"Well, at the cellular level…certainly. But I don't know how that would be evident on the surface."

"What about body heat? Could a replicant's body temperature be higher than normal?"

"I suppose. But how would we distinguish that from a fever caused by the meningitis?"

"You think someone up here is infected?" Kelly asked, injecting himself into the conversation.

Frank sighed, "Its, um…possible."

"Well if you're looking for a way to detect it, I would suggest a blood test."

Armand coughed, "Yes, well I was just telling them that we don't have enough…"

"I heard," Kelly interrupted. "I'm not talking about using the chemical detection kits. I'm thinking something a little more crude."

"What have you got in mind?" Frank asked.

They listened quietly as Kelly recalled what he'd seen in the warehouse just prior to their rescue. He detailed how the pools of blood and bits of alien flesh had behaved, moving along the platform to assemble themselves into a larger creature. He described how the fragments tried to escape from the flames once Spence had ignited the fuel.

Frank and Viktor looked at him in disbelief.

"It's absolutely true. I saw it too," Armand said quietly. "Happened exactly as he says."

"Seems to me that if we drew a blood sample from an infected person and subjected it to a threat – a searing hot metal rod perhaps – it would behave the same way…try to 'protect' itself."

"I have a better idea," Kelly asserted. "One that I know the crew would buy into. One that *everyone here at this site* knows will surely work."

They listened intently as Kelly detailed the plan.

"You think it would work?" Viktor asked Armand.

"I think it would. I saw it, too…again, exactly as Kelly described it. I think he's right!" Armand seemed to grow more certain of the plan's success with each statement.

"It's simple and seems foolproof," Frank agreed. "OK! We give it a try."

"I could test it first on a sample taken from Edgar. He's been dead less than half an hour so there should still be cellular activity. If it works, we could do the rest of the testing in the hangar. Let everybody see. I think that would go a long way to restoring at least *some* trust." Armand paced as he spoke, clearly glad to have something to work with.

"Once that's done, we limit the crew to the hangar and the CSC. We'll have to keep that manned to keep tabs on things below in the warehouse and to maintain contact with Seattle. We'll assign four-man crews."

The mood in the small room lightened considerably now that they'd developed a workable plan.

"So, it seems there's just one more crisis that needs to be handled."

Armand and Frank looked at each other curiously as Viktor reached into his pocket. He held aloft the small plastic case that usually stored his flavored toothpicks, shaking it vigorously. "I'm out."

For the first time in over a week, they laughed.

≈ O ≈

Frank leaned against the bulkhead in the hangar and watched as the last of the group was tested. It seemed the entire crew was just as eager to re-establish some level of normalcy after days of constant and acute stress. Most had actually been eager to participate and clear themselves from suspicion, although there were initially some holdouts. These, too, ultimately saw the wisdom of the test and finally joined in.

Those that had already been tested stood in small groups, each nursing a small cut. Their guard was still up but they were at least mingling now. Even Hildy seemed less anxious, although she was still refusing to allow Armand to set an IV in her arm for the magnesium sulfate drip. But she was at least taking in fluids again, now that the crew had begun melting then boiling snow in the hangar to provide them with sterilized drinking water.

Frank smirked. One of the guards had just provided a gallon of water to Richard and his men, who remained locked inside the equipment room. He derived a great deal of satisfaction from the irony that Richard's men were now confined to the very room from which they'd tried not so long ago to implement their plan.

Frank felt some of the tension drain from his neck, marvelling at how simple the test was and the positive impact it was already having on the crew's morale.

It was simple really. Each man provided a blood sample, collected in a small plastic container, by slicing the tip of a finger. Doc let them do this themselves, if they preferred, to alleviate any concerns – however unfounded – about being infected during the process. The sample was placed into the microwave, which was then run for several seconds to cause the expected reaction by any tainted cells. No reaction meant no infection. Of course, the converse was also true.

The beauty of it was that there was no doubt the test would work. They'd all witnessed it not so long ago when someone had tried to infect Hildy by tainting her soup. Any infected crew members would soon be exposed.

In fact, Edgar's tainted blood *had* reacted. The organism had thrashed about wildly, throwing the container around inside the microwave oven as its cells began to cook. It had taken less than ten seconds to get the reaction. They'd removed the container with a set of long tongs and taken it outside to be destroyed.

They'd demonstrated this to the crew prior to beginning the test, using another sample of blood from Edgar, to bolster their confidence in it. After that, most cooperated willingly.

Each crewman was isolated in an open area just outside the hangar as his or her blood was being tested. Two guards were prepared to immediately torch anyone who tested positive. Those cleared by the test were segregated at one end of the hangar until all testing was completed. With each attempt, the crew collectively held their breath as the microwave began to hum, exhaling in unison after several seconds when no reaction was noted.

Armand strode over, "Okay, that it. That's the last one."

"Thanks, Doc. Why don't you try to get some rest?"

"That's my plan." Armand said wearily.

"Have you seen Anders?"

Armand frowned, "Not since we started getting the test together. Why?"

"But you tested him, right?"

Armand furrowed his brow, "You know, I don't really remember..."

Frank shook his head, "I don't remember seeing him go through."

Armand held up his own bandaged finger. "Should be easy enough to tell."

"Right. Go get some rest."

Frank watched as Armand made his way across the hangar. He noticed that about half of the crew seemed more relaxed as they mingled and chatted lightly. The others seemed less certain but still appeared much less stressed. The signs were subtle but they were there. For many, it was simply that their faces were no longer so taut – their expressions less tense. Only Robert seemed to have separated himself from the rest, standing quietly by the main hangar door. Frank made a mental note to check on him later.

He didn't know whether to be troubled or relieved that the test had cleared all of the crew. Not identifying a replicant further deepened the mystery of how Edgar's food had become contaminated. But there was nothing more that could be done right now. At least the test results had made the challenge of re-integrating the crew a lot less daunting.

Frank gave them another moment. Now that they were all verified as 'clean', he wanted to go over some new rules that would hopefully ensure that they remained so. But he knew instinctively that they needed this moment to 'heal'. The coming days were sure to present more challenges as they waited for a rescue that might never come. It was going to be more important than ever that they operate as a team.

THIRTY-FOUR

"Is it true, about Anders?"

Viktor stared at Richard through the large open window of the equipment shed door. A guard stood nearby, making sure that Richard's team stayed put within their makeshift cell and that none of the regular site crew tried to get in to exact revenge.

"Yeah, it's true."

"You can't keep us locked up in here," Richard insisted. "We've got no weapons and no place to retreat to. If that thing shows up, we're sitting ducks."

"Sorry, Richard. I let you out of there and these guys will tear your men to shreds. They're still plenty pissed, although I can't for the life of me understand why," Viktor said, his voice dripping with sarcasm.

"Be sensible, Viktor. You can contain us in the damn helicopter if you want, but you *have* to give us a chance."

"Like the chance *you* gave *us*?" Viktor regretted it the instant he said it. He caught the smirk on the guard's face as he lingered nearby. The man had obviously heard him.

Viktor had been working to get the crew to accept Richard's team, now that they were in the same boat. But the crew wasn't having it. Many of the men were still pissed that they'd been marked for execution and had no intention of letting it go. Now Viktor's own words belied the fact that he felt the same way, despite his efforts at reconciliation. Unfortunately, keeping them locked up was still the best course of action.

"Vik, we just lost Sun Ah. Kevin's taken a turn for the worst too."

Viktor clenched his teeth wondering why Armand had chosen this very moment to blurt this out. He wanted so badly just to scream and strike someone. It wasn't so much Armand's poor timing. This was just another small fracture in the dam. But things just kept going from bad to worse. He was extremely tired and supremely edgy.

Armand closed his eyes and drooped his head, waiting for Viktor to reply. Viktor felt the steam evaporate from him as he realized how tired Armand was too. In addition to the rest of this crap, the doctor was doing his best to treat the sick with no medicine and prevent the meningitis from spreading. It was an impossible task.

"I'll be right there, Doc."

Armand nodded and returned to his sole remaining patient.

"You see, Dick," Viktor said sarcastically, "It could be worse. At least in here you won't get sick."

Richard glared at him through the window.

≈ o ≈

Sun Ah had been wrapped in a blanket and Viktor instructed two men to carry her body outside. Cholsu was weeping quietly and mumbling in Korean as he gently rocked back and forth on his heels. Hildy was trying to comfort him but he seemed oblivious to her.

Kevin's face was pale as he shivered under the blankets. Viktor wanted to go over and say something encouraging to the guy but was afraid to risk it. He couldn't afford to get sick.

"Doc, you gotta try and get some rest. You've got just the one patient now. Let Charlie handle him for a while."

"I'm afraid I've got two patients." Armand said.

Viktor swore in Norwegian then crinkled his brow curiously. Kevin was the only obvious patient that he could see. Sun Ah's recently occupied cot lay empty just a few feet away. "Where's..."

Armand's pale face revealed the answer even before Viktor could finish the question.

"Oh, no, Doc. Not you too."

≈ O ≈

Kelly kept glancing nervously behind as they snaked their way through the compound. Pamela walked in front of him, her whole body visibly shaking with fright. He couldn't blame her…they hadn't been able to locate Anders and two other crewmen for several hours, which didn't bode well.

"I'm right behind you," he kept repeating softly, hoping she'd be reassured by the sound of his voice. After the third or fourth time, she slowly turned around.

"I'm ok. Honest."

"OK," Kelly replied. He was impressed. She was obviously scared shitless. But, to her credit, she was forcing herself ahead. Kevin, the site's primary meteorologist, had fallen ill this morning. With him incapacitated by meningitis, she was the only one who knew how to translate the complicated weather data.

Viktor had sent this small team to the tower to get a better idea as to when the weather should be clearing up. Based on their original estimates, the winds should diminish significantly within the next two or three hours.

He would normally have preferred to wait until they'd located the missing men but the rest of the crew was getting anxious. Most of them had nothing to do, giving them way too much time to focus on their situation. A bit of good news, no matter how insignificant, would get them to focus on something positive and would do much to boost their spirits.

Kelly had thought it was not worth the risk and initially fought Viktor. But Viktor finally persuaded him to make the quick trip. Perhaps it *would* be good to have something positive to focus on. But now that they were on their way, he was beginning to reconsider.

Pamela still held her left arm in a sling from the gash that she'd received some days ago down in the warehouse. Kelly smirked at the thought of Doc assuming a Kung Fu stance and lashing out at Pamela, fearing he, Charlie, and Hildy were under attack.

Pamela had actually been damn lucky. Under the same circumstances, Kelly knew that *he* wouldn't have held back. If it had been him rather than Doc wielding the knife, Pamela wouldn't be alive right now…and *he* would be a murderer.

Two days ago, it would have been unthinkable. But now… The smirk faded from his face as quickly as it had come.

Kelly stiffened as there appeared to be a commotion up ahead. A moment later, he relaxed as he realized that it was just Geoffrey pausing at the stairway at the base of the Met tower, giving the others a chance to catch up. He held the nozzle of his flame unit to one side away from the others, like a trained marksman. The hissing of the unit's pilot light seemed way louder now in the quiet of the empty facility.

"You guys good?"

"Yeah. Let's do this," Kelly replied.

Pamela just nodded as she absentmindedly rubbed her sore shoulder.

Geoffrey opened the door and peered up the staircase. "C'mon."

They slowly filed into the tower, Geoffrey in the lead and Kelly in the rear. The window that had been shattered during the helicopter crash had been covered with plywood. It stopped the wind but it was a poor insulator. A thick layer of frost had accumulated all around it and the air in the tower was icy cold.

"Where do you want us to start?" Geoffrey asked, as he scanned the various consoles scattered about the room.

Kelly stood at the top of the stairs waiting for instructions but Pamela said nothing.

"Pam?" he prodded.

On the other side of the room, Geoffrey peered out the tower window as windblown snow whizzed by below.

Kelly took a few steps into the room. Pamela had neither moved nor spoken in the few seconds since she'd entered the tower. Her head was cocked to one side slightly as though listening to something. Kelly stopped and strained to hear. Despite the howling of the wind outside, he could just hear a faint crackling, popping sound. It had a distinctly wet quality to it, like the sound a large cricket would make being crushed under foot – magnified hundreds of times. He cocked his head from side to side trying to locate its origin.

Pamela suddenly swung around and leapt at him, hitting him in the face with a giant crab-like claw that now existed where her right arm used to be.

≈ O ≈

Brent closed his eyes and rolled his head, trying to stretch the tension from his neck. He frowned at the thought that he was only half an hour into his shift.

The CSC was quiet. The other guys on watch with him were wandering the room, checking equipment. They'd all been 'cleared' by the test but still preferred to keep their distance from one another.

The monitors glowed and flickered as the security cameras continually scanned various sectors of the complex. But there hadn't been anything interesting to see in days.

He closed his eyes and imagined a fresh, hot cup of coffee. God, he'd kill for one. Although coffee was available, he didn't dare drink any. He was too afraid of what else might be in it.

He opened his eyes at the thought and shivered involuntarily. Like everyone else, he was doing his best to not think of the creature. He stared at the ceiling for several seconds, cursing fate for bringing him here. The pay, which had previously seemed too good to be true, was suddenly no longer so appealing.

His eyes scanned the displays. Nothing. Every camera angle depicted the same damn thing as it had for the last forty-eight hours or so. The crew appeared to be relaxing casually in the hangar…well…as casually as they could under the circumstances. The various topside corridors were all empty. Nothing was happening inside the warehouse. Even the monitor showing the vessels interior showed no signs of activity.

Brent suddenly bolted upright. He peered intently at the last monitor. Until now, the vessels interior hadn't been displayed on any of the screens. Something inside had activated the motion sensors.

His heart pounded in his chest as he scrutinized the monitor, looking for any movement. He reached for the phone on the desktop without removing his gaze from the monitor.

The phone rang and rang. Brent slammed the phone into its cradle in irritation then dialed another number.

"I'm not sure what, but something's happening," he said urgently. "You'd better get in here right away, sir!"

He hung up and stared at the monitor intently as he waited for Frank to arrive. He would know what to do.

THIRTY-FIVE

They stared at the monitor in awe. By the time they'd arrived in the CSC from the hangar, the creature was frantically whipping about below in the vessel's bridge. It was amazing how gracefully it moved for such a large beast. Its multiple arms executed different tasks in coordinated, synchronized movements. Each motion flowed into the next, as though it were thinking several steps ahead as it scurried about the cabin.

They watched it for several minutes as it raced about the bridge, opening crevices and compartments that they never even knew existed.

Frank swore and slammed his fist onto the console.

"How are we going to stop it?" Viktor asked.

Frank watched as the beast silently removed several damaged tellurium nodes. In a flash, it inspected them and tossed them aside then disappeared for several minutes.

Frank buried his face in his hands as he thought. He suddenly dropped them to his side revealing a look of grim determination.

"Vik…you stay here and keep me posted," he instructed. "Johan, you…"

He looked around the CSC, "Where the hell is Johan?"

Brent stood up, "I dunno, sir. He never answered his office phone. Tried him several times before I finally called you."

Frank cursed. He'd already lost Anders…he couldn't afford to lose another Security Chief.

"Track him down and get him in here."

Brent nodded and frantically began dialing.

"Where the hell are you going?"

Frank paused and looked Viktor in the eye, "Maybe Dick had it right all along."

"Sir, look!"

Brent was standing and pointing urgently to the monitor.

They didn't see him at first. He stood just outside the range of the camera.

The creature returned carrying several tellurium nodes. It scampered about replacing the damaged ones that it had removed. It wasn't until it had almost completed its task that they saw him.

They looked at each other for confirmation, each hoping that they weren't seeing what was clearly evident on the monitor. But there was no denying it.

Brian stood next to the creature, operating the ship's equipment as adroitly as if he'd been one of the vessel's original crew. There was no obvious communication between the two but they were clearly operating to the same game plan.

Frank ran his fingers through his hair and sighed. Then he turned to leave.

"What's the plan Frank?"

Frank stopped and turned around. Viktor stood in front of the console looking perplexed.

Frank cringed inwardly. For the first time ever, he and Viktor did not appear to be on the same page. It should've come as no surprise, as tired as they all were. Nobody was operating on all cylinders anymore.

"We've got to make sure they can't escape. We can't let them…" Frank paused, searching for the words. "We've got to destroy them. If that organism makes it out of here…"

Viktor nodded, finally grasping Frank's meaning. He reached for his cell phone, "I'll keep you informed."

Frank nodded and turned to leave. He'd taken only a couple of steps when he paused again and turned around.

He walked quickly over to Viktor and placed his hand on Viktor's shoulder. "If I'm not back or you don't hear from me in the next fifteen minutes..."

Viktor quickly looked around the room and nodded his understanding.

They parted silently, Viktor watching until the door closed behind his friend.

The CSC was quiet as the other men in the room struggled to accept what they'd just witnessed. It was highly unnerving.

None of them had ever witnessed a more final goodbye.

≈ O ≈

Brian worked feverishly to replace the damaged tellurium nodes with those that Arkt had retrieved from other sections of the ship. He marveled at their design. They were technologically complex yet their construction was remarkably simple. He held one aloft and studied it.

Like a microchip, it outer casing revealed nothing of the maze of circuitry inside. But he could clearly see a schematic of the device in his mind. He was amazed and somewhat embarrassed actually that the scientists on his own world hadn't been able to figure them out.

He closed the lid of the recessed compartment and pressed several touch-sensitive switches in rapid succession. He knew the ship now almost as well as any other member of the Shem crew. He could hear the faint hum of the component behind the compartment door and see its faint glow through the thin metal construction. Once he'd verified that it looked and sounded normal he moved on to the next one.

He still didn't fully grasp Arkt's plan but he trusted the Shem. He knew from the brief glimpse that Arkt had given him into his mind that the Shem's intentions were honourable and unselfish.

He knew that Arkt, too, greatly feared the Ishtaq organism and was determined to wipe out the monstrosity before it caused irreparable harm to the planet. Arkt understood that failure to prevent its spread on this planet ultimately put other planets at risk, especially if the Shem spacecraft remained intact. Arkt was ashamed of the fact that the Shem were responsible for its creation, even if it was accidental, and was determined to stop it at all costs

Arkt was working near the center of the room, his multiple arms gracefully manipulating nodes and tools with such speed and agility that Brian found himself wishing that he, too, had four hands. Arkt suddenly stepped back and the shimmering column that they'd seen during their test several days ago reappeared. But it seemed fuzzier now. As if reading Brian's mind, Arkt touched a couple of the tiles and the column became clear and bright. The lighting along the walls grew brighter too vastly improving the visibility on the bridge.

Arkt scanned the room quickly then strode over to the far wall. He reached up and touched an overhead section and a seamless door melted away, revealing a concealed compartment. The space within it was dark and Brian knew that its nodes were no longer operational. He also knew that they'd stripped the nodes already from all the unnecessary systems. There were no more to be had.

Then he remembered that *that* wasn't quite true.

Brian touched Arkt's arm and the Shem turned to face him. He opened his mouth to speak then realized that this wouldn't work. He might be able to understand Arkt's speech but his own vocal chords weren't designed to make many of the sounds needed for Shem language. As he searched for a solution, he saw the computer and monitoring equipment that they'd set up to support their last experiment.

Brian quickly found a marker, tore a page from a reference manual, and began writing the strange characters of the Shem right over the typed English text. Arkt understood.

"How many?" Arkt uttered.

Brian started to write his response but Arkt touched his hand to stop him.

“Speak,” Arkt said in Shem.

Brian paused, confused. Surely Arkt would know that while he could understand Shem sounds, he wasn’t physiologically equipped to make many of them.

The realization struck him like a lightning bolt. The same would obviously be true of the Shem.

“They would be in one of the labs above us,” Brian said slowly in English.

Arkt seemed to ponder the situation for a moment. “You stay. I will go.”

Brian shook his head. “No,” he said firmly. “We stay together.”

Arkt hesitated then bowed slightly indicating his agreement.

“Wait,” Brian yelled. He sat at the computer and logged on.

“No time,” the Shem said.

“If I don’t tell them what we plan to do they might interfere.”

“Then do it quickly.”

Brian nodded and began typing commands furiously into the computer.

≈ O ≈

Viktor marveled at the sight of the Shem. The grace with which it moved seemed impossible given its size and build. Just as amazing was the fact that Brian and the alien creature were communicating in different languages – Brian speaking in English, Arkt in Shem – but seemed to be having no trouble understanding each other.

“I’m sorry. But I just can’t believe what you’re telling me.”

“I get it Viktor. I really do. I know I’ve been gone for a while but I’m telling you that I’m not one of those things. Neither is he,” Brian insisted, gesturing to Arkt.

"Look, you've seen what the Ishtaq can do. Do you really believe that such a monstrous organism would be capable of creating such a complex and wondrous spacecraft?"

"Ishtaq?"

"It's what the Shem call the organism. This craft is theirs. It belongs to the Shem. *They* built and piloted it…not that hideous, destructive organism."

Viktor sighed in exasperation. He badly wanted to believe Brian. But it was tough to accept that the creature hadn't found and replicated him down there. He'd been missing a long time. Anything could've happened.

The Shem spoke at length to Brian, who finally nodded and hung his head. Then he lifted his gaze and stared straight into the camera. "By now, you know that this creature is comprised of many parts…that each part of this organism can form a whole if it has to. Every part of this thing will fight to survive if threatened. We've all seen that, right?"

"Yes," Viktor admitted reluctantly. "Thanks for reminding me."

"Let's show them," Brian said to Arkt.

The Shem knelt as Brian stepped aside. The mid-section of Arkt's biosuit turned from black to light gray to pale green and a small light blue hand emerged from within. The biosuit formed a tight seal around Arkt's hand, which shimmered with a silvery metallic glow as Arkt held it out with his fingers extended.

"Ready?" Brian asked.

Arkt spoke, apparently indicating that he was.

Brian grabbed Arkt's outstretched hand and gently separated one finger from the rest as though preparing to remove a splinter from it. With a quick motion, he raised the heavy wire cutters that he'd retrieved from the tool bag and snipped. Arkt's three remaining fingers curled into a tight ball and his hand trembled violently as the severed digit fell to the floor but the Shem didn't make a sound. Brian picked it up and held it in front of the camera as Arkt retracted his hand into his biosuit.

"What the hell is he doing?" Brent shouted.

"If Arkt here is infected, then this," he said, holding Arkt's lifeless finger aloft in the jaws of the wire cutter, "…will react to this."

Brian lit a portable blowtorch and seared the finger for several seconds, rotating it to ensure every inch of it was burned. He dropped it onto a cleaning cloth once he had sufficiently demonstrated that there was no reaction, respectfully and gently rolling it into a tidy package.

Brian handed the tool to Arkt, who grabbed it with one of the biosuit's smaller forelimbs, and offered up his own hand. Brian yelled loudly as Arkt snipped off two of his fingers with a single snip. He grabbed a cloth from the workbench to bandage his hand as Arkt retrieved the fingers from the floor. Over the circuit, they could hear one of the men in the CSC gagging and cursing under his breath.

Arkt said something quietly. "Yeah, well I guess you have a higher tolerance for pain than I do," Brian shouted, shooting Arkt a dirty look.

He handed Arkt the lit torch and the Shem torched Brian's detached fingers. He quickly wrapped their charred remains in the same cloth that held his own former digit.

Brian grunted and groaned as he cradled his hand. "You know as well as I that if those body parts were imitations that they would have fought to survive. They'd have sprouted legs or tentacles or something and would've tried to get away. So, you know now that neither of us is one of those things. You've *got* to believe me."

Viktor stared at the screen still torn. It was a pretty convincing display for sure. Still, with all the freakiness that the organism had already demonstrated, he couldn't shake the lingering doubt that this wasn't just another of its tricks.

"Viktor, please!"

Viktor stared at Brian's image on the monitor. Beads of sweat ran down Brian's forehead and the pain of his injury shone clearly on his face. The urgency in his pleading also seemed very real. If this was a replicant…if the organism could copy a person this precisely, then they were screwed anyway.

Viktor snatched his cell phone and dialed, shoving aside his doubt.

Brian and Arkt watched him on the monitor. "You did not tell them the plan." Arkt said.

Brian edged closer to the Shem, "Because they'd try to stop us."

THIRTY-SIX

Frank watched as Richard's team connected the hoses that linked the cylinders of deadly gas to the Halon fire suppression system. There were still a number of crewmen missing and likely trapped below. The burden of command weighed heavily on him as he prepared to order the deaths of any survivors that might still be unharmed down there, even though it was unlikely that anyone could've evaded the creature after all this time.

A cloud of gloom descended upon the crew in the hangar. From their perspective, the timing of Frank's decision couldn't have been worse. The atmosphere in the hangar had been improving steadily since the blood test had cleared them all and they were beginning to gel again as a team. But as soon as Frank ordered the deadly cylinders moved back into the equipment shed his intention was obvious.

Hildy begged and pleaded with Frank to wait. She kept insisting that Brian would somehow find a way out. Frank didn't have the heart to tell her what they already knew…that the Brian she knew no longer existed. Her pleas grew more urgent as the last cylinder was put in place inside the shed.

As the clanging of the metal bottles died away, Hildy finally realized the futility of her words. She sobbed quietly as Charlie gently led her away to another part of the hangar.

Frank paused before entering the equipment shed. The entire crew had assembled to watch as Richard's team transported the cylinders inside. They were visibly upset and seemed to be waiting for an explanation.

Frank struggled for the words but they wouldn't come. "It must be done. I'm sorry," he said finally as he turned to enter the shed. It was all he could manage.

As he watched Pruit connect the last of the hose, he berated himself for his inability to be more sensitive to the crew's needs. They were scared for their own sakes and struggling to accept the impending execution of any comrades trapped below. But despite his desire to say something comforting, he was simply too fatigued from the events of the last week. Right now, it was taking all his will to carry out the plan that would end the lives of several of his crew, some perhaps unnecessarily.

Richard sat on a large tool bin staring at Frank as he caressed his injured leg. His gaze belied pity and understanding.

Frank stared back. He felt remorse now for having attacked and crippled Richard. He still thought that the man was a gigantic pile of dung. But Frank was also beginning to see things from Richard's perspective and was starting to question his own motives. Maybe fighting for their survival *was* the wrong thing to do, given the extraordinary abilities of the organism. Maybe it *would* be necessary for them to all die here to ensure the complete destruction of this thing.

Frank watched Richard interact with his men. The bastard's demeanor had softened somewhat since realizing that he and his men were also now expendable. Strangely, Richard's men seemed to understand and accept it. Maybe it was time for Frank's crew to do the same.

Pruit approached Frank. "That's it. Whenever you're ready."

Frank nodded. Again, he felt the need to say something to assuage his guilt and appease any troubled thoughts the team might be experiencing. But again, words failed him. There are apparently no 'right words' when sending others to their deaths or, more accurately, sending death to them.

There was no sense in dragging this out. "Go."

With a single syllable, he set the plan in motion.

≈ O ≈

Viktor swore and slammed his cell phone onto the desktop. "Why the hell isn't he answering?" he asked, irritated.

"The signal's always been spotty in the equipment shed. Too much electrical interference," Brent stated. "If he's in there, you might not reach him."

They glanced at the monitor but Brian and the Shem had already departed. They would be making their way to the lab now to recover the extra tellurium nodes they needed. They had seemed pretty damn certain that they could destroy the organism if they could get the vessel working. Viktor had his doubts. But he had to admit that he really knew nothing about the capabilities of the Shem or their vessel.

He rapidly calculated the odds. If Brian was right and the gas were released, then the organism within the warehouse would be destroyed. But that didn't eliminate the threat topside. Brian claimed that the Shem could kill the organism completely *throughout* the facility. It could be just a ploy to keep themselves alive but Viktor really didn't think so. The more he thought of their macabre display earlier, when they'd cut off an appendage to convince him that they weren't infected, the more he was convinced that they were telling the truth.

The conclusion hit him suddenly and forcefully. Brian and the Shem represented their best chance of killing off the organism completely. If they were asphyxiated by the chlorine, then the chances of keeping the thing contained were greatly diminished

Viktor sprang for the door. "You keep trying," he shouted as he sprinted down the hallway.

Brent picked up the phone and redialed as the door slammed behind Viktor.

Pruit moved from cylinder to cylinder opening each valve to start the flow of the gas. He had linked the six bottles in series feeding them into a single terminal line. It ended at the pump that was designed to discharge Halon into the warehouse in the event of a fire. With this setup, it would be extinguishing something else entirely.

Pruit moved to the final bottle. He paused as he placed his hand on the final valve that would introduce the chlorine gas into the system, sending it into the warehouse below. Frank nodded somberly for him to proceed.

Pruit opened the terminal valve. The gas hissed from the bottles, announcing that the flow had begun. In less than five minutes, the warehouse would be saturated with poison.

They listened in silence as the gas hissed through the lines. Frank half expected to smell the chlorine but there was no hint of it in the air up here.

He looked at his watch. It had been almost a minute since they'd started the flow. The gas should be visible on the monitors in the CSC…a white fog of death falling silently from the ceiling. He reached for his phone to call them for confirmation.

"Stop! Turn it off! Turn it off!" Viktor tripped as he burst through the door and sprawled out on the floor. He looked up urgently at Frank as he struggled to breath.

Frank immediately yelled for Pruit to close the valve as he rushed to aid Viktor. The man wouldn't be telling them to stop without a good reason.

Pruit looked at him uncertainly but closed the valve to stop the flow.

The hissing stopped.

"What's going on?" Richard asked, swinging his legs over the side of the chest.

They listened as Viktor quickly explained, then made their way to the CSC.

≈ O ≈

Robert watched in wonderment until the door closed behind Frank and Viktor, baffled by their decision. Releasing the gas would surely kill the damn creature in the warehouse. Doing so seemed like a no-brainer. Why wouldn't they want to eliminate the threat? Hadn't they cleared everyone up here? Didn't that mean that the creature below represented the last remaining danger?

He groaned as he remembered that this wasn't necessarily true. Nobody had been able to locate Anders since early this morning. It was rumored that one of the topside Norwegians was missing too, although Robert didn't know who it was. But there was just too much uncertainty now. Everyone was tired and it was difficult to keep things straight.

Robert sighed as he took a seat by the door, resting a rifle between his legs. This latest development was extremely troubling. Just when things had seemed to be looking up…

For the first time in quite a while, he had been actually feeling pretty good about himself. During one of their darkest moments, he'd been instrumental in getting the crew to accept the reliability of the test. For the first time in a very long time he'd felt a sense of purpose and gratification. He'd made a significant contribution not just to his own well-being but to that of the entire topside crew. Frank had even told him privately that he'd just saved the day.

He hadn't felt this good about himself since he'd perfected that bacteria in Seattle, the one that could break down the crude oil.

Earlier this morning, he'd been riding high. But subsequent events had soured his mood. Sun Ah's death from the meningitis, Doc getting sick, the ill-advised decision to stop releasing the gas into the warehouse… Uncertainty and paranoia had bubbled to the surface inside of him with renewed intensity.

The extreme contrasts of his moods, coupled with fatigue, was fraying his nerves. He began contemplating various ways to remove himself from this dreadful situation. After much deliberation, he finally decided. The more he honed the details of his plan, the more convinced he became that it was perfect. It was only a matter of timing now.

If they weren't going to be smart about this them screw them.

He stood and cracked open the door. He could just barely make out the dark shape of the helicopter under its tarp. He'd just need a pilot. And he already had the perfect one in mind.

THIRTY-SEVEN

They waited for several minutes, staring at the monitor. Brian and the alien had left the bridge hurriedly to retrieve the nodes from the lab and had neglected to shut down the vessel's computer. That made Frank nervous. If one of the ghastly creatures found its way in there before the two of them got back, they might find themselves watching the damn thing take off, perhaps to land in the middle of Times Square or some other major population centre.

"Wish they hadn't left the lights on," Viktor said over Frank's shoulder, obviously thinking along the same lines.

"Tell me again what Brian said."

"All he really said was that the alien, the 'Shem' he called it, had the technology to destroy the organism, *down there* and *up here*."

Frank stared stone-faced into the monitor trying not to let Viktor see his scepticism.

"If they had the technology to do that, then why didn't they destroy it before?" Brent asked.

"I don't know. It must've surprised them. They obviously didn't land here intentionally or the pods would've remained attached to the main body. Maybe by the time they realized what was happening it was every man for himself. ...or every Shem...or whatever." Viktor tried to sound confident but even he was having doubts now. Maybe this was all just a trick. Maybe he shouldn't have stopped them from gassing the place.

"Look!" Brent stood and pointed at the monitor. Arkt was re-entering the bridge, three of his hands holding tellurium nodes. Brian was draped over one of the Shem's larger arms and wasn't moving. Arkt quickly set him down and moved to an area behind the shimmering ship's computer.

Brian lay on his back gasping. A pink foam-like substance sputtered from his lips and formed around his mouth as he struggled to breathe.

"Shit," Frank mumbled. "He must've inhaled some chlorine."

Arkt returned carrying a heavy, jet black blanket. He spread it out onto the floor and unfolded it, revealing the outline of a biosuit, minus the arms in the back. Arkt lowered Brian into the suit and sealed it. He seized one of the smaller hands of Brian's suit and lifted it, placing one of his own palm to palm. A thousand tiny connections automatically linked the two suits allowing Arkt to operate Brian's suit from his own. He quickly set the suits environment to accommodate Brian's needs then left him there, bounding around the room to replace the rest of the damaged nodes. Midway through his task, he paused.

Arkt grabbed a marker and tore a page from the manual. He wrote something and flashed it at the monitor. There, in perfect English, were two simple phrases. 'He will be alright' and 'I will be right back.'

"Amazing," Frank uttered in fascination.

Viktor felt his previous confidence restored as he watched the creature work. The rest of the crew also seemed to relax a bit. Arkt finished installing the nodes and returned to check on Brian. Two seconds later, he was back at the monitor.

"Is there anything that we can do to help?" Viktor asked.

"No," Arkt wrote. "But I can't do this without his help. He needs a little more time."

"How long?" Frank asked, amazed that they were even having this conversation.

"Twenty minutes."

"How will you destroy the creature?"

"Only one way. Massive explosion. Very high heat."

"What?!" Brent stepped backwards, tripping over the chair and falling to the floor.

"Calm down," Frank yelled at him. He turned back to the monitor, "There must be some other way!"

"No other way. I am sorry," Arkt wrote. "Must completely destroy Ishtaq. Also, must destroy this vessel. It is badly damaged but still capable of terrestrial flight."

Arkt glanced in Brian's direction then slowly and methodically wrote one last note. "I wish we could have met under better circumstances."

"Wait! Wait!" Frank urged.

But Arkt had already moved out of the camera's range.

≈ O ≈

Brent was shaking visibly as Viktor tried to calm him down. "There *is* no other way, Brent. You've seen what that thing can do. We *can't* let it get out of here."

"I…I don't want to die," he mumbled quietly, his voice cracking.

"None of us do. But think of your family back home. Do you really want to put them at risk? Do you want *them* to see what *we've* seen here?"

Brent looked directly at Viktor as his eyes grew misty. "No."

Brent looked around the room as he got to his feet. He brushed himself off as he mustered what was left of his dignity. "What do we tell the others?"

"Nothing."

They studied Frank, waiting to see if he'd say more.

"We can't stop them," he said gesturing toward the monitor where Arkt had just been. "Even if we could, I'm not so sure at this point that we should. You heard Richard earlier. Despite all their precautions, they still had no idea how or when one of theirs got infected back at Dunford."

He walked into the Security Chief's office, emerging again after several seconds holding a bottle of vodka.

"In less than an hour, this will all be over. It'll be quick and painless."

Frank poured three small glasses and handed them to Brent and Viktor. "What good will it do the rest of the crew to know?"

Viktor nodded and held his glass out. Brent reluctantly touched it with his own. Frank did the same.

"Salute," Viktor said quietly as he downed his drink, the other two following his lead.

Viktor set his glass down firmly, indicating that he wanted a refill.

"If it's all the same to you, I'll pass" Brent said quietly, setting his glass on the counter behind him. He snapped open his holster and pulled his pistol out. He hefted it quietly in his hands. "I think I'm going to go for a walk outside," he said.

"Brent, don't..."

"It's his choice, Vik," Frank muttered quietly, holding Viktor back.

Brent nodded his thanks and moved to the exterior door. He paused for several seconds with his hand on the handle before turning again to face them.

"Would one of you be willing to give me a hand? Not sure I can do it on my own."

Frank swallowed hard but nodded, "If you're sure about this."

"Yeah," Brent exhaled.

Frank set his glass down and moved toward the door.

≈ O ≈

THIRTY-EIGHT

Kelly opened his eyes and looked around, trying to get his bearings. He scrambled to his feet, ignoring the pain all over his body as he remembered Pamela's attack.

He was at the foot of the staircase leading up to the Met tower. His assault rifle was nowhere to be seen. Fortunately, his pistol lay on a tread a few steps up.

He crept quietly up the staircase listening intently. But it was quiet. He peeked over the lip of the top stair, grabbed his pistol, then immediately hunched back down, pressing himself into the stairway.

Pamela's torn body was leaned over what was left of Geoffrey. Kelly had gotten just the briefest of glimpses but the image was vivid and unmistakable. Although he'd seen it before in the confines of the warehouse, it was no less horrific.

He glanced at his pistol. Experience told him it was no match for this creature. Better to live and fight another day.

He felt torn as he began to creep back down the stairs and wished desperately that he had a more potent weapon. He wanted to kill this thing now rather than have to worry about finding it later, not to mention that there would be two of them once it had finished with Geoffrey.

The horrid image of the creature taking over Geoffrey's body wouldn't leave his head.

Kelly suddenly stopped. Geoffrey had been carrying a flamethrower.

He started back up the steps. At the top, he peeked again. The Pamela-thing had dragged Geoffrey to a spot away from the broken window, apparently seeking a warmer spot.

The creature had almost finished the job of replicating Geoffrey. One by one it began to retract the tentacles that it had sunk into the man's flesh. Geoffrey's skin began to exhibit the normal pinkish hue rather than the pale grey it had had just a minute ago.

Kelly cursed himself. The odds had suddenly gotten much worse. Now he'd have to deal with two of the creatures with only his pistol. Perhaps he still had time to make a run for it.

The Pamela-creature suddenly caught sight of him in the doorway. In an instant, she whirled around and screeched, launching a rugged tentacle from her abdomen and swinging it at him like a thick barbed whip.

Kelly dodged, barely escaping it as he dove for his assault rifle on the floor just a few feet away. The creature anticipated his move and flicked the gun away with its tentacle. It surged toward Kelly, who fired several shots from his pistol into the thing's face. The creature recoiled and retreated, shrieking loudly.

Kelly made for the door. Again, the creature anticipated his move and swung its tentacle to intercept. The thick appendage connected with his chest sending him flying. Kelly slid across the floor and slammed heavily into the console. He saw his pistol on the floor midway between himself and the foul beast and dove for it. This time, it was the Geoffrey-creature that kicked it away.

He was out of options.

Kelly dove for the door. As he sailed through the air, he twisted his body to minimize the pain and damage when he landed on the stairs. He reached out for the railing as it loomed. But it abruptly stopped and receded. He wondered why as his back slammed heavily against the top few stairs.

But his curiosity was quickly supplanted by the realization that the creature was pulling him forcefully back into the room by a tentacle wrapped around his ankle.

Kelly grabbed desperately for the door frame seizing it firmly with both hands as the beast pulled at him harder. His muscles bulged as he strained with the effort and he knew instinctively that he had just seconds before the thing overpowered him. He looked around frantically for something he could use as a weapon and spotted the assault rifle on the floor off to his right. He was doubtful that he could reach it but he had no choice.

The creature tugged repeatedly trying to break Kelly's grip on the door frame. With each tug, it could sense Kelly's strength beginning to ebb.

Kelly timed his move. The instant the creature relaxed its grip between tugs, he released his grip on the door and spun his body. He landed on top of the rifle and was barely able to grasp it before the creature began dragging him rapidly across the floor toward itself.

Kelly raised the rifle and fired a short burst, riddling the beast with several rounds. The creature released its grip and screeched again. Kelly fired a few rounds at the Geoffrey creature too, which had begun to move toward him to help the other beast. As both creatures screeched and wailed, Kelly bolted for the door again. He turned to fire at them again, hopefully giving himself the precious seconds that he needed to escape.

He just caught a glimpse of it between the two creatures as they prepared to charge at him together. He had no time to consider alternatives.

As the creatures prepared to pounce upon him, he quickly aimed and fired what was left of his ammo into the bright red tank leaning against the wall. The flamethrower exploded, engulfing the tower in a tremendous fireball.

Viktor leaned against the console and poured two more glasses of vodka as he waited for Frank to return. He was glad that Frank had volunteered to help Brent, saving him from having to make that choice. He didn't know if he'd be capable of shooting a man, even if it *was* what the guy wanted.

He set the bottle down and looked up at the clock. It had only been 5 minutes since Arkt had informed them that they would all soon die in a fiery explosion.

Viktor raised his glass to his lips. He'd planned on waiting for Frank but the urge to numb himself was overpowering.

The room suddenly jolted as if the complex had been hit by a small earthquake. But Viktor recognized the sensation for what it was. It hadn't been that long since they'd felt it.

The last time though, the explosion had leveled the garage.

≈ O ≈

The hangar shook as the explosion rumbled through the complex. Much of the crew dove to the floor trembling, waiting anxiously for whatever would happen next.

The exterior door burst open and one of the guards came rushing in, half-panicked. "The Met tower just exploded!"

A murmur swept through the hangar but nobody seemed to know what to do.

From their cell within the equipment shed, Richard's crew cursed and murmured noisily as Richard made his way to the door and stuck his head through the small, pane-less window. The single guard stood with his back to them, the butt of his rifle resting on the floor.

Richard strained to see the guard's face, hoping it was Gundersen. He would be malleable and indecisive without a strong leader around, especially given this unexpected crisis.

Richard signaled to his men, urging them to protest more loudly.

"Hey! You need to let us out of here!" Richard purposely injected a hint of panic in his voice, hoping to mentally disarm the guard.

The guard looked at him but shook his head vehemently. Still, Richard was pleased to see that it *was* Gundersen.

"Are you just gonna leave us in here to die if the whole place goes up?! C'mon! Let us out, man!" Richard ratcheted his feigned panic up a notch. Some of his team started in behind him, demanding that they be let out.

Gundersen took it for a minute but was clearly growing confused about what to do. Richard covertly urged his men to continue their rant, gesturing to them with his hand behind his back.

Finally, Gundersen appeared to have had enough. "Shut the hell up," he yelled, sticking the muzzle of his rifle into the window.

Richard seized the weapon by the barrel and tugged at it forcefully. Gundersen panicked and squeezed the trigger, firing a short burst into the equipment shed. Richard released his hold on the barrel as he and his men dropped to the floor.

Gundersen stared in shock at the door, surprised that he'd actually pulled the trigger. "Everybody ok in there?" he asked after several quiet seconds. He could hear Richard's men cursing him as they slowly rose to their feet but relaxed a bit once it was clear that he hadn't shot anyone.

"You son of a bi…." Richard paused, interrupted by a commotion in the room behind him. He turned as one of his team came charging for the door.

"Chlorine! He hit the damn tanks!"

Gundersen's eyes widened in horror as the faint odor of chlorine confirmed the man's accusation. Richard's men surged toward the door, some of them already coughing and sputtering from the poison.

"Let us out! Now!" Richard demanded, shaking the door fiercely.

Gundersen fumbled nervously for the key, dropping them on the floor. He quickly recovered them and unlocked the door. Richard's men poured through, knocking him over.

Many of the crew had gathered near the equipment shed, several with their weapons drawn. They watched with uncertainty as the prisoners surged from the makeshift cell.

"Everybody out of the hangar," Richard yelled. "The gas is leaking!"

Most of the crew ran for the hallway leading into the CSC. Others rushed to the exterior door, making their way outside.

"Give me a hand," a crewman yelled to Robert, who stood near the main hangar door.

Robert flinched, startled, as Liam gestured wildly for his help. He smiled, realizing that he couldn't have planned this any better.

Liam was the co-pilot that had flown in with Richard's team. And since Richard's team had remained sequestered within the hangar since their arrival, the chances of him being infected were minimal.

Robert looked around the hangar. It was every man for himself as the crew scrambled frantically to escape from the hangar as it filled with poison. In the confusion, they wouldn't notice until it was too late to stop him. He touched the pistol on his belt and felt an unexpected resolve wash over him. This was his moment.

Robert rushed to help Liam get Armand and Kevin to their feet. Each draped the arm of one of the sick men around their neck and half-dragged them from the hangar. The smell of chlorine had already permeated the hangar as they stumbled out into the cold.

Robert made sure that he exited first. The windblown snow and semi-darkness of dawn made it difficult to see anything. Perfect… He was banking on the fact that Liam would defer to Robert's familiarity of the facility to guide them to safety. He was hoping that the urgency of the situation would prevent Liam from realizing until it was too late that Robert had separated them from the group.

"This way," he shouted behind him.

Liam followed. Robert led them to a small outbuilding that stood apart from the main facility. He forced open the door and entered, followed immediately by Liam supporting Kevin.

Robert set Armand down atop a wooden crate and quickly drew his gun, leveling it at Liam as he flicked on the light. Liam set Kevin on a table and turned to find himself staring into the dark muzzle of a pistol inches from his face.

THIRTY-NINE

The engines whined in protest as Liam powered them up. From his seat in the back, Robert could see the main rotor slowly beginning to turn. The process seemed to be taking a lot longer than usual.

"Let's go," he yelled impatiently at Liam. He kept his weapon trained on the pilot.

"I'm going as fast as I can," Liam shouted back angrily. "In case you didn't notice, this thing's been sitting out in the cold for a few days."

Robert looked around anxiously expecting the others to rush out of the building to stop them. He checked the safety again to ensure that it was off. He hated the thought, but he would not hesitate to shoot anyone that tried to prevent them from taking off.

Seconds later, the helicopter was hovering.

Liam maneuvered it slowly away from the buildings as the wind tossed them around.

"Get us the hell out of here! Now!" Robert glared at Liam and poked him in the shoulder with the muzzle of his rifle. He'd holstered the pistol once they gotten inside the chopper, opting for the heavier firepower. It was easier to keep it trained on the pilot from back here and would be more of a deterrent for anyone that tried to stop them. Fortunately, nobody had.

His stomach lurched as Liam rotated the collective, causing the chopper to rise quickly. He felt a profound sense of relief as he watched the compound recede behind them.

Liam flew in silence for several minutes glancing occasionally at the radio. He'd been expecting someone from the site to contact them, urging them to return. But the radio remained silent. It was only after achieving their cruising altitude that he remembered that the tower had been destroyed.

Robert adjusted the microphone inside his headset. “How long to McMurdo?”

“We don’t have the range for McMurdo,” Liam responded. “We’ve got to refuel at Warner.”

Robert swore. He hadn’t planned on that. He would need Liam’s cooperation to get the chopper refueled. They would be making an unscheduled stop at Warner. If the crew there refused to refuel them, they’d be stuck again in the middle of nowhere. He couldn’t have that.

“Listen, Liam. I’m sorry. I hate that it had to come to this.”

Liam stared at Robert through a small mirror installed near his head, allowing him to see into the cabin behind him. Robert lowered his weapon slowly and deliberately, exaggerating his movements so that his intentions would be clear.

“Look. We need to get to McMurdo. We need to tell them what’s happening. We need to…”

“They already know what’s happening,” Liam replied coolly. “This isn’t about warning anybody. It’s about you saving your own ass. So, you can stop trying to justify it.”

Robert’s heart sank in his chest. He knew it was true and turned his head away, unable to look Liam in the eye. He realized at that moment that he actually hated himself.

All his life, he’d lived in fear…fear of physical pain…of rejection…of failure…of ridicule. He’d worked constantly to inoculate himself from it over the years through countless excuses and alibis that justified, at least in his own mind, his unusual behavior. It had been awkward at first but eventually he’d gotten good at it. Over time, he’d even lost the guilt that he used to feel with every new lie. It was all supposed to be temporary, a thin veil designed to prevent others from seeing him as he truly was.

But each untruth was more acrid and corrosive than the last. They became inextricably meshed until they became one giant lie that he was forced to perpetuate lest anyone should see the real Robert.

But with just a few words, Liam had exposed him. He felt suddenly naked and ashamed. He eyed the rifle leaning against his leg and wished he had the courage to take his own life. But he was afraid of that too.

A sudden movement out of the corner of his eye brought him instantly alert. He turned his head ever so slightly to get a better look.

A dark brown boot lay on its side in at the rear of the cabin, its top disappearing beneath the edge of a tarp. It looked at first to be lying there haphazardly, as though it had been discarded by an owner who no longer needed it.

Then, it moved.

A hand emerged to hurriedly pull the boot back under the tarp.

The fact that they had a stowaway on board was frightening enough. But only Anders had a pair of boots like that.

"Liam." Robert spoke quietly through the headset.

"I see it," Liam replied just as quietly.

"What do we do?"

Liam immediately banked left turning the chopper in a slow, wide descending turn. "I'm setting her down right here."

Robert looked out the cockpit windshield at the surrounding terrain. They were approaching a line of rocky hills, the only distinct geographical feature visible for as far as he could see. Being stranded down there was definitely an unpleasant prospect. But it was still preferable to being trapped up here with one of those damn things. Anders had been missing for over a day. While nobody had said it directly, most of the crew suspected strongly that the organism had gotten to him. The fact that he had been hiding quietly inside the helicopter, apparently waiting secretly for an inevitable trip to McMurdo, seemed to remove all doubt about it.

Robert turned again to look at the tarp and was surprised to find his view blocked by a pale gray curtain. In the split-second it took for him to realize that he was staring at a jacket just inches from his face, Anders had his hand around Robert's neck.

Robert dropped his rifle and grasped Ander's wrists trying to break free. Anders brought his face within inches of Roberts and stared at him impassively. The skin on Anders' face pulsated and bubbled with several small blisters.

Robert pounded harder trying to get the Anders-thing to release him.

Liam banked sharply throwing both passengers off balance and slamming them into the side of the helicopter.

The Anders-thing glared at Liam threateningly. It tossed Robert to the rear of the cabin and turned toward the pilot. Liam flew erratically, trying to keep the creature off balance. But with each wild maneuver, the creature spawned a new appendage that grasped whatever happened to be nearby to steady itself as it moved inexorably toward the cockpit.

Robert watched in horror as Liam unbuckled himself in one fluid motion, flung open the door of the helicopter, and leapt out. The creature screeched in rage and turned its attention again to the rear of the aircraft.

Robert lay motionless on his back and cried out, searching the floor for his rifle. But it was out of reach.

The creature moved slowly toward him, barely impeded by the jerking of the pilotless helicopter as it fell from the sky.

Robert reached for the bright orange pouch strapped to the seat in front of him. He zipped open the Velcro and fumbled with its contents. The creature wailed and swayed as it relentlessly made its way to the rear of the small cabin.

Robert removed the small plastic safety cap that covered the muzzle of the flare gun. He aimed it at the creature and cringed as he prepared to fire. He hesitated, realizing that the single flare wasn't going to kill it.

His brain processed things with incredible sharpness and rapidity. Through the windshield, he saw a beautiful patch of sky through a break in the clouds, the horizon dimly lit by the rising sun. The ground was rushing up to meet them but, surprisingly, the chopper remained generally in level flight. They would surely hit the ground hard and Robert understood that he was unlikely to survive the impact. He was surprised to find himself relieved by the thought. In truth, he didn't *want* to survive it.

But the creature might survive.

With sudden clarity, he understood what he'd done. This thing was a terrible threat to everything he knew. It would be his fault if it escaped. He resolved to not let this happen.

The creature was very close now. Robert looked up as it loomed menacingly over him. He raised the flare gun and pointed it at the creature's head. Beyond the creature's misshapen, grotesque head various hydraulic, electrical, and fuel lines ran throughout the aircraft, attached to the fuselage overhead. If only he knew which ones were which. He followed them quickly to a point overhead where several of them ran parallel and close to one another. He switched his aim and fired.

The flare imbed itself into the fuselage amidst the piping. It burned bright and hot, melting the metal tubing and ultimately rupturing several of the lines. Robert got lucky…one of them happened to be pumping fuel to the engines.

The fuel hissed into the cabin under high pressure through a tiny fracture. It atomized into a fine cloud that rapidly expanded instantly filling the cabin with a fine volatile mist. Ten microseconds later, the white-hot flare ignited the cloud. The helicopter exploded in a giant fireball just seconds before impacting the ground.

≈ O ≈

FORTY

Viktor was trying to quiet the riot created by the nervous crowd in the CSC. Almost thirty of the crew were assembled there, each having something urgent to say. Viktor had never seen such pandemonium or felt so inept at addressing it.

A shot rang out and the room grew suddenly silent.

Frank stood near the main console, his pistol raised and a small cloud of debris raining down around him from the ceiling. "Everyone shut the hell up!"

He surveyed the group sternly. "Gundersen, what the hell is going on?!"

"It wasn't my fault," Gundersen yelled. "If they hadn't acted up…" He pointed to some of Richard's men, who began to protest loudly again.

"Shut up!" Frank yelled, slamming his palm against the top of the console hard enough to cause the monitors to flicker in protest.

Richard stepped forward, "Here's exactly what happened."

Frank listened as Richard described what had occurred in the hangar.

Frank sighed, "Did anyone think to open the main hangar door to vent the gas?"

The crew looked sheepishly at the ground. Even Richard seemed to have lost his usual cockiness. "That would've been good," Richard said awkwardly. "Guess we were too busy at the moment trying not to die."

Frank pondered the situation for a moment. It was no big deal that they hadn't opened the hangar door. They could do that at any time from the outside. The arctic winds would clear any chlorine from the hangar in no time. A more immediate concern was the number of crewmen who were now unaccounted for.

"Where's the rest of the crew?" Viktor asked suddenly.

Richard looked around at the group assembled in the CSC, suddenly realizing that not everyone was there. "I don't know. It was difficult to see outside. Some of them must have gotten separated.

"OK. You, you, and you," Frank said, pointing to the three nearest men, "Get outside, open the hangar door, and get your asses back here." He pointed to two others, "You two come with me."

"What the hell is that?!"

A crewman in the midst of the crowd was pointing excitedly at the console. The room fell silent at the strange spectacle displayed on the monitor.

Arkt had returned to the vessel's bridge and was manipulating controls on the shimmering column. Brian stood unsteadily behind the Shem.

Brian approached the remote terminal and looked into the camera. His face was pale and a thin line of pinkish saliva, dried and crusty, ran down one side of his mouth. His damaged eye was now glazed over with a pale white film like spider's webbing. He looked ghastly.

"Hello, Frank. I see you're not alone. Do they know?"

Frank hunched over the monitor and stared back, "There hasn't been time."

Brian nodded, his good eye reflecting his understanding of Frank's situation.

"It won't be long now."

Frank pursed his lips and nodded. The crew continued to mutter behind him as they watched the alien creature and their co-worker race around the vessel's cabin. Without even turning around, he knew that others were looking at him, waiting for an explanation. He could almost feel the glare of their eyes boring into the back of his skull. Through the corner of his eye, he saw Viktor standing close, his face a mask of anxiety. It was something that Frank had never before associated with the man.

Frank remained hunched over the monitor for several seconds after Brian had moved away. He couldn't bear to bring himself to turn and face the crew assembled behind him. He didn't know how to tell them that, in just a few short minutes, they were all going to die.

≈ O ≈

Kelly awoke to the smell of burning wood and plastic. He lay in the darkness, once again trying to remember where he was and how he had gotten there. His whole body was in pain yet he had no recollection of how he had hurt himself.

Kelly propped himself up on his elbows. He was looking up a staircase, the top of which was engulfed in flames. Slowly it came back to him.

He got up and opened the door behind him. The explosion had knocked out the power leaving the hallway dark. Kelly almost didn't care. He had a splitting headache and searing pain on the left side of his face. He reached up to touch it as he reconstructed the last few moments and realized that his face was pretty badly burned.

After a quick fruitless search for a weapon, Kelly headed down the dark hall toward the CSC.

≈ O ≈

Pruit grabbed his penlight from his belt and shined it around the room. "Where the hell are we?"

"We're in the Haynes building, near the Met tower," Tom answered. "We must have overshot the CSC."

"But at least we're inside," Charlie said. "And we can get to the CSC from here. It's just out that door and down the hall to the left."

Kim leaned against the wall and mumbled something in Korean. Whatever it was, it sounded forlorn and hopeless. Hildy walked over and grabbed his hand but she didn't know what to say.

"What are we waiting for?" Tom asked, moving toward the door. He stopped suddenly and looked down. "What the hell is this?"

Pruit shone the light down revealing a white, mucous-like substance covering the floor.

Kelly shuffled slowly down the hallway, his pace hampered by an injured knee from his second fall down the stairs. With each step, the skin on his face and neck around his burns pulled taut sending waves of pain through his head. But he fought through it, intent on getting back to the others. He had had no clue about Pamela…other replicants may still be hiding among the crew.

He paused to catch his breath, leaning against a white fire alarm box. He opened the small metal door and looked inside but someone had already removed the fire axe that had been hanging there. He swore and almost slammed the door shut in frustration but managed to restrain his anger at the last second, closing it quietly. No sense alerting anyone or anything to his presence.

He started down the hall again then abruptly stopped as he realized where he was. He peered into the room through the small portal in the door to confirm it. Sure enough, he was just outside of the room that Doc had turned into an infirmary since they'd arrived topside.

Kelly put his hand on the door to push it open, then paused. There was no sense going into the room if he'd lost the vial. He began patting at the pockets of his jacket, hoping he would still find it there – the little bottle that Brian had given him days ago when life had been somewhat normal. He swore under his breath when he didn't feel it, fearing that the damn thing had fallen from his pocket during his scuffle in the tower. But as he brushed his hand one last time against the fabric of his jacket, he felt its unmistakable shape.

He quickly thrust his hand inside and pulled it out to confirm that it was the bottle of catalase. He stared at if for a second and breathed a sigh of relief. It seemed like a hundred years ago since Brian had asked him to hold onto it during their 'illegal' drink in the lab. He wondered briefly how Brian and Parker were faring…a fleeting thought that departed as soon as it had arrived. He had more immediate concerns.

He quickly put the bottle back into his pocket and entered the lab, hoping he would find the rest of the stuff he needed.

≈ O ≈

"They're called Shem. They are the original builders and operators of the spacecraft. The organism attacked them too a long time ago, causing them to crash here."

"How many of them are there?" Richard asked in amazement.

Frank relaxed just a bit. This was good. As long as they were talking about the alien creature, they wouldn't be asking about Brian's last statement.

He dropped his chin to his chest and contemplated his own impending death. He'd always believed in a Higher Being and had tried to live an honest and upright life but he had never really been 'religious'. He hoped that would be enough. He began to silently mumble a prayer, just in case, hoping that he wasn't too late.

"There's just the one," Viktor said, responding to Richard's question.

The crew stared at him in obvious disbelief.

"Is something wrong?"

One of the crew raised his hand slowly and pointed at the monitor.

Viktor turned to look just as the second Shem emerged from behind Arkt and attacked.

≈ O ≈

FORTY-ONE

Kelly exited the infirmary, moving more slowly now to protect his fragile package. He had just the one device and neither the time nor the chemicals to fashion another. He wasn't even sure if this one would work.

He looked at it dubiously, a collection of glass tubes and beakers held together by medical tape. It rattled lightly as he walked as the glass fragments suspended within the liquid clattered against the beaker like crushed ice in a cold drink. But the glass was already warm to the touch due to the reaction of the peroxide and hydroquinone, belying the fact that this was no summer cocktail. All he had to do was shatter the inner test tube to release the catalase into the mix and stand back.

At least that's how it had worked before when Brian had demonstrated it...

But Brian had only shown them the one time and Kelly hadn't exactly been focused on memorizing the process. Plus, he wasn't sure he'd be able to break the glass tube inside without shattering the outer glass as well. But it was all he had and it was better than nothing. It wasn't likely to kill the creature if he encountered it. But, if it worked, it might buy the precious seconds he'd need to escape.

He nearly dropped the device, startled by the shrill female scream two doors down.

≈ O ≈

The second Shem held a small, thin instrument resembling a curved blade, its ends jutting forward and away from it like miniature ram horns. Arkt suddenly sensed its presence and turned to face his former shipmate as the newcomer raised the implement. The tips of the device flashed a bright blue and Arkt was instantly thrown backwards, landing on his back on the metal floor. The arms of Arkt's biosuit went limp and the black sheen drained from its skin.

The second Shem moved toward the shimmering column ignoring the immobilized Arkt. Its hands quickly flitted about the surface of the computer entering several rapid commands. It suddenly turned and rushed to the far side of the bridge, where Arkt had recently replaced several of the tellurium nodes, and began undoing Arkt's work. The vessel's interior dimmed significantly, making it difficult for the crew in the CSC to see inside the ship.

"What the hell is it doing?" Brent asked quietly.

≈ O ≈

Kelly peered through the small portal. The window was fogged over but he could just make out three or four human figures huddling against the far wall. From their posture, he surmised that whatever was frightening them was just inside the door through which he was peering.

"Grab the shovel! Grab it!" a man suddenly yelled.

Something in the room brushed against the wall very close to where Kelly was crouched. He eyed the makeshift weapon in his hands and realized that he had no idea how he was going to use it. The fragile beaker had to remain unbroken for it to have any chance of working so he couldn't exactly throw it.

He realized that he also had no idea how long it would take for the chemical reaction to happen. It had seemed like just a few seconds when Brian had done it. But he was dealing with a much greater quantity of liquid and a less certain construction.

The shouting in the room grew suddenly more urgent and several shots rang out. Large holes appeared in the wall inches from Kelly as two of the shots missed their target. The creature hissed and screeched as other bullets found their mark, giving Kelly a better idea of where it was located inside the room.

Kelly burst through the door holding the device over his head. He froze. Even his previous experiences with the creature down in the warehouse and up in the Met tower left him unprepared for the spectacle before him.

A monstrously large creature stood just a few feet away, its back toward him. Perched atop a thick trunk that extended six feet over its torso were three human-like heads, each closely resembling a former Langstadt Station crew member. They faced in different directions, the forward-facing head eyeing its prey at the far end of the room while the nearest one glared at him, its mouth forming a jagged snarl.

Kelly ducked as something whizzed by his face, narrowly missing him and spattering as it slammed into the door. He glanced quickly across the room in several short glances, afraid to take his eyes off the hideous multi-headed monster. He saw it just in time to avoid another projectile that it launched at him.

Hovering over the door was a large and vicious looking spider. It appeared to be Carlson's tarantula but it was twice the size. It hung from the top of the door, menacingly waving the pointed tips of its forelegs in his direction as it hissed loudly.

It turned its attention alternately from Kelly to the small knot of people trapped in the far corner of the room. It was clearly guarding the door, cutting off their only means of escape. A thick bright green fluid oozed from a deep crevasse that ran along the length of its spine. Near its back end, a pair of spindly appendages was collecting the fluid and forming it into a sphere, readying itself for another attack.

Kelly glanced back and forth between the two creatures. Both seemed focused on him now leaving him unsure which represented the more immediate threat.

A tentacle sprouted from the chest of the larger creature and charged toward Kelly, its tip sprouting into a three-pronged, hand-like appendage as it rapidly closed the distance.

Kelly tucked his fragile weapon into his gut and dove toward a stack of wooden supply crates as a puddle of bright green fluid splashed across the floor in the area where he'd just been standing. The spider creature hissed again loudly, seemingly pissed that another of its orbs had missed its target. Kelly watched in awe as the fluid flowed from the point of impact toward the larger creature, where it was quickly absorbed.

The tentacle slammed into the top crate with a loud crack, violently shattering it. It swiftly changed direction and smashed a second crate sending wooden splinters everywhere.

Kelly dove behind another set of crates as the tentacle reduced a third crate, completely eliminating his previous cover.

He scanned the room frantically as he realized that the spider-like thing was no longer guarding the door. The larger creature left him no time to dwell on it as it bounded toward the fresh crates and effortlessly shoved them aside. Kelly lost his grip on the fragile glass bomb, dropping it roughly onto the floor as he dove behind the final stack of crates.

He could hear the other crew members firing and yelling but his own dire situation demanded all his attention. He searched the floor for his weapon but saw nothing but shards of wood and cans of food from the smashed crates. He seized a large shard, wielding it like a knife.

The tower of crates was suddenly gone, smashing into pieces against the wall as the creature cast them aside with a single shove. Kelly stepped backward but found himself against the wall with nothing more between him and the larger creature. It slowly drew near, two of its heads snarling at him. It coiled its barbed tentacle around him like a snake, pinning his arms to his sides. Kelly stabbed at the tentacle with the wooden shard but could do little damage given the limited range of motion of his arms. The beast lifted him off the ground and drew him near as large blisters sprouted along its flesh.

The creature suddenly released him, shrieking loudly.

Kelly rolled away as soon as he hit the floor, tripping over a shovel that was leaning against the wall as he scrambled to put some distance between himself and the beast. He grabbed it as he sprang to his feet, wielding it menacingly.

But the creature was moving away, twisting and writhing in pain. Steam rose from its backside and the far wall twinkled with the sparkle of a thousand tiny diamonds. It took a moment for Kelly to realize what had happened.

His makeshift bomb had exploded, sending shards of glass and steaming hot fluid everywhere. The creature had taken the brunt of the impact and, ironically, had protected Kelly from the shrapnel.

The creature flailed and charged away from Kelly seeking vengeance on whatever had caused it such pain. Its forward-facing heads searched the room while the rearward head, half of covered with scalding hot fluid, shrieked and wailed, its eyes betraying its confusion.

Kelly quickly bolted for the exit, now open and filling the room with icy air. The spider thing was still nowhere to be found and Kelly could only hope it wasn't lying in wait, planning to ambush him. But the door represented one of two options right now and the second one – fighting the beast armed only with a shovel – was much less attractive. He gripped the shovel tightly, poised to strike just in case, as he scrambled through the exit.

≈ O ≈

FORTY-TWO

Brian watched the unfamiliar Shem for several minutes, knowing exactly what it was doing. Re-shuffling the nodes would divert power to the ship's engines and undo much of what Arkt had done to turn the vessel into a giant bomb. Brian also knew that this Shem was a replicant. No genuine Shem would jeopardize so many others to save itself.

Brian glanced quickly at Arkt, who remained motionless on the floor. The weapon had disrupted the functioning of the biosuit but Arkt himself remained unharmed inside. But Arkt wouldn't be much help against the Ishtaq without the suit. While highly intelligent, the Shem were small and physically not very powerful. The biosuits providing them with surrogate strength and stamina. Brian would have to stop the Ishtaq-Shem on his own.

He quickly weighed his options. There weren't many…and all of them were likely to get him killed. He'd be ok with that if he knew that he'd wipe out the Ishtaq as well.

The imposter Shem was busy at the computer, studying the ship's status. From the display, Brian could clearly see that the vessel was too damaged for space flight. Unfortunately, it retained enough capabilities for terrestrial flight. In less than an hour, it could easily reach any of a hundred densely populated areas.

As if reading Brian's mind, the Shem began reviewing the earth's topography. Fortunately, the images – captured when the ship had crashed hundreds of thousands of years ago – showed none of the population centers that had come to dot the landscape since.

Despite the significance of the moment, Brian felt a sense of wonder at the astoundingly clear and beautiful images of an earth not yet tarnished by man. The oceans in particular were of the deepest blue-green and shimmered with an almost electric quality like vast neon signs.

Electricity…

Brian's epiphany was so sudden that he stepped back involuntarily and had to steady himself, as if he'd been physically shoved. He scanned the bridge, assessing the function of each of the power nodes. Unfortunately, none would suit his purpose. The system was well designed to guard against any of them acting as a single point of failure.

The vessel shuddered suddenly. A deep and steady rumble gently shook the spacecraft and a low, muffled droning sounded from below like a helicopter turbine gearing up for flight The engines began cycling through start-up, the pitch and volume getting higher and louder.

Brian could feel the heavy machinery coming to life beneath him. He backed away silently until he was sure that he was out of earshot, then he sprinted down the corridor.

≈ O ≈

Kelly had never thought of the arctic cold as refreshing. But right now, it was about the most refreshing thing he could've felt. The cold air soothed his burned skin and helped to cool him down following the exertion of his fight and flight. He stood in the middle of a clearing staring back at the building from which he'd just emerged. The door remained open but, so far, neither of the ghastly creatures had come out after him.

"I guess they hate the cold."

Kelly jumped and raised the shovel, startled.

"It me, Kel," Tom yelled urgently, raising his hands to shield himself.

Kelly lowered the shovel. Kim, Hildy, and Charlie huddled together in the cold several yards beyond Tom.

"Oh, man! Are you ok?" Tom asked, noticing Kelly's injuries for the first time.

Kelly looked at the others, "Anybody see what happened to the smaller thing?"

"I started firing at it as soon as the larger thing attacked you. I don't think I hit it but it dropped to the floor and took off. We didn't stick around to find out where it went."

Kelly nodded. "We'd better find some shelter."

"No way! Ain't none of us going anywhere inside. Those friggin' things are all over the place!"

"We can't stay out here," Kelly yelled. He stopped and looked curiously at Tom.

"Why aren't you guys in the hangar with the rest?"

Kelly listened as Tom filled him in about what had occurred in the hangar.

"So, where's everybody else?"

Tom shrugged, "I think they're in the CSC. We got separated from the rest and overshot it. Ended up in there." He tilted his head toward the building from which they'd just exited.

Kelly thought for a moment then gestured for the others to come closer. They did so hesitantly.

"The chlorine should've killed off anything by now. I'll go into the hangar and open the main door to clear the air inside. Soon as its safe, we go back into the hangar and try to contact the others."

They looked at him doubtfully but nodded.

"Do you really think the chlorine worked?" Charlie asked nervously. "Cuz, I'd much rather freeze out here than face that thing again."

"Me too," Hildy said firmly.

"Yeah, well me three," Kelly mumbled seriously. "But we can't stay out here. It may be a balmy minus twenty degrees right now but it's going to start getting really cold soon."

He looked toward the hangar then back at the others. "I'm ready to kick some ass."

He turned and marched off toward the hangar, hoping that his bravado was enough to distract the others from the fact that, other than a shovel and a rifle with no ammo, they had no weapons.

≈ O ≈

The whole building was shaking. The crew in the CSC looked around in dismay, leaning on desks or against walls to steady themselves as picture frames and desktop items dropped to the floor.

"I think it's trying to take off," Viktor shouted in disbelief.

Frank ran to the door and flung it open. The weather had cleared and the winds had finally died down giving them decent visibility for the first time in days. The vibration loosened up the snow and ice causing the ground to look fuzzy and out of focus. Sharp loud cracks filled the air as ice that had been in place for decades on the warehouse roof was suddenly disturbed. A few other brave souls ventured out behind Frank to see what was going on.

A particularly loud crack rifled through the air like a sharp peal of thunder. The ground several yards away swayed and then dropped several feet revealing the outline of the vast roof that covered the long-hidden warehouse complex below. In several spots, the hue of the ice was changing rapidly and a thin vapor was rising steadily into the cold air.

Frank cursed loudly and turned. "Go! Go! Go!" he shouted, pushing the others back toward the building. He continued to yell as they entered the CSC, urgently screaming at the crew to exit from the other side.

The room shuddered and heaved suddenly, knocking most of the crew to the floor. From his hands and knees, Viktor peered out the door toward the warehouse just in time to see the roof surge upward and then collapse noisily into the warehouse canyon. Ceiling tiles and framing fell all around them as the room shook violently.

The lights and monitors suddenly blinked out, immersing the room in total darkness. Seconds later, light poured back into the room as the wall nearest the warehouse completely collapsed. The debris, and several men who had been using the wall for support, disappeared into the chasm of the widening crater.

Viktor cursed in Norwegian and scrambled frantically to his feet. The shaking stopped so suddenly that he lost his balance and fell onto his back. He lay there in shock expecting the worst as a light snow descended into the room dotting and stinging his face.

≈ O ≈

They waited in the distance as the hangar door opened noisily, its metal coils and springs protesting loudly from the cold and lack of use. Kelly rolled under the door from inside as soon as it was big enough for him to squeeze through. He sprinted out toward the others and exhaled loudly.

"No doubt about it. There was enough chlorine in there to kill off anything." He huffed and puffed, trying to regain his breath. He hated the fact that such little exertion had tired him so much. He'd kept himself in good shape…at least until all this shit happened. He wiped his sweating brow with the back of his hand, wincing as he brushed his burned flesh. With that small reminder of what he'd been through in just the last hour, he suddenly didn't feel so bad about being winded.

Hildy stumbled and fell as the ground began to shake. The tremor started off slowly but quickly grew violent enough to knock them all to the ground.

They looked around anxiously, trying to make sense of what was happening. Loud cracks filled the air as the permafrost heaved and splintered.

"Look!" Tom pointed toward the hangar with one hand as he struggled to steady himself with the other.

Steel beams and sheet metal were falling from the ceiling, clearly visible through the wide-open hangar door. They cringed at the sound of a loud boom as a thick white cloud rushed into the hangar.

"The other chlorine tanks must've ruptured," Tom yelled.

The interior of the hangar suddenly filled with light as a large section of the roof completely collapsed, followed by the far wall. The white cloud quickly dissipated as the chlorine flowed into the unseen abyss.

All around them, buildings swayed and moaned against the unexpected strain. Another large crack was followed by the collapse of the CSC building to their right.

A strange, warm wind reached them from between the two buildings.

The violent shaking settled into a calm, rhythmic vibration. It was still quite strong but decreased enough to allow them to stand.

"What do we do?!" Charlie asked anxiously.

"Over there," Kim shouted, pointing to a small outbuilding behind them.

Kelly weighed their options as he scrutinized the small shed. It seemed far enough away from the other buildings to offer them some protection. "Go!" he yelled, helping Hildy to her feet. The others stood dumbfounded and uncertain.

"I said go!" Kelly demanded more urgently. He gripped Hildy's arm and practically dragged her with him to the shelter.

≈ O ≈

Frank grasped a metal beam jutting out from the collapsed wall to steady himself as he peered over the rim of the crater. Debris from the warehouse roof and from what had once been Decks 2 and 3 covered the spacecraft.

The thrust of the engines lifted some of the wreckage and ejected it from the canyon. Large pieces of framing and sturdy sheet metal fell almost silently about the compound, the impact muffled by the snow.

Even from this distance, the heat from the engines was overwhelming.

"What do we do?" Viktor asked urgently.

"I have no idea!" Frank replied, gesturing with his hands across the expansive crater. "How are we supposed to stop *this*?!"

Steam vapor rose into the sky as the icy canyon walls crackled and sizzled from their first ever exposure to heat.

"We've got to get out of here," Viktor urged. "We need to let them know back at McMurdo so they can destroy it!"

"How the hell are we going to do that, Vik?! We no longer have a radio! Even if we did, we no longer have power! We've got *nothing*! I don't think we…"

Frank suddenly shifted his position and peered into the distance. He could just make out the remnants of the hangar through the rising fog. Just beyond it sat the tail boom of a helicopter.

He smacked Viktor in the chest with the back of his hand. "C'mon! There *may* be a way!"

FORTY-THREE

Brian crouched in the walkway near a vast bank of complex machinery as debris rained down onto the spacecraft. He wasn't really concerned about the hull collapsing…he knew the ship could take the punishment. But he couldn't stop his human instincts from reacting to the loud noise.

He swore under his breath. He thought he'd have more time. But the replicant Shem seemed intent on departing with all possible speed.

He grabbed the utility knife from his belt and plunged it into the plastic gallon container of mineral spirits. He'd grabbed four bottles of the stuff from a stash of equipment and supplies that they'd pre-positioned inside the vessel months ago to support their experiments. The white liquid spilled over his hands, pants, and boots as he sloppily cut the top completely off the jug. Ordinarily, moisture was anathema in the arctic cold. It expedited the loss of body heat and could quickly result in hypothermia. He'd normally be quick to wipe it away or change into dry clothing. But now he took little notice…in a minute or two it just wouldn't matter.

He ran his hand over a section of the wall in a circular motion, opening a concealed door. Behind it, two tellurium nodes hummed quietly as they provided power to the massive engine. A small bulkhead separated the two nodes and they were spread apart further than he would have liked but there was nothing he could do about that.

Brian lifted the bottle chest high and took a deep breath, hoping it wouldn't be his last. Then he heaved the fluid onto the electrified components.

≈ O ≈

Kelly entered the outbuilding still dragging Hildy behind him. She screamed as soon as he flicked on the light.

Kelly shoved her backward and raised the shovel, ready to strike. He lowered it slowly as he realized why she'd screamed.

"Watch the door," he instructed Kim, who remained half in and half out of the doorway.

Two men, completely wrapped in blankets, lay in the center of the room…one on a table and the other across several crates. He approached them cautiously.

"That's probably not a good idea," Tom insisted anxiously.

Kelly ignored him and moved slowly toward the men. He recognized the nearer of the two as Kevin, the site's meteorologist. The flesh of his face was a pale blue and ice crystals had formed on his skin. Kelly knew the guy was dead even before he felt for a pulse. He turned and faced the others, shaking his head to communicate the guy's status.

He moved over to the second man, who lay on his side with his back to the door. Kelly gently grabbed the man by his shoulder and rolled him onto his back. Hildy and Charlie both began to sob even before Armand's face was visible. They'd worked with the doctor for a long time and recognized his physique even under the thin blankets.

Kelly checked for a pulse. The women's sobs grew in intensity as he slowly backed away, shaking his head. They stood in one corner and hugged each other.

Kelly looked around for a weapon. As much as he wanted to console them, ensuring their survival was a more urgent task at the moment. He grabbed a crowbar and hefted it. He flung it toward Tom, who caught it and eyed it doubtfully.

Kelly shrugged. It was better than nothing.

Tom joined him as they rummaged around the room for any other means of defense. There wasn't much…just some Coleman heaters and a small tool bag filled with mechanic's tools. Kelly grabbed a hammer and a long, sturdy screwdriver.

Hildy suddenly gasped and ran toward Armand's body. "He's still alive!" she shouted. "I saw him breathe! I saw his breath!"

Charlie rushed over and quickly ripped open the blankets. She placed her head against Armand's chest and listened.

"I hear a heartbeat! It's very slow and faint but it's there!"

"Grab those blankets," Kelly yelled at Tom, pointing at Kevin's stiff body. Tom hurried over and, after a brief hesitation, stripped the blankets and brought them over to the women.

They quickly wrapped the extra blankets around Armand as Kelly filled one of the heaters with fuel. He primed it, punched the ignition switch, and the machine came to life.

"Close the door!" he yelled at Kim, who promptly replied.

"We can't…at least, not all the way," Tom asserted, "We've got to vent the room or the fumes from that thing will asphyxiate us all."

Kelly grabbed a narrow crate and jammed it into the doorframe. The winds blew the door open again and Kelly grabbed Kim by the front of his jacket, placing him against the door. "Keep it just like this," he instructed, "…and keep an eye out."

Kim nodded and peered through the open slot in the door.

The temperature in the room was already climbing as the women rubbed Armand's exposed flesh, trying their best to warm him.

"Give me a hand," Kelly yelled to Tom.

They carried Kevin's body and placed it outside. Kim, Hildy, and Charlie looked at them in shock as they re-entered the room.

"If he's one of those *things*, I'd rather not have him thaw out in here."

Charlie and Hildy looked at each other. They glanced quickly down at Armand then tentatively stepped away.

Kelly shrugged in resignation as they looked to him for guidance.

"Maybe we should put him outside too," Tom suggested, his voice suddenly filled with apprehension.

Hildy's mouth dropped open in horror but she said nothing. Charlie stood beside her, the grimmest of looks on her face.

Kelly studied Armand's face from a distance. It was hard to imagine a man as docile as Doc harboring such a hideous beast inside. Still, he was suddenly just as uncertain.

If it had been anyone else, he wouldn't have hesitated. He would've placed the dying man outside to succumb to the harsh elements. It wasn't likely he'd survive anyway and it would've been the most logical thing to do to protect the rest.

But not Doc K… There was no finer example of a human being anywhere on the face of the planet in Kelly's book.

"No. We give him the benefit of the doubt," Kelly finally said. "But he'll be on a very short leash."

≈ O ≈

Brian picked himself up and verified that he wasn't seriously injured. The mineral spirits had erupted into a fireball as the liquid shorted out the high-powered nodes, sending him flying. His collision with the opposite bulkhead dazed him but left him otherwise unharmed. He made a mental note to stand to one side for the next one.

His action had had the desired effect though. Both nodes were destroyed and the affected engine, now deprived of power, slowly collapsed back to its rest state.

Brian grabbed the remaining jugs and ran over to the next engine. The computer would have already alerted the replicant Shem to the malfunctioning engine. If he were lucky, the creature would consider the breakdown a result of the crash that occurred millennia ago rather than an act of sabotage. That would buy him the time he would need to disable at least one more engine. Then, he would be out of time. The unlikely failure of a second engine would be sure to elicit a hostile response from the creature.

He hurriedly sliced the top from another gallon and opened the panel to expose the engine's power nodes. He heaved the fluid into the compartment, turning away at the last second.

He fared better this time, although he'd had to thrust off his jacket which had gotten soaked by the spirits and had burst into flame from the resulting short circuit and fire. But this engine, too, wound down and collapsed.

He had no time to admire his handiwork. Brian bent down to retrieve the remaining two gallons only to realize that he'd set them down on the other side of the flaming compartment. He grit his teeth and dove through the flames, rolling on the floor to the other side. He got to his feet quickly and reached for the gallon jugs, surprised to see them inexplicably receding from this reach.

He found himself suddenly floating above the floor, just inches from the ceiling, in the grasp of the replicant Shem.

Brian quickly twisted his body, writhing frantically to free himself. Fortunately, he hadn't zipped up the sweatshirt that he'd been wearing beneath his jacket and was able to wrangle himself free. He braced himself for impact with the floor but the creature scooped him up with the other large biosuit hand before he'd fallen very far.

The Shem raised him high and flung him against the bulkhead down the corridor. Brian careened off the wall and landed hard on the floor fifteen feet away, getting the wind knocked out of him. The Shem was immediate on him again. It grabbed him and raised him high horizontally then suddenly righted him and brought him in close.

As he hung there facing the creature, its two smaller biosuit arms seized him by the legs. The front of the biosuit changed from shimmering black to light gray and then a pale blue-green as two Shem hands emerged from behind it. They twisted and turned slowly as they inched toward Brian. The Shem's skin pulsed unnaturally then split in several places as small tendrils erupted from beneath the surface.

Brian screamed and shook violently, trying to free himself. But the biosuit's four arms held him securely. He turned his head away and clamped his mouth and eyes shut in a last, futile gesture of defiance.

He felt a sharp pain explode all over his body as the darkness took him.

FORTY-FOUR

They'd finally reached the helicopter.

The spacecraft's engines continued to drone from the canyon below, their pitch changing occasionally ever so slightly. They paused for a minute to catch their breath then began removing the tarp that covered the chopper's cockpit.

Once it had been pulled back sufficiently, Viktor opened the door and entered. Frank came over to the same side of the aircraft and waited while Viktor flicked the switches to activate the helicopter's electronics. He stuck his head out the doorway after several seconds, "It's working!"

Frank waited impatiently as Viktor attempted several times to contact McMurdo Station. He looked off at the low mountains in the distance to the south and wondered if they were blocking the signal.

"I've got somebody," Viktor yelled suddenly, startling Frank.

"McMurdo?"

"No. Another aircraft."

"Two six seven three this is Langstadt station…We have an emergency. Do you copy?"

The voice on the other end was sporadic, broken heavily by static. Frank looked up at the sky, cursing the atmospheric conditions that were inhibiting their communications as Viktor tried repeatedly to reconnect with the other aircraft.

Suddenly, Viktor jumped down from the cockpit and shoved Frank to the side. Frank fell into the snow and rolled onto his back. Viktor had one knee on the ground and was aiming his weapon at something. Frank turned his head to see as Viktor fired a short burst.

"Stay where you are," Viktor shouted.

A second figure emerged from a small shed in the distance and ran toward them yelling something. He stopped when he reached the first man, who was stood holding his arms up to show himself unarmed.

"Vik! It's Kelly! Don't shoot!"

≈ O ≈

His entire body tingled uncomfortably as he regained consciousness. As his faculties returned, so did the terror.

Brian fought with all his might to awaken. Even before he'd fully regained consciousness he carefully scrutinized his hands, looking for some clue that they were no longer his. Other than the numbness that permeated his body, he didn't feel any different. He touched his face and searched his mind but everything *seemed* normal.

He flinched as a strange guttural groaning noise started behind him. He fought to stand but couldn't coordinate his movements and fell face down on the floor. He turned his head slowly and saw it.

The replicant Shem was lying on its side just a few feet away, its tremendous frame quivering. The front of the biosuit was completely open revealing the creature inside. Other than its arms, which were covered with small lifeless tentacles, it looked like a normal Shem.

The replicant's head was pitched backward, its mouth agape as if it were trying to scream. Its low groaning indicated unmistakeably that it was still alive.

Brian fought with renewed vigor to get to his feet. He managed to get himself to his knees but the effort left him on the verge of blacking out again.

"Do not fight. That makes it worse."

Brian fell onto his back and closed his eyes. Had he really heard Arkt's voice?

"The feeling will pass soon, if you lie still."

He was only vaguely aware of the sensation of being lifted and carried as he succumbed again to the blackness.

≈ O ≈

The atmosphere in the cabin was tense. Viktor and Frank stood by the door as Charlie and Hildy stood at Armand's feet. Kelly planted himself between the two groups casually brandishing an over-sized screwdriver. Nobody spoke for several minutes.

"So, where's everybody else?" Kelly finally asked, trying to break the ice.

Frank shrugged, "Out there somewhere. There were about a dozen others in the CSC who managed to get out…no idea where they ended up."

"So, it's just the two of you? Where you been hiding?
"Look, Kel. You don't need to worry about us. We've been together the whole time. I can vouch for Vik and he can vouch for me!"

"That's great," Kelly said sarcastically, "…unless you're *both* one of those things."

"If we were, we'd just attack you right now, Kelly. If we haven't been able to stop it with assault rifles, do you honestly think that screwdriver would do the trick?" Viktor reasoned.

Kelly seemed to relax a bit but was clearly not yet fully convinced.
"How about you?" Frank asked cautiously. "Where are the others that went with you to the Met tower?"

They listened as Kelly told them of his fight with the creatures.

"So, who's to say you're not one of those things now?" Frank asked skeptically. "You telling me that you were able to fend off two of them things? It took ten of you to do it down in the warehouse!"

"No," Hildy chimed in. "It was Kelly who attacked the creatures in the storeroom. He saved us."

"That's right," Charlie affirmed.

"Or maybe he was saving himself." Frank conjectured as he continued to eye Kelly suspiciously.

"Now wait a damn minute!"

"Enough!" Viktor yelled, stepping between the two. "This isn't helping!"

"What's his condition?" Viktor asked, gesturing toward Armand.

"Not good. He's very sick and suffering from hypothermia. Who knows how long he was out here." Charlie's gaze fell. "If we don't get him some real help soon…"

Frank moved toward the door and peered out. In the distance, he could see Tom and Kim dragging a heavy piece of ground support equipment from the damaged hangar toward the helicopter.

"Looks like they got it," he stated casually. "Shouldn't be long before they've got the engine pre-heating. We should be able to fire it up shortly."

"Are you sure Tom can fly that thing?" Viktor asked doubtfully. "He's really only been up a handful of times."

"Well, Ken says that he's a quick learner. Hopefully it's enough."

Frank closed the door, "Anyway, he's all we've got. Nobody else has a clue on how to fly it."

They waited in silence as Tom hooked up the pre-heat equipment.

"They're on their way back," Kelly announced a few minutes later. He looked at his watch, "We just need to hang on for a few more minutes. Then, we can get the hell out of here."

The whine of the spacecraft's engines suddenly reached a new intensity as if to taunt them.

They looked at each other anxiously.

Frank scrutinized the helicopter in the distance then casually looked over at Viktor, who held his gaze for a brief moment before turning away. They both understood the situation.

Even if the engine heater worked…even if they got the helicopter started…*even if* Tom had acquired enough knowledge and skill from his impromptu training to pilot the chopper…they wouldn't *all* be making it out. The helicopter was simply too small.

FORTY-FIVE

He was back on the bridge, lying near the ship's computer. The shimmering column towered above him – an imposing electronic obelisk.

Brian propped himself up onto his elbows and looked around. The numbness had subsided significantly and he felt more steady. Arkt, who was busy on the far side of the room rearranging the nodes yet again, walked over as soon as he saw that Brian had revived.

"Not much time," Arkt said weakly.
Brian nodded.

"I have restored the nodes to their previous configuration. This will allow you to detonate the vessel."

Brian swallowed, wishing desperately for some water to soothe his completely parched throat. Arkt watched him as he tentatively got to his feet. He held one of the crescent-shaped weapons in one of the smaller biosuit hands.

"Ishtaq?" Brian asked.

"Immobilized for now. The Ishtaq has a much higher degree of molecular activity within its cells so the effect of the weapon is more pronounced. It will take longer to recover. Its biosuit will no longer function."

Arkt's original biosuit lay on the floor in the spot where he'd fallen following the attack by the replicant Shem not so long ago. It was useless now, the ability of its cells to process electrical impulses irreparably damaged by the replicant's weapon. Arkt now wore the biosuit that had temporarily housed Brian, helping him to recover from the effects of the chlorine gas he'd inhaled earlier.

"Brian…"
Arkt had never said his name before so Brian was instantly alert.

The front of the biosuit slowly faded, fully exposing Arkt inside.

"I am done. You must finish this."

Brian nodded his understanding. Arkt had already been severely weakened during the Barquii Fal process, when he and Brian had shared their knowledge. From the moment Arkt had initiated it, he had begun to die.

It was actually unheard of for the Benefactor Shem to survive this long after the Barquii Fal. Although he couldn't be sure, Brian suspected that Arkt's subsequent longevity was due to the fact that the knowledge transfer process hadn't been fully completed.

But whatever the reason, the effect of the weapon following the replicant's attack, the effort it had taken Arkt to change biosuits, and the energy he'd expended retrieving Brian from the clutches of the imposter had sapped the last of his strength.

"I'll finish it," Brian promised, looking into Arkt's dark eyes. "Journey well, my friend."

Arkt's head nodded almost imperceptibly. The sheen faded instantly from his eyes and Brian knew immediately that Arkt had passed. He felt immensely saddened by the fact that he would never get the chance to know the Shem better. He shook it off. There was no time to waste.

Brian manipulated several of the tiles amidst the ship's computer and studied the vessel's status. Arkt had set the remaining engines to a high idle and had restricted the flow of coolant, causing their temperatures to reach unsafe levels. All Brian had to do was shut off the flow completely and bring the engines to full power. This would require him to circumvent multiple safety protocols designed to prevent this from happening, but it could be done. In fact, he wasn't surprised to discover that Arkt had already made several of the necessary adjustments. In less than two minutes, the ship would detonate, leaving a crater in the ice almost a mile wide.

Brian manipulated the controls to begin the process. As he waited for the prompt to begin the next sequence, he retrieved his organizer from his jacket pocket. He flipped it open and stared briefly at his favorite photo that he'd taped there months ago. In it, he and Hildy were sitting on a brilliantly blue ice shelf, their feet dangling. A field torch illuminated their faces in the fading sunlight while a vast green ribbon of the Aurora Borealis flashed in the heavens behind them.

Brian set the organizer on a nearby shelf, taking his eyes off the photo just long enough to manipulate the controls each time the system prompted him to initiate the next sequence. He knew he'd have less than ten seconds once he entered the final command. He planned to spend them searing the image into his mind.

≈ O ≈

Frank closed the cabin door. He smiled as best as he could and waved to the passengers inside. Hildy and Charlie waved back meekly, their faces masked with fear and doubt. Armand lay across their laps. It was the only way they could fit him in.

Frank stepped onto the helicopter's skid and stuck his head into the cockpit.

"Guess I'll see you around, my friend," he said, smacking Viktor on the shoulder. Viktor smiled wanly. "We'll be back soon as we can to get you. You hang tight, eh?"

Frank nodded and winked. They both knew any further rescue was highly unlikely. Viktor had said it solely for the sake of the other passengers.

Frank leaned across Viktor and peered into the passenger compartment, "We'll see you back at McMurdo."

"Um, I think we'd better go," Tom said nervously, pointing out the cockpit window.

Several men were running toward the helicopter in the distance. They waved their arms and yelled, clearly wanting to catch a ride.

Frank smacked Tom on the thigh, “Go,” he shouted, as he backed out of the cockpit.

He jumped to the ground, closed the door, and backed away to join Kelly and Kim, who had also volunteered to stay.

Tom geared up the engines and the small helicopter gently lifted off the ground, hovering tentatively. The skids slammed into the ground a couple of times as the helicopter bounced around.

Kelly swore as he crouched into the snow, willing the aircraft to fly.

Seconds later, Tom rotated the throttle, raised the collective, and the helicopter lifted sharply into the sky.

They watched it for a moment as it receded to the south before returning to the warmth of the outbuilding.

Some of the men in the distance collapsed into the snow, defeated, as others marched dejectedly toward the shelter of the cabin.

“What about them?” Kelly mumbled.

“What about ‘em?” Frank shrugged as he replied.

“They could be…you know…”

Frank watched the helicopter shrinking into the distance, the sound of its rotors barely audible now. The ground still vibrated as the spacecraft’s engines idled less than 50 yards away.

“Quite soon, my friend,” he said, walking toward the edge of the abyss, “It won’t make any difference.”

≈ O ≈

Brian looked once more at the photograph as he prepared to enter the final command that would obliterate the site and destroy the heinous organism that threatened the planet. It saddened him that many good and innocent people would also die, but it couldn't be helped. He'd succeeded in detaching himself emotionally from the crew, even Kelly his dearest remaining friend, and felt confident that most of them would have understood – would've chosen to die – if it meant the complete destruction of the damned organism. He was glad that they were unaware of what was about to happen and that the end would be quick.

He grabbed the organizer from the shelf and drew the picture closer. He ran his fingers gently over it as if to caress Hildy's cheek.

He looked up quickly as a short, warbled tone screamed for his attention. A small section of the ship's computer was flashing a bright blue light. He moved closer to read the Shem-script and took a step back in surprise. The ship's sensors were warning him of the approach of an object directly overhead.

"*Must be a helicopter from McMurdo,*" he thought, frowning at the thought of taking even more innocent lives. He certainly wasn't about to alter his plan. There was just too much at stake.

He heard it before he saw it and was just able to jump behind the ship's computer in time to avoid it. The barbed tentacle slammed into the column and was immediately repelled by the computer's energy field – a safety feature designed to protect the device from an incidental hard blow.

Through the semi-transparent column, Brian could see the pale blue skin of the Ishtaq-Shem as it moved slowly toward him, its barbed tentacle waving through the air above it. Somehow, the much smaller size of the infected Shem without its biosuit seemed even more terrifying and menacing.

Brian reached out quickly and rotated the middle section of the column, bringing the appropriate input tiles within his reach. The Ishtaq-Shem surged forward, bending the tentacle around the column to reach its prey. Brian rolled again, keeping the column between himself and the creature as the tip of the appendage forcefully struck the floor. He attempted to rotate the middle section again in his direction but the Ishtaq-Shem had seized it with a free hand and held it fast. Brian cursed loudly as he frantically scanned the room. But there was nothing within reach that he could use as a weapon and there was no way he'd be able to outrun the Ishtaq-Shem.

The creature seemed to understand this too. It hesitated, studying Brian.

Brian felt his skin crawl as he realized that the eyes of the Ishtaq-Shem were silvery and dull. It was scrutinizing him carefully, but its gaze kept returning to Brian's damaged eye. From the knowledge it would've gained from its Shem host, the Ishtaq would appreciate what it meant. It would fathom the additional knowledge it could gain from such a host – a Ben Him Hist…an Inheritor of Shem tribal knowledge. It would crave it.

Brian backed away slowly, circling the column and trying to keep it between himself and the creature. The Ishtaq countered Brian's moves, trying to avoid having an obstacle between itself and its coveted host. As it moved, the end of the tentacle transformed from a barb into a hand with three thick, highly articulated fingers. The appendage slowly lengthened, its hand wavering in the air as it reached toward Brian.

Brian gave one last look around the bridge for a way out of his mess but came up empty. He was out of options.

≈ O ≈

FORTY-SIX

Viktor tried repeatedly to raise McMurdo on the radio as Tom piloted the aircraft. The chopper bucked and weaved against the winds, which had thankfully subsided some. After several tries, his headset crackled to life.

"Langstadt Station, this is in-bound two six seven three from McMurdo. Glad to finally hear from you."

Hildy and Charlie looked at each other with a glimmer of hope, the first they'd felt in what seemed like a very long time.

"Two six seven three, this is site Deputy Commander Viktor Sandersen. Do not, I repeat, DO NOT approach the site! We are airborne and heading your way. Suggest we rendezvous at..."

Viktor suddenly threw off his headset as a sharp squeal shrieked loudly through the earphones. The others did the same as the chopper bucked wildly.

"What the hell was that," Tom shouted over the noise of the engines.

Viktor shrugged, his face a mask of surprise and exasperation.

Behind them, Hildy shook her head trying to clear her ears, shaking her head rapidly left and right. She saw it out of the corner of her eye through the small portal. She would have missed it completely had it not been for the sudden burst of static and noise that had caused Tom to inadvertently bank the chopper sharply to the left in his haste to shed his headset.

She leaned over to get a better look and leaned forward to grab Viktor's jacket. But Armand's weight across her lap restricted her movement. She quickly grabbed a pen from her breast pocket and threw it at him.

Viktor flinched then turned around, an annoyed look on his face.

Hildy pointed urgently out the window. Viktor shifted his gaze and his eyes suddenly widened in surprise.

He gestured to Tom to circle around. Tom shot him a questioning look but complied.

They gasped at the scene before them, several miles distant but seemingly right in front of them.

A second Shem craft was just settling over its stricken sister ship, rotating slowly as it sank into position. It was somewhat smaller than the earthbound vessel and had a very different exterior configuration but it was clearly Shem.

As he stared at it silently, wide-eyed and apprehensive, Viktor found himself thinking back to his conversation with Doc in the cafeteria. Maybe nuking this place *wasn't* such a bad idea. But as he watched the new spacecraft position itself over the warehouse he knew that it was too late for that now.

≈ O ≈

Kelly watched in awe as the second vessel descended. It made no noise whatsoever even as its engines stirred up a massive cloud of snow and ice. Behind him, Frank and several others watched equally awed while a few others cowered in fear inside the cabin.

As soon as the vessel settled into place, a large door on its underside slowly opened, receding into the ship. The entire vessel hummed as a column of snow and ice rose into the air toward it as the ground vibrated.

≈ O ≈

Tom banked the helicopter sharply and increased its airspeed aiming for a rise of low hills a few miles away as his passengers craned their necks at the windows, trying to see what was happening behind them. Viktor thought briefly about protesting Tom's maneuver but something told him that getting away was probably the best thing they could do right now.

"What the hell?" Tom murmured as they crested a small ridge.

Viktor reluctantly peeled his eyes from the side window to see what had caught Tom's attention. He was shocked to see a Trac Crawler lumbering slowly southward below them, already about five miles from the site.

"Where the hell are they going?" Tom asked incredulously. "There's nothing out here."

"They're just trying to get away.... same as us."

The Crawler stopped. Three men jumped out and scattered, running in different directions as the helicopter raced overhead.

"What the hell did they do that for? They'll freeze out there!"

"I think that's what they want." Viktor said after a moment's pause. His response was barely audible over the headset and Tom wasn't sure he'd heard correctly. Once he realized that he had, his eyes widened in fear as he began to grasp Viktor's meaning.

"What do we do?" He asked, half panicked.

Viktor shook his head as he noted their coordinates on the flight computer, "They won't get far. We have to get to McMurdo."

He returned to the side window to watch the new vessel. "We'll send a crew out to deal with them later," he mumbled.

Various parts of the hovering Shem vessel began to pulsate with light and, though he couldn't be sure, Viktor thought he saw something rising from what used to be the warehouse. "...unless it no longer matters," he said quietly to himself, a sinking feeling in the pit of his stomach.

≈ O ≈

Brian moved slowly toward the column, closing the gap between himself and the Ishtaq. The counterintuitive move seemed to momentarily confuse the creature and it paused, assessing its prey.

When he judged himself to be close enough, Brian charge toward the Ishtaq. The creature braced itself as a second tentacle sprouted from its torso and charged, together with the original appendage, to intercept him. At the last second, Brian swerved and dove headlong into the shimmering column.

The protective shield of the ship's computer repelled him, throwing him backward through the air. He collided with the bulkhead and fell to the floor on the brink of consciousness.

Brian cursed inwardly. The protective barrier was designed to protect the ship's computer from being struck inadvertently with excessive force in the event of an in-flight accident. It operated with just enough force to repel any projected threat. He'd hoped that if he'd hit it with enough force, the shield's repulsion energy would be strong enough to kill him.

It was all he had left. He lay in a heap as the Ishtaq lumbered toward him, satisfied that its quarry had no fight left.

A bright blue curtain of light suddenly surrounded him, filling most of the bridge. It stung Brian all over his body, which convulsed and tossed him around like a mannequin, banging his head repeatedly against the floor. Just an arm's length away, the Ishtaq was convulsing even more wildly. The bright blue capsule of light moved across the floor until it encased the ship's computer. Even in his agony, Brian experienced a profound sense of relief as he understood what it all meant. There could be no other explanation.

They were taking it away.

He'd clearly been mistaken earlier about the arrival of a helicopter from McMurdo. It had to be another Shem vessel. It must be anchored directly overhead and was depriving the Ishtaq of its sole means of escape by removing key components from the crashed vessel, making it incapable of flight. Once this was done, they'd no doubt get to work ensuring the complete annihilation of the organism – probably using either the nostufal-hikkal or hikdt. Either one would do it.

Brian closed his eyes and allowed himself to slip away secure in the knowledge that he hadn't failed. He'd contained the Ishtaq just long enough. His Shem brothers would take it from here.

FORTY-SEVEN

They watched in amazement as the hovering Shem vessel retrieved various parts of its counterpart buried in the ice. Rapid flashes of light streamed from the opening beneath the vessel striking the spacecraft on the canyon floor, carving it up. The extracted pieces rose gently from the stricken ship and drifted silently up into the cavernous opening beneath the hovering ship. Most of the salvaged sections were quite small and some were barely visible.

"Are those nodes?" Kelly wondered aloud.

Frank didn't reply. His gaze was fixed upon the largest of the sections that had been carved from the vessel below and was ascending slowly skyward. Even from this distance and through the veil of the light he recognized the shimmering column that comprised the ship's heart and soul. But there was something else there too.

He squinted and formed his hands around his eyes to block the glare coming off the snow as the sun began to peek over the horizon. Two or three smaller objects floated slowly around the computer as it rose. They were significantly larger than the tellurium nodes – if that's what the other objects were – but still only half as big as the column in the center. They rotated slowly around it like oversized electrons orbiting the nucleus of an overblown atom. One of the orbiting objects appeared to have four appendages that distinctly resembled the outstretched arms and legs of an average sized man. It disappeared into the belly of the Shem vessel before he could confirm his suspicions.

The flashes of light stopped as abruptly as they began and the hatch dropped slowly back into its place, sealing the vessel.

"I think I saw a man in there," Kim stammered.

"I saw it too," Kelly replied after a moment.

Frank nodded imperceptibly.

The extreme edge of the hovering vessel changed abruptly from a steady pale blue light to a quivering lime green and a loud, severe tone filled the air like feedback from an over-modulated amplifier. The men staggered in the snow and covered their ears trying to block it out.

A series of short, sharp reports rang out as small, flare-like objects shot from the periphery of the hovering vessel. They started from two opposinh edges and jetted rapidly to the ground, boring deep into the ice until only their trailing edge remained visible. A thin pulsating filament rose skyward from the tail of each buried flare to its point of origin along the vessel's edge, glowing with the same lime green as the spacecraft's periphery.

More flares burst from the spacecraft in rapid succession. They moved along the edge of the vessel in sequence, starting from where the first two flares had jettisoned, and arced around the ship's circumference along opposing paths that terminated on the opposite side of the spacecraft, where the initial flares had originated.

The buried flares formed a wide circle that completely encompassed the site.

The obnoxious tone ceased, leaving a deafening silence in their wake.

Frank studied the flares buried in the ice beyond the canyon. Their spacing was perfect, each equidistant from its two closest neighbors. He followed the arc of their deployment, rotating his body until he could just see the nearest flares behind Kelly and the rest of the crew that stood transfixed near the shed.

"It must be a mile in diameter," Kelly exclaimed in awe.

They turned again to face the spacecraft as a loud clanking noise demanded their attention. As they watched, the end of each filament that remained attached to the edge of the vessel began to move slowly downward toward a large glowing disc located along the vessel's underside. They stopped when they reached its edge.

After a brief pause, the glowing disc detached from the spacecraft with another loud clank and descended, the filaments remaining attached and traveling with it. It stopped midway between the vessel and the ground forming a large green matrix over the complex not unlike an oversized birdcage.

"I don't think I like this," Kelly mumbled nervously as he traced the filaments overhead from the disc to the ground half a mile beyond them.

"It's leaving!" one of the men shouted in the distance as he fell against the shed.

The vessel had indeed begun to climb. In just a few seconds it had doubled the distance between itself and the disc that formed the top of the birdcage. It moved off at a steady pace until it formed a dark shadow behind a cloud bank. Seconds later, it was gone completely.

The disc began to rotate slowly, emitting a low gentle hum. The filaments maintained their spacing but began to pulsate more brightly and with greater frequency.

"I think the show is over," Kelly murmured.

Several of the men turned quickly and began to run toward the nearest boundary of the flare line. Kelly, Frank, and a couple of others watched them as they fled, knowing instinctively that it was already too late to run.

They watched the spinning disc as its rotation gathered momentum, the thin filaments no longer pulsating but glowing a steady bright green.

Frank put his arm around Kelly's shoulders and sighed deeply. "Never figured I'd go like this," he mumbled quietly.

"Me either," Kelly replied, returning the gesture.

Seconds later, they were vaporized in a brilliant emerald green flash.

≈ O ≈

Tom closed his eyes, temporarily blinded, and tried to picture the scenery that was before them just a second ago. Fortunately, they were high enough where he didn't have to worry about hitting anything.

"Take her down!" Viktor yelled.

"Are you crazy?! I can't see a damn thing!"

Viktor grabbed the cyclic and forced it forward and eased up on the collective, putting the helicopter into a sharp descent.

"What the hell are you doing?!" Tom yelled.

The chopper lurched as the shock wave struck it from behind. Warning klaxons sounded inside the cockpit as key systems failed.

"We're not going to make it," Tom shouted as the ground rushed up to meet them.

≈ O ≈

"What the hell was that?" the co-pilot yelled into his mouthpiece as he shielded his eyes from the light.

"Hang on," the pilot warned, bringing the helicopter into a rapid descent.

"What are you doing?"

"Taking her down."

"But we'll be at the site in fifteen minutes!"

"I'm sorry, Mister Raymond. But I've got to set her down until we can figure out what the hell's going on. I have absolutely no idea what caused that flash and I am *not* flying us into it blind."

Xavier started to protest but changed his mind as the helicopter suddenly bucked and dropped due to an unexpected and violent bit of turbulence. He sat back in his seat and tightened the restraints against his chest. They'd be pissed back at headquarters if his mission was delayed. But they could be damned. He'd spent the last three days getting out here from Seattle, bumming rides on any aircraft that happened to be heading this way. It had been a very long, uncomfortable, and tiring trip and he wasn't about to end it in a crash just thirty miles from the warehouse.

≈ O ≈

Hildy woke to the touch of a hand on her face. She tried to pull away but something was holding her in place.

"It's ok. You're ok."

She opened her eyes to see Viktor hovering over her holding a bloody cloth.

He waited for a minute, allowing her to get her bearings.

"Don't move around too much," Viktor instructed. "You've got a nasty bump on your head and probably a concussion."

Hildy nodded feebly. She looked down and gasped, startled to see a pair of legs laying across her lap. It took a second for her to remember that they belonged to Armand.

"Everybody else ok?" she finally asked.

Viktor sighed, "Charlie is still out cold. Knock on the head, same as you I would imagine. Doc seems the same as when we left." He gestured with his thumb toward the cockpit. "I wouldn't go in there, if I were you."

Despite the warning, Hildy strained to see. Fortunately, Tom's body was mostly obscured by Viktor and the back of the pilot's seat. A large bloodstain spattered what was left of the windshield.

"Any idea where we are?"

Viktor pursed his lips and shook his head. "Only about ten or fifteen clicks from the site. You know…middle of nowhere."

Hildy relaxed her body and sighed. "Guess it's better this way than…. you know…"

Viktor nodded. "I'm sorry."

She touched his hand, "Not your fault." Hildy looked at Armand and Charlie, "With any luck, they just…won't wake up," she said quietly.

"I could help that happen, you know."

She looked at him quizzically, missing his meaning until she finally noticed that he was resting one hand on his holster. She stared at it numbly. "Ordinarily, I couldn't imagine it. But now…it's not a *terrible* idea."

"I'll be right back. I've got to get something to drink."

"I could go for some water too."

Viktor nodded again and forced open the chopper door. It creaked loudly, its frame bent by the impact.

He began scooping snow into a metal container. He'd melt it for drinking water with the portable Coleman stove he'd found stashed away among other equipment in the cargo hold.

He stood and arched his back, listening to his spine crack. He turned to re-enter the chopper then paused.

He felt it even before he heard it…the distinct heavy wump-wump-wump of a helicopter rotor. He moved away from the wreck of his own chopper and scanned the sky. A large helicopter was flying northward. Its flight path and the fact that it was descending meant the flight crew would have a hard time spotting Viktor's downed chopper.

Viktor ran to the wreckage. Hildy had heard it too and was already searching the cabin for the flare gun. "I can't find it!" she shouted desperately.

Viktor swore and jumped onto the ground, intent on opening the cabin from the other side. As he passed the cockpit door, he was suddenly struck by a thought. He quickly threw the door open and hopped into the co-pilot's seat. He scanned the instrument panel but it was dark. He opened first one panel then another, frantically searching for the breakers. He quickly reset them all and portions of the instrument panel glowed to life. Fortunately, that included the radio.

He quickly donned his headset. "Mayday. Mayday. Mayday. This is..." He searched for the proper procedural wording but his mind went blank. "It's Viktor Sandersen, dammit! Is there anyone on this station?"

Viktor strained to hear a response through the heavy static. After several anxious seconds, it finally came through.

"Good to hear you, Vik! This is McMurdo two six seven three. What's your location?"

Hildy listened as Viktor guided the pilot to their crash site. The heavy thumping of the helicopter grew louder until the whole cabin of the wreck began to shake. Adrenalin surged through her, causing her head to throb almost in sync with the sound of the approaching aircraft.

"Such a beautiful sound," she whispered despite the pain.

FORTY-EIGHT

"Well, *you're* sure looking better," Viktor exclaimed as they entered the room.

"Still feeling pretty lousy. But from what I understand, I'm damn lucky to even be here."

"You sure had us worried there for a while," Hildy said handing her crutches to Viktor and sitting on the end of the bed.

Armand smiled weakly but genuinely.

Hildy poured some water and put it to his lips. He drank slowly, clearly savoring every drop of the cool liquid.

"Fever's finally coming down," Hildy said, flicking through Armand's chart.

"Yeah. I'll be alright."

They chatted idly for a few minutes, skirting the elephant in the room as Armand adjusted his bed.

"So…," he finally said, "Is it dead? I mean, did we destroy it?"

Hildy jumped down from the bed onto her one good foot. "You know what? If you guys are gonna talk 'monster' I'm going to go visit Charlie."

She kissed Armand lightly on the forehead, "I'll come back later."

Armand smiled, "I'll look forward to it," he mumbled quietly.

Viktor waited until the door closed behind her then sat down on the edge of the bed. He patted Armand's hand gently, "Mostly. There's just one loose end to tie up."

"What do you mean? Armand asked cautiously.

"Well…everything at the site was completely…obliterated. I mean, there is absolutely nothing left. But the pod that the Japanese discovered near Mizuho..." Viktor sighed loudly and started to pace, "Unfortunately, they loaded the damn thing onto a vessel. Left the coast two days ago."

"What?! That's insane! It's…it's terrible! It's…"

"I know, Doc. But don't worry. They've got a plan. In fact," he glanced at the clock, "They should be taking care of it in less than an hour."

"How?"

"Submarine. They've been racing like hell to intercept for a couple of days now. Caught up with the ship around mid-morning."

"Vik, they can't do that!" Armand bolted upright, swinging his legs over the side of the bed. He grabbed his aching head with both hands, fighting through the pain.

"It's too late, Doc," Viktor said irritably. "Look, I don't like it any more than you. But if we have to sacrifice the vessel's crew to stop this thing for good, well…we really have no choice."

"No! That's not it at all!"

Viktor looked at Armand curiously.

"For God's sake, think! If they torpedo that ship, they'll blow that thing to shreds...shreds that will be scattered across a very large patch of ocean! Shreds that'll be consumed by all kinds of sea life!"

Viktor's eyes widened as he realized the implications, "Oh my God! Thousands of fish will become infected."

"The sea will literally become a vast ocean of potential hosts! Once it starts there will be no stopping it!"

Armand jumped off the bed but Viktor had already beaten him to the door. As he struggled to free himself from the hospital monitors and intravenous tubes, a long-forgotten passage from the Bible's book of Revelation ran through his mind; "*…and the angel poured out his vial upon the sea and it became as the blood of a dead man and every living soul died in the sea.*"

FORTY-NINE

Captain Gregory Martel eyed the Nisshin Maru at maximum magnification. Thankfully, the deck was empty, the crew taking advantage of the lousy weather and hunkering down inside the warm, dry interior. He was glad for that. In less than 90 seconds, his torpedoes would break the ship in two and end the lives of the 30 or so men comprising its crew. Not seeing them on deck de-humanized the ship…just a lump of machinery in the middle of nowhere. It made his unsavory task somewhat easier to swallow.

He listened to the Weapons Officer, or 'Weps', in the background verbally verifying that the torpedoes were operating normally as they sped to their target. He acknowledged receipt of the information, his confirmation barely audible. Weps was used to that. The Captain was completely focused and wouldn't relax until the target had been destroyed. He'd been like that in every attack drill they conducted together…with live torpedoes from his boat screaming toward a live target, there was no reason to expect him to behave differently now.

Weps didn't understand the order at all. The Alaska was a boomer – a ballistic missile boat that was supposed to keep quiet and stay hidden. Instead, their boat was about to make a whole lot of noise, something that would surely go against the grain of any boomer man. Something like this should be done by a fast attack sub like the Mississippi, which had been their escort until just a day ago. Unfortunately, the Mississippi had been forced into port by a serious mechanical issue leaving the Alaska on its own.

They'd been working to intercept the Nisshin Maru for two days and were perplexed by the order to sink the unarmed cargo vessel almost immediately following their initial contact report. But the Captain would do his duty, as would every man on the boat, confident in the fact that the Commander of Submarine Forces, Pacific had a good reason for wanting them to do just that.

Captain Martel flicked the switch that activated the camera that would record the destruction of the Nisshin Maru. The vessel rolled in the heavy swells, its crew completely ignorant of their impending doom.

"Conn this is Radio! EAM confirmed as authentic! Abort! Abort! Abort!"

Captain Martel backed away from the periscope in surprise. He quickly grabbed the 1MC – the ship's internal intercom – and keyed the transmitter.

"Weapons! Conn! Abort warshot! I say again, abort warshot!"

"Warshot abort, aye!" Weps echoed.

The Captain cursed and wiped the sweat from his brow. That had been damn close.

They'd received the emergency action message, or EAM, just as he'd ordered the launch of the two torpedoes. Under normal circumstances, the Captain himself would've seen to the decoding and verification of the message as authentic. But, with two 'hot fish' steaming toward a live target, he'd left the task to his Executive Officer.

The destruction of the Nisshin Maru was going to make one hell of a racket – something any boomer Skipper would be loath to do – so the Captain had chosen to take the shot from as far away as possible. By keeping as much distance as possible between his boat and the target, they stood a better chance of slipping away undetected if they inadvertently drew the attention of an unfriendly sub that might be in the area. Fortunately, this had also provided him with the precious few extra seconds he needed to get the EAM decoded, allowing him to abort the attack before it was too late.

"Conn! Weapons! Mechanical malfunction, tube three! Unable to abort warshot!"

Captain Martel cursed loudly. In less than a second he'd weighed his options.

A hot weapon normally received updated targeting information through thin wires that kept the torpedo connected to the submarine until the torpedo's internal tracking system acquired the target on its own. Once that happened, the wires would be cut automatically and the torpedo would home in on its target independently. In the event of an aborted attack, the lines could be severed manually and the weapon would sink harmlessly to the bottom of the ocean.

Unfortunately, a malfunction was preventing this. With only seconds before the torpedo acquired the target on its own, Captain Martel had only one option.

"Manually detonate warshot!" he commanded, resting his face against the padding of the periscope. He barely heard Weps confirming the command.

Captain Martel cursed silently again and again as he waited for visual confirmation that the torpedo had exploded.

Seconds later he had it. He felt a chill down his spine when he saw how close the torpedo had actually come to striking the vessel. Several hundred pounds of explosive sent a towering column of water skyward only one hundred yards or so from the vessel's port side. Seconds later the Alaska's crew heard the deep rumble and felt the heavy vibration of the detonation. Several of the crew exchanged glances, glad that they'd likely never be any closer to such a blast.

But the crew of the Nisshin Maru had been much closer.

The deck of the Nisshin Maru was suddenly illuminated by floodlights as dozens of crewmen scrambled about the deck on both sides of the ship. They peered over the railings searching for the cause of the tremendous blast that had just shaken their ship. Some of the crew pointed to the spot in the water where the blast had obviously occurred, the water still churning and foaming.

One crewman scanned the area with a pair of binoculars. Captain Martel froze involuntarily as the man seemed to lock onto his periscope in the distance, seeming looking the Captain right in the eye. But a moment later the Japanese crewman was scanning another area of the vast ocean.

Captain Martel quickly surveyed the surface area above his boat, satisfying himself that no other vessels had been in the vicinity to witness the debacle. But his submarine had just caused one hell of a racket. It was time to verify that there weren't any unexpected surprises waiting for them below. It was time for him to hide his boomer again.

"Down scope," he ordered, "Sonar, any other traffic in the area?"

"Negative, Conn."

The Captain turned to his Executive Officer, "Mr. Jackson, take the Conn."

Captain Martel strode off to his stateroom. He was pissed. He couldn't wait to hear their explanation for this fiasco when they pulled into port next month.

FIFTY

Xavier Raymond slumped back in his chair as he listened to the discussion. The video conferencing center here in McMurdo was nowhere near as plush and comfortable as what he'd gotten used to back at headquarters. He was surprised to realize that he actually liked it all the more for it. There was something about being out here in the field, free from the endless line of corporate happy-horseshit, that was liberating. Out here, all that mattered was getting the job done.

On the screen in front of him, the Chief of Axis Corp's Operations, Gilbert Sullivan, was seated at the head of a long table surrounded by a dozen other important looking men. "We're still pushing the nuclear option with the Pentagon but so far they haven't committed."

"What is so hard for them to understand?!' Viktor shouted, rising from his chair. He'd already forgotten the guy's name and really didn't give a damn. "This isn't about just some damn potential international incident! There *is* no other option, at least none that will ensure the complete annihilation of the organism!"

"Viktor is absolutely correct," Xavier stated firmly. "The original team in '93…Dunford three years ago…and now Langstadt Station. How many more chances do they think we are going to get to destroy it?! What happens if it gets loose on that ship or the Japanese suddenly become spooked and decide to just dump the damn thing overboard? What then?!"

"Look. At some point, they'll see it our way. We've just got to give them a little more time. Right now, they're probably just trying to avoid the negative publicity and controversy that would inevitably result from an A-bomb going off in the middle of the Pacific."

Xavier leaned forward in his seat, "In normal times, I'd get that. But right now, what's actually *in* the middle of the Pacific is far more dangerous! It won't affect a single locality or region. This thing has global implications!"

"Damn right!" Viktor chimed in firmly. "Right now, we have a Japanese cargo ship in the middle of the Pacific carrying *the most dangerous* cargo it could possibly carry while your government casually discusses how to stop it – like it's just a boatload of Cuban refugees."

Gilbert raised his hands in mock surrender. "I don't know what else to tell you guys. We are doing all we can to push hitting it with a nuke. It's in the hands of the Joint Chiefs now."

Next to Gilbert, another man was casually flipping through a small blue binder. Xavier recognized it as the initial report that he'd sent just yesterday.

"You can flip through it a thousand times, Ellis, but it's not going to change."

Ellis closed the binder cover with a heavy flip. "I guess I just find it hard to believe that absolutely nothing remains of the site. I've been there. The place was huge. How can there be *nothing*?"

"The pictures don't lie," Xavier said coolly. "Whatever process they used to destroy the facility generated a ton of heat but no real explosion…no blast to scatter debris around. It literally vaporized the station, leaving just a big hole in the ice."

Ellis slumped back in his overstuffed chair and grunted, "Big hole…" he muttered sarcastically. "The damn crater's almost two miles in diameter. Our physicists estimate that the temperature at the epicenter had to have been several million degrees."

Xavier nodded, "Wouldn't doubt it. The shock wave caused by the pressure differential nearly knocked us out of the sky from over 30 miles away."

"Well, the international community is already screaming at us for answers," Gilbert said irritably, shifting in his chair. "As far as the whole world is concerned, we've *already* set off a nuclear device in the middle of nowhere, Antarctica. What the hell is the reaction going to be when we actually *do* set off a nuke?!"

"You mean *two* nukes," Armand piped in.

The men on the video screen looked at each other uncomfortably. "What do you mean?" Ellis finally asked.

Armand released the wheel lock on his wheelchair and rolled over to a map on the wall. "Everyone seems to have forgotten that right about here," he said, jabbing the map along the northwest coast of the Antarctic continent, "lies the fourth pod, submerged in about a thousand feet of ocean. If the Pentagon is going to hit the Nisshin Maru with a nuke – and they had damned well better! - then they need to hit this one as well."

"He's right," Xavier chimed in. "We can't afford to ignore it. They have to hit them both at once." He looked around the room then stared into the camera, "I don't know about you, but I won't be able to sleep at night as long as I know that this damn thing is lying on the ocean floor. Hell, I may not ever sleep well again as it is!"

Viktor pursed his lips and sucked on a mint toothpick, which the General Store here at McMurdo thankfully happened to have in supply. His thoughts returned to the Trac that he'd seen travelling south as they passed overhead in the helicopter. A subsequent search located the vehicle – abandoned – about twelve miles south of Langstadt Station. At least two sets of prints led away from it and out into the tundra but the occupants hadn't been found. The thought sent a shiver down his spine and he shuddered involuntarily.

Nukes would certainly take care of the Nisshin Maru and the submerged pod. But what were they supposed to do about two or more missing, potentially contaminated men? Viktor considered raising the question again but ultimately decided against it. They'd already discussed it to death and were no closer to a solution.

The meeting ended after a few more minutes of aimless discussion. Viktor, Armand, and Xavier moved together quietly toward the cafeteria. None of them were hungry. Still, going through the motions of having a meal would focus their thoughts at least temporarily on something other than the threat that still hovered over the planet.

They sat quietly and mindlessly nibbled on their food, the silence only occasionally punctuated by an automatic comment about the quality of the food or about how well Armand was recovering. Viktor made a feeble joke about putting Armand in for a purple heart for being wounded while fighting the enemy, but it fell flat. It was too close to the truth.

As they sat finishing their coffee, the majority of the food on their trays cold and untouched, Xavier fished a cigar out of his pocket. He snipped one end off and stuck the other in his mouth. He lit it and puffed on it several times, releasing a large cloud of fragrant smoke over the table.

"You know those things'll kill you, don't you?" Armand asked dryly.

Xavier chuckled, "So I hear."

Viktor sighed deeply, "Got another one?"

Xavier dug into his pocket and drew a second cigar out, passing to Viktor. "You want one too?" he asked, nodded at Armand.

Armand looked around the cafeteria, amazed at how normal things looked and sounded. All around them, workers droned on about their mundane work day. Some complained about the food or accommodations at the site or bitched about having to work the midnight shift out in the arctic cold. Others laughed over a bad joke or over some insignificant occurrence that had momentarily thrown a little life into their otherwise dull routine. One group in particular was being especially raucous, drinking beer and playing cards at the far corner of the room. Their boisterous laughter would often drown out the griping and whining of the malcontents. Armand wondered if he'd ever feel that carefree again.

But even as the thought lingered in his mind, a vision of Hildy and her baby crept in. She'd be heading home in the next day or so, blissfully unaware of the floating time-bomb heading for Asia. She was doing alright now…at least physically. She was getting the treatment she needed and the fetus in her womb appeared to be healthy and strong. He smiled at the thought of her holding a newborn.

The thought of new life sparked a something within him and, for the first time since their arrival at McMurdo, he felt fresh hope. He began to feel confident that time would eventually heal him - that he would one day begin to enjoy life again, even if the thought of the Ishtaq never completely went away.

Armand smiled at Xavier, still proffering the cigar, and shook his head, "No, thanks. I think I'll just take my chances with whatever else life decides to throw at me.

FIFTY-ONE

Hildy stood at the window staring up at the Northern Lights. She had once thought them to be among the most beautiful sights she'd ever seen. Now, they brought her little joy and did nothing to quell her sorrow and fear.

She thought of the night when she and Brian had first expressed their love for each other. It was a night not unlike this one…a billion stars shining brightly in a clear sky muddled only by the streaming green hue of the Aurora Borealis. He'd snapped a photograph of the two of them, their faces shining brightly in the lantern light as the sky silently danced behind them. It would always be one of her fondest memories.

She glanced down, suddenly realizing that she'd been softly stroking her belly with both hands. She felt the hot tears welling up behind her eyes as she imagined raising her son alone. She was torn…simultaneously conflicted by fear and loneliness at the thought of rearing their son on her own yet comforted by the thought that a part of Brian remained with her. She fought back the tears, determined to focus on the positive.

Hildy turned at the sound of a gentle shuffling behind her, surprised to see Charlie approaching her slowly. She was staring at Hildy in a weird, unnatural way and Hildy felt goosebumps spring up all over her body. She stepped back involuntarily until the cold window pane was pressing against her back.

"Charlie, what's wrong?"

Charlie stopped in the middle of the room, her eyes rapidly scanning Hildy's face. "They wanted me to tell you…they thought it would be easier coming from me…but I don't know how to say it."

Hildy felt a chill run up her spine, "Charlene, what is it? You're scaring me!"

"I'm sorry. I don't mean to. But I can hardly believe it myself…"

Charlie moved closer and seemed to be fighting tears. "He showed up out of nowhere. He doesn't remember how he got here or where he's been the last few days. He seems to be ok, at least medically. But…"

"But what, Charlie?! What the hell are you talking about?"

"She's trying to tell you that I'm not dead."

Hildy gasped as Brian entered the room. He wore a heavy robe and slippers that had obviously been issued by the infirmary but, other than a patch over one eye, seemed unharmed.

She studied him from across the room, which was suddenly spinning around her. She staggered and reached out for the wall to steady herself.

Brian stepped toward her, hesitantly at first before breaking into a sprint. He reached her just in time to catch her as she collapsed.

Brian listened to the humming and thumping of the machine as it moved over his body. He focused on its rhythm, using it as a form of meditation. He stared up at the bright white walls of the tunnel just inches from his face and grinned, remembering a time when an MRI procedure hadn't gone quite so smoothly. He'd been just fine for the first twenty minutes or so. But then he'd made the mistake of opening his eyes. It had taken all of thirty seconds for him to freak out and shimmy his way out of the machine in a panic, much to the annoyance of one medical attendant and the unrestrained laughter of another.

Things were certainly different now. His ability to handle being cooped up in a tight space was just one of the many changes that he'd undergone in the last several days.

His memory had been murky when he'd arrived at McMurdo but it had improved significantly, especially during the last twenty-four hours. He stared into the bright light and thought about all he'd been through, trying to fill in the few remaining holes.

He remembered lying on the deck of the second Shem vessel. It wasn't cold and hard like the one that had been lying dormant in the Antarctic ice for so long. It was firm but pliable and conformed to the footfalls of the Shem as they walked. Even as he lay there, it adapted to the contours of his body and adjusted its temperature to a comfortable warmth that was perfectly tuned to his natural temperature.

They hadn't intended to retrieve Brian or the Ishtaq-Shem from the stricken vessel. They should have been just two more unfortunate casualties. But they'd been too close to the ship's computer and had been inadvertently recovered along with the valuable device.

The energy generated by the field that had salvaged the computer had caused significant damage to his central nervous system. Left on his own, Brian would've been permanently and completely paralyzed.

But the Shem had placed him in a chamber to rejuvenate his body. They'd introduced billions of microscopic organic machines into his body that worked to repair his damaged nerves and ruptured muscle fibers. But they also did far more. They eliminated the bacterial meningitis that had just begun to settle into his brain and destroyed the cancer cells that had recently begun to spawn in his pancreas.

And as the micro-machines worked their magic within his body, the Shem scanned his mind.

Their technology had advanced significantly in the time since Arkt's spacecraft had crashed on earth. This time, they 'connected' with him artificially, using electromagnetic and spectrographic means that left no physical damage. Through him, they'd learned things that they hadn't been aware of…like the fate of Arkt's crew and the full, awful potential of the Ishtaq.

The final communique the Shem had received from Arkt's vessel eons ago, as the ship had been crashing to earth, had been frantic and incomplete. Additional information that they'd extracted from the computer that they'd salvaged from the crash was just as fragmentary.

They'd turned to Brian as a last resort. Through his experiences, they realized that they'd seriously underestimated the destructive organism that their brothers had accidentally created and to which many of them had succumbed.

They understood more clearly now what had to be done.

Brian faded in and out as they travelled. He remembered the Shem being highly agitated but couldn't recall why. When he finally awoke, they were discussing something that had just occurred in the waters below them.

As he eavesdropped, still unable to move, he realized that a submarine had attempted to sink the vessel but had somehow failed. The Shem realized that a nuclear strike was the next likely course of action. It was the only weapon in man's primitive arsenal that could completely annihilated the organism.

"We're half-way through. You doing ok in there?"

"I'm good," Brian replied absent-mindedly. Since his exchange with Arkt, he was able now to focus his mind completely on multiple concurrent tasks. As the MRI technician chatted with him, he could dedicate a small part of his brain to the conversation while he continued to replay and re-assess his experiences aboard the Shem vessel.

"Ok. Let me know if you start to feel anxious."

"I'll be fine," Brian stated matter-of-factly. "Take as long as you need."

The MRI machine began clanking and chunking along again, the rotating section of the apparatus now at his feet. He wasn't supposed to be able to feel the magnetic energy being emitted by the machine but he could.

As they healed his flesh in the Shem chamber, the micro-machines automatically regenerated nerves and muscle fiber that had atrophied with age. As they erased the ravages of time, they'd unintentionally heightened the sensitivity of his senses, tuning them to a finer degree than he'd ever before experienced.

Brian didn't need the machine to tell him he was in perfect health. He could sense it. He could focus his attention on any of his internal organs or systems and run a mental diagnostic in just a few seconds. Compared to the advances of the Shem, the human MRI machine was so primitive.

He smiled as he thought it, amused by the irony that he'd automatically thought of the device as a mere 'human' machine, as though his encounter with Arkt had transformed him into some sort of Shem-Human hybrid.

He endured the cumbersome, slow process knowing that it was all that the doctors had available. He was doing this for them. They needed to assure themselves that he was unharmed and – more to the point – normal.

Brian studied the machine. He could see its inner workings in his mind's eye as though the plastic and metal casing around the machine were no longer there. With one major tweak and a few simple ones, the machine could be made so much more capable and efficient. How could they not see that?

He realized as soon as he thought it that this would be the best way for him to use the knowledge gifted to him. He could commit himself to advancing human medicine…to alleviating pain and suffering. It was a much more attractive alternative to the many, less beneficial applications he could dream of for using it. It felt like the best way for him to honor Arkt.

The thought of his Shem acquaintance returned his musings to his time in the rejuvenation chamber aboard their vessel.

As the Japanese vessel sailed below them, the Council had debated their options. They couldn't use the nostufal-hikkal – the weapon that had completely vaporized the warehouse site. The deployable devices were designed for use on a solid surface such as soil, rock, or ice. Retrieving the pod was a possibility, but one of the Japanese crew might already be infected. After much discussion of their options, they finally decided upon a course of action. Still weakened from his injuries, Brian drifted off without hearing their plan.

He awoke again a full day later. He knew exactly how long he'd been unconscious without having to be told. He could move now, although the Shem urged him not to. But he could at least speak.

They were in orbit. He could see the bright white Antarctic continent far below them, a large white pearl amidst a beautiful blue ocean.

The Shem who oversaw the final stages of his treatment was Bar'wii Forn. She chatted with him for hours as she retrieved the bai'aq – the Nano-machines – from his body.

She told him how they'd retrieved the pod and the human crew from the Japanese vessel using the larniq – the tractor beam-like device that had inadvertently brought Brian aboard. They'd sterilized the seaborne vessel to ensure no trace of the Ishtaq was present then sliced it in two, sending it to the bottom.

The crew was being treated, a few at a time, in the same way that Brian had been to repair any damaged tissue. But for several of them, the stress of the energy beam had been too much. Those that had died had been released back into the water, once they'd verified that they hadn't been infected by the Ishtaq. To the Shem, it had seemed the most natural thing to do.

As for the sole remaining Ishtaq-Shem, they'd placed it into a separate chamber to freeze it. Once they'd returned to the deep cold of space to begin their journey home, they would jettison the creature into the sun at their closest approach…a fitting tribute to the brother they had lost and final end to the terrible organism they had inadvertently created.

The ship later returned to Antarctica and retrieved the final pod. It had required much more effort to salvage as it was submerged too deep – beyond the limits of the larniq. But they finally succeeded in raising it via other means. Both pods were now attached to the underside of their vessel.

They'd successfully revived two of the four Shem, one from each of the pods. The other two had succumbed to their injuries long ago. Among them, one of the dead within the pod recovered by the Japanese had been infected. Had the human vessel made it home, they would surely have precipitated a global disaster.

Brian wept. Hearing of the loss of the Shem filled him with intense emotion as he recalled his shared experiences with Arkt. Although she was already well aware of what had transpired between Brian and Arkt, Bar'wii Forn had let him tell the story without interruption.

After he'd finished speaking, she'd told him how they'd watched the Barquii Fal process through his eyes as they scanned his memory. They were fascinated by it as the procedure had never been done before with one who wasn't Shem. It made some of their crew uncomfortable, knowing that an alien species now possessed so much of their knowledge. Although their war with the Rhnem Rimni Tii'rq had occurred so long ago, they still carried the memory of its effects on their planet and people - the experiences kept alive and fresh through the many Barquii Fal that had occurred since.

The Council had debated for a long time about what to do with him. Many had voiced their preference to keep him aboard, certain that man would use their knowledge for selfish and perverse purposes. But two of the Ancients among them, moved by the depths of Brian's affection for Arkt, had ultimately convinced them otherwise. The Lum Ha Niq persuaded the others to trust that Brian would guard their knowledge and use it for good.

They'd decided to return him to earth – to any location of his choice – just as soon as his health was fully restored. He hadn't hesitated to tell them where he wanted to go.

"OK, we are all set."

Brian mumbled his thanks to the MRI tech as he sat on the edge of the table, not caring that his backside was completely exposed through the wide-open medical Johnny. The technician blurted out several instructions regarding what was next but Brian barely heard him. He was trying to remember his final moments with the Shem, a period in his past that still had several holes.

He stopped listening to the technician to devote all his energies to digging up any lost fragments.

He remembered the Shem assembling around him as the ship descended toward earth. Having no word for 'goodbye', each Shem bade him farewell in their way – quietly uttering a single word or short phrase that had a deeply personal meaning between them and their departing brother. It would serve as a personal reminder, an intimate token of affection to be reflected upon by both parties until they met again one day. They would be the first words they would share on that occasion, a personal greeting reaffirming their mutual affection and assuring the other that they hadn't been forgotten.

Brian had planted each phrase in his mind. He knew already that he'd have no trouble recalling them if the time ever came to use them in greeting, no matter how far in the future that day might be.

As if reading his mind, Chief Council Lum Ha Niq Muella Bin Darqu Dun – the equivalent of the ship's Captain – gently nodded his head and quietly uttered his farewell.

Brian remembered smiling and fighting the urge to physically embrace the Shem. That was not their way. He only vaguely recalled nodding in acknowledgement and uttering his own farewell.

He remembered Bar'wii Forn and the Chief Council accompanying him to the hangar bay for his short trip back. No-one spoke. They had already said the last words they were supposed to say to each other.

Brian jumped down from the MRI table and started the walk back to his room, annoyed that he couldn't remember his final moments aboard the Shem vessel. He paused at a window and looked out, wishing that it was a night sky rather than daylight that met his gaze. He opened a door and stepped out into the cold, clad only in his Johnny and slippers. But he barely felt the chill.

He scanned the sky hopefully but saw nothing. He smiled though, somehow knowing that they were still watching.

Hildy hung up the phone and took a long drink of water.

"That's good. You need to stay hydrated." Charlie refilled Hildy's glass and set it beside her bed.

"So, what's mom and dad have to say about their baby girl coming home?"

Hildy smiled weakly, "They're thrilled of course, especially when I told them that I'd be home for good."

She looked down at her abdomen, "And they're absolutely thrilled about being grandparents, although they're obviously leery about Brian."

"They'll learn to love him just as you did," Charlie stated confidently. "He's a great guy. And I think he'll make a wonderful daddy."

Hildy smiled more enthusiastically. "I think so too."

They grew quiet as Fox News flashed an alert on the television against the far wall.

"The crew of a Japanese cargo vessel that had been missing since Sunday has been found by a small Japanese fishing boat. An international consortium of vessels has been searching for the missing ship since it went silent Sunday morning, failing to keep to its regular communications schedule. Strangely, the missing crew was located almost fifteen hundred miles northwest of where they were expected to be.

Initial reports are sketchy, but it appears that none of the crew members have any memory of what happened to their vessel or how they arrived on the island. For more on the story, we go to Michael Hersch, our FOX news affiliate in Yokosuka..."

Charlie picked up the remote and turned the television off. "I think we've had about enough of *that* for a while." She grabbed an extra pillow from the cabinet and placed it on the chair near Hildy's bed. "You want me to stay with you?" she asked tentatively.

Hildy sighed lightly, "No. Thanks. I'm ok."

"OK. I'm going to go and let you get some rest. I'll come by again later. You need anything before I go?"

"No. You've pretty much taken care of everything." Hildy reached out and grabbed Charlie's hand. "Thank you so much for everything, Charlie. You've been a wonderful friend."

Charlie smiled. "We've been through a lot together, you and me." Charlie gave Hildy a hug. "I'm glad that you were there for me, too."

Hildy watched Charlie leave. She glanced at the clock and sighed. In less than twenty-four hours, she'd be on a flight home. Brian would join her a few days later, after he'd been declared healthy and unharmed. Well...mostly unharmed.

The thought made her cringe. He hadn't yet told her what had happened to his eye and she hadn't asked. She wasn't so sure she really wanted to know. Just the thought of what *may have* happened opened the door to all the other hideous images that she was fighting so hard to suppress.

She closed her eyes and thought of home, trying desperately to relax. She imagined lying on the soft, green grass on a hill overlooking the seaside, Brian lying by her side and gently caressing her burgeoning belly. She imagined the warmth of the sun on her face and the light breezes that carried the fragrance of Spruce and Blue Anemone, the fragrant flower that grew abundantly in her hometown. She imagined sitting on the porch of her parent's Tudor home in Trondheim, looking down at the home of friends and family in the valley below, their son sitting on Brian's lap and giggling as daddy tickled his belly.

It took a while but Hildy finally drifted off to sleep, her lips curled into a slight smile. She hadn't looked forward to something this much in a very long time.

Epilogue

Brian lay in bed and stared up at tiny lights that dotted the ceiling. He'd removed the fixture from the top of a fiber-optic sign that he'd taken from the break room, allowing the tiny cables to project thousands of tiny specks above him like a field of stars. He watched them sway ever so slightly on the ceiling, mesmerized by the effect, as he contemplated the world of the Shem. He never tired of viewing the scenery of their planet – some scenes so much like places here on earth while others stood in stark but beautiful contrast.

He fixated on a single dot, imagining that it represented their star in the night sky. But he knew the actual sphere of their sun wouldn't be visible to the unaided eye in our night sky, hidden behind tremendous clouds of interstellar dust and phosphorescing gases. He determined that he'd visit the Mauna Loa observatory in Hawaii when he could, intent on viewing their star.

He awoke an hour later, surprised but pleased that he'd finally fallen asleep. He sat up in bed, bothered by a strange dream that was already beginning to fade from his memory. He focused on it, sensing that it held some deep meaning.

In his dream, he had been in their home, a quaint Norwegian farmhouse nestled into the side of a lush green hill. From another room, he could hear the sound of laughter…Hildy and their son. Little Ben was just beginning to talk and she was playing a game with him, holding up flash cards with bright pictures on them and saying them aloud. He'd repeat the words back to her and she'd clap and cheer, eliciting smiles and giggles from the boy.

He saw daddy peeking into the room through the door, which was slightly ajar, and called for him.

Hildy looked up at him and smiled as he entered. He picked up the lad and hugged him close while Hildy put the cards back into the box. She stumbled as she got up, spilling the cards all over the floor.

Ben giggled loudly from daddy's arms as Brian teased her, telling Ben what a big mess mommy had made.

Suddenly, he pointed down at the floor, "Chi iri."

Hildy smiled wildly, "That's right, Benny! Cherry!" She picked up the picture of a bright red cherry and repeated it.

Ben shook his head no and pushed the card aside, "Chi iri!"

They went back and forth several times as Hildy tried to get him to say the word correctly. Each time, he said it in exactly the same way.

Finally, he leaned back in Brian's arms and stared firmly into his father's good eye, as if understanding despite his youth that the other was a prosthesis. "Chi iri!" he insisted.

Brian jumped to the floor, his heart pounding in his chest as the memory suddenly returned.

He'd been standing before Lum Ha Niq Muella Bin Darqu Dun after receiving farewell words from the rest of the crew. The Ancient Once regarded him solemnly for several seconds, his gaze piercing Brian as though he were looking right through him.

Brian waited. It was customary that the farewell words be initiated by the one remaining behind. Finally, the Ancient One bowed his head ever so slightly, "Chi 'iri."

Brian smiled as a wave of hope and excitement flooded through him, instantly erasing the unease that had been plaguing him since he'd arrived at McMurdo. He hadn't noticed it initially but felt it growing inside him as life at the station went on as usual for everyone else.

Brian couldn't stop smiling, immensely comforted as he quietly repeated the parting words of the Ancient One… "Chi'iri" – 'return'.

He remembered now…he had returning the Ancient One's bow and uttered his own farewell words, "I will be waiting."

Brian got dressed suddenly anxious to put his arms around Hildy. He so badly wanted to tell her but knew that he couldn't. With all she'd been through, he doubted that she'd be as enthusiastic or find the same level of comfort in the Shem's parting words.

"Chi 'iri."

The Shem would be back.

THE END

I sincerely hope you have enjoyed reading 'Ishtaq: The Second Vial'. If so, I would really appreciate a short on-line review. Your help in spreading the word is gratefully appreciated!

If you would like to receive notifications and updates on my upcoming books and become eligible for pre-release specials and give-aways, please visit me at:
www.tgifournier.com

About the Author

Thomas G. Fournier is a former intelligence analyst and reporter, having proudly served in the U.S. Marine Corps, National Security Agency, Central Intelligence Agency, and with foreign intelligence services abroad. He currently lives with his wife, Mona, in eastern Connecticut.

Made in the USA
Las Vegas, NV
17 May 2021